DEAD RINGER

HEIDI
BELLEAU

SAM
SCHOOLER

D1057040

RIPTIDE
PUBLISHING

Riptide Publishing
PO Box 6652
Hillsborough, NJ 08844
www.riptidepublishing.com

Dead Ringer
Copyright © 2015 by Heidi Belleau and Sam Schooler

Cover art: Dion Marc, facebook.com/Dion.Marc.Creations
Photographer: Marisha Dudek, marishadudekphotography.com
Editors: Sarah Frantz Lyons, Chris Muldoon
Layout: L.C. Chase, lcchase.com/design.htm

ISBN: 978-1-62649-338-4

First edition
October, 2015

Also available in ebook:
ISBN: 978-1-62649-337-7

DEAD RINGER

HEIDI
BELLEAU

SAM
SCHOOLER

RIPTIDE
PUBLISHING

To all the fuckups, shut-ins, and queers.
We live.

TABLE OF
CONTENTS

CHAPTER
ONE

Brandon was craving a cigarette by the time he pulled up in front of Dahlia's house.

No, screw that. A whole *pack* of cigarettes. So many cigarettes that the chain store clerk down at the Fifth Street Speedway would give him that dead-eyed judgey valley girl stare every time he came in for the next year.

Dahlia's ancient blue Mercedes had a squeaking rust spot around the back brake, and the mechanic at the impound place had told Brandon to "jam it in real hard a couple times, you'll knock it loose," but Brandon was pretty sure the thing would up and just give out if he tried that, so he eased it down, circling the fountain a couple times before he let it coast to a stop at the bottom of the wide, white steps leading into the house. The whole house was wide and white, even more monstrous than he remembered it being, and he wasn't sure if he was looking forward to getting lost in it again or not.

Right now, he was leaning toward not.

In the trunk, he had three suitcases—the entire contents of his shit life—and his wallet. And his laptop, which was also a piece of shit. His new set of keys were tagged with the real estate office's name and number, plus an advertisement on the flip side that said "WE'RE YOUR NEIGHBORS."

Yeah, right. They sure were his neighbors . . . when they wanted him to pay up.

Brandon left the suitcases for now and ripped the tag off the keys with his teeth on the way up the steps. He got the door unlocked and nudged it open with his hip.

God, it smelled like her.

Brandon knew from the bullshit junior year psychology course he'd gone to three classes of that scent was the strongest sense when it came to remembering things—or so they said. They had to have it wrong, though, because for a hot second he *forgot* that she was dead, and he caught himself waiting for her to come around the corner from the kitchen the way she always did, ankle-length flowing skirt billowing around her legs and her wiry grey hair in a long, youthful side-braid.

Apparently he had a good reason for not putting much stock in psychology.

Shaking it off, he spun the keys in his hand, then locked the door behind him to keep out any wandering, ambitious, rude as fuck paparazzi. Couldn't they have some kind of statute of limitations on their hounding? Like say, if someone hadn't been in a movie in, oh, *sixty damn years*—then they couldn't bother them anymore?

And that was assuming they were here for Brandon's grandmother, and not his grandfather, who not only hadn't done a movie in sixty damn years, but also hadn't been *alive* in sixty damn years.

Didn't they have a new generation of Kardashians to stalk?

"Yo," he called to the house, which seemed to echo strangely without her in it, even though all her furniture and possessions were exactly as she'd left them, reflecting sound the exact same way they always had. The familiar layer of dust on them was as much from her being in the house with her forgetful cleaning habits as her being gone.

Her monetary assets were to be divided amongst her various charities. Dusty house and dusty contents went to her sole grandson and heir, Brandon Ringer.

Which sounded nice enough, until you realized that the property taxes alone for this place were more than a high school droupout fuckup like Brandon made in a *year*. The real estate office clerk had been polite enough, explaining that Dahlia had been a "lifelong valued client" of whatever the manager of the place was. But then the clerk had laid the real shit down: the fact that paying for the annual maintenance of this place had taken a bite out of Dahlia's admittedly extravagant budget. Brandon would be lucky to cover a month on his average yearly income.

And that was when he wasn't "between jobs," as she used to call it.

Which he was, currently.

How the hell was he going to pay for this fucking place? Not like he could afford any kind of upkeep—which that bottle-green swimming pool out back desperately needed, and same to Dahlia's beloved garden, left to grow wild—or the aforementioned taxes, or the utility bills. He knew how much the house cost to heat and cool, plus electric and gas and water . . . Bare minimum would be a chunk of change that he wouldn't be able to scrape from anywhere. He couldn't even afford to *sell* the place with the insane up-front retaining fees realtors asked for houses like this. It didn't matter that it was on the outskirts of Hollywood, not even downtown or in one of the more historic areas—this was rich people hunting grounds, and Brandon was, as usual, the odd one out.

He *could* sell, he guessed, he had the *ability* to sell, if he hired someone without retaining fees, but not unless he took a bargain basement as-is price. Which would then leave him homeless and without enough liquid finance to support himself, no matter how sparsely he was living.

And he just knew it would end with some weird fetishist buying the house so they could brag over shrimp cocktails and overly expensive, sommelier-suggested water (yeah, that was a thing now) that they lived where *James Ringer's wife* had lived. As if she weren't even her own person, just some extension of *him*. Plus Brandon would have to personally make all the necessary changes it would take to transform the place into something marketable—AKA, get rid of all the hippie stuff and replace it with chrome and air or whatever was in fashion.

Replace everything left of Dahlia.

He couldn't do that, not for any amount of money.

No, Brandon was stuck here, stuck with the old oak fixtures and the potpourri smell and the basement full of props and paper ghosts. No job and a handful of unpayable bills was better than no job *and* no house *and* a handful of unpayable bills. Probably. At least if they shut off his heat and electricity, he could use the house's huge not-to-code fireplace and his grandmother's expansive collection of scented candles to get by. Better than a homeless shelter. A million times better than his parents' place, not that they would let him back in if he was down to his last cent.

He walked the whole of the house, and by the time he'd passed the same mid-century starburst clock in the middle of the cross-section between the two wings three times, he realized he was looking for something he wasn't going to find.

It wasn't Dahlia. He wasn't delusional. Just . . . *something*. He hadn't lived in this house for a little over a year, not since he turned eighteen. It wasn't that Dahlia had kicked him out or anything. It was just that she was more like a roommate than a mother-figure or the guardian the court had deemed her to be, and once Brandon was supposedly an adult, he'd decided it was time to stop being a drain on her and move the hell out.

He regretted that now that she was gone. Of course he did.

Not the money part—the part where he didn't have her to hand him an Amex and tell him to get what he needed, anymore. He wasn't that much of a little bastard. He missed *her*. Missed . . . fuck, he missed that he hadn't been here, if that made sense. He missed that he'd lost a whole year of saying goodnight to her when she was still up at four in the morning, and of finding her asleep out by the pool with a half-potted plant next to her and a dish full of flavored cigarette butts. He missed all their midweek movie marathons where they never watched his grandfather's stuff. He missed her mixed drinks that she always handed to him with an, "I know, I know, you're not old enough to drink" speech and a dismissive, disgusted flap of her hand.

When he'd gotten the official legal notification the house was his now, it said it was part of "the Ringer estate." It didn't even have her name on it.

But she was all over in here. Maybe his grandfather's name was on the paperwork, but this was Dahlia's house. Brandon gave himself a shake, ignoring how his fingertips kept twitching, itching for a cigarette to calm him down, chase away the flutter of nerves from god knew where. Dahlia had always had a no-smoking-in-the-house rule, and Brandon had one more place to look before he would give himself the a-okay to go out and smoke.

If he didn't go down there now, he never would.

He needed to make sure nothing downstairs had been fucked with. Who knew what these rich Hollywood lawyers did when they were checking out properties. He'd toyed with the idea of hiring someone to do it. Letting them come in and catalogue. It seemed like the best possible solution. Brandon wouldn't have any idea what the hell he was looking at down there. Whether it was worth anything or not. He'd been down there once, just because his mom told him not to go look. It hadn't been his mother who'd found him, though—it had been Dahlia, and she'd told him, strained, that that place wasn't for looking around in. She'd never gone down there, not once, the whole time he'd lived with her.

The door to the basement was off the kitchen, between it and the room with the ancient upright piano neither Brandon nor his grandmother ever played. It had come with the house, and Dahlia said it seemed sad when she tried to move it, so there it stayed, gathering a few more token inches of dust.

Just like everything in the basement. His grandmother's "collection," which had been the subject of dozens of cold calls over the years from people seeking to buy it.

Brandon had never seen copies of his grandfather's movies in the house, and since he'd never had any desire to put himself through watching James Ringer "act" anyway, he'd never looked for them on his own, either. So he didn't recognize most of what he was looking at when he flicked the lights on.

The stacks of softening, yellowed newspapers announcing JAMES RINGER DEAD were kind of obvious, but the other things not so much: the boxes labeled with various film names and "PROPS" could have been from any film set, as far as he was concerned. Same with the costumed mannequins.

But all right, the butter-soft leather motorcycle jacket, framed and hung on one of the walls with a light placed directly over it, he did recognize. Sort of. Those cheesy commemorative magazines he saw on the newsstands periodically about James Ringer's life and death often featured it prominently, and cheap pleather versions of it were a fixture of bagged Halloween costumes year after year.

He ran his hand over the plastic display case closest to the base of the basement steps. Inside were stacks of monogrammed cigarette packs with pictures of his grandfather's face and a few poker chips here and there, scattered around a Las Vegas postcard that said A NIGHT

WITH MR. RINGER in faux-neon print.

Framed photographs took up an entire row of shelving on their own. Brandon edged down the center of the aisle, irrationally afraid of touching them.

His grandfather's face stared at him from every angle. From every angle, too, Brandon had to look at his long legs, his slim shoulders and slimmer hips. Dahlia had candids, set shots, staged shoots—and in all of them his grandfather had that same wicked, curling smirk but strangely vulnerable eyes that had gotten him named Hollywood's hottest boy.

Brandon turned his back on them, sucking in a breath. He didn't need to be down here looking at all *this* in order to see that mouth. He saw it in the goddamn mirror every day.

Suddenly ill at ease with the idea of being here, surrounded on all sides by someone he'd never even known, someone whose footsteps he could feel behind his heartbeat, he headed back to the stairs and gripped the railing until his knuckles turned white. He didn't need to be down here at all. Coming here was pointless. What did he care if any of this shit had been moved, broken, stolen?

He gave everything else a cursory look from the stairs, anyway, telling himself he owed it to Dahlia to at least make sure there wasn't a leak in the ceiling or some shit. Just because she never came down here didn't mean she hadn't had a connection to it. A connection that had nearly fucking ruined her with grief for sixty years, yeah, but a connection nonetheless. The framed posters that dominated the right-side wall were still lined up evenly, undisturbed, and the shelves of chewing gum boxes, license plates, and Zippo lighters were all as neatly organized as ever. Organized and dusty and—not forgotten, but definitely abandoned.

Dahlia hadn't talked about any of this after Brandon had wandered down that one time, but his parents, before they decided he wasn't their kid, had told him that after James died, people had been calling Dahlia at all hours of the day, either offering to come and buy weird as shit things like tissues James had used or his cigarette butts, or—conversely—offering to give *her* something of his they'd held on to. People had left memorabilia on her goddamn front porch.

"She *did* buy some, too, Lisa," his dad had said, when his mother broke off to dab her eyes. She was economical and strict, and she and Dahlia didn't get along, but if Brandon could say one thing about his mother, it was that she was never cruel to Dahlia.

She'd just never spoken to her, either.

"I know she bought some," his mom had retorted. "But all those people forcing them down her throat . . ."

Brandon couldn't really get why Dahlia *bought* all the stuff, unless she'd planned to sell it all and live off that money once the money from James's work and endorsements ran out. That made more sense than the motivations of the weirdos who thought she wanted her dead husband's collectibles left on her front porch.

Maybe after James Ringer died, Dahlia—and all the rest of them—had just wanted to remember him as a young and square-jawed and handsome fantasy, instead of how he'd really been, alive, or how he'd died: torn to shreds and skin full of gravel, twenty feet away from his crumpled motorcycle.

Or maybe it just felt better to her to have it all in her basement safely tucked away instead of sitting on display in Planet Hollywood where people could gawk at the remains of her personal tragedy—everything James Ringer had taken from her, first with his playboy running around and then with his equally reckless, selfish death—while they stuffed their faces with overpriced cheeseburgers. Or maybe hoarding her dead husband's junk was another tick on long list of discovered quirks, right after her obsession with New Age medicine and those spinny spaghetti wind chimes people hung from trees.

Whatever the reason, it was too late now to ask her. Too late to let her tell him her secrets, confess her regrets.

She'd left this place to him. This house, and everything in it. So now it was his problem, and his decision.

He stood there with a hand on the railing and looked out over it all, the whole big basement stuffed full, and figured maybe his first idea—getting someone in here to catalogue it—was the best thing to do. He wouldn't have to look at it, and he could sell it off to the people who slavered all over eBay. Then, once it was gone and he had the money from it, he could move out. Suck it up and sell the house—as it was, he still wouldn't change it even if it did mean getting a worse price—and not think about the people who bought it and the bragging they'd do with their extra-dry, extra-olive $100 martinis in the backyard, lounging by the newly pristine swimming pool and thinking about how rich they were.

They would tell stories about this place, and all Brandon could think was that he'd spent the better part of three years here, spilling macaroni on the floor in the middle of the night and swiping booze from the cabinet in the dining room. They would comment on the gorgeous mid-century modern features, just like the lawyer had, and Brandon would know this was just the house he grew up in. It wasn't magic, it wasn't special.

The person who had made it special was gone.

So he'd sell it.

He flicked the lights off, plunging his grandfather back into darkness, and went upstairs.

Decision made.

Dahlia's old lounger was still in the same place it had always been: on the patio overlooking the pool, with an over-full ashtray of lipstick-smeared cigarette butts beside it. Brandon brushed a layer of crumpled leaves off the seat and fell in.

He flipped open his laptop and lit a cigarette while he waited for it to boot up. That first whiff of tobacco, combined with the familiar smell of the garden and the pool, had his eyes stinging with grief. Like hell he was going to cry, though. He sucked hard on the cigarette and stubbornly blinked his eyes until the feeling passed, until the more immediate concern of a mild cigarette-induced coughing fit sufficiently distracted him. If he got sentimental now, he was fucked.

His laptop chugged and whirred, but finally hacked up an Internet browser window. For a moment, he stared at it blankly, cigarette hanging from his lower lip. What the hell was he supposed to type?

James Ringer collection. Dahlia Delair . . . net value collection? How much is it to get someone to look at old ju—stuff?

He moved the cursor into the little box and typed:

PAWNING OFF MY DEAD RELATIVE'S MOST PRECIOUS POSSESSIONS LIKE A CALLOUS GOLD DIGGING LITTLE

ASSHOLE?

It was accurate as all hell, but he wasn't sure how much use it would be to a search engine. He tapped his cigarette on the lounger's edge, selected the text, and hit delete.

Maybe just PAWN SHOP?

Was just about to hit "search" when he remembered that bald asshole on TV who always lowballed people and fed them lines of bullshit about how their precious heirlooms were gonna take up shelf space for months and he'd never be able to find a buyer and it all wound up meaning that he was only gonna offer less than half of the appraised value.

Aha! APPRAISER.

Brandon would just skip the pawn shop asshole and his flapping gums. Go straight to someone who priced this shit for a living instead of trying to sell it to vacationing suckers.

Okay, millions of results. Not helpful.

HOLLYWOOD MEMORABILIA APPRAISER LOS ANGELES.

He hit "enter."

Now he was onto something. The first result was for *Silver Era Collectables: Hollywood Memorabilia Bought, Sold, and Appraised. Professionally accredited.*

Perfect.

He got out his phone and dialed the number on the screen.

"Silver Era Collectables, this is Harry speaking."

Okay. Okay. He could do this. He took a deep breath.

"Hi, my name's Brandon R—" No, better not to use the last name in case this guy was shady and had paparazzi on speed dial to supplement his income. "Brandon. My grandmother just died and she's got this basement full of my grandfather's old Hollywood stuff and I was wondering if you had someone who could come by."

"Well, son, I only do house calls for larger collections. Otherwise it's best if you pack it all up in a box and bring it down to my store."

Brandon thought back to the basement, expansive and packed wall-to-wall, that first view as the lights flicked on that reminded him of that warehouse in Indiana Jones. "Oh, it's large, all right."

"Well . . . hmm. What is it your grandparents have, then?"

Brandon opened his mouth to speak, but the guy railroaded him. "I should warn you though, son, that I don't buy those collector plates they sell on TV. Really, I don't buy anything they sell on TV or in stores. No reproduction lunchboxes, no velvet posters, no collector coins, no decorative plates, no commemorative *anything*. So you keep that in mind now and then tell me what you still got to make my drive worthwhile. Elvis? Marilyn Monroe? Lauren Bacall? She's a hot item right now." He cleared his throat, as if picking up on his own callousness.

But then, who was more callous, here? The man for whom this was just business, or the no-good unemployed loser selling off his dead grandparents' legacy to pay some trifling bills? Dahlia had cared enough to keep all of it even if she didn't want to look at it.

Hadn't been *able* to look at it, he reminded himself.

Because it was all stained with James Ringer.

No, he needed to just get rid of it. No dilly-dallying.

He opened his mouth, and—

"Well?" Harry cut in, smarmy and impatient. "You dead over there, kid? Or are you just coming to terms with the fact that all you've got on your hands is a basement full of Granny's worthless commemorative junk?" He chuckled. "Chin up, bud, there's always eBay."

Brandon nearly crushed his phone in his fist. "I'm Brandon *Ringer*," he said through clenched teeth, pronouncing the word so forcefully that the G stopped being silent. "My grandmother was Dahlia Delair. Her late husband—my grandfather—was James Ringer. *The* James Ringer. I don't know how much of a 'hot item' he is in your business, but I've got a basement full of his stuff and it sure as hell ain't *commemorative junk*."

There was a full thirty seconds of stunned silence on the other end of the line. "O-oh!" Harry finally managed to get out. "Mr. Ringer, sir, I didn't realize! You didn't say! Of course I'll come by. Of course. I'd be honored to appraise Ms. Delair's collection. I'll come personally. At your earliest convenience! I'll have my assistant move some appointments around, I'll—"

Brandon hung up on him.

Didn't know whether he was more disgusted with Sleazeball

Harry, or himself.

Over the course of their conversation—if you could even call it that—his cigarette had burned down to a stub, so he ground it out on the patio stone and tossed it in the general direction of Dahlia's ashtray.

That settled that, at least. Oh, he was still going to get rid of the collection, but there was no fucking way he was going to sell it, not even for eight figures, because if Harry was an example of "professional and accredited" in this morbid business, then no amount of hand-washing would ever get Brandon's hands clean after shaking on a deal with any of them. He'd be better off donating it to a museum or something. Better off stuffing it in garbage bags and leaving it out back to rot than selling to fucking Harry, but at least a museum wouldn't be looking for a fat paycheck.

Speaking of money.

Back to square one. Broke. No job, more bills than he could even comprehend. The stack of them he'd found in Dahlia's old writing desk had all been marked to be paid in the next few months. Property taxes for the year, homeowners' insurance, a petty fee for the local homeowners' association. Pretty much the only way Brandon could make those on actual time was to sell his liver, so he'd gotten extensions, but not for long. He had a whole house full of stuff he wasn't desperate enough—yet—to sell. Couldn't sell the house without selling the stuff, or at least having enough money to put it in storage.

He wasn't desperate enough to sell his liver, either.

So he opened the search engine page again and typed in: MAKE MONEY FAST.

Then added, + NOT A SCAM.

And - SALES JOBS.

The first page of results were scams, of course. *I make 20,000 dollars a day using my computer!* and the like. Brandon wasn't gullible, and he wasn't greedy enough for the dubious promise of $20,000 a day to tempt him into ignoring his suspicions, either.

Three more pages of bogus results later, and he was about to give up on the whole enterprise when he saw it: *Confident and outgoing young women and men wanted! Live your own life, set your own hours, never have a boss again! Cam models always needed!*

So apparently promises of unimaginable wealth didn't crank his proverbial chain, but the thought of no bosses, of *living his own life*, did.

Lighting a second cigarette, he clicked the link.

CHAPTER
TWO

*L*ive your own life.

The first time Brandon heard it, he was probably thirteen or so—right around the age when the things adults said about you started to get under your skin.

"That boy is the spitting image of his grandfather!"

Outsiders always said it to his face, loud and proud, excited to see a cherished long-dead cult celebrity they'd only known from movie posters and biography channel specials live on in his genetics.

People who knew James Ringer more intimately—Brandon's parents, Dahlia's friends, the occasional paparazzo, and the hoi polloi of old Hollywood—all whispered it under their breaths or behind their hands, like an ill omen.

As he grew from a boy into a young man, he heard it more and more often.

And not always in flattering terms.

"He looks like that damn James Ringer. You watch out or he'll wind up like him, too!"

"You know where your grandfather's devil-may-care attitude got him, boy?"

"Just because he looks like James Ringer doesn't mean you have to indulge him like he's a celebrity. I don't even think we should indulge celebrities like celebrities! You saw how that *turned out, Dahlia!"*

James Ringer had been a Hollywood darling in the early '50s. A "hot item," like Harry had said. Everyone wanted a piece. He'd had seven starring roles in a short period and was at the peak of his celebrity when he'd crashed his Triumph Thunderbird and died instantly, leaving behind his beautiful young actress wife and their infant daughter. He was twenty-one.

Brandon was just recently nineteen. He wasn't superstitious at all, didn't inherit his mother and father's toxic Christianity or Dahlia's less-toxic but still completely woo-woo new age beliefs, but after a whole life hearing how much he resembled his grandfather, how much he was destined to *become* his grandfather, he couldn't shake the bone-deep conviction that once he turned twenty-one, he would die, too.

Every time he'd managed to convince himself it was all bullshit, something would go wrong and he'd remember just how many traits he and James Ringer shared: absolutely no special skills or talents, but looks good enough to let them skate by on first glances; the inability to make their faces hold an expression that looked anything other than sardonic and slightly bored for more than two minutes, which usually took care of any second glance they got—well, Brandon got—and the propensity for sleeping around.

Like, that wasn't a *bad* thing, in and of itself, but the problem was the only times Brandon really slept around were when it was necessary. And the only times James Ringer slept around—was rumored to have slept around, whatever, he obviously did it—were all when he was already with Dahlia.

God, he hadn't deserved her.

And neither had Brandon.

Maybe that was why he cared so little about his future, cared so little about putting money into savings or getting an education or any of that shit. What was the fucking point in pretending he was going to go anywhere? He'd even grudgingly admit that in some respects, he was worse off than James Ringer, because when *he* died, there wasn't anyone who was going to be framing his face or keeping his likeness in their basement for the rest of their lives because they missed him. His grandfather's lingering fame was because he'd died so young, so tragic, and so publicly, but Brandon had exactly two contacts in his cell phone, and one of them was the cell phone company. And the other one, Dahlia . . . well.

The only person who would've missed him had left him to miss her.

Live your own life, the advertisement for cam modeling promised. Not the life his parents had tried to force him into—the one where he conformed and quit smoking and straightened up his posture and got a good job and wasn't a filthy fucking queer. Not the life his grandfather's own had left him feeling fated for: dead at twenty-one, guttered out like a candle that—unlike for James Ringer—had never even burned.

His own life.

The way things were now, that was as much a pie in the sky promise as twenty thousand dollars a day.

In that moment, Brandon didn't care.

He knew what "cam modeling" was a euphemism for, of course. Jacking it or fingering himself on the internet while perverts watched and got off and maybe gave him instructions what to do.

No big deal; he was no stranger to whoring his body out, after all. Before Dahlia had come and collected him, driving all the way to North Dakota from LA and back in her Mercedes, he'd sucked his fair share of dicks to make rent. It was better than fighting tooth and nail for a job at Walmart, and better still than going to fucking conversion therapy like his parents wanted.

Cam work would be a walk in the park, compared to that. No fighting about condoms. No kissing gross dudes who hadn't brushed their teeth. No worrying about his backup plan if someone got a little rough or decided he wasn't done when their hour was up.

Yeah, he could do this.

The battery on his shit laptop was just about dead, so he slammed it shut, put it under his arm, and headed inside for a power source.

Paused in the doorway to chip off his cigarette on the door frame, because even if Dahlia was dead, he wasn't about to start smoking in her house.

His suitcases were still in the car, but he was too keyed up about the possibility of a job to bother pausing to grab them or unpack. Instead, he just found his laptop charger and headed straight for the wing of the house where the bedrooms were.

For this, he'd use one of the impersonal guest rooms. No family photos, no tchotchkes, no smell of Dahlia. Just a sprawling king-sized bed with an over-the-top pile of decorative pillows and a framed piece of samey modern art that was probably worth more than what most white upper middle class non-celebrity people had hanging in places of honor in their living rooms. Maybe he could pawn *that*. If Dahlia had hung it in here out of the way, in one of the ten rooms she kept locked so the maid didn't have to come in and clean up as often, then obviously it didn't mean much to her. A gift from a suitor, maybe, or just one of those handouts celebrities got from designers and artists and corporations—because who better to give free stuff to than multimillionaires, right?

He shoved at least eight decorative pillows onto the floor, plugged in his laptop, and hopped onto the bed.

The site was clean and mostly black, with greyed-out shots of girls' asses and guys' abs and feet in high heels and the occasional tanned and artfully oiled sideboob. Most of the information was for people who wanted to watch, but down on the right was a gold panel that said SAW OUR AD? JOIN HERE. Brandon skipped past the top of the page, which was the general "if you're not at least eighteen, please leave this site" warning.

Down below were two graphics side-by-side, one of a cute pouting girl in a corset, arms squeezed together in that coquettish way that made her cleavage stand out, and the other of a grinning, shirtless dude, hands stretched out to the side to show off his heavily muscled chest, the bulges of his biceps. Yeah—Brandon didn't look like that. He knew exactly how he looked—duh—and had seen the unavoidable ad copy and talk shows that had said his grandfather was "unconventionally handsome." Square-jawed, "expressive" eyes, the whole nine. His face was fine. His body . . . Well, he wasn't this guy. He was leaner, had a naturally slim waist and small shoulders, and he'd never done the weight training thing like the jocks in his high school had. He wouldn't fall on his ass lifting boxes and shit, and that was enough for him.

Whatever. The website even said: SKINNY? FAT? FLAT-CHESTED? SMALL DICK? YOU DON'T HAVE TO BE A MODEL TO BE A CAM MODEL.

People liked all kinds of bodies. He already knew he could sell his. There was no point in dwelling on the what-ifs of internet creepers' sexual preferences.

MAKE A 60% BASE COMMISSION AUTOMATICALLY!!! said the type below the shirtless guy graphic. GET PAID TWICE A

MONTH.

He scrolled through the FAQ section, skimming questions like, "What can I do to increase my viewers?" and "Why do I only make 60% base rate?" to get down to, "What kind of camera is best for shows?" because his laptop had a webcam built in, but its pictures were grainy and pixelated, and he doubted he was going to make much if he looked like he was a model made for an 8-bit video game.

Oh well, it'd have to do for now, because if he waited long enough to run to Best Buy before he went through with this, he'd probably come up with some bullshit reason not to, and then he'd wind up sucking dick anyway. Maybe once his first paycheck came in he could take some of it to upgrade his equipment.

He clicked SIGN UP, which brought him to a form where he filled out his sex, age, and body type, then checked boxes on a list of acts he was willing to perform for the camera. All solo, of course, because Brandon sure as hell didn't have any friends, let alone ones willing to do dirty things on camera with him.

Online banking info was next, and then it was time to pick a username and upload photos.

WHEN CHOOSING A USERNAME, REMEMBER:

- PICK SOMETHING UNIQUE

- THAT REFERS TO THE MAIN DRAW OF YOUR SHOW

- SUGGESTIONS FOR WOMEN: LACTATINGLADY, BBW_MILF, BROWN$UGAR, GYMNASTFORU, ETC.

- SUGGESTIONS FOR MEN: GAY4PAYSTR8, UNCUT_BOYTOY, POWERBOTTOM, LATINLOVER, ETC.

Well, Brandon wasn't lactating, and he was pretty sure "brown sugar" was just racist pervert speak for black women. He wasn't gay for pay, he didn't lift, and his dick wasn't circus-freak impressive. He'd done some assplay, but he was in no way a power bottom. He didn't have any hardcore or impressive kinks to speak of, and he wasn't sure if there was *anything* he knew to do to make his show "stand out."

BROKE_BOY was taken—surprise—and BROKE_BOY_WHO_REFUSES_TO_PAWN_HIS_GRANDMAS_STUFF was too many characters.

BOY_FUCKED_BY_REAL_ESTATE_TAXES was also too many characters, and kind of misleading, he guessed. Now a little helpful bubble popped up on the side of the application box and told him he could try using Urban Dictionary if he was "having issues committing to a name."

"Fuck you too," he told it, and backspaced. So he didn't have any unusual kinks, and no one was going to find "BILLSREALLYSUCK" intriguing enough to check him out. The only thing he could think of, the only thing people ever noticed about him, the only thing unique about him at all . . . was his grandfather. His resemblance to his grandfather.

He squinted out at the pool, watching the lapping water. JAMES_RINGER by itself seemed too plain and probably creepy.

JAMES_RINGER_CAM. Too generic? Also—just as creepy as plain old JAMES_RINGER. And, damn it, too many characters.

JAMES_RINGER_LIVES.

Again, too many characters. And too reminiscent of the dogged conspiracy theorists who used to call Dahlia's house demanding to see proof of his grandfather's death certificate and listing off pages of reasons why he couldn't possibly have died in the accident, and why Dahlia was harboring him in the house, protecting him from media storms and scandals and the goddamn sun itself.

He tapped his fingers on the keys, twisting the words around in his head. Yeah, he didn't want to give anyone the idea that James Ringer was anything but gone and on his way to forgotten. So . . . maybe not "James Ringer *lives*," but . . .

DEAD_RINGER.

Heck, it was even a pun.

Ta-da. He clicked FINISH, and it took him through to a poor man's YouTube-style dashboard. There were, of course, no helpful/obnoxious popups to guide him around the thousand widgets on the page, but he could make most of it out himself. There were section heads: CURRENT SHOW over a big black box in the center, SCHEDULED SHOWS off to the right, CALENDAR on the bottom left, PAST SHOWS along the very bottom, PAY STUB on the bottom right, and up top, VIEW PUBLIC PROFILE.

Aw, shit, this thing wanted a profile, too?

Well, he was already here. Might as well go all the way. Plus, it wasn't like he was ethically bound to be *himself* on here. Probably no one was themselves on a site like this. It was all about show. What kind of show would the Dead Ringer put on?

No good deadbeat with a famous face. Will debase self for cash.

Delete, delete, delete. There were people that would fish in, but the kind of people who hung around to watch self-pitying bastards tended to be nutcase socios, and yeah, no thanks. Brandon dealt with enough of those just from living around Hollywood.

He itched for another smoke. Rubbed his fingers on the keyboard to quell the need to crush the soft end of a cigarette between the tips of them.

Okay, the site wanted a picture, too. That he could do.

He fired up his shitty webcam and twisted sideways, pulling his sunglasses low and taking a grainy picture of his sharp jaw, his brown hair falling into his covered eyes. Uploaded it. His only viable asset, documented for the world to jerk off to. And speaking of jerking off . . . he clicked through his computer's hard-drive absently, and sure enough, found a few dick pics and bathroom selfies in an unmarked folder. Leftover presents for an ex-sugar daddy who'd turned out to be an even bigger deadbeat loser than Brandon, and, *unlike* Brandon, a liar to boot. Well, hopefully the pics could make him a few bucks now. Better late than never, he supposed, but it was hard to believe it when "late" had left him hungry and having weird fever-dreams about giving in and calling Dahlia to ask for a few hundred bucks. He could've lived for months off that, but he could never let himself do that to her. Not after he was sure James Ringer had done that exact thing: leeched off her and then gone off to fuck around, only around when he needed something from her—not money, maybe, but a wholesome family photoshoot when his reputation needed a boost, definitely.

There were thousands of paparazzi photos to prove he'd never paid her the amount of attention he should have, too busy ritzing it up with his costars and hell, even some of his movie crews.

No matter how bad of a spot Brandon had ended up in—and he always seemed to end up in one, and it was always his fault—he'd never called her. And if he didn't do this money thing right now, he was going to wind up in a bad place again, this time with no one to call.

Maybe beggars couldn't be choosers when it came to nutcase

socios. He re-typed the bio line he'd just deleted two minutes ago and hit "save" before he chickened out again.

At least this way he wouldn't get anyone wasting his time with flirting or romantic overtures. Nutcase socios would take what they wanted, metaphorically toss some cash at his feet, and leave.

Just how Brandon liked it.

CHAPTER
THREE

P arties, like everything else in Percy's ridiculous excuse for a life, had *rules*.

The rules were as follows:

You couldn't skip them, no matter how miserable you were feeling that day, because then people would talk.

You couldn't sulk or scowl, no matter how much pain you were in or how much the people around you were being shitheels, because then people would talk.

You couldn't overstay your welcome, even if the party was happening in your house, because then people would talk.

You couldn't enjoy yourself too much or too visibly, even in the unlikely event the party was a great time, because then people would talk.

Make an appearance so you didn't look too much like the family's dirty little secret. Leave, so you didn't make people too uncomfortable with your presence. Smile constantly, so nobody thought you were bad company. Don't laugh or talk loudly, just in case somebody thought you were drunk or showing off.

Be seen and not heard, essentially.

Yes, that.

Percy couldn't drink, but he held a glass of cognac at every party, because that was what his father did, and if Percy's stiff hands were empty, people would *talk*. There would be rumors of alcoholism, of medication abuse, of . . . well, any affliction people could think of. Percy was no stranger to that. Most people in his parents' social circle weren't privy to what Percy had, but they certainly made a habit of guessing. Outlandishly.

Of course, Percy had tried to tell his parents that if they were just honest that it was nothing more interesting than juvenile idiopathic arthritis, the whole issue would be moot, but that would ruin the mystery. Or something.

His knees ached. The drink in his hands felt as heavy as if he was holding a fifty pound dumb bell. It was always fine for the first half hour or so, a struggle for the second half, and then intolerable after a full hour. Coincidentally, that was also how dealing with the people at these events went. Percy mostly skirted the outside of the throngs of people, making slow circuits to keep his joints from locking up and to keep it looking like he was properly interacting when his parents glanced up to check where he was.

He was a twenty-one-year-old man, and his parents still kept an eye on him at parties. Lord.

At the midway point of the night, when talk was beginning to wind down from shallow greetings, "how are you"s, and platitudes, turning to discussions about sales figures, the latest millionaire facing an audit, and, in his mother's case, her current debutante client's wedding plans, Percy retrieved a tiny plate of fruit from one of the tables in the ballroom, careful to make sure there wasn't any pineapple on it. The last thing he needed was to have an allergic reaction in a room full of people who would assume it was E.coli or hepatitis or cancer. Most likely cancer. Whatever was most dramatic.

His body couldn't be counted on to hold the plate in one hand and the glass in the other, and he wouldn't dare be seen asking for help, so he stacked the plate on top of the glass, then picked up the whole structure and carried both that way, hoping he could make his way to the seating area without anyone drawing attention to him.

The large majority of the tables were full or at least claimed by groups of men with expensive suits and slicked hair, standard fare for his father's friends, most of whom were good ole boys: accountants at the same firm where he worked, or other white collar former fraternity brothers, all of them united by old money, bad cologne, and overinflated salaries with egos to match.

Near the back of the room, though, was a ten-seater table with only one occupant, a young woman Percy's age who looked roughly as bored and miserable as Percy felt. He headed that way.

"May I sit?" he asked. The woman glanced over at him and nodded with a quirk of her lips. Percy mumbled his thanks and sank down in the seat on the other side of the table to pick at his food.

He'd expected to be ignored, but to his surprise, she leaned over a moment later and said, "If you're not drinking that, can I have it?" She gestured at his cognac.

Percy blinked, then pushed it toward her. "It's cognac," he warned, and she gave him a dry *no shit* look before she tossed back a healthy mouthful.

"Not bad," she said, surveying the glass. "Cognac's not your thing, Mr....?"

"Percy. Just Percy's fine." The fact that she didn't know his name was refreshing. "And no, it isn't." *But if I don't have a drink in hand they can accuse me of not having a good time.*

She set the glass down and stuck her hand across the white tablecloth. "I'm Kovie."

It took a second for Percy to understand she wanted to shake.

That... never happened. Ever.

He lifted his hand, letting her see his contractures, the awkward way they pulled his pinkie down and how his muscles were collected in the cup of his palm, knotting up the tendons and flesh there. But she didn't pull away. Didn't look down.

Her grip, when they shook, was firm, and her fingertips were calloused. It hurt, putting pressure on his already-tense muscles, but it was good, too, this time. "Sooo what are you into?" she said, after another mouthful of her pilfered cognac. She had black curly hair that was cut close, and was wearing twinkling handfuls of chunky gold and pearl bangles that stood out against her dark skin and clinked merrily every time she moved. "Or did you get dragged here by the 'rents, too?"

Percy studied her for a moment. Wondering if her reaction would be exactly as he expected. "My mother is our hostess this evening."

Her eyes grew wide in recognition. "Oh!"

Ah yes. There it was.

That "Oh, it's Percy. *The* Percy. The *sick boy*," gasp.

At least she didn't say it. At least she didn't coo, or furtively try to excuse herself.

"I hate these things," she said instead. "But I guess you're used to them, huh?"

"I wish I weren't," Percy replied, then flinched at his own honesty.

Just because she seemed trustworthy now didn't mean she wasn't about to go blabbing about how ungrateful and unsociable he was.

Her laugh was low and genuine, a relief. "I'm trying not to let myself get there just yet. I'm only here because my mom's out of town for work and my dad—" she gestured subtly to the table of businessmen "—didn't want to show up alone. You know. Oh, the horror of not having an escort on your arm."

"You should have told him that if it was that much of an emergency, he could have just hired one," Percy said under his breath.

Kovie choked on her sip of cognac and slapped a hand over her mouth. Percy didn't have time to wonder if he'd offended her—she was giggling, her dark eyes glittering. "God," she sighed, "you would've made the rest of these things so much more interesting. Are you going to anything next month?"

Percy opened his mouth to tell her he was going to go to everything, he always did, but Hazel's familiar voice, dripping with concern, cut him off.

"Percy!" she said, coming up behind him. She gave him a terse, close-mouthed smile, and didn't bother hiding her surprise when she cast a look at Kovie and said, "I see you've . . . met someone."

Yes, Percy supposed that was the one thing he could be grateful for was that his parents had never tried to push him into sitting at the kids' table or into attending the social gatherings popular with their friends' children. He'd never been encouraged to have friends, so he simply . . . hadn't bothered trying to make any. The fact that he was sitting with someone was practically a novelty—that she'd engaged him in friendly conversation and he actually wanted to participate rather than feeling compelled to was as common as a planet-wide cataclysm.

Hazel laid a light hand on his shoulder, being cautious not to squeeze him, as usual. "I'm sure we can find you somewhere empty to sit, Percy."

"Oh, no no, he's great here, I'm not waiting on anyone," Kovie chimed in. She half stood from her chair and offered a hand, bracelets swinging. "I'm Kovie Mittelstaedt, nice to meet you."

Hazel took her hand off Percy's shoulder to shake, her wrist limp. "Mittelstaedt," she said, with an odd tone. Then she cleared her throat. "I'm Hazel, Percy's caretaker. I hope we haven't inconvenienced you."

"Nope, seriously, I'm here all alone too and Percy here was giving me some desperately needed company." Kovie flashed a brilliant smile and sat again, lifting the cognac glass. "Plus he got me a drink. What a gentleman." Her smile turned a little more secret, and she aimed it just at Percy, who flushed. How could he not?

"Well." Hazel cleared her throat again. "Percy, you should be eating more than that, since you skipped dinner. And, thank you, Miss, mm, Mittelstaedt, but Percy must be going now." She slipped her hand under Percy's elbow, the way she always did, the way he hated, "helping" lever him out of his seat when he could have done it fine himself, with a little more effort. "Come on, Percy, we'll find somewhere—"

"Um—no, it's okay." Kovie's grin was gone, and her eyes flashed to Hazel and back to Percy, the muscles over her jaw flexing. "Take this one. I can go." She held Percy's eyes for a moment longer, until he nodded, then stood, collecting her little pearl-colored clutch and Percy's cognac glass. "Have a nice night, Percy. Hazel."

"You too," Percy said, forcing himself to smile.

"Yes, you too." Hazel released his arm and sniffed, taking Kovie's vacated seat. "Oh, Percy," she said, reaching over to fix the fold of his suit. "If you want company, I can always stay closer to you at these parties. You know I'd rather be nearby in case . . ." She waved a hand, indicating what she surely thought were millions of things that could go wrong. She was a former registered nurse, Percy knew, and had worked in one of the first children's wards his parents had put him in. They'd hired her full-time once Percy had reached that in-between state of too healthy for the hospital but too sickly to be solely under the care of his parents, a state he'd never passed through. "I don't want you to have a miserable time."

"I'm not having a miserable time," Percy protested, careful to keep his voice even. *Or at least, I wasn't.* "We were just sharing some small talk."

"Please don't make a scene," Hazel chided gently, talking like a ventriloquist now. "People are looking."

Percy took a deep breath through his nose. Forced himself not to flex his hands or twist his head on his neck. "Maybe I am getting a little tired. All this standing and walking around. I should say goodnight." Go back upstairs to his suite, to his movie collection and his books. He'd gotten a remastered signature edition of James Ringer's third movie in the mail this morning, and right now, he couldn't imagine anything nicer than going upstairs, making tea in his kitchenette, and camping out on the couch to watch the three hours of B-roll footage and extra interviews. Chances were he'd already seen most of the content on YouTube and messaging boards and Tumblr, but seeing it on the TV would be a totally different experience. You just couldn't compare a miniscule 280p video with the picture quality on a full television screen.

Hazel sighed and smoothed her skirt down. She always dressed up for these parties, too. Percy remembered the pinched look on her face when she'd shown up in high heels to the second party after she was hired, and she'd had to tell him his father requested she "look the part" in front of guests. It was remembered moments of solidarity like that which made him want to forgive her constant hovering.

"You'll do no such thing," she said. "I told you, I'll keep you company. Your parents don't want to close down until nine. Going upstairs two hours early isn't acceptable." She heaved another sigh and stood. "You should eat."

Percy glanced around for Kovie, hoping she'd come back so he didn't have to sit here with Hazel watching him take every bite. But no, Kovie had heard Hazel call herself his caretaker, and was likely as far away as she could get by now.

Hazel seemed to know what he was doing anyway. Out of the corner of his eye, he saw her put her strong workwoman's hands on her hips. "There are some cold cuts on the main table. Go and get some, and then, since you want company that obviously *isn't* me, find a group of men to mingle with, all right? Your parents won't like it if we both sit over here looking so antisocial. We'll suck all the party out of the room." She said "we" in a sickly sweet way that made it abundantly clear "we" was Percy.

She meant well, he knew. And he was also all too aware of how depressing his presence was at every party, how he moped in corners and looked ungrateful for all the extravagance. How people avoided him, then whispered to his parents what saints they must be, to be a lifetime support system for someone like him.

He *knew.*

"Fine." He ducked her evaluating look, picking apart a strawberry.

She reached over, nudging his hand away. "Percy, come on. Stop that. Use a fork. Are you really having that terrible a time?"

He shrugged, then hurriedly shook his head before *that* comment—or lack thereof—could escalate into another discussion with his parents about whether or not the limits his *condition* put on him merited a prescription for antidepressants. "No."

"Percy . . ." She tipped his chin up. He *hated* that, God, he hated it. It made him feel three years old, every time. "You know I only want to take care of you."

Yes, I know. That's your job. "I know."

She searched his eyes, then patted his shoulder. "Go and get some food, all right? Later, I'll draw you a bath with those Epsom salts you like."

"Sure," he murmured. She patted him one last time and bustled off to do her own showing around. At forty-six, she was in the middle age range for attendees, and seemed to get along well no matter what group of people she spoke to. She always had him as common conversational ground, after all.

He went back to picking his strawberry into pieces, his appetite having deserted him. The very idea of walking over to get cold cuts made his stomach turn.

Find a group of men to mingle with, she'd commanded. The one next to him, the one Kovie had indicated, would do; at least that way he wouldn't have to do any more walking than strictly necessary. Percy stole a look at them and found someone had brought out a deck of cards and they were lazily playing poker as they talked. One surfaced after his hand was dealt and snapped his fingers at one of the catering company's girls, asking for more whiskey.

Snorting, Percy halved a grape, trying to figure out how to while away the next hour—and then the men next to him burst into raucous laughter and he heard one of them say *James Ringer.*

His heart double-thumped.

He froze and stared hard at the grape, then slid his gaze sideways, covertly watching them and straining to listen over the myriad noise from the rest of the party-goers.

"Tell 'em, Harry," one of the men said, absently twisting his Rolex around his wrist. "Tell 'em."

"He just hung up on me, the little prick," Harry said, sneering. "He sounded all of fifteen, thought he was a big man, you know. Told me I'd be missing a *huuuge opportunity* if I didn't come look at his shit. Of course, once I gave him the usual spiel about not wanting any commemorative crap his grandmother bought on the TV, suddenly he's calling himself James Ringer's grandson—his actual grandson!— but now the offer to come see the collection is mysteriously off the table. How convenient, right?"

They all laughed again, passing around new rounds and slapping the table as they guffawed on and on about how smart and wily and rich they all were.

And the whole time here was Percy thinking, What if it *had* been James Ringer's grandson? It niggled at Percy some, that even a self-proclaimed expert like him didn't know whether or not James even had one and, if he did, where the boy—man now, obviously—was. But that was a spectacularly invasive thing to know, he thought, even for someone like him, who hoarded encyclopedic James Ringer information like an apocalypse-happy survivalist. Dahlia had been private about her personal life after James's death, but Percy knew that she and James had had one child, a girl. So the secret grandson had every chance of being a reality. And what if he was? What if he had Dahlia Delair's house and inheritance to himself now? What if there was a huge, priceless James Ringer collection out there in her attic, waiting to be discovered, and this moron *Harry* had laughed it off and passed it over for the sake of his ego?

It would be exactly the sort of collection Percy would want to get his hands on.

To do what with, he wasn't sure. Donate it maybe, to a museum where it could be appreciated and cared for and contextualized, versus pieced out and sold off and scattered into private collections across the world.

Or he could purchase the entire collection and treat it as a personal investment—one that wasn't his trust fund from his grandparents, which was stuffed away in a bank and which his parents had only recently allowed him grudging access to, since he'd reached adulthood.

Or he could keep it all to himself as a fuck you to Harry and every other one of these ignorant, egotistical men.

Or he could just hoard it, not because it was worth a fortune and bragging rights, but because it was James-fucking-Ringer's stuff, and if he could never meet the man or occupy the same Earth as him or see another new movie with him in it, then at least he could have this one big thing. Because this wouldn't be like any other collection out there. If it was Dahlia Delair's—and he knew it was a big *if*, he did, but that wild frantic hope was seizing up inside his chest and making it difficult to breathe—then it wouldn't be mass-produced collectibles. It would be things she'd cared about. It would be things James Ringer had touched. Things he'd *owned*. That collection would be ten times rarer and more important than That Interview, and *that* had taken Percy months and months to track down a copy of.

Somehow, he got out of his chair and made his way over to the poker table. Somehow, he found himself speaking in a loud, clear voice.

"What if it really was James Ringer's grandson?"

And in that moment, Harry looked up at him, taken by surprise with a completely unguarded expression, and it turned out all Percy's speculation had been for naught, because he could see it right there on the man's face, plain as day.

It had been.

Not that Harry would admit it. He shook off his brief look of shock and lifted his head, his greased hair catching the low lighting from the chandeliers overhead. "It wasn't. It was just some pranking little shit who thought he had a bigger pecker than he does." His eyes skimmed down Percy's front, suggesting Percy was much the same. On the way back up, they caught on Percy's hands.

Percy set his jaw and took advantage of Harry's silence. "Or it was a wasted business opportunity that cost you a valuable personal connection to old Hollywood *and* a fortune in profit," he said, snapping each crisp word. He sounded like his father, and he hated it, but he saw some of the other men at the table raising their eyebrows and sitting back, their attention on him—and *not* on his hands. On *him*.

"Well!" Harry sputtered, his hand clenching on his whiskey tumbler. "That's your opinion, son. And you're welcome to it. Maybe you can track down this Mr. Ringer yourself if you're so sure!" He chortled meanly, which got the other assholes at the table laughing, too. "Don't bother yourself with the *expert's* opinion!"

"I will." Percy lifted his chin. His heart was racing, either from adrenaline or anger. Either way, it was the most he'd felt in a long time. "And I would, if the opinion was actually expert."

He turned on his heel, careful not to overbalance himself, and left, striding through the ballroom and across to where Hazel was sitting, drinking champagne. "I'm going upstairs," he told her, and watched her eyebrows raise at his tone. He'd learned a long time ago not to take a tone with her, but the same boldness from talking to Harry was carrying over, and he wanted to go. He *wanted* . . . "Good night."

She managed a, "Don't forget to take your doses," aimed at his back. Percy waved over his shoulder and tried not to look like he was hurrying, his heart still pounding in his chest. He wasn't stopped by anyone on the way out, as per the usual, but Kovie gave him a tentative, questioning smile from her spot by the door.

He waved at her—a real wave—and mouthed "good night." Her smile brightened and she nodded. *You too.*

Then the heavy ballroom doors thunked closed behind him, and he was alone in the quiet darkness with himself and his mind full of James Ringer.

Their house was old and the walls were thick. The sound of the party faded as Percy made the trek down the long, ornate hallway, toward the kitchen and the stairwell leading up to the second floor, where the bedrooms were. Percy had the entire east wing of the house to himself—a bedroom, library, bathroom, and sitting room of his own. Hazel's rooms were next to his, and on the other side of the enormous stairwell, in the west wing, were his parents' rooms, which Percy hardly ever set foot in.

He knew he should be thankful to have his own space within their house—as Hazel liked to remind him, most people with his particular "affliction" and resulting disability didn't get their own space even as adults, were more often stuck in their childhood bedrooms or sent to live in filthy group homes. It was hard to feel thankful though, when even with his own space, he felt like he was under close watch and tight control.

He even suspected, sometimes, that Hazel had installed a keylogger on the laptop he'd gotten for Christmas. For a long time, his parents hadn't told him the exact nature of his illness; the doctor had named it for what it was, but he might as well have been speaking Greek for all it meant to Percy at the time. His parents, rather than explaining, had just told him he was "challenged" and needed extra care. But then, when he was thirteen, he'd gotten his own laptop so he wouldn't have to sit in the downstairs den with their old Dell desktop, and he'd Googled his test results. Read things.

When he tried to talk about it with Hazel, she'd gasped in horror and taken the laptop, telling him he didn't need to cause himself more anxiety by reading "nonsensical things from doctor search engine and his army of naturopaths" on the Internet. He'd protested, but then she'd added something about online bullying and how excessive stress could cause a flare-up that would land him back in the hospital (again), and Percy was just such an *easy target* . . .

Of course, that meant he hadn't been able to do his homework unless he was in the company of his parents, so in the interests of spending as little time with him as possible, they'd made Hazel give it back to him. It had since been replaced by a newer model, but he wasn't about to fool himself into letting any of that convince him his privacy was safe.

Which made finding jerk-off material about as tricky as it must have been pre-Internet.

Doubly so for a closeted gay kid, who couldn't even rely on old standbys like Victoria's Secret catalogues or *Sports Illustrated*.

Nothing wrong with googling "James Ringer," though, was there? Nothing incriminating about that.

Too bad he didn't know the name of whoever had called Harry. James's Wikipedia page mentioned Dahlia Delair, of course, but anyone could find that. Percy had every biography published, had accessed web archives and forum pages from the very beginning of the Internet. He knew everything there was to know. And if Dahlia and James's girl had married, then it was likely the mystery grandson wouldn't have his grandfather's surname. He could be anyone, anywhere, impossible for even someone with Percy's knowledge to find.

Percy sighed, scrolling through the James Ringer search results mindlessly. He'd visited all the sites before, most of them—including HOTTEST SILVER SCREEN CELEBS DATABASE—multiple times. He'd never seen any mention of a grandson, but then, even the "reporters" at TMZ probably had a line where celebrities and the people related to them became irrelevant, or not profitable anymore. The unnamed grandson of a man who'd been dead for sixty years probably crossed it.

The link caught his eye, either because he'd just been thinking "dead" and there it was, or because it was unclicked blue nestled in among the oft-trawled purple.

Widow of '50s heartthrob James Ringer dies in Hollywood hospital.

He scanned the article. "*Dahlia Delair, silver screen star and widow of cult icon James Ringer, died today at Good Samaritan Hospital . . .*"

So that much checked out, at least.

Of course, a con-man had as much access to these same web results as Percy did. It was entirely possible that he'd seen news of the death, concocted a story, and then . . .

Tried to sell something he didn't even have to sell?

But the article didn't say anything about a collection. It barely mentioned anything personal—just gave brief detail about the drama of James and Dahlia's passionate, whirlwind relationship, sounding more tabloid and gossipy than mournful. There was no mention of valuables, or an estate, or anything financial.

A collection, Harry had said. If it was anyone but James's grandson, that would mean, unfortunately, exactly what Harry had been talking about: collectible plates bought from QVC and "memoir" lighters emblazoned with James's face.

But if it *was* the grandson?

Percy could only imagine. There was so little unique, personal memorabilia around. Newspapers, sure. Movie posters. A couple props. But not nearly as much as there was for some other celebrities:

no outfits sold at auction, no journals, no personal photos, no letters, no cars, nothing. It was like somebody had taken everything James had once owned and burned it all rather than let anyone get their hands on it.

Or it was stowed away somewhere, protected by the grieving person to whom it'd mattered most.

Somewhere a desperate skeezeball relative could stumble across it and realize there was a quick buck to be made.

James Ringer collection, he googled. *James Ringer grandson. Ringer estate Hollywood.*

Nothing.

Good thing Percy hadn't burned the bridge with Harry, the one man who had a connection to the supposed grandson—oh no, wait, he'd done exactly that.

Fuck. So much for that sense of victory he was getting high on.

He slammed his laptop shut, furious with himself, then hissed with pain as the shock ricocheted up his arms, into his already-tense joints.

Take your doses, Hazel's exasperated voice reminded him.

Yes, Percy. Take your doses. Sick boy. Good for nothing leech. Take your doses and stay stuck up here in your suite forever.

And here he'd been dreaming of financial independence, of making his own money and his own life?

What a fucking joke.

He lurched into his sitting room to do exactly what he'd wanted to earlier: pop one of James's movies into his Blu-ray player and settle in for a long night of regret.

Five minutes into the opening credits, he remembered his fucking pills.

CHAPTER
FOUR

P UT SHOE ON UR HEAD, one of the anonymous chuckleheads
instructed. Brandon gave him the finger. Aaand there went his
viewer count, down by three.

Par for the course. Brandon could usually get up to around fifty
people at the start, but they all dropped like flies by the time the free
"preview" portion of his show was over. The anonymous chuckleheads
never actually asked for a private room, never pushed past the paywall
or left tips, but their antics and his having to deal with them drove
away his actual potential paying customers.

But then, he *had* picked a bio line that he *knew* was going to
attract sociopaths. Trolls were a kind of sociopath. Just not the paying
kind he was hoping for.

One of his potential paying customers asked him to take his shirt
off, bitch.

"Since you asked so nicely," he quipped, rolling his eyes, and peeled
his T-shirt off. Down one more viewer for the attitude. He sighed
and sat back a little, getting his full chest and some of his stomach in
the shot. He flexed the meager muscles in both, even if it was the last
thing he wanted to do. He'd learned over the past couple weeks how
to angle his desk lamp so the light caught just right on his (mostly) flat
stomach, making him look more toned than he was.

A lot of effort to put in for piddling paychecks that barely
managed to cover the water bill on this place. The site had made good
on its promise to pay him sixty percent, but sixty percent of almost
nothing was still a shitty cut.

His timer ticked down. Seventy-six more seconds he had to
entertain these people and hope when he went private for a buck a

minute, they'd want to come with him.

Yeah, right.

After three full weeks of trying this, he had to admit it—he was no fucking good at trying to please people. He didn't like being ordered around, and it wasn't like any of the viewers ever asked *nicely*, or tacked anything resembling a suggestion or a "please" onto any of their weird-ass requests. No one seemed to care that he looked like his grandfather, either. He'd tried mentioning it his first couple shows, hoping to hook in some fetishists, since that seemed like his best market, but all he'd gotten in response was someone yelling about how they wanted to see cum on his face RITE NOW.

That was pretty tame, considering. If he managed to get anybody past the pay wall, the real shit would start. People asking him to put weird fucked-up shit up his ass. People asking him to eat his own cum. People asking him to step on things with his bare feet. People telling him to cry or beg or occasionally laugh at them.

His plan had been to just get on camera and jack off, but that wasn't enough for the free people, let alone the payers. Maybe all those other people—LACTATINGLADY and UNCUT_BOYTOY—had something to back up their usernames, and Brandon did, too, but no one gave a single shit about *his* so-called "unique marketable quality." Maybe if he was a lookalike for Brad Pitt or whoever the kids were losing their shit over these days.

Okay, probably not Brad Pitt. Brandon was pretty sure he'd cycled out of reliable wank fodder part of his brain at least a year ago, if not more.

Eight seconds left. More and more of his viewers disappeared, off in search of a new camwhore to taunt and troll. A paltry four remained when the clock hit zero.

Well, four was better than zero, at least. If they all stayed for a half hour, he'd stand to make seventy-two dollars. It'd cover some groceries, at least, which was good because he was getting sick of eating through Dahlia's aging stash of preserved food that had apparently been kicking around since the seventies. The woman really was a hoarder.

He blew a kiss to the camera like an asshole, then realized what he'd done and mumbled, "Thanks for sticking around," all while studiously avoiding eye contact.

After that, it was a dose of what was pretty much his routine: he made sure his lamp was angled and he jerked off a little, lost his boner, then cycled through anything that wasn't Brad Pitt to try and get it back, which was hard enough without being surrounded by the smell of Dahlia's potpourri. His viewer count had dropped to three by the time he finally managed to come, more sweaty and sticky than actually enjoying his orgasm.

He told the remaining three thanks and clicked out fast so they'd get billed for sure, then slumped in his desk chair and grabbed for some tissues to clean his stomach off. He'd thought this would be easier than sucking guys off in motel rooms or in the backs of cars, but it was harder, because—and maybe this was weird—Brandon actually liked having another person there, even if he had to fake liking the sex itself. He didn't feel connected to faceless viewers on the other side of a chat window, and all the one-star reviews and shitty comments he was getting on his site profile proved they didn't feel connected to him, either.

Well, there you go, a creeping little thread of disappointment whispered. *You're just no good at camsex.*

"Yeah," he muttered, slapping his laptop closed. "Add it to the fuckin' list."

No matter how done he wanted to be with camming, a sad, sad check-in on his bank account drove him back to the site the next day. He'd take his untalented self and at least finish up this week's shows. If he had to find something else after that . . . Well, he would think about that later.

He was in the middle of rubbing baby oil on his feet for the camera when things changed. One of the six guys he had watching his show just then up and asked him in the show's chat room if he was ready to ditch this shitshow and have a good time that'd be worth his while.

Brandon was so surprised by how candid that comment was that he fucking laughed aloud. "What, and miss out on giving myself foot massages?" he asked, only barely suppressing the urge to call them *creepy* foot massages.

Although maybe his tone of voice betrayed his meaning anyway, because his foot fetishist viewer dropped out of the room with a snide "ur feet r wasted on u gayboy."

He didn't even have nice fucking feet. What was *with* these people?

Not the *make some real money* person, though—he repeated the question, and Brandon sat back, staring at the camera while a few other viewers complained and then dropped off the viewing list. He'd been asked that question plenty of times before, usually in dive bars by guys with beer breath leaning into his side and asking if he wanted to get outta here, find somewhere better, maybe get off. "Maybe," ha, sure.

But what could a dude on the Internet have in mind?

Like the guy had heard him, an invitation popped up on the lower right side of his screen.

HLLYWD_DBLES HAS REQUESTED A PRIVATE SHOW. ACCEPT?

Brandon watched as yet another person dropped out of his current show.

What did he have to lose?

He leaned forward and clicked ACCEPT, ending the show he was in. The camera flickered, his lighting dimming before it picked back up—and, to his surprise, there was a camera open on the other side of the line, showing a white office wall with one of those typical office modern art paintings that were so ubiquitous you couldn't tell anymore if they were the real deal purchased for thousands of dollars in a gallery or just something off the shelf at Walmart. Movement off to the right, then a leather chair rolled in, someone's hand directing it in front of the camera.

The hand's owner sat a second later, filling the whole of the camera's view.

He was wearing a suit. A flashy, crisp suit with a platinum tie pin. Not exactly the kind of person Brandon expected to be watching his shows. He didn't even have his dick out, for fuck's sake. His hair was the kind of dirty blond that looked badly dyed, and it was slicked back with gel that shone in the office's overhead lights.

"Uh, hey?" Brandon greeted. "Is this some kind of FBI investigation kind of thing? Because I'm legal."

The man chuckled, and even just the sound of it dripped sleaze. "I promise you I am *not* a cop. But I'm glad to hear you're legal, because

I've got a little business proposition for you."

Well that sounded *totally* legit. Brandon moved to close the window before he let this guy waste any more of his time.

"It's not a scam," the guy said. Which, yeah right, but hell, the guy was paying by the minute. Why not play along? Maybe this was all just a set up for a new and weird fetish. In any case, sticking it out and listening to him for as long as he could jabber on would earn Brandon more of a paycheck than he'd gotten in weeks. Not so much of a waste of time after all.

He toweled off his feet. "Fine. I'm listening."

"Well, before we go any farther, I'm gonna have to ask you to dial back the attitude."

Brandon rolled his eyes. Another one of these. "Sure boss. Whatever you say."

The guy pinned him with a look—severe, dead-eyed, Brandon couldn't tell. It lost its bite thanks to the webcam. But his voice was a weird combo of stern and jolly uncle when he said, "Boy, all those reviewers had it right." Brandon bristled. "Now, don't give me that look. This is a business, son, and in business we bend over backwards to help our clients. *And* our talent, of course."

"Your talent," Brandon said flatly.

"That's right. My name is Vince." He said it with a sort of grandioseness to it, like Brandon was supposed to walk out and see it strung up in lights down on Vine, illuminated and immortalized forever. He knew how names like that tasted, and Vince wasn't one of them. Then Vince went on, and the next thing he said held some interest, however canned and used car salesman it sounded: "I work for a boutique escort service called Hollywood Doubles. We strive to provide our clients with a sterling Hollywood experience, and employees like you are the first step."

Brandon squinted at him. Maybe he'd be taking this more seriously if the whole room didn't stink like artificial coconut. "What exactly does 'employees like me' mean? Because A, I'm not your employee, and B, you just told me I have a piss-poor attitude, so what's that gonna do for your *sterling* customer service?"

"You are definitely a risk," Vince replied. "But a risk I'm willing to take."

"O . . . kay."

"Let me tell you about the company."

At the private show rate of $2.99 a minute, Vince could tell Brandon whatever he liked. He gave a nod and waved his hand in lackadaisical invitation.

Back to the script again. Brandon could even see Vince's eyes flicking down to the desk in front of him. "At Hollywood Doubles, we provide our discerning clientele with a uniquely star-studded— if you'll pardon the pun—experience: escorts who look, sound, and act like their favorite stars. We have men and women working for us who look like Hollywood A-Listers, pop and rap stars, reality TV celebrities, and everything in between." He paused, maybe hoping for some kind of reaction from Brandon—awe? enthusiasm? giddy glee just to hear about the opportunity?—and when he didn't get it, he just barreled on. "What with you looking like the late and great James Ringer, we would love to welcome you into our roster. Old Hollywood has a slightly more niche appeal among our clients than current A-list celebrities, but our Marilyn Monroe does exceedingly well for herself and I'm sure you can, too."

"Well if *Marilyn Monroe's* on board . . ." Brandon drawled.

Vince gave him an unimpressed look. Shrugged and sighed. "Maybe your being such a damn hothead will serve you. I don't think James Ringer was too good at niceties either."

"You're the expert." Brandon spun in his chair, not sure whether to be bored or excited.

Vince didn't respond to that one. "Obviously, since this is escort work we're talking about, the job will require a little bit . . . more from you than cam shows." Back on message, then. "But our agency is quite exclusive and we screen clients with care and consideration before we book appointments."

What a spiel. He must have hired a PR person to write up this bullshit, because no way his greasy ass could have come up with it. "I've hooked before," Brandon said, aiming for shock value. If the guy wanted to think he was some high-rolling pimp . . . "Sucked some dicks. Sold my ass. And I sure as hell didn't need anybody *screening my clients*." He said the last with an exaggerated wiggle of his fingers.

"So, with your experience, you must be considering my offer, then. Tell me you're considering my offer."

Brandon tilted his face away so Vince couldn't see any hint of whatever grudging expression was there. The guy was kind of pathetic, but he hadn't batted an eye at Brandon's rote "yeah, I was a filthy teenage hooker" routine.

No. Maybe. No. Yes. No. Maybe.

The job would definitely a change from camwhoring, but was it the *right* change? It was still sex work, which in Brandon's estimation *still* wasn't as degrading as dealing with customers in retail or food service. But it still meant his personality defects posed a problem, especially if his "clients" were paying out the nose for his "boutique" service. It was way more than a buck a minute they'd be picking bones over if they didn't like Brandon's attitude. Or Brandon assumed it would be, since it was an escort service getting him the work instead of a shady Craigslist ad or a meaningful press of his tongue in his cheek at the right guy in the right bar. More money, though, would mean having to answer to a boss. A boss who would tell him how to act and criticize him when he didn't obey and could fire him if he fucked up one too many times. A boss who also knew he was participating in illegal activity.

"How much does this gig pay?" Brandon asked. That was the real deciding factor, wasn't it? His reviews on the cam site was getting shittier and shittier every day, enough to make him not even want to *look* at his laptop, let alone sit his ass in front of it and slather butter on his jawline or put socks on his ears or who knew what the next request would be. So the way it was looking, his next job would either be this or sucking dicks in back alleys. Again.

At least no one else would be taking a cut of his profits.

"It varies," Vince said, glancing back down at his hands. His shoulders moved as he made an attempt to subtly ruffle pages, but his webcam microphone picked the sound up clear as day. "We have what we call 'star quality tiers' for our performers, and our newest performers tend to start at our beginners' tier, but . . . well, like I said, people such as yourself have a niche clientele. So when you join—"

"If," Brandon cut in, bristling.

Vince beamed a wide, plastic, I Can't Believe You're This Much of an Asshole! smile at the camera. Brandon preened. "*If* you join, you'd be starting automatically on our second tier, which begins at a rate of three hundred dollars per hour, with sixty percent going straight to you."

So, the exact same as the cam site was getting. Well *that* was promising. "I already make sixty percent," Brandon drawled. Why not hedge a little? Pull Vince's strings, see how far he was willing to take this. "I'm pretty sure I could slap m—James's name on a shitty WordPress website and put some shots of my ass up and do exactly what you say you're gonna do for me."

There went the smile. "We do more than bring in clients. We screen them, provide transportation and security personnel, and we ensure our performers work in comfortable settings and get perks like food and drinks on the client's dime."

Was it sad that Brandon's stomach grumbled at the idea of free food? That more than anything else was tempting.

Still.

He leaned back in his chair, idly rubbing his fingers over his stomach. Pretending to work through the numbers in his head. Vince didn't know half his checks from the cam site didn't make it out of the teens, and he didn't need to. "I want seventy percent."

Vince raised one obviously-waxed metrosexual eyebrow. "You *do* realize most escort services split earnings seventy-thirty—as in, seventy going to the agency—or worse, don't you? And that's *without* providing the kind of perks we do?" He paused, smirking. ". . . Or is the camwhoring paying you that well?"

"I get by," Brandon said stiffly.

"Sure, kid. You want to go ahead and try it out on your own again, be my guest." Vince waved a hand; fat gold rings glittered on half his fingers.

God, Brandon hated him.

Did he really want him as a boss?

Of course not, but he didn't want *anyone* for a boss, so what was the difference between this greasy scumbag on one hand and a smiley be-your-pal chucklefucker on the other? At least Vince was real with him, didn't hesitate calling him a little shit or telling him exactly how bad his attitude was. He wasn't the type to smile and smile and smile and then up and fire him with a laundry list of offenses. Brandon's last boss had ostensibly fired him for getting back three minutes late from a lunch break, but as soon as Brandon had gotten riled it had been open season for pointing out all the shit he'd done wrong in his entire working history.

"Sixty-five," Brandon said. He was ready for Vince to slam the webcam off, roll his eyes and give Brandon another shove-off or a quip about what a useless whore he was.

That was why it surprised the hell out of him when Vince leaned forward and said, "Deal."

CHAPTER
FIVE

Brandon wasn't sure what he expected Hollywood Doubles' offices to look like, but it wasn't this: a squat brick building with a multi-name sign plastered on the front. Hollywood Doubles was listed on the bottom left in a plain, non-slutty black font on white, and that *definitely* was not what Brandon had expected.

He'd googled the place after getting off the call with Vince, because he wasn't a moron, and their site had been extensive, but he'd expected something a little more . . . a little *more* than the hotel-y carpeted hall that smelled like cleaner and vacuum bags, and the single door at the far end of it. A Hollywood Doubles sign was tacked to it, identical to the one outside, and Brandon took a deep breath, yanking the collar of his jacket up higher before he knocked.

"C'mon in!" a cheery voice called. When he stepped inside, it was into a miniature lobby, stinking of the same kind of ostentatious sleaze Vince had dripped with. Totally impractical ultramodern chairs lined one wall, and at the center of the room was a huge, sweeping wood and glass sculpture that was apparently also a desk. The voice belonged to the middle-aged woman sat behind it, dressed imposingly sharply but with a big, friendly smile as at-odds with her outfit as this room was with the dowdy office building that housed it. "Are you Brandon Ringer?" she asked, like it wasn't really fucking obvious. It kinda warmed him to her.

"That's me."

She turned, tapping away on her clacking desktop keyboard. "Mr. Cassano is just waiting on one more person to join us for your meeting, so if you'd have a seat? Can I get you coffee? I think I can dig up some tea, too, if you'd like. Don't know where I put that box . . . "

She bent down before Brandon could reply, riffling through one of her desk drawers, so he retreated to the chairs, sitting on the one that looked least likely to bust and dump his ass on the floor.

He meant to say no, don't worry about me, but then the receptionist was on her feet and heading back through the door into the rest of the office. She came back with a steaming mug of tea that read WISCONSIN JUNIOR SPELLING BEE CHAMPS '07 and handed it to him. "Uh, thanks," he said, fumbling it for a second with the same kind of awkwardness he'd had when he was thirteen and his cousin had a baby she wanted him to hold. "It looks . . . nice."

"It's genmaicha," she said proudly. "My sister brought it back from Korea. It's Queen Bee's favorite." Queen Bee, of course, being one of the agency's top girls, a Beyoncé lookalike who Brandon had seen splashed all over the front page of the site like the royalty her name said she was.

Tea dispensed, Theresa left him to it, returning to her desk, where her phone's notification light was blinking red. "Hello, Hollywood Doubles, this is Theresa speaking, can I help you?"

Brandon watched her until he realized that was pretty creepy and busied himself with the tea instead. He didn't drink tea a lot. Dahlia had, but it was always something weird, brewed with a flower in a pot, or bought from the vegan stand that got set up down at the nearest gas station sometimes until the station's owner—who was apparently not a vegan—called the cops on them for solicitation. Whatever genmaicha was, it was good, had the same bitter bite black coffee did.

Theresa was busy as fuck with the phones. It seemed like every time she hung up, there was another call on the line, and she'd answer with the same cheerfulness. Brandon half-listened until he heard her telling one customer about their prices, and then he tuned in fully. Six hundred an hour for . . . someone. Who knew. Brandon wasn't sure he would get that high in the price tier, but it sounded appetizing all the same, and it couldn't hurt to fantasize a little about making twenty-four hundred bucks off four hours of work.

Well, not really that much. Not after Vince took his cut.

Still, more than he'd ever made in one day.

He raised his mug to his lips when Theresa glanced over at him. She grinned, then answered the phone again, and he chewed his lip.

He wasn't used to middle-aged women grinning at him unless they were flirting.

He didn't *think* Theresa was flirting.

Maybe in her line of business, being cute and smiley with every man you came into contact with was a requirement. Brandon might not be a john, but maybe she couldn't turn it off.

Would he end up acting like that?

No way.

He was hired to be a double for James Ringer, and James Ringer was a dour motherfucker of a heartthrob, haughty and brooding and unreachable. Brandon knew that much from the posters. He'd be fine. Theresa seemed pleased by him just sitting over here staring into his tea. All he had to do was bring that same persona to his appointments— whether Vince personally liked it or not. Vince just signed the checks. As long as the johns got their dicks sucked by a convincing lookalike, that was all that mattered.

Easy.

The doorbell for the office chimed and Theresa's head snapped up, her warm, inviting smile plastered firmly in place.

And in through the door strode one of the most stunning women Brandon had ever seen.

Half a foot taller than Brandon in towering designer heels, wrapped in a huge white fur coat. Pristine. Her hair was ice blonde, her darker eyebrows sculpted and high, her lips matte red, and—

"Marilyn Monroe," Brandon blurted out.

She swung around, her huge diamond studs twinkling. Everything about her *sparkled*.

Brandon should probably have closed his damn mouth at some point.

"They call me *Ms.* Monroe," she corrected, voice equal parts proud and sex kitten. Her gray gaze roved once up and down his body, assessing him. "You must be the new boy." She reached out one hand, her red nails absolutely fucking immaculate, and Brandon, under her spell, clasped it.

If he was a dopey straight boy, he'd have kissed her knuckles, but luckily he wasn't, so he managed to escape the encounter with at least a tiny shred of pride left.

"You are quite the little doppelganger," she said, and for the first time in his life Brandon didn't find the observation insulting. "Nice." She motioned with one hand, drawing him up out of his seat. Another motion had him turning like an idiot so she could look at him from all angles, and when he was back and facing her, she had an approving smile tucked in one corner of her full mouth. "*Very* nice."

He blushed.

There went the last of that dignity he'd been guarding.

And boy did she notice. Her smile spread, amused, but somehow not at his expense. "I'm the—hmm, how do I put it—manager for the 'Silver Screen' contingent here at Hollywood Doubles. Vince is good with marketing the Lindsay Lohans and Katy Perrys in this business, but not so much with the Rita Hayworths or the Josephine Bakers . . . or the James Ringers. Luckily for us, despite his various shortcomings, he has the business sense to know when he's out of his depth, which is why I'm here." She turned to Theresa, and that slice of an approving smile spread wider, like she was beaming Theresa with all her warm appreciation at once. "Can you tell him we're ready to come in?"

"Already did," Theresa said with a wink.

"You are a doll. I never say that enough," Ms. Monroe cooed.

"You say it *too* much," Theresa tittered back.

Okay, now *that* seemed like flirting.

Ms. Monroe pulled off her coat, and when Theresa gestured for it, draped it elegantly across the side of her desk with a wink. She beckoned Brandon to follow her through one of the lobby's doors.

He thought she'd take him to Vince's office—Brandon couldn't wait to see how rich and tacky that room was—but instead she lead him into a large, warehouse-like space with racks of clothing and a photography setup. Beds, chaises, fat satin pillows, and high-end designer chairs were strewn around the place, scattered between lighting jigs, tripods, and rolled up backdrops. *Props.*

Vince stood in the center of the room, where a portrait studio setup was ready, lit, and waiting, with a twitchy-looking photographer.

"You're late," the photographer said, nose wrinkled.

"You're on my schedule, kid," Vince corrected. "My people are never late."

"Yeah, well, I got another shoot in forty-five minutes, so right now, they are."

"Another shoot? What, some emaciated cokehead fifteen-year-old need headshots for her 'modeling' career?" Vince rolled his eyes.

Ms. Monroe frowned at him. "Don't be mean. And don't underestimate fifteen-year-old girls," she said icily.

Brandon watched Vince stumble over his response, and watched the photographer struggle with being caught between them before finally forgoing reacting at all to duck and fiddle with his camera. *Damn.* Now Brandon felt like *way* less of an idiot for how he'd acted in the front office. It was obvious who was really in charge here.

"Even so, time is money, so let's get to it. Brandon, strip down, please." Without a second glance, Ms. Monroe strode over to a rack of clothes set out nearby and started fingering through the pieces with quick, decisive motions. Flick, *no*, flick, *no*. "I did a little Google image searching before I came in today. I think we can get away with some of the earlier Elvis pieces—" she pulled a pair of pale blue jeans "—maybe some of the stuff we bought for Paul Newman before he ran off with a client like pretty woman. It's a shame I couldn't find a suitable replica for Ringer's famous leather jacket . . ."

The leather jacket hanging in Dahlia's basement. Brandon had to bite his tongue, because no way would he hand it over to skeezy Vince, but Ms. Monroe? He'd probably gift-wrap and hand-deliver it if she asked.

So he'd just have to not mention it. Because there was no way, either, that he was going back down in that basement.

But shit, that reminded him. He wouldn't talk about the jacket, but that wasn't going to keep Ms. Monroe and Vince from figuring other stuff out. He might've gotten away with only looking like his grandfather, but after he'd been disowned, he'd dumped his father's last name and retaken Ringer to match Dahlia's legal surname—well, that and as a fuck you to his parents—and Ms. Monroe at least was more than sharp enough to put two and *obvious* together.

"You're still dressed, Brandon," Ms. Monroe chided as she turned around, arms loaded with clothes on hangers.

"S-sorry," Brandon sputtered, forgetting the identity problem for now, and quickly stripped.

For a guy who'd been camwhoring for weeks on end, it was

somehow hideously embarrassing. He had to force himself not to cover up.

Ms. Monroe pursed her red lips. "You're male clientele, am I correct?"

Brandon nodded rapidly, hugging himself around the middle. Suddenly he felt about twenty pounds heavier. He didn't like the look she was giving him. Or maybe he was just cold in this fucking room. Yeah, that one. His nipples pebbled, his leg hair standing on end.

Her expression softened. "You need to work out more, then. I'm not asking you to compete with The Rock, but people have an ideal image in mind when they hire from us, and here," she tapped her pointer finger on his bicep, "and here," his stomach, "will need some tightening." She passed behind him to set the outfits down on the long table close to the shoot set, and tapped him again on her way, above his waistband on the small of his back. "Here, too. But don't you dare change a thing about that full little ass of yours."

"Yes ma'am," he said, arms shooting down straight to his sides. He clenched his hands into fists, forcing himself not to fidget.

"You're so cute," she said. "Too bad you're gay and I don't mix work with pleasure." She turned to the photographer. "Until he settles into a workout routine, Brandon will just need a touch of Photoshop. A *touch*, Derrick. Subtle. Can you manage that?"

He threw her a disgruntled look. "Yeah, sure, lady."

She leveled the same look at Brandon over her shoulder. "He says that, but he tried to give me a thigh gap. *Me*."

"Uhh," Brandon said, not sure he was either invited or qualified to add anything.

Vince cut in for him. "It'll be done." He waved a hand at the outfits. "I'll leave you to it, just come find me in my office when this is all finished." Obviously he knew when he was in way over his head—and so did Derrick, who stared longingly after him as he made his quick exit.

"Brandon." Ms. Monroe held out a pair of high-waisted tighty-whities. "These are for you. You don't need any help filling them out, I hope?"

Brandon gave a quick glance to his own boxer-briefs. "Uhh," he said, again.

She smiled and rolled her eyes good-naturedly. "Just give yourself a rub and get yourself half-hard. Don't overdo it, though, it's not classy."

"Classy," he echoed automatically, taking the underwear when she shook them once.

The next hour passed in a weird haze. He got half-hard on command. Ms. Monroe strutted on and off set, did his makeup, and fixed his hair, combing it back into a perfect pompadour. Guided him with her professional touch to tilt his chin this way, cant his hips that way, flex this and suck in that. Derrick occasionally barked out orders to do this and do that and stand this way because the lighting was better, but there was no questioning who was really in charge.

Underwear photos first, from the front *and* back—a shot that required him to arch his spine and thrust his ass up like some CockyBoys twink—then she had him in jeans and motorcycle boots. A white undershirt. A tight tee with the sleeves rolled up. The *Jailhouse Rock* black leather jacket, which Ms. Monroe couldn't hide her dismay about. She even had him light a cigarette and smoke the whole thing while Derrick snapped away. For the last shots, she handed him a pair of black plastic-rimmed glasses. "Trust me," she said, when he made a face at them. "Put them on."

"Yeah, yeah," he said, and did what she told him to. He'd have probably done the same if she'd handed him clown shoes or a tube of lipstick to smear himself with. He remembered seeing an interview at three in the morning on motel cable about some journalist who'd been writing a book on Marilyn Monroe, and they'd talked about seeing her turn on "the glow." Now he knew exactly what that meant, except Ms. Monroe had hers on *all the time*, and Brandon was totally helpless against it.

At the conclusion of the photoshoot, Ms. Monroe thanked Derrick with a kiss to both cheeks—which he hadn't earned, dammit, and double dammit Brandon was *not* jealous, he was *not*—and then told Brandon to get dressed in his street clothes and meet her in Vince's office.

Vince's office was as hideously over the top as Brandon had imagined, maybe even worse. He had a huge, gleaming iMac, which he turned so Brandon and Ms. Monroe sitting across the desk from him could both see the screen.

It was a profile template, much like the ones Brandon had snooped through before he'd come here.

Vince unflinchingly asked him the standard questions to fill it out—men, women, or both, (men only, which Ms. Monroe expressed disappointment at since apparently the silver screen guys did more female business than most—excepting "Tim" Clooney), did he top or bottom (either, he didn't give a shit as long as the money was good), did he have any unique talents (uuhhh), what was his ideal date (fondling each other in the back of a movie theater, which for as glibly as he said it went over surprisingly well with both Vince and Ms. Monroe).

Everyone at the agency needed an off-brand but recognizable working name—Ms. Monroe, Tim Clooney, Queen Bee, Zak Efron, Cady Perry.

"Oh, and your real name, obviously," Vince said, pushing a form across the table for Brandon to fill out his banking info.

Fantastic.

He took the pen—it was from a strip club called Dish 'n Dine, which, *seriously?*—and ran it between his fingers. LAST NAME, the form said. Right as he wrote the curly end of the "R" in Ringer, he had a weird moment of nervousness. Jeez, what, was he worried they were going to tell him to take his genetics and get the hell out of there?

He finished the form and passed it back.

Vince sighed and turned it back around to face him. He jabbed a bejeweled finger at LAST NAME. "No, kid, your *real* last name."

Ms. Monroe took a sharp breath in.

Brandon closed his fingers around the pen. He thought he'd felt exposed in the photoshoot, but no. *This* was exposed. "That is my real last name."

"You're shitting me," Vince said. His fingers twitched like he was going to reach for Brandon or something, so Brandon looked up, and got to watch in slow-motion as Vince took him in with renewed interest. "You're related?"

"His grandson." Brandon flicked the papers. "There. I signed. Stage name—"

"No, no, hold on a second there, kiddo." Vince put his hand over the papers and leaned forward, his beady eyes fixed on Brandon. "Sure, the lookalike deal rakes in good business, but do you have any idea how much you could make if we marketed you as the real deal? James Ringer's flesh and blood, his next of kin, the closest—"

"That's fucking gross," Brandon snapped at the same time as Ms. Monroe said, "I don't think that's a prudent idea."

Brandon's anger fizzled out. "You . . . don't?"

"Of course not. Vince, think about what you're saying. If we bring that sort of media attention to this business, what do you think is going to happen?"

"Profit margins through the roof," Vince said dreamily. "A bigger office." He slapped the desk. "We could finally poach Mia Kunis from that horrible parody company."

"*No.*" Ms. Monroe's soft-looking hands were tight on the arms of her chair, and she met Vince's thunderous glare with a slightly wide-eyed but no less stubborn one. "Vincent, no, this is simply not going to happen. If that's what you want to do with him, I won't abide hiring him."

Brandon almost, *almost* opened his stupid mouth and said he was okay with it.

Which he wasn't.

God, he had no idea why he was even *considering* saying okay. Desperation didn't account for what outing himself publicly would do. Operating under the radar as a random jackass kid worked because people assumed he was too poor and too much of a punk to be a descendant of Hollywood royalty, but if TMZ or someone got ahold of the fact that James Ringer's grandson was a) not only a thing that existed, but b) was whoring himself out *pretending to be his grandfather* . . .

"Think of the business opportunities," Vince whined. "The merchandise. The advertising. It'd take this place to a whole new level. We have star quality now, but to have the real James Ringer would be . . ." he spread his hands out "*super*star quality."

There went Brandon's short fuse again. "I'm not fucking James

Ringer," he snarled, and only realized afterward how bad that sounded. Well, whatever. He'd said it. "I'm *not* him. You want me to pull the act, I'll pull the act, but don't for one second think I actually am him or I'll go out those doors and be perfectly happy selling my ass on the Internet again."

Ms. Monroe made a faint noise, but when Brandon looked, she was composed, her lips pressed together. "It isn't a good idea. When Brandon does his job, that will be enough to make you your money."

Vince's frown deepened a second before he turned full charm on Brandon. "Kiddo, come on. You can see how good of an opportunity this is, right? So you're not him, but you could rake it in. We just take a few more photos, print out some novelty birth certificates that show you're related . . ."

"Oh my god," Brandon said, and stood. "You know what? I'm—"

Ms. Monroe's hand landed on his forearm. "No, Vince. Brandon, sit down." He wavered, fed up and about to say screw it all, he really would go sell his ass on the Internet, but she mouthed *please*, and, well.

He sat.

Vince was red all over his face and down his neck, but he let the name thing go.

Brandon had a feeling it was just for now.

Anyway, Brandon Ringer was both too close and not close enough to what they wanted for a stage name—was that the right term?— and they couldn't run with plain James Ringer. "Rights issues," Vince explained, with a pinch between his thick eyebrows that suggested the right of celebrities—and Brandon—to control their names and images was a persistent and worsening irritation.

"We should stay with a J, though," Ms. Monroe said. "For recognizability."

Vince pushed for Jimmy, but Brandon vetoed that because the last thing he wanted was people treating him like he was a little kid, and Ms. Monroe backed him up. Again.

Jim Ringer it was.

Vince typed it into his profile, and on they went.

Unlike the camwork website, Brandon wasn't expected to come up with his own ad copy, for which he was infinitely grateful, so long as Vince stuck to the guidelines and didn't go parading him around as the long-lost ball of Ringer genetics. Ms. Monroe thankfully did the bulk of the work on that part of his profile, calling him brooding but vulnerable, masculine, and sensitive. Described his square jaw and soft, inviting mouth and sad eyes. His sexy, "real" body. His rugged old-fashioned body hair. ("No manscaping for you," she told him. "Thank god," he muttered. "But a little trimming wouldn't hurt." *Great.*)

What felt like ten hours later, the grueling process was finally over. Vince hit "save draft" on Brandon's profile. "That photographer—Darren? Derrick?—should have your photos processed and ready to upload in a couple days top, and after that, you're in business. Keep your phone on, because that's how our dispatcher will get ahold of you."

"And when you get a client call, try to keep in mind what I dressed you in today," Ms. Monroe added. "Clients aren't just buying that resemblance of yours—which, to them, will be charmingly uncanny, but not enough to keep them sated. They're buying the whole package." She gestured to her own retro wiggle dress and blonde bob. "Attitude, mannerisms, charm. Your main priority is character. Good character means good customer service."

Which meant good tips, Brandon hoped. He didn't doubt Ms. Monroe brought in more than enough. She may have had a foot and a half on the real Marilyn Monroe, but he had to admit, everything else about her, attitude included, made up for that minor factual discrepancy, and then some.

At the end of their meeting, Vince shook his hand, and Brandon had to resist the urge to wipe it off on his jeans.

Ms. Monroe led him out into the hallway and gave him a kiss and a big, sweet perfume-smelling hug, and it reminded him so weirdly of Dahlia that he wished he could just let her hold him forever, wrapped in the warmth of her fur coat. "Remember what I said about clothes." She pulled away and cupped his face, that knowing smile back in the crook of her mouth. "You'll do just fine."

He sure as fuck hoped so, because he didn't have a lot of options left.

CHAPTER
SIX

No search results found. Try removing extraneous words like "the" and "a" from your search for more results.

Percy frowned at eBay's cheery, colorful notification. There were no "the"s or "a"s in his search. It was the same as it had been for the past few weeks: *James Ringer collection sale Dahlia Delair.*

Whoever this mysterious grandson was who'd called Harry, he wasn't making any moves on the websites Percy checked. Craigslist, eBay, the usual group of eclectic and overpriced Hollywood auction sites . . .

Items had been pouring in on all of them since Dahlia Delair's death, thousands of consignors predictably trying to capitalize on the trendy tragedy of it, but they were nothing that couldn't be scavenged from any casual '50s collector's display cabinets. Nothing worth more than passing attention, and *certainly* nothing from a personal collection.

He supposed it should have discouraged him from thinking the man who had contacted Harry was really James's grandson, but, for some reason, his faith never wavered. It was more likely the man— boy?—had been frightened away by Harry's off-putting attitude. It was heartening to know the person in possession of a collection Percy wouldn't dare put a price on wasn't willing to sell out to someone so seedy for a quick buck.

Unless, of course, he'd found a *less* seedy private buyer.

The very thought of that made Percy's chest squeeze—of that collection vanished and out of his reach forever. It wasn't as though there weren't other silver screen stars' collections that would surface later, but this was *James Ringer,* owned by *Dahlia Delair.* And unless this Schrödinger's grandson of his became famous in his own right, there wasn't anything left to stir the media's attention. James would fade to grainy, unprofitable afterthought.

But not for Percy.

Chewing on the inside of his cheek, he closed eBay and tried a general Google search, as fruitless as the concept seemed. All the immediate results were about Dahlia Delair—no grandson—and her funeral and the dissolution of her estate to various charities—no grandson—but there wasn't a single word about a collection being sold or donated. Percy had checked each of the estate articles when they started pouring in, hoping he would see James's things had been given to a museum or donated to a charity to be showcased or auctioned for proceeds. Even getting to *see* piecemeal bits of it would have been enough to whet Percy's appetite. Having the option to buy some was a cherry on top.

Or it would be, if he could *find* anything.

But he couldn't.

There was the Wikipedia article, the IMDB listing, the Hottest Silver Screen Celebs website, the biography pages insisting he was secretly gay—no, of course he wasn't, and Percy was one of the very very few people who knew that for certain—and analyzing every sideways glance or sigh captured on camera, moving or still. YouTube compilations of his best scenes. Torrents of his movies. Those quote aggregator websites that half the time attributed the same quote to eight different celebrities. Websites selling T-shirts and lunchboxes to rockabilly girls.

It was all about him, but it was all so *impersonal*.

Maybe that was what Percy was really after, striving to find this collection. Something personal. Something he could touch, that he could hold and put his fingerprints where James's were.

Like the . . . oh, all right, that was hilarious or maybe sad or maybe that fucked-up mix of both. New search result on page six: an advertisement for a lookalike escort whose whole schtick was looking like the guy while he . . .

Keylogger be damned, Percy clicked the link. He could always plead misclick to Hazel and his parents later, if they asked. Just to be thorough, he clicked through every other link on the search result page. There. Hardly his fault that in his thoroughness at following every link available to him that he'd also clicked through one that directed him to a less savory result.

Wow, what it directed him to.

"Jim" Ringer wasn't just a lookalike, he was like a reincarnation. The same blue-gray eyes. The same square jaw. Even the same persistent, barely-there three o'clock shadow that made that jaw look unbelievably sharper. And made his mouth look fuller.

Percy's hands flexed in a way that had absolutely nothing to do with pain.

The pictures were *gorgeous*. So much bravado in them, and pain, but there was humor there too. That cocky, boyish smile, just like in screencaps from Ringer's less melodramatic films. He was so soulful and hungry, clutching at the collar of his all-wrong black leather jacket. It was left split open to reveal his chest and stomach, which weren't the sculpted, oiled perfection in all the other "escort" ads Percy had seen popping up on the sides of his browser windows. He had a thin, fine trail of dark hair leading down from his navel, and his stomach was flat, but his muscles were soft, too. More like a classic leading man than a modern gym bro, but then, that made sense.

And his ass looked ripe enough to bite into.

Percy covered his eyes, embarrassed that he'd even *thought* such a thing.

God, though, it was so true.

He closed the picture slideshow as abruptly as slamming an embarrassing book shut, and thought he was out of the weeds, but then he saw it:

Jim's Ideal Date: Catching a flick with my best guy and sitting waaaaay in the back where it's too dark for anyone to catch us necking.

He may have been too humiliated by himself for a boner before, but that little phrase clearly won out, blowing his shame and his self-control out the window.

Images of James Ringer fumbling at him in the dark of the cinema, his mouth tasting like popcorn and Dum Dums while something black and white splashed across the screen, or, oh, the two of them at the premiere of one of James's films, where they'd snuck away to be together, had him clutching at his dick through his slacks, pawing at himself with that same horny, endearing lack of finesse he pictured eternally young, lazily lovely James Ringer would have.

God, *God*—

A knock sounded at the door of his suite.

"Percy!" Hazel called, her voice distinctly agitated. "Telephone! Percy!"

Making a strangled sound, Percy tore his hand off his crotch. "Coming! Just a moment!" He slammed his laptop shut. Made his way to the door and opened it just the barest crack. The last thing he needed was for Hazel to cop on to what he was up to. "Yes?" he asked her.

"Telephone," she said, and held out the receiver. "It's Miss Mittelstaedt."

Percy instantly felt his misery flee him. "Thanks!" he gushed, and reached out for the phone.

Hazel pulled it back and pressed it to her chest. "Percy, do you know much about her? Her family?"

"No. Should I?"

She sighed. "Let's just say Miss Mittelstaedt is not the sort of person your parents would want you associating yourself with. Tell her to call you on your cell phone from now on, if you must continue speaking to her."

"S-sure," Percy stuttered, before he even realized that it was her own fault for not leaving Percy and Kovie together as they were, happily, long enough for them to trade email addresses or cell numbers, giving Kovie no option but to call the family line, which Percy was obviously forbidden to answer since it was never for him, and his answering his parents' calls was "offputting" to the caller, his father said. Still, the almost-apology kept tumbling out of his mouth: "It won't happen again."

"That's right. Good boy. I'll be in with your dinner soon. Don't talk too long, you know how conversation tires you out." She put the phone into his hand.

No sooner had the door closed than Kovie was drawling, "She's always pleasant like that, is she?"

Percy spared a glance at the door, then moved farther back into his suite to make sure he wouldn't be overheard. He hoped Kovie hadn't overheard Hazel tell him Kovie was the equivalent of the neighborhood riffraff. "Always, yes." He breathed out a laugh. "You get used to it."

"I wouldn't count on that with me," Kovie replied. "Never been one for niceties. Speaking of which, how about we skip the small talk? My dad was talking about you—" not nicely, Percy guessed by her tone, "and let it slip that you were a classic movie nerd. Bit of a James Ringer fanboy?"

You have no idea, Percy thought, giving his closed laptop a fearful glance like it was about to come to life and snap his dick off. "Y-yeah," he admitted.

"Cool! Well, you know Los Feliz? Downtown? They're doing a Friday night noir double feature with a cash bar, and me and some friends are going. You wanna come along?"

Percy's heart swelled, a grin breaking out across his face. How long since he'd been invited somewhere? Never, actually, because before his diagnosis it had all been carefully arranged playdates with other rich well-connected boys, and after his diagnosis it had been homeschooling and his parents, then Hazel, keeping him cocooned in bubble wrap. Some of the neighborhood parents had invited Percy at first, when he was really young and before the contractures had shown up, but to be invited to the movies by people his own age without it being orchestrated by somebody's mummy or nanny . . . that was new.

"Yes," he said, way too fast. Kovie didn't laugh or mumble something derisive, though, which was briefly heartening. "Yes, definitely."

"Awesome." Her voice was warm and genuine. "You can probably out-trivia any of these basic nerds I'm friends with, so I'm looking forward to seeing you show off."

"Who says I'm going to show off?" He couldn't remember the last time he'd done that, either.

Now Kovie laughed. "I'll make you! You have to show the rest of these boys where it's at."

Boys? Plural? Did she mean something by that? Did she know about Percy?

She went on before he could get too deep into anxiety. "I mean, I have my ladies, too, but the guys think they're kings of everything, all the time."

He tucked the phone into his shoulder and blew out a long breath. Raised it back up to say, "Are you sure you want to bring me in just to crush their fragile egos?"

Kovie's pause was longer than expected. When she did speak, it was uncharacteristically hesitant. "That's not . . . you know that's not what I meant, right? I want you to come because you're the only thing that got me through that awful party."

"You want to make it up to me, is that it?"

"No! God! Don't your parents pay for therapists for you like all us other rich kids?"

Her frankness surprised him into laughing. "Yes and no. My parents have a therapist on call, but he only ever wants to talk about *my illness* and the limitations it causes me. My whole personality, defaults and talents and all, is all about *my illness*, apparently."

And being blunt didn't stop with therapy: "Sooo what do you have?"

"Juvenile idiopathic arthritis," Percy said, rubbing the fingertips of his free hand together. It was a habit he'd gotten into over the years to help alleviate his stiffness. "It wasn't so bad when I was younger, but it gets worse as you get older, and I've always been sickly, so . . ."

"Hence the homeschooling?"

Percy blinked. "I didn't tell you that."

"I asked my dad after he mentioned you." Her tone tipped a little ashamed. "I wanted to know more about you. I didn't, like, specifically ask if you *were* homeschooled, I just asked what your deal was."

His *deal*. Yes. Well, his deal was that his parents obviously wished this was still the 1950s—for all he loved the films, he recognized the era's problems—and they could quietly send him away to a filthy institution, where he could be abandoned and forgotten without social repercussions. In fact, they'd be lauded as merciful and generous, the same as they were now.

He was a twenty-first century child locked away in the attic, that was his deal.

"Percy?"

"Hmm?" He shook himself out of his thoughts.

"I'm sorry I pried."

"It's no bother," Percy answered automatically.

"Yeah, no, it obviously is, so I'm sorry. You don't need to be fake with me, okay? I can handle being told how it is. I wanna know the real you, not the person you think you have to be to fit in with 'high society.' And in return, I can promise the same thing, okay? Here, I'll tell you what about me *my* family has sworn to secrecy: I had an abortion back when I was sixteen. My mom paid for it. Then they paraded me around in this community purity ball so everyone would be *sure* to know I was still a sweet untouched virgin."

Percy wrinkled his nose. "I'm making a disgusted face," he said, because he felt like he needed to not be *silent*, even if he didn't have anything to say, exactly. And damn it, now he was sure Kovie had overheard Hazel, so he hurried to clarify, "At the purity ball thing, not the utterly commonplace medical procedure."

Kovie laughed. "You sound like a Planned Parenthood brochure. I like that in a guy."

"I like you too," Percy said.

"So you're in for Friday?"

"Definitely."

"I'm driving," she said. "I have someone else to pick up, too, but she's in your area-ish, so I can pick you up a little after five if you want?"

Being picked up from his parents' house for a—well, a not-date, but still a social event nonetheless—was not something Percy had bothered to imagine, but now he wondered how it would go over. If his parents would watch from the foyer windows, wondering who this girl was, whether she was appropriate for him to be seen with, wondering where she was taking him and what they were going to do there.

He smothered a smile.

"So are we on or what, Mister James Ringer's number one fan?"

Percy flushed, and was overcome by the sudden temptation to tell her about what he'd found tonight.

Maybe eventually. They could laugh about it over drinks, and in return she'd tell him about whatever handsy sixteen-year-old had gotten her pregnant. That had to be a story.

And she would tell him. He knew she would. For the first time in *so* long, he felt like he could bare parts of himself no one got to see, and she'd not only accept them—and him—she'd offer things in return. Not because she felt sorry for him. Not because she was trying to make it up to him. Because that was what friends did.

They could be friends.

Maybe they were already friends.

He couldn't help it anymore—he *grinned*. Big and bright, until his cheeks hurt. "Yeah, we're on. A-little-after-five *sharp*. Don't forget to bring me a corsage."

"You got it," she said, her matching grin evident in her voice, and hung up.

Percy forgot to, for a minute. Just stood there clutching the phone like a moron, staring down at it and wondering if it was possible he'd hallucinated the whole conversation.

Good things like this *never* happened to him. If he had a reliable pincer-grasp, he'd have pinched himself.

But he didn't, so he'd just have to accept it was true.

Man, wasn't that just the darndest thing.

He grinned to himself as he returned to his computer, fully intending on looking up what Los Feliz for their double feature so he could brush up on his trivia in advance. Of course, the minute he opened the thing, he was staring James—no, "Jim"—Ringer in the face again.

He blushed, typed *Los Feliz* in the search bar, was about to hit enter . . .

And then he bookmarked Jim Ringer's site—not that he'd ever get the balls to call or even want or *need* an escort service—but, you know, just in case.

Yeah.

CHAPTER
SEVEN

Brandon woke up to the sound of his cell phone ringing. He peeled his face off his pillow and blearily slapped a hand across his bed, finally finding the phone buried in sheets. It stopped ringing before he could answer the call, but immediately lit up with another call from the same number. Disoriented and annoyed, he pressed Talk and growled, "What?"

"Morning, Brandon!" Theresa's bright voice came through. Brandon startled upright, almost banging his head off the headboard. "How are you today?"

"I—uhh, good."

"That's great to hear. I told my sister you liked that genmaicha! She said she's going to bring back more over Christmas, so you'll have to come in and see me." She said that like she had utter certainty he'd still be around at Christmas. Uh huh. He did appreciate her polite denial of his obvious problems. "Anyway, down to business! I have not one, but *two* bookings to tell you about. Fast out of the gate, you are!"

"You're shitting me," Brandon said, then flinched. "I mean, uhhm, that's great. Awesome. Thank you."

"You're welcome, sweetheart. So, the first is a current client, the second is a new joiner, but both have been pre-screened by the agency already. Client one, Alfred, wants to meet tonight. He's arranged for you to have a couple drinks in the hotel bar where he has a room. No special requests other than wanting you clean—" she cleared her throat delicately "—inside and out. If you take my meaning."

One douched asshole coming up, Brandon thought dryly. He'd have said it, too, if the person on the other line was Vince, but he wasn't that much of a prick to disrespect Theresa that way. "Gotcha," he said, instead. "Will do."

He heard her clack away on her keyboard for a second. Then, "We'll send a driver—um, Cyrus most likely—to pick you up at four p.m. Please be ready for him. He's your security personnel, and he's certified in first aid. He'll drive you to and from appointments in a company car, like I said, which helps protect your identity should a client try to get inappropriate." She rattled off the address he'd given Vince, and he confirmed that was where he'd be. Right up until the county kicked him out for unpaid tax liens. "All right! Any other questions about today for me?"

"Nope," Brandon said.

"It's okay if you have them," she said gently. "I know you all tend to get thrown in and you're expected to fend for yourselves, but I try to help as best I can."

"Aw, thanks, mama." He switched his phone to his other ear. "So who's guy number two? I know you're being super nice, but I also know you probably have four other calls on hold right now so I don't want to take up any of your time."

She let out a guilty laugh. "You're my first priority, but . . . yes. This darn phone! Anyway, your second client is named Harvey. He actually just joined up, but his references from a few other agencies check out. You'll be his first impression of Hollywood Doubles, so Vince and J—ahem, *Ms. Monroe* both wanted to stress the importance that you therefore make his night extra special so he comes back to see us again."

Suck up to him. Or suck him off. Or both. Possibly at the same time. "Understood. I'll, uh, do my best."

"I know you will, sweetheart. He wants to see you Tuesday afternoon. He has a room at a hotel, he assures us, so that's where you'll meet him. A driver will pick you up at one p.m. if that's all right."

"I think I can be out of bed by then."

She chuckled. "All right, Brandon. I can't send you their files while you're still under probation—confidentiality is very important at Hollywood Doubles, you understand—but I'll email you a debrief file for you to look over as soon as we hang up."

"Thanks. Appreciate it." He doubted he'd even look at the emails, but that didn't mean he had to rub Theresa's nose in it. He wasn't a *complete* waster.

Overall, Brandon wasn't sure if his chosen ensemble would have passed Ms. Monroe's standards. It wasn't the classy hooker clothes she'd put him in for the shoot. It was an eclectic mix of the stuff Brandon used to wear to catch guys on the street—aka leather pants, loose-laced motorcycle boots, and a tight white shirt—along with a denim jacket he'd found in one of Dahlia's stuffed closets. It smelled like mothballs, but that was nothing a liberal spraying with cologne couldn't fix, he didn't think . . .

Well, whatever. He knew how the seedy side of this went, and within ten minutes of meeting him, all any guy would smell was sex. Hollywood Doubles might think of themselves as "boutique," but there was no question why both of these guys wanted to meet in hotels. Once their pants were off, it was all the same thing, faux-fancy office or no.

They may have convinced themselves they were hiring him for his famous face, but it was all a pretense, a pretty lie. What they wanted was a willing ass they didn't have to work too hard for.

Brandon was that.

Cyrus arrived that afternoon right on time, his black sedan pulling up the drive just as Brandon was finishing off his cigarette. He chipped it off on the wall, tossed it into the garden, and strolled down to the car, climbing into the back seat.

"To the hotel, Jeeves," he quipped. It came out limp and watery. Brandon's heart was pounding all of a sudden. Cyrus, who was mid-forties maybe and had a buzzcut and one of those faces that looked permanently disgruntled, twisted around in his seat, but Brandon looked deliberately out the window, paranoid the guy would somehow see the fucking jackhammer in his chest.

Maybe he saw something else, because he just turned back to the front and pulled away from the curb, heading back down Dahlia's long driveway to the main drag. This was the same, too, only instead of riding a bus and getting shitty scandalized looks from old ladies who noticed the cum stains on his pants or saw his smeared Walmart eyeliner, he was avoiding Cyrus's occasional gaze in the rearview. Whether it was judgey or not, he didn't know, but he assumed. What kind of person lived in a house like Dahlia's and needed to sell his ass to get by? That was what Cyrus was probably wondering.

Wondering where it had gone wrong. What Brandon had fucked up, and how badly.

Whether he was a tweaker or a junkie, or a gambling addict, somebody who couldn't be depended on, who was as likely to rob his driver as he was to actually show up to an appointment. Somebody who would puke in the back of his car.

Or maybe he wasn't as judgmental as Brandon was making him out to be. Maybe he just had a shitty resting face and thought Brandon just had a lot of student loans. Maybe he sympathized; maybe he had an English degree and was working for an escort agency to pay it off. Maybe he had a kid who was a junkie, and he was paying for their rehab by driving on the side.

Maybe they were both strangers to one another, each silently theorizing about the other.

Or maybe Cyrus wasn't thinking about Brandon at all.

The hotel Cyrus finally pulled up to was all mid-century class with shiny brass and thousands of bright bulbs lighting up the overhang. Cyrus pulled up without comment, handed his keys and a tip to the valet, then escorted Brandon into the hotel bar.

"I'll keep my distance, but make sure you get eye contact with me before you go upstairs. I'll follow you up on the next elevator and be outside the door if you need me."

"Man, I don't need a bodyguard," Brandon scoffed to him.

"Good. Maybe you can tell the boss that so I can work with the girls instead of babysitting your fairy ass." Cyrus went in ahead of him and took up a seat at the far end of the bar, ordering something from the bartender right away. Brandon curled a lip at his back, anything vaguely charitable he'd been thinking in the car flying right out the window.

He hadn't read the debriefs Theresa had sent him, so he had no idea who he was looking for. Ah well, not like he didn't have experience hanging around at bars looking vaguely slutty until a guy approached. He ordered a whiskey and draped himself back against the bar, surveying the room. Playing it cool, letting the "client" come to him. He liked the feel of that.

It didn't take long for Alfred to reveal himself. He wandered in with a jacket folded over one arm, gray hair and gray slacks and a gray vest over a white shirt, a little paunchy, an honest-to-god American flag pin stuck over his heart. At first, Brandon thought he was just some random old dude here to shoo his poor queer ass out of his swank hotel, but then he sat next to Brandon, not looking at him, and said in a low smoke-raspy voice, "Jim?"

"Yeah, sure," Brandon replied. It wasn't hard to slip into the cocksure, moody guy his photoshoot prints had promised, especially since it was mostly him, only less "vulnerable" and "sensitive." "You're Alfred?"

"Yes, I am."

"Good. Buy me another drink. Whiskey on the rocks. No cheap shit."

Alfred raised his bushy brows. "You need a stiff drink to stomach me, son?" he asked, and Brandon couldn't tell if he was joking or sincere. Whatever his intention, it made Brandon bristle. He had no interest in flattering this guy's ego or playing his therapist or laughing at his "jokes" or any of it.

"Forget the drink," he said. "Let's go upstairs."

"If it's all the same to you, I think *I'll* have another one," Alfred said, dryly. He ordered a rum and Coke. They didn't talk for the interminably long time it took for the bartender to slide it over. Brandon looked disinterestedly around the bar while Alfred drank, pretending like he wasn't even there. "All right." Alfred slammed his glass down on the bar. "Let's get this over with."

My thoughts exactly. "You're the boss."

He made eye contact with Cyrus, who snarled back, then headed upstairs.

Hopefully Alfred had stamina befitting his feeble age and this really would all be over soon.

Once in the room—which Brandon had to admit was pretty damn nice—neither of them bothered with any more pleasantries than they had down at the bar. Alfred, sitting in one of the room's two plush red armchairs, had Brandon strip down in front of him, then gathered him in between his knees, wordlessly kneading his ass and leaving a wet, mouthy trail down his torso.

"You don't kiss?" he said at one point, and it was barely even a question, more a statement of resignation. Brandon shrugged. He hadn't really considered it. Nobody had ever paid to kiss him before.

"You can if you want," he said.

Alfred considered it a moment, then shook his head. "Nah."

Instead, he sucked on Brandon's nipples and stroked his hole, making hungry noises the whole while. Brandon never touched him. Never cradled his head as he suckled, like he'd done as a teenager with the other boys he'd fucked around with. Never stroked his shoulders tenderly or thrust his dick with need. Barely even moaned, other than a few bit-back involuntary noises. He didn't *perform*, but Alfred didn't seem put off by that. He'd paid for Brandon's body, and that was what he got. He played with Brandon at his leisure, touching and turning and stroking, then finally told him to go to the bed.

So much for Vince's focus on winning personalities.

Brandon was relieved to be pushed face down. Relieved even more by the fact that Alfred didn't undress, just zipped down his fly and rolled a condom on.

Pushed in.

Brandon clutched at the blankets, forcing himself not to think uncharitable thoughts about boner pills or to have anxiety-fueled waking nightmares about how long this might go on because of them. They were unfounded, anyway. It wasn't, like, teenager-fast rabbit humping, but it wasn't drawn out, either.

It was . . . punctual. Considerate. He couldn't really complain.

He thought after Alfred unloaded inside him that he'd get up, zip up, and leave, but instead he splayed himself out over Brandon's back, kissing his skin almost frantically. Brandon stiffened, way more discomfited by this than getting fucked in the ass, but didn't struggle. Alfred seemed suddenly emotional, and Brandon didn't want to trigger any kind of episode or outpouring of feeling. No sudden moves.

After a while, Alfred seemed to calm down some, his breathing slower and more measured. He grabbed Brandon by the chin, turning his face so that his left cheek rested on the mattress, and laid one last kiss on Brandon's stunned, slack mouth. "You really do look like him," he said. "Guess that's as good as it gets."

Brandon breathed out hard, because he couldn't breathe in. Didn't think his lungs would hold it. Hold anything, even water, even though he felt like he was drowning.

"Yeah," he said dully. "I guess it is."

CHAPTER
EIGHT

For the minimum outcall of two hours, Brandon made three hundred and ninety dollars after the agency got their cut. He also got a lukewarm review, which Theresa ever-so-helpfully forwarded to him with a chipper but stern, *Make sure to take these critiques into account before you meet your next client. Remember to shoot for the stars!*

Alfred had called him unenthusiastic and cold. Had complimented his body, but thought his dress sense inappropriate. Expressed embarrassment about having to be seen with him in public because of that, and worry about having his name on the hotel's room roster.

Two stars.

Brandon told himself he didn't care, that the money was as good at two stars as it was at ten, and who gave a shit what some wrinkled old john like Alfred thought, but for all the pep talk, he still felt like a complete fucking failure.

He smoked four cigarettes while he waited for Cyrus to pull into the driveway for his next pickup.

They didn't even say hello to each other. Brandon lit a fifth cigarette right there in his back seat. Cyrus snarled again, beady, judgmental eyes staring Brandon down, but he didn't say anything. Good. Fucking asshole. What kind of guy took a job driving and protecting—well, "protecting," Brandon hadn't seen him once he'd gone upstairs with Alfred, and he'd been gone by the time they were done—gay hookers if he had a fucking problem with it? Seemed shady as fuck to Brandon.

Then again, Alfred's review made Brandon sound . . . just like that.

Cold.

Unenthusiastic.

Why was he even there if he so obviously hated it, Alfred had probably wondered. Or maybe not. Maybe his apathy toward Brandon as an actual person had extended beyond sex, and sending in his review had just been like sending in a review on a vibrator that crapped out the second it was out of the box.

Whether Alfred wondered or not, it made Brandon think about it. Obviously he had reasons for being there. A lot of them were reasons he couldn't help, like Dahlia's need to have a big house where she could be as isolated as possible from the rich, nosy neighbors around her, and the fact that California liked charging taxes out the ass, but the rest of it?

The rest of it was just Brandon. And apparently he wasn't good enough for this, either, whether he affected cocky, pouty-mouthed distance or let his own distaste at the situation show. He was just as bad at this as he had been camming, as he had been working retail and fast food, as he had for his one brief stint working for an under-the-table lawn care company where he'd lasted three weeks before blowing up at his boss for telling him he was lazy for getting heatstroke in hundred-and-four-degree weather.

How long before Vince decided two stars wasn't worth hanging on to him? How long before he decided sixty-five percent was too much for the puny amount of effort Brandon was putting in?

It wasn't that Brandon *wanted* to hate it or do a bad job, he just . . . It was the same cycle repeating itself. Brandon didn't have a problem with wanting to be good at shit, but being told he wasn't good enough, do this, do that, pander to customers, pander to the bosses, pander to everyone. This was just more of the same, and it didn't make him want to do better.

How was he supposed to act bubbly and seductive and personable when he knew all he was there for was to be a convenient hole? A stand-in? It was in Brandon's goddamn job description. He was a double. Hooking on his own, he'd just gotten down on his knees and offered his ass knowing what he was in for and how to do it, but here it wasn't *good enough*. Alfred had made that clear, as at odds as it seemed with what he'd wanted when they were fucking.

By the time Cyrus pulled to a stop in front of the hotel—different hotel from Friday but just as swanky—Brandon had gone from resolutely not thinking about Alfred's review beyond remembering what an asshole he was to deciding he could at least try a little harder. He'd already dressed differently per Theresa's email, had ditched the leather pants for jeans and was wearing a blue button-down with the first four buttons open over a white tank. It was as close as he could get to the outfit his grandfather had worn in one of his "down home" photoshoots that, despite dedicated avoidance, Brandon encountered everywhere on the Internet, the one where he and a radiant, pregnant Dahlia lay in the grass with their dogs, drinking technicolor pink lemonade and blowing cigarette smoke into the perfect summer sky.

Friday's explanation of Cyrus's routine was evidently all Brandon was going to get. Cyrus strode in ahead of him without a word and went to the bar, already striking up conversation with the bartender like they were old friends. Brandon rolled his eyes, then remembered, right, he was going to try ditching the attitude today, and went to the opposite end of the bar.

"What can I get you, sugar?" Another tender leaned over her station, her glossy cherry-red hair catching the overhead lights.

"Whiskey, please." He quarter-turned in his seat, leaving his legs tipped apart and his body open to anyone coming in from the lobby. He figured he'd be able to spot Harvey as easily as he'd spotted Alfred.

He wasn't.

At ten past their appointment time, Brandon was starting to wonder if he'd been ditched, and equally wondering if he was supposed to pay for his own drink in that case. A couple people trickled into the bar, mostly tourists, and once a wide-eyed teenager who ducked out the second Brandon's bartender cleared her throat with a pointed finger.

At fifteen past, the bartender was giving *him* looks, too, but then her eyes flicked from him up and over his right shoulder, behind him, and Brandon turned and, yep, this was Harvey. He had the same "is this the hotel manager" look, outfit included, but beyond that?

Nothing was the same.

Where Alfred had been standard passably decent-looking old dude, wrinkled liver-spotted skin and a neat row of white, probably denture teeth, Harvey was handsome enough to be on the cover of one of those magazines that talked about golden years and living as your best self after fifty. He had broad shoulders and a strong jaw and salt-and-pepper hair, and he was holding a thick-fingered hand out to Brandon.

His eyes were bright gray and steely.

"Harvey?" Brandon asked, clasping his hand. The guy had calluses. He was wearing cologne—the nice kind. Brandon couldn't help but admit he could actually see himself attracted to this guy outside of the job, maybe even enjoying sex with him.

Harvey held the handshake for a few silent seconds, then nodded. "James."

"Uh, it's Jim, actually." Brandon said it as politely as he could. He wanted five stars this time, and with a guy like this? He could see that happening, for sure. So he shifted toward Harvey, letting his shoulders slump into a relaxed, uneven slope, letting one arm rest along the cool wood of the bar. He tried for Ms. Monroe's tiny curled grin and let his gaze rove down Harvey's body. "It's real nice to meet you."

Harvey smiled back. Nothing really special or sparkling, but Brandon felt warmed all the same, after the way Alfred had been in front of other people. Harvey surprised him again by sitting down next to him, close enough that Brandon's canted leg brushed his thigh. "Miss?" he asked, holding a hand out to the bartender. "Two more of what he's having."

"You got it."

Brandon's glass wasn't emptied yet, but he took the second with a bashful, grateful smile, muttering about Harvey being considerate. It wasn't hard to sound like he meant it, either. Having a drink in his hand meant he didn't have to come up with topics of conversation. Shit, had those been in Theresa's debrief emails?

He could google when he got home. *Publicly acceptable things to say to the old dudes you're about to fuck.*

Or maybe he could just read the fucking debrief emails.

"Don't say much, do you?" Harvey asked.

Brandon slanted a purposefully amused glance his way, hand curved around his tumbler. "Usually don't need to."

Harvey laughed low in his chest. "I'll bet. You probably have to beat 'em off with a stick."

Brandon definitely flushed from *that*. His first response was a self-deprecating *yeah, right*, but he bit it back. This wasn't about what Brandon Ringer would say. What would *Jim* Ringer say?

"I prefer to forego the stick, personally." He flashed Harvey a big, shit-eating grin.

"Let's go upstairs," Harvey replied, without laughing. His expression was so intense Brandon's knees went liquid.

Well, that was one way to do it.

Brandon didn't bother catching Cyrus's eye on the way upstairs, playing the part of entranced boy for Harvey. That was easy, too. This was *all* so much easier than it had been with Alfred. He wasn't sure whether he could attribute that to his increased experience, effort, or just to the fact that Harvey was way better looking. Brandon was almost looking forward to fucking him. Or being fucked, which seemed the more likely option with a guy like Harvey.

Either way, this was on track to suck a lot less than last time.

Harvey stayed close to him in the elevator, shoulder to shoulder, hands to himself, and let Brandon out ahead of him on their floor. Brandon swiped the key card for the room and pushed inside, the familiar rush of hotel-recycled cold air greeting him. It woke his body up a little, a counterpart from the warmth he'd felt standing so close to Harvey—or was that the whiskey in his belly?

The door clicked shut behind them.

"Got you where I want you now, don't I, you tease?"

Brandon spun around with a wink, ready to live up to the name with a shimmy and shake, maybe while unbuttoning his shirt, but stopped up short when he caught sight of Harvey. That intense look, again, but it looked a lot less like arousal this time.

Brandon's breath caught in his throat. He tried to laugh it off. Threw out the first canned lines he could think of. "Oh, I can tease all you want. Call it a specialty."

Harvey didn't laugh this time, either. "I'm well aware." He shrugged his suit jacket off and laid it over the small table in the room's short entrance hall. Then he undid his tie slowly, deliberately, with capable, mechanical motions, and inexplicably, Brandon's whole body went ice cold.

"Strip," Harvey said.

"Uh, hey, how about we take it a little slower, huh handsome?"

"You'd like that, wouldn't you, James?"

"It's Jim," Brandon insisted. Didn't know why he kept insisting it—not like he cared about "image rights" especially since he was probably the owner of James Ringers' now—but for some reason it seemed crucial, just then, more than any other insistent moment in his life, to make it clear to Harvey that he was his own person. A double. Not the real thing.

Not James Ringer.

"So this is what you do, is it? Get unsuspecting men all worked up with your act then dance out of reach? Go back to the thousands of women who fawn over you? Is it a power thing, turning men?"

"T-turning? What? No man, no. Sorry. I thought you wanted me to play coy, that's all. You'll . . ." He gulped. "You'll get what you paid for." To prove he wasn't playing around, he immediately flicked the rest of the buttons on his shirt open. Let the shirt fall to the floor.

"Now the rest," Harvey instructed. "James."

Was this some kind of roleplay? Shit, why hadn't Brandon read the debrief?

He stripped down efficiently, then stood there like an asshole, arms at his sides, open to Harvey's scrutiny.

"Your dick's not even hard," Harvey said, disappointed.

No fucking shit, Brandon thought, and then, *Two stars. Cold and unenthusiastic.* Getting fired. Again. Going hungry. *Again.* "I can—"

"No need." Harvey moved forward. "I know what you're about. You can't get hard, right? So the only way you can have sex is . . ." He trailed off, reached around Brandon's body and took a rough handful of his ass, fingers clawing into his cleft.

Nothing like Alfred's fumbling but well-meaning, gently handsy grasp.

Yeah, Brandon was missing Alfred right around now.

"You need to get fucked, so you force yourself onto men minding their own business. Make them want you." He grabbed Brandon's wrist, now, and pressed Brandon's clammy palm to his groin. "*Look what you do to me.* Now what are you going to do about it, tease?"

Brandon pushed through the sick panic. "You, uh, want me to suck you off? Ride your dick? Something else? What'll it be?"

Whatever it was, he'd do it. He'd do it, and he wouldn't complain, and then he'd get the fuck out of here.

Harvey's hand shot out, catching Brandon's upper arm in a vise grip. He walked Brandon like a disobedient child to the foot of the bed, then shoved him forward. "I want you to *apologize* to me, James. For what you do. What you always did. Do you even care?" He pushed Brandon face-down on the bed and dug his fingers into his arm. "Your father was long gone, but mine wasn't." He breathed out through his nose and slapped Brandon hard on the ass. "What do you think he thought of your sick, coy little pictures? What do you think he thought when he found that magazine? What do you think he did? And there you were, galloping around with your pretty girls pretending you didn't *ruin my life.*"

"I don't know what you're talking about," Brandon wheezed. Damn it. Right after he said he wouldn't complain. He shoved his face into the comforter. "T-the magazine. I'm, I—" Shit, what did he say? He didn't have the faintest idea what magazine Harvey was even talking about. Or what the guy was doing, rambling on about his dad.

Harvey twisted his arm. "Apologize!"

"Fuck!" Brandon was too stunned stupid to fight it this time, and he went limp under Harvey's weight. Thought for a second about calling Cyrus—but no. This was his job. And it wasn't like Harvey wasn't at least right about something: that James Ringer had run around with any girl who gave him doe eyes, flirting and fucking his way into jobs and dinner parties and premieres and anywhere, *anywhere*, but somewhere that was good for Dahlia.

He felt kind of sick thinking it, but . . . well, he *understood*. He was just as bitter at his grandfather for the same damn reason.

So he let Harvey call him whatever he wanted. Did it really matter, in the scheme of things?

Harvey slapped his ass again. "I said apologize!"

"I'm sorry!" Brandon shouted, not trying to yank his arm back. He could do this, too, could apologize the way James Ringer should've to Dahlia. All he had to do was lie here and say he was sorry—and he was, he was sorry about Dahlia, too—and that was what it would take for him to get out of this fucking hotel room. "I'm sorry, okay?"

"No you're not." Harvey's nails bit into his skin as he wrenched Brandon's arm again, giving him no space and no leverage to move away if he tried. "But you will be."

For all Harvey's talk, the sex wasn't nearly as bad as what had gone down before it, although maybe that was a low bar to cross.

Brandon found a rhythm where he said "sorry" on every thrust, and Harvey seemed to get off enough on the abject humiliation of it that inflicting pain was no longer as necessary.

But Brandon still had bruises. The thick fingers he'd noticed when Harvey shook his hand were imprinted on his hips, turning a deep blue. The kind of bruises that would go through the fucking rainbow before they faded. He touched them while Harvey did his belt back up and pulled his jacket on. Stopped in front of the mirror and smoothed his hair back. His eyes were just as cool when they found Brandon's in the mirror. "Say it," he said.

By now, it was automatic. "Sorry."

Harvey snorted. "You're starting to sound like you mean it. You'll get better. Next time you'll say it and you'll be sincere." No, no, no matter how much he thought James Ringer deserved it, no fucking way, *no*— "It was good enough this time, though." Harvey smoothed his jacket down and left without a second glance, the door clicking shut behind him.

It was really pathetic that Brandon immediately wondered if "good enough" was five stars.

Really pathetic, and really fucked in the head.

So this was what he got for trying, huh? He didn't try, he was cold, he did try, he ended up with a nutcase who thought he actually *was* his grandfather. He'd been dragged into boss's offices plenty of times, shaken by the scruff of the neck and told he needed to be different, to change, to be something more, but he never knew how to *be* that. And he didn't know now.

He curled up where Harvey had left him, pressing his fingers into the blooming bruises, but he didn't have the luxury of wallowing alone for more than a couple minutes before a sharp rap sounded on the door.

"Let's go." Cyrus. "Check-out's at three."

Brandon couldn't let Cyrus see him like this—couldn't stand to have his eyes on him, thinking *you deserve this* just like Harvey did—so he picked himself up and went to the bathroom, washing away the blood from where he'd bitten his lip and working his hair into order. He dressed, buttoning his shirt all the way this time, and slid his sunglasses over his eyes, hiding them from view.

How many paparazzi photos showed his grandfather looking exactly like this? Fat round sunglasses keeping the shadows of his face secret, his mouth tight and blank of expression as he went here or there, sometimes with Dahlia, always with stony-faced bodyguards.

How much had *he* hidden?

Brandon doubted it was something like this. His issues had to have been all rich Hollywood boy problems, like, oh, my wife saw the article about me running around with five other girls, oh, this gorgeous babe I banged is pregnant, how much do I pay her to keep quiet? Or, in Dahlia's case: when do we reveal? Oh, which car do I drive today? Which script should I decline at my leisure because my pretty face can always get me better? How will I spend that check the cigarette company wrote me for flashing their brand?

Cyrus rapped on the door again. "Hey, Ringer! You alive in there?" Fucker sounded amused by it, like it didn't matter either way to him. Brandon could have been murdered and stuffed in a dry-cleaning bag under the bed by now.

It seemed weird he hadn't been. Weird that he had to put this face on and go out there and pretend what had just happened to him wasn't terrifying and offputting and invasive in ways he hadn't known were possible. That he wasn't still thinking about how he understood, in some small way, how Harvey felt, looking at James Ringer and the waste of space he'd been, how he glided through it all without shit sticking to him and then dumped it all on Dahlia to carry for the rest of her fucking life. And he hadn't been prepared for it, not in the slightest, not even with his previous . . . experience.

Harvey, the way Harvey wanted to play, was new and terrible, and Brandon couldn't even articulate *why*.

He pushed through the door.

"You look like shit," Cyrus said immediately.

"Thanks. You look great, too. Let's get the fuck out of here."

By the time Cyrus dropped Brandon off, he was pretty well settled on the fact that he needed to email Theresa and tell her about Harvey. That was why he gave the agency a cut of his pay, right? For them to screen clients and weed out the bad ones. Harvey was a bad one. He may not have raped Brandon or caused lasting damage, but whether he was right about James Ringer or not, that cold feeling in Brandon's chest wasn't going away, and in fact, his hands were trembling, and he felt claustrophobic and jumpy, like Harvey was going to be waiting in the front hall when Brandon finally managed to get the key to work in the lock of Dahlia's front door.

It took four tries.

His laptop was on the desk in the living room, its damaged fan whirring loudly, and as badly as Brandon wanted a shower, he wanted to get this over with first. Get some kind of control over this whole shitty thing, no matter how retroactive. Sure, he couldn't take this back, but he could prevent it from happening again, and once he accomplished that, he'd be able to move past it. Get over it.

Eventually.

He'd just email Theresa, let her know how tonight had gone down, how Harvey had set off alarm bells and been rough with him in a threatening gonna-get-worse way, and that he didn't want him as a client anymore. Harvey was a first-timer, right? So it wasn't like Brandon would be offending a long-time client or one of Vince's buddies.

Theresa had given him a business card with her HD email on it, but Brandon had no idea where it was, so he popped into one of her debrief emails to get it—

And then the word "rough" caught his eye.

It was Harvey's debrief.

Enjoys rough play and D/s, including humiliation. Please email me before Tuesday if this will be an issue for you and we will work out a solution that fits for both of you.

Brandon sat back in his chair. Sagged against the back of it.

Enjoys rough play.

Humiliation.

Please email me before Tuesday.

If he'd read this email when he was supposed to, would he have emailed her? Probably not; he needed the money. But he'd have gone in prepared for what was to come. He'd have been better able to do his job. Maybe the reason he was so shaken up was because of how Harvey had done a complete one-eighty once they were alone together.

Maybe Harvey at the bar—charming, personable, flirtatious—was his actual personality, and Harvey in the room—domineering, terrifying, humiliating—was all just a sexual act. A play, just like the email said.

Could Brandon really fault Harvey for wanting to do a little roleplay with someone he *thought* was on the same page? It would be no less ridiculous than getting upset with the guy for pretending to be his teacher at school once they were alone together, or, hell, asking Brandon to call him Daddy or Mr. Freeze or Nicolas Cage, if that was what had been pre-arranged.

It *had been* pre-arranged.

This was all Brandon's fault. If he'd have read the email, he would've known ahead of time to expect to get thrown around. He'd have been ready, mentally prepared. Could have played along, really shown Harvey a good time. Fuck, all his fighting and whining . . . Harvey had to have thought that was part of Brandon's acting.

But then, Harvey had said Brandon was "good enough," though. So he couldn't have ruined the experience for him too badly. Maybe he could still recover. Really outperform himself next time, get into it. Let Harvey chat him up at the bar and then get on his knees right away when they went upstairs, pander to what Harvey had paid for.

One thing was for sure: he wouldn't have a problem sounding sorry.

CHAPTER
NINE

Friday came after a week that felt both too fast and like it dragged on endlessly. Percy had never experienced genuinely looking forward to a social event, and couldn't remember worrying this much about one.

He was still excited, though. Excited enough that for the first time in a long time, getting out of bed that morning wasn't excruciatingly difficult. He wondered if this was how healthy people did it, woke up with a smile at the ceiling and a stretch and then rolled (almost) effortlessly out of bed. His joints did their usual complaining, creaking, and popping as he got to his feet. The air in his suite was always warm and treated by the three humidifiers installed in all the rooms except his library, but the wood floor always managed to give him a cool shock each morning.

This morning, it didn't damper his mood one bit.

Not even Hazel's grumbling could get to him. He bucked up the courage to ask for fried eggs instead of scrambled, and jam on his toast, and endured her sighing lecture about managing the sugar in his diet before he politely but firmly repeated his request. The faint trickle of guilt at the back of his throat was worth the way she drew herself up, looking surprised, then nodded curtly and left to do as he asked. He ate alone, doing some last-minute cramming for tonight's movies. After clearing his dishes, he retreated to his bedroom, where he spent an embarrassing amount of time trying to plan an outfit.

It wasn't as though he actually got to purchase his own clothes— his parents mostly did collective, seasonal orders from designers that were in vogue, so he always had something deemed appropriate to wear to all the galas his parents took him to, but this was different.

This wasn't dressing to impress friends of his parents. This was dressing to be himself. To go out with people he wanted to like him.

The very fact that he could come home tonight with *multiple* friends his age was enough to make his hands shake. Well, more than usual.

By the time he settled on something nice but not overly dressy, it was almost four-thirty, and he was keenly aware he'd teased Kovie about being on time. Hurrying to button his shirt just made it more difficult, and as he was concentrating on slowing his breathing and flexing the weak muscles in his wrists to maneuver his fingers more efficiently, there was a quick knock on his suite door and then Hazel was bustling in in what Percy recognized as her pre-dinner routine.

She froze at the same moment he did.

He'd been so preoccupied finding something to wear, he hadn't bothered to put away the discarded possibilities. They were all on his bed, stacked absently in haphazard piles. His chosen shirt hung open over the black undershirt he'd put on, and his dress slacks were on, belt already done up. His shoes were resting beside his mirror.

"What are you doing?" Hazel asked, in the same sort of tone with which someone would say, "Is that a live grenade in your hand?"

Percy swallowed. Met his own eyes in the mirror. Then Hazel's. Why hadn't he done this earlier? "I'm going out tonight. The woman who called last week, Kovie——Miss Mittelstaedt—she was—" *Damn it, say a complete sentence!* He cleared his throat hard and squared his shoulders, turning to face her. "The woman I was talking to at the party, Kovie Mittelstaedt, invited me out to a theater tonight with her friends. I'm being picked up in ten minutes."

Hazel's voice was artificially calm. "And you didn't think to tell me this?"

Oh, right. That was why.

He wouldn't lie—it was nice to see her sugary sweet, I'm-talking-to-a-child voice fade into simmering anger.

"I didn't think it was necessary. I'm an adult. So is she." *I don't need your permission.*

Hazel set down her armful of miniature tablecloth and cutlery on Percy's side table and faced him, hands on her hips. "Yes, you are both legal adults," she said, snapping her teeth on the *t*. "You've reached the age of maturity, Percy, I know, and you're taking better care of yourself now than ever before. I know that can make you feel empowered, and independent, but you're not *like* her, Percy. Does she have someone to make her breakfast every morning because she's not capable of it? You couldn't even plan an outfit on your own without making a mess of it." She cast a pointed look around the room. Percy flushed. "You can't possibly think you are an 'adult' in the same way she is. She probably has a *job*, Percy. She probably does her own laundry, and makes her own meals, and isn't dependent on treatments and medications. She isn't fragile. And yes, that means she gets to plan her own schedule. Is she the one picking you up?" Percy clenched his teeth, and Hazel raised her eyebrows. "See? Sweetie, come on, she has a driver's license. She can make her own schedule because she is capable of taking herself places she wants to go, and won't have to keep an eye on herself so she doesn't worry her parents when she has a medical emergency—"

"I could do that too!" Percy exploded, before he could think better of it. "I *could* drive, if you would just let me *learn*. I could get a license." Yes, the gripping would be difficult, but that didn't mean he was *incapable*. He was so, so sick of being thought of as incapable—by his parents, by their guests, and by Hazel.

And he was scared that Kovie, too, would come to see him that way.

Scared she will?

Or scared you *will?*

Hazel tsked gently. "Percy, calm down. You need to manage your stress. Don't you remember what Dr. Marietta said last time?" She tutted again and sighed. "And you want a driver's license now?" she said, like he was a little boy who'd asked for a pony and a flatscreen TV *and* a yacht for Christmas. "Does this Kovie think you had one?"

"Uh . . ." Percy thought back. No, she hadn't asked. She'd just . . . offered. But it hadn't seemed weird at the time. "No," he admitted tersely.

"Exactly. See? If she thought you were the least bit independent—if she thought you were so normal and so much of an independent adult—she would have told you a place and a time and assumed you'd meet her. But she didn't. Already she's babying you. Do you really think she sees you as her equal? It's a pity date, Percy." Hazel's big brown eyes were genuinely sad, the laugh lines around her eyes dimpling in with each word. "She feels sorry for you, and I don't want you to have to sit through that, knowing how she must think."

"No," Percy protested. No, Kovie was honest. She'd asked about his disabilities up front because she wanted to know him, not because she thought less of him. She'd shared her own family secret with him. She wouldn't invite him out under false pretenses.

But Hazel only seemed more convinced. She came to him and put her hands lightly on his shoulders. "Yes, yes. Oh, yes, Percy, I know you don't know many people your age, but you have to understand it's very trendy for them to be politically correct now. She saw how awkward you were the other night and she felt sorry for you. Because you're so sick and lonely. So she invited you out. But she didn't invite you out as a peer." She rubbed Percy's shoulders. "I'm glad you think the best of her, but she invited you out as a project, as an object of pity, like I'm sure she was for someone, once. She'll drive you there, and then she'll introduce you to all her other normal friends, and they'll all be so kind to you, and then she'll drop you off here again and her need to be a good Samaritan will be satisfied, and she won't call you again. Or she will, but she won't be nearly so accommodating, because secretly some part of her will *want* you to say no. And then how much of an adult will you be, Percy? How much of her equal will you be?"

She sighed one last time, strode across the room, and started woefully picking up Percy's strewn clothes and laying them over her arm to put back on the hangers. Percy's hands stung just looking at how many he'd need to put clothes back on. "Who will care for you after she's doted on you for one night and then left you, Percy? Not her. She has a life to live, her *own* life, and she won't have time to drag you along and make you comfortable and tend to your social anxieties and chauffeur you around, and you'll be right back here. With me. And after all I do for you, all the meals I've cooked and laundry I've done and prescriptions I've fetched and appointments I've driven you to, you have the nerve to say you don't need to tell me where you're going and with whom because you're an *adult*? What if something happened? How would I take care of you?"

"I . . ." Percy's throat thickened. His knees ached. He didn't bother telling Hazel it wasn't a *date*, because everything else she was saying . . .

He wanted to be strong. To be independent. He wanted to be thought of as an adult, as Percy, not just Percy Charles, the sick boy.

But what if he'd been so desperate for someone to see him like that, he'd seeded affection and genuineness into Kovie? What if he was only projecting his wants onto her, and Hazel was exactly right? He couldn't bear for Kovie to treat him like that. Like a child. Like a breakable—breakable—like a *purse puppy*, carried around and brought out to show how it could fit into a teacup and how it shook all the time.

"I didn't mean it like that," he finally managed. "I'm sorry, I just thought, I thought . . . I thought you wouldn't let me go, if I told you."

"And did you ever consider that the reason you're so sure of my answer is because you know it to be correct? Tell me, Percy, did you even take your pills this afternoon?"

God, he hadn't. He'd been so busy trying to decide what to wear and how to present himself, so busy furiously brushing up on movie facts he already knew in order to make a good impression, that he'd completely forgotten.

"And did you remember you have an infusion early tomorrow morning? Will Kovie be driving you to that after you've spent a late night out with her?"

"I wouldn't be out that late," Percy protested, but by now it was half-hearted, worn down, no matter how much he hated himself suddenly, fiercely, for wilting under her criticism.

"How can you even say that, Percy? You're depending on her for a ride. Did you ask her what time she planned on bringing you home by? Did she ask *you* what time you needed to be home for? No, of course she didn't. Which would mean you would be stuck waiting for whenever she felt like bringing you back." Hazel's voice escalated as she went on, and Percy fought the urge to cover his ears, yank his shirt up over his head to shut the buzz of it out. Then he really *would* be acting like a child." What if she had a couple drinks? What if she and her friends decided to go dancing and you were in too much pain to? Do you really think you would speak up and tell them to bring you home? Stand up to that peer pressure? Of course not. So who would be driving you home? Me? But you weren't planning on telling me you were going out in the first place!"

Stop. Stop it.

What if Kovie wanted to go out after the movies? What if her friends wanted to get drinks, or go for a midnight dinner? Would he want to impose on her by asking her to leave her friends and bring him home early? Be a total drain on her good time? It was true that with his pain and the fatigue that came with it, he only ever had a few hours of energy in him at a time, and that was assuming he'd rested all day in preparation, which he *hadn't.* He'd been on his feet, up and down, trying on clothes, for at least an hour. He was lucky he wasn't already in bed because of pain.

Honestly, he hadn't even remembered he was supposed to be in pain until just now.

Gravel crunched outside, the telltale sound of a car's brakes squeaking. Percy and Hazel looked out the window at the same time to see a late '60s Mustang slide to a smooth halt. "She's already here," Percy mumbled, despite knowing he'd lost the battle.

"That's all right, sweetheart. I'll go down and tell her for you that you can't come out. I'll even say it's my fault that I *forgot to tell you* about your appointment early tomorrow morning. That way you won't lose face, hmm?"

It really was generous of her. Such a convenient half-truth, so much better than him having to admit like a child that he hadn't gotten permission to leave the house, hadn't remembered his limitations and planned appropriately around them. Better than admitting to anyone other than Hazel—who understood, didn't judge, just took care of him day after day—that he and Kovie *weren't* on the same level. He nodded, dropping down onto the edge of his bed. He couldn't even look at Hazel. "Thank you," he mumbled.

"Don't even think of it," Hazel said softly, ruffling his hair as she laid the pile of his clothes on his bed beside him. "What else am I here for? I'll just pop downstairs, let her know, offer your apologies, and then I'll be right back up to clean up this mess, then make you dinner. Your favorite. How about perogies and chanterelle mushrooms? What say I draw you a bath tonight too, hmm? I can tell your knees are swollen."

Percy nodded again, not saying anything. He could feel tears gathering in his throat and behind his eyes. He wondered if he could get a cry in between the time she went downstairs and the time she returned.

He couldn't, of course. But it wouldn't be the first time she'd seen him cry.

He held off on crying until he was safely settled in the bathtub. He wasn't *alone*, not with Hazel breezing in and out, finding excuses to come in and check on him and prod at his bruised ego, but at least he could dunk his head under the hot water to hide the evidence. If she noticed, she didn't comment, having accomplished today's fill of reminding Percy what a child he was.

After a long soak, she helped him out of the tub, draped him in a towel, and left him.

His folded pajamas, baby blue and specially and unnecessarily tailored from hypoallergenic, silky-soft material to keep from irritating his skin, were waiting for him on the bed, and on his bedside table was a glass of water and his pills.

He stood there a long time, with his towel wrapped around his head and shoulders like a toddler, and just *stared* at them.

The pills were whatever, he had genuinely forgotten to take them and they were, yes, essential to his quality of life, but the pajamas? The pajamas filled him with a kind of rage that had his hands *shaking*. He was not a child. He was capable of going into his drawer and selecting his own pajamas.

While he was at it, he may sometimes need help getting in and out of a deep bathtub, but he could run his own bathwater. And true, he was tired from being on his feet all day, but he could've put away his own clothes, too. Could have, except Hazel had already done it for him, everything folded and pressed and returned to its proper place in dresser or closet. He hadn't even had the *chance* to do it himself. They all just *assumed*.

It was a recurring theme.

What he'd said in the heat of their fight—that he could have earned a driver's license, could be able to drive . . . it was *true*. If Hazel just gave him the chance, if his parents gave him the *chance* . . .

But they didn't. They never had. And tonight, he'd lost the chance to prove he could go out with friends, with people who cared about him, who liked him. Not because they were all at some stuffy event together, but because of *him*.

He yanked his drawer open and pushed the pajamas Hazel had selected for him back into it and grabbing a set of blue silk ones instead. He didn't have a preference one way or another, really, but at least these were his choice. His.

He was about to pull them on when he heard . . . a tapping? At his window?

The sound took him so much by surprise that he forgot to finish dressing, which meant that when he opened the window and leaned out, he was completely naked.

And Kovie was standing on the lawn.

"Hey loser!" she called up to him. "How's the tower? Your dragon wouldn't let me come in and see you." She blinked, and then one of her eyebrows crept upward. "But I *definitely* see you now, dude."

Percy's face went hot. "Oh! Uh! J-just a second!" He ducked away from the window, yanking the pants for the pajamas over his scrawny legs.

Kovie was still standing in his yard when he returned to the window. He didn't know why that surprised him so much.

"We missed you tonight," she said. "They had a trivia thing between films, you would've swept it."

"S-sorry," Percy mumbled, feeling guilty all over again.

"You better be!" But Kovie was smiling, like all was forgiven—no, like forgiveness wasn't even necessary in the first place. "Now I'm down here with this stupid corsage and nobody to pin it to."

Percy's mouth dropped open. "You bought one?" Now he *really* felt guilty.

"Duh," Kovie said. "Unlike some people, I keep my promises. Remember? A-little-before-five and a corsage." She held it up with a pointed look. Percy couldn't make out the floral intricacies of it, but it was bright purple—the same shade as Kovie's dress. Still in its plastic clamshell container. "So what happened to you really?"

Really, he'd let Hazel talk him out of living his own life again. "I dunno," he said. "Cold feet, I guess."

"Is this the first time you've had someone come to your window in the middle of the night?" she asked.

"Uh, yes?"

"Hmm," she replied. "Sounds to me like you're in need of some belated teenage rebellion, then."

Percy wasn't sure whether to laugh or scoff—at himself, not her. He settled for saying, "I have an appointment early tomorrow morning. And as romantic as it would be, I don't think I'm really up for climbing the drainpipe down to you."

"I hope you're a good catch, then." She lifted her arm before Percy could tell her not to and beaned the thing straight up to him, with enough force that it smacked off his chest.

He fumbled to grab it, crushing the plastic a little, and gaped down at her. "Where the hell did you learn to throw like that?"

She shrugged. "I like javelin throwing, and my stepmom Braeden and I are in an extreme Frisbee club. Also, I played football when I was in high school. You're looking at the star sophomore quarterback. Dad hated it."

"Sounds to *me* like you have enough teenage rebellion for us both, then," Percy said, turning the clamshell over in his hand. The corsage looked delicate and sweet and fragile. He almost didn't want to touch it.

"It's not a comic book figure," Kovie called from below. "You're supposed to take it out the box, I promise. Unless—oh, shit! You're not allergic to any flowers, are you?"

Percy shook his head absently, wedging his fingers under the clamshell's tabs to open it.

"So what do you suggest I do?" he asked, arranging the corsage around his wrist. It took effort, but he managed to avoid crushing any petals.

"About what? The corsage? I dunno, wear it to bed? Take a selfie with it on? Whatever."

"No, about the teenage rebellion. My dragon—as you call her—knows your face." *And your name.*

"Oh, *I* don't want to be your rebellion. You never grow past that. It'd be like me marrying my high school boyfriend, the weed dealer with the greasy ponytail. No no no, you find someone positively terrible and preferably temporary to rebel with, and then when you're done, I'll look wholesome as fuck by comparison. Your dragon will be *begging* for you to come out with me."

"Do you have your ex-boyfriend's number, by any chance?"

"Ha! No, but you can look it up. Last I heard, he got arrested for streaking at a Mets game." She planted her hands on her hips, staring up at him. "That's definitely your color."

He flushed. "You can't tell from down there."

"I have *excellent* style. Of course I can tell."

He laughed. Briefly, weakly, but it felt good.

"Hey Perce," she began, and it made his heart squeeze. Nobody had ever given him a nickname before, not since before he got sick. Not a genuine, affectionate nickname anyway, the kind that didn't come from infantilizing him because of his condition. "Are you . . . are you okay?"

"I—" He gulped. Refused to think about anything, refused to examine the question or why she was asking it or what the answer to it was. He threw his hands wide and plastered on an obviously fake grin. "Of course I am. I'm rich!"

"So was James Ringer." She flashed him a weird and not at all fake half-smile. "I should go. Tell me when I can come around again without getting you in trouble, okay? I wrote my number there." She nodded to him, and Percy turned the clamshell over to see a phone number written in black marker.

It wasn't your fault, he wanted to say, but she didn't seem like she thought it was. She didn't seem like she thought it was his, either. Shit happens, he thought she would say, if he asked. Shit happens and we get caught up in it.

"Will do." He waved sadly after her as she walked away into the darkness of the grounds. Her car started up a minute later, its engine purring up at him from the very end of the long driveway.

He wasn't sure how sound her advice was in actuality, but it sure seemed good in theory. The spark he'd felt standing up for his independence, no matter how brief and small, had warmed him from the inside out, sandwiched between the crushing guilt. It certainly wasn't a weed-dealing boyfriend, but it was *something*. A step in the right direction?

And that step, along with the name she'd thrown in at the end, had him opening up his laptop and navigating to a by now familiar page.

Jim Ringer at Hollywood Doubles Escort Agency. Since Percy couldn't seem to meet people the normal way—not isolated as he was by his illness and by Hazel's micromanagement—and since, for the same reasons, he evidently wasn't permitted to leave the house even if he did meet one, maybe he could get his rebellion delivered, like ordering in a pizza.

Preferably temporary, Kovie had said. Percy was inclined to trust her advice.

What was more transient and temporary than a business relationship based solely on a financial transaction? Perhaps not *solely*, if this Jim Ringer knew half as much about the real James as Percy did. And he must—in order to play James Ringer, this man had to know him well. Had to have watched his films, analyzed them, noted his body language, the way he had a lazy accent to his voice sometimes, when he was smoking or relaxed. He knew James had in fact gone by Jim to close friends and to Dahlia Delair, and *that* was selective knowledge only brought about by reading the most obscure interviews James had given.

If Jim was anything like other professional impersonators, then forget the collection, even forget all the rare memorabilia Percy had—he could have a slice of James Ringer right in front of him, for him to touch.

Not that it would even be about sex. Obviously that was what this man did for a living, but Percy would be content to have him sit on the couch and discuss *Break of Dawn* with him. God, to have someone to share his passion with who wasn't on a barely frequented Internet forum.

And what a way to rebel, too! He could just hear himself now: *"Well, Hazel, you said I was too strange and pathetic and stunted to make normal friends with normal people, so I paid for one, just like how my mother and father paid for you to parent me."*

It was absolutely one hundred percent crazy, the whole damn plan, but after a night as desperately miserable as tonight, Percy was willing to give crazy a try.

CHAPTER
TEN

Theresa emailed Brandon bright and early Thursday morning with Harvey's review.

He gave him four stars.

And then, in the little box that said, "Please share your comments about your Hollywood experience!" he ripped Brandon apart. The words stung more than the bruises on his hips.

"Ringer clearly cares more about his personal image than pleasing his client. He seems incapable of taking criticism or direction and is a painfully slow learner. He's obviously in love with the sound of his own voice and expects everyone else to be in love with it as well, all with minimal effort on his part. He is very attractive and he knows it, lording it over other men. I hope with time and patience he can learn humility more appropriate to his station in life. My experience was good enough to warrant a second visit, but I'll be expecting better."

"Did this asshole just call me 'uppity'?" Brandon asked his computer screen, hands vibrating with anxiety. He'd chalked the whole experience up to roleplay thanks to Theresa's email, but even in his review Harvey seemed incapable of keeping Brandon and James Ringer separated into two people. What the hell did "station in life" mean? It was a *job*, not a designation. Not that he'd ever held down a job classier than this one for more than a couple months, but *still*. Harvey talked like this job was who he *was*.

Okay, no. Okay. Maybe this was all part of the roleplay for Harvey. He was probably just trying to get his last kicks in.

Theresa's follow-up was cheerful. *"Be sure to take these notes into account next time you meet with this client! The fact that he wants to book again is a good sign. See, you're getting there! :)"*

Ha, right. The four stars paled in comparison to Harvey's actual review of him. *In love with his voice.* Bull*shit* he was. He'd been *trying* to be charming after Alfred's review. But apparently he'd been too charming, or something.

What did these people want from him, God dammit? Shut up and take it or flirt and earn it? Or what? Smile but not actually be happy? Flirt but not in hopes of making men desire him? He scrubbed his hands through his hair, wishing he could puke. At least it was another five hundred bucks. That plus what he'd earned from Alfred was enough to pay the electric and water and buy him food that wasn't plain white bread with Miracle Whip and Kraft Singles. It wasn't fur coat and diamond earrings money like Ms. Monroe was making, but it was a start.

He just had to put up with a lot of fucking bullshit to get it.

Theresa wasn't part of that bullshit, though, so he emailed her back a quick thanks and got up to go make coffee and smoke a cigarette or four. No sooner had he lit the first one than his phone was ringing, and it was—Theresa?

Switching cigarette and phone from hand to hand, he tucked his cell in the crook of his shoulder. "Hey?"

He was half-expecting her to say there was a problem with the way he'd said "thank you," but it was Theresa, so of course she didn't. "Good news!" she chirped. "He just called in, or I would've sent it along with your email. You have a booking for Monday!"

Brandon almost dropped his cigarette. "Seriously?"

"Looks like! Vince has a tech lady who helps us get our site links on Google, and he said your page had a bunch of hits this week and got up to page six of search results, so he expects clients will start rolling in. Looks like he's right!"

"That's, uh, that's great." What was even better was that Brandon was going to read the fucking debrief this time. "Monday?"

"Mmhmm. At two. His name is Jeffrey, and I'll send along the rest of the information as soon as I have it written up."

"Sounds great," Brandon said, injecting some enthusiasm into his voice. It wasn't too hard when he focused on the "yet another five hundred bucks" part of this. "Thanks a lot, Theresa."

"Of course!"

The debrief, when Brandon got it an hour and a half later, was concise but thorough. Jeffrey was younger than both Alfred and Harvey, but apparently had an over-inflamed sense of his own importance and/or checkbook, because his "any special comments for us?" section just said, *Be prepared to wow me and maybe you'll earn a little something extra ;) $$$.*

Brandon had no fucking clue what to do with that. He'd thought he had it all figured out before Harvey, but now he was terrified that if he tried to be charming again he'd wind up with another scathing review. The thought of trying to act *exactly* like his grandfather—like, by watching his movies or interviews or commercials or whatever—made him feel sick, because it was already hard enough sometimes to see himself outside of what other people saw him as. He didn't want to act exactly like James Ringer anyway. This was a job where he was supposed to act. Actors put their own spin on things. Didn't they?

Now if only he could figure out which way to spin it so he didn't offend and/or disappoint every client . . . And this debrief didn't have any hints as to what Jeffrey expected for his version of James Ringer, just general information and that weird-ass comment. Half Brandon's life could be described as "winging it" and now . . . Now he wasn't even sure he *could*.

But he didn't have a choice.

Jeffrey was pretty bland as a client, but luckily he was also talkative and demanding, telling Brandon exactly what he wanted and when. It was easy to follow along with his instructions and nod along when he started talking about his four businesses and the fact that he was getting into trading Bitcoin and blah blah blah.

"A little something extra ;) $$$" turned out to be a $200 tip that was all Brandon's to keep. And Jeffrey's review? Four stars and "pretty quiet in multiple situations if you know what I mean ;)."

Well yeah, he'd been quiet. He hadn't been able to get a word in edgewise even when he *wasn't* sucking the guy's dick.

Whatever, Brandon would take it. He would take it and fucking run with it.

And suddenly, he had a lot of room to run. Theresa had been right—after Jeffrey, her next booking call was for two more clients, their appointments on back to back days. Then she called him again later that day with a third booking. Every call made something squirm uncomfortably in Brandon's chest, something he didn't want to put a (pathetic) name to, but he read each debrief diligently and even wrote the appointment times and names on Dahlia's ladybug dry erase fridge calendar.

He showered and trimmed his body hair before every appointment, even started carrying a tin of Altoids in his back pocket. He dressed the same he had with Harvey, but kept an eye on how many buttons he had open, and actually did things like making sure his belt and his shoes sort of matched. No one commented on it, in person or in his reviews, but he stuck with it out of principle, reminding himself that Ms. Monroe would be disappointed if he didn't. He wished they could go for coffee or something so he could pick her brain about stuff, ask for advice on clients like Harvey.

Maybe on clients in *general*. Because according to Brandon, all three of that week's appointments went pretty well, but only two of them rated him above three stars, and neither of those were fives. The third rated him two stars, and his comment was, "Eh." Just "*eh*." That was more infuriating than having everything he'd done wrong listed for him. What the fuck was he supposed to get out of "*eh*"?

Brandon had a half-nightmare of a dream about calling Vince up and saying, "I fucking quit," all big and dramatic, complete with shirt-removing for no reason. Then Brandon woke up and felt sick to his stomach and like a quitter, which he wasn't. He'd never once quit a job. His jobs were over when his bosses arbitrarily decided he'd hit the last level on "not good enough." He'd never quit, and he wasn't willing to start.

When Brandon compiled the meaty quotes from all of his reviews so far, they contradicted each other, like all the rest of his feedback. Too talkative. Not talkative enough. Too flirty. Shitty at being coy. Drank too much. Didn't want to sit and drink and socialize.

At least none of them had said he wasn't good at being Jim Ringer. No one had mentioned the Hollywood angle at all, except Alfred on that very first "date," who'd murmured "you look like him, at least" like it was the world's smallest consolation prize.

But maybe the Hollywood angle was all bullshit. Maybe these guys really didn't care if he was good at pretending to be James Ringer so long as they got a pretty mouth around their dick. Booking someone from an agency online was less risky than finding someone on a street corner. But then, the age range of his clients did skew "old enough to have jerked off to James Ringer when he was still breathing," which suggested the resemblance was *some* kind of draw for them. Or maybe it was just brand recognition. Better a recognizable figure they'd had fantasies about—had some kind of connection with—versus a complete stranger with a passably hot body, even if on closer glance the resemblance wasn't as strong as it first appeared. Maybe just that degree of familiarity was enough.

That Saturday morning, his cell phone woke him, and he peeled his face off the couch cushion. The TV was still on from the night before, and his plate of pasta had congealed overnight and smelled like rotting basil. And—fuck, the phone! He scrambled for it, recognizing the ringtone he'd set for Theresa.

"Hey!" he said, way too loudly.

Theresa laughed. "Well, isn't someone in a good mood! I'm about to make it better. How do you feel about doing an appointment today?"

"Uh, today? Yeah, uh, yeah. Just, uh. Need to shower. Brush my teeth."

"Can you be ready in twenty minutes? The client wants you at his home in less than an hour." She lowered her voice conspiratorially. "And judging by the address he gave me, Brandon, he's *rich*. Old money rich. This could be a really good chance for you!"

She was right. Jeffrey had been old money rich, and a potential repeat of that experience—minus the constant self-important chatter—was appealing as hell. Especially if Brandon could impress the guy enough to make it a regular occurrence.

"I—yeah." Brandon glanced at Dahlia's ornate metal wall clock, his body already protesting a lack of both morning caffeine and morning tobacco. "Yeah, I'll be ready."

He made it by the skin of his teeth, showering and dressing in record time. He lit a cigarette on the way out the door, ignoring

Cyrus's glare, and smoked it and a second one through on the way to the client's house. Shit, he'd hung up on Theresa too fast to even ask the guy's name, and he'd turned data off on his phone to save money on his plan, so he couldn't check to see if she'd sent him a debrief email. Great. Fucking great. All his excitement drained away. He couldn't *wait* to wind up pinned to the wall by a self-important old money rich dude who'd just discovered *the help* hadn't bothered to learn his illustrious name.

Or maybe he needed to suck it up and think fast. Maybe the pessimism was just the lack of caffeine talking.

He jiggled his knee, staring out the window in a mix of awe and dread as the houses grew larger and more ornate. This was the way old money neighborhoods were: the biggest and most expensive houses, belonging to the most upper-crust families, were cloistered in the middle, and the more the neighborhood fanned out, the less important people were. The very edges of them were populated by people who were basically like those sucker fish that clung to the undersides of sharks, hoping for a free ride.

But these houses?

These *were* the sharks.

"Must be a real freak of a shut-in today," Cyrus commented mildly as they drove. "Most tricks don't bring their whores home to the family."

Which was sort of true, if cruelly stated. Even in his limited experience, all of Brandon's meetups had taken place in hotels, a different room each time so that none of the hotel managers caught wise and banned him. What kind of person called up an escort agency and asked for a guy to be at his house in less than an hour? Brandon was a person, not a fucking pizza.

"Seriously, what's your fucking problem?" he muttered, but Cyrus either didn't hear him or pretended not to, which was fine by Brandon.

He silently seethed about the one-hour thing for the rest of the drive, wondering if Cyrus was thinking the same thing about him. If he was, he showed a previously unseen amount of self-control, because he didn't say a word until they pulled into a driveway and up to the biggest wrought-iron gate Brandon had ever seen, with poles as thick as his fists and curling waves of metal washing down toward them, designed to keep the sucker fish out. Or the paparazzi, depending on who lived here. The gate was ajar, letting the car through to drive up a pristine white driveway. The grass was way greener than it had any right to be in the middle of an endless California drought—probably had built-in automatic sprinklers and owners who had no regard for the rest of the state turning brown—and Brandon spied gardens around the side of the house, along with a separate building. A garage or a guest house, probably, or hell, who knew, maybe it was an entire house for this dude's alligator skin shoes. With a yard like this, Brandon wouldn't put it past him to indulge in other nonsensical and/or selfishly terrible luxuries.

Cyrus rolled to a stop at the foot of the steps heading up to the front door. They were just as white as the driveway, bordered on either side by perfect black soil and little round bushes. A manicured climbing vine was mounted on a trellis by the cream front door. The house itself was all sweeping, elegant arches, classic architecture from what Brandon could tell, probably around the same age as Dahlia's, albeit it *way* nicer and more timeless.

"You're four minutes past," Cyrus drawled from the front, interrupting Brandon's—shit—open-mouthed staring. "Starting it off right, huh?"

"You're the one who drove me here," Brandon snapped back. And he repeated it from earlier: "What the fuck is your problem?" Cyrus didn't answer, so he yanked his sunglasses down over his nose, really, *really* missing his coffee now, and shoved his door open. It was embarrassing, how intimidating just the stupid house was. Brandon knew for sure the john wasn't the one keeping the yard looking like this. Did he call everything else in half an hour ahead, too? Just call and expect his yard to be trimmed, his cars—Brandon was sure he had a bunch—to be washed, his groceries to be bought and stocked automatically, his newspaper not only brought to his door but delivered each morning on a silver platter next to his daily, overcomplicated breakfast order, like that woman from *The Devil Wears Prada*? Instant service.

Five minutes past, now. "Fuck," Brandon muttered, rubbing his fingertips together. He needed at least three more cigarettes to make up for caffeine, but he was shit out of luck now. He jogged up the steps, taking them two at a time when they got closer together and smaller as they approached the door.

He rang the doorbell, then knocked twice for good measure, and took a step back, fidgeting with his hands before he let them settle behind his back, fingers hooked together. He was mostly expecting a maid or a butler, so when the door opened and there was a *kid* standing there, it was all he could do to keep himself on the fucking doorstep instead of turning tail and hauling ass out to the car.

Had Cyrus brought him to the wrong house? On purpose? Seemed low even for him.

What the fuck was Brandon supposed to do with a *kid*? Was this some kind of sick—God, he wasn't even gonna think about it. No fucking way. It had to be the right house, and this had to just be some kind of misunderstanding. He was never going to live through this job if he let it make him that cynical and twisted.

He didn't know how long he stood there like an idiot without saying anything, but the kid was looking at him open-mouthed, too, pale and wide-eyed. *Really* pale. Jesus, did Brandon look that scary?

"Uh," Brandon said. "Is . . . is your dad home?"

The kid coughed—hacked, really, like he was about to spit a lung out—then shook his head. "It's me. You're Jim, right? It's not my dad. It's me. Please come in before someone sees you."

What.

Brandon—okay, yeah, he backed up. Just a step. "No fucking way," he said, pure disbelief, even though he already knew from the determined look the kid had on his face that he was telling the truth.

Irritation replaced that determination instantly. "Get inside before someone sees you," he repeated, in this kind of waveringly firm voice. Brandon opened his mouth, and the kid's expression closed further, his eyes narrowing, his lips trembling a little. "*Please.* Please."

Well, fuck.

Brandon stepped inside, into a huge, soulless front foyer that made his kid-client look even smaller.

"Follow me please," he said, then added, "Take off your shoes there, but bring them with you."

It took all Brandon's willpower not to snap back, *Yes, your highness.* He toed his shoes off and took them in one hand, fingers hooked into the heels. His socks didn't match—and the kid fucking *looked at them*, full-on looked for a couple seconds, then lifted his eyes to Brandon's. Shit, Brandon did not come here to have his fashion sense evaluated by a judgey teenage boy.

"Are you even legal?" he blurted out.

"Your company screens clients," the kid replied with a roll of his eyes. "Please don't talk anymore until I tell you."

It was like Harvey, and unlike him. Like Harvey because the kid was rude and superior and treated Brandon like so much disposable trash, like Brandon had something to be sorry for.

Unlike him because Brandon didn't feel threatened by this kid at all. Not even a thread of fear, just plain old annoyance. He wasn't afraid of what this kid was going to say in his review of Brandon. He wasn't even afraid of what Theresa might think of his continuing inability to impress anyone, because surely she would see the kid's age on his paperwork and laugh just like Brandon wanted to.

Or, he would want to, if the little shit didn't turn his back on Brandon and motion over his shoulder with curled fingers, like Brandon was a poodle. The urge to take off came back full-force, but honestly? Brandon was kind of . . . *curious*, too. There was no way this kid owned this big house all by himself, right?

I own Dahlia's.

Deciding to let himself be interested, Brandon padded after his client, down a long entrance hall with marble floors and to a huge set of stairs. The second floor was distinctly separated into two sections, the one immediately at the top of the stairs and the one on the far side of the house. They were gapped by the staircase, and Brandon's client didn't even look at the far side. Brandon did, though, trying to see if it was lived-in, or if it had been left to die and gather dust, like Dahlia's bedroom, recently, and the basement, always.

"Come on." The kid was glaring at him from down the closest wing's main hallway, gesturing with one hand again. "Quickly." His glare deepened when Brandon scowled at him, but he waited until Brandon joined him to push the second door on the left side of the hall open. He nodded Brandon in ahead of him, then slipped in behind him and closed the door behind them and locked it with a quiet sigh.

When Brandon glanced back at him, he was resting his forehead against it. Not for long, though—he met Brandon's gaze a second later and straightened up. Not that it did much. He was probably a good three or four inches shorter than Brandon on a good day, and his skinniness didn't help at all. He was seriously scrawny; the bones in his wrists pushing up under skin were so pale Brandon could see the blue of his veins. And his hands . . . his fingers were just as thin, and some of them were pulled together, like something was bent deep inside his palms, a string pulled too tight.

"I can't believe it," he said softly to the door. His accent was posh, educated, with that perfect enunciation that set Brandon's teeth on edge. "I can't believe I went through with this, and I can't believe that for all my effort, I got *you*."

With any of his other clients, Brandon would have played it cool or coy, tried to get the john back on his side with a bit of flirtation or a less subtle hand down the pants distraction.

But with this kid, he snorted. "What, were you hoping for a whore whose socks matched?"

The kid turned to face him fully and tossed him a pissy look. "Tell me, is this the kind of professionalism you use with all your clients?" He sounded half patronizing but also half disappointed, like he was upset about more than wasting his money, and Brandon didn't know what to do with that other than bristle. The kid went on before he could retort. "If you're going to be this bad at your job, the least you could do would be this bad while still halfway resembling James Ringer."

"Ex*cuse* me?" Brandon squared his shoulders. "I look *exactly* like James Ringer, kid." It was weird, he'd never been almost proud to say it before, but with this kid questioning him, all he wanted was to own it, to shove it in his face and go, *uh, yuh-huh, I do.*

"My *name*," the kid bit out, "is Percival Charles. And I didn't say you don't *look* like James Ringer, I said you don't *resemble* him. Have you even seen his films?"

That threw Brandon for a loop.

His reasons for not watching them were obvious and a lifelong effort, but he couldn't tell Percival Charles any of that. Which made him look like a complete opportunistic asshole.

It was only then that he noticed the enormous flat-screen television on the wall to the left of him, the one with ceiling-high shelves of Blu-rays, DVDs, and VHS tapes. *Thousands* of movies. Thousands of them. And on one long shelf, Brandon caught sight of patterns he recognized from the basement's posters and promo material. An entire section of shelving dedicated to James Ringer's filmography. Some of them were doubles, even triples, some had silver edition and limited collector's stickers . . .

Holy shit. This kid actually hired him because he wanted *James Ringer*. In a way none of the others did. Not just to fuck him, but— what? To *talk* to him? Spend time with him?

Shit.

He stared down at his hastily thrown on outfit: ripped jeans and button-down shirt, nothing like the movie posters or DVD covers he'd ever seen. His mismatched socks and sleep-tousled hair. None of it even remotely *resembling* James Ringer.

He'd gotten used to being himself. He'd gotten so used to people expecting sex without paying much attention to the James Ringer part—except Harvey—and then rating him for *his* personality that he'd come in here without even trying to be his grandfather.

"Shit," he said, shoulders sagging. "Shit, man. I'm sorry. Percival."

"Not as sorry as I am," Percival muttered. "You know, I knew it was a stupid idea, but for a minute there I actually . . . when I saw your pictures I . . ." His lip trembled. He shook his head once, hard, and clutched at his elbow, then stumbled over to the leather sofa facing his TV setup. Sat gingerly. "When I found you online, saw your pictures, I thought maybe even if I didn't wind up, you know—having sex, I guess, I know that's your job . . . But I thought at least you'd be someone who would *understand*." His sad face turned fierce. "But you can't. How could you? You don't know anything about him." He flashed narrowed eyes at Brandon, the wobble vanishing from his voice. "*Obviously*."

"I—" Brandon snapped his mouth closed. Needed to get ahold of himself *right now*, before he said something to ruin not only this but the rest of his shitty job, and potentially the rest of his shitty life. Because wouldn't *that* be exactly the story Vince wanted it to be? Splashed everywhere, all his secrets leaked by some rich kid rolling in money who didn't get one thing his way. This kid probably couldn't even comprehend how dire Brandon's financial situation was, and Brandon didn't think he'd care if he could. He could see TMZ's headline now: *"James Ringer's only grandson gets desperate! Get the inside scoop on him sucking dick for food!"*

Percival held a hand up. The awkward bend of it was even more apparent from this angle. "Getting you out of here is going to be the difficult part."

Brandon raised his eyebrows. "I just got here."

"Yes, and—and now you're *leaving*, as soon as I can figure out how to smuggle you out the door again. I'll pay your fee, don't worry about that. But this was obviously a mistake."

It wasn't even about the money. Brandon should have been happy to hear he could walk away from this whole mess and still get paid, but being given the chance to flee like he'd wanted to downstairs only made him more desperate to prove this was *bullshit*, sending him away because he didn't "resemble" James Ringer enough, without even giving him a real chance. Brandon could do better than this. He'd just gotten caught off guard, like with Harvey, but this time, he could still recover. He could do better than this, he'd been doing so fucking well even if he was miserable half the time and confused *all* the time. He could stick with this, salvage this, before it became another black mark on his record.

He had to prove it. Not to Percival—to himself. Had to prove everything his bosses had told him about being just a pretty face wasn't true. Had to prove he wasn't only (barely) making it thanks to the same talentless, capitalizing cruise on easy street that James Ringer had made a career of.

So he did the only thing he could think of. Stepped back into the cycle he'd found himself trapped in, time after time after time.

He got down on his knees at Percival's feet. "Please," he said, soft and breathy, like he'd rehearsed for when Harvey called him back for seconds. "I'm sorry. Can we start over?"

CHAPTER
ELEVEN

A
ll Percy's breath whooshed out of him at once, because though the tone was painfully put-on and Percy did not believe for one second that Jim's apology was genuine, that *voice*.

The accent was all wrong, of course, but the voice . . . there was that same smoky come-hither James always used in quiet scenes.

Percy didn't realize he hadn't responded until Jim reached for his belt, and then he made an embarrassingly high noise and slapped at Jim's hands. "No!" he squeaked. Clearing his throat, he added, "I don't need fake apologies from you. I didn't hire you for this. I just need you to leave."

Before Hazel found out. Before his parents found out.

What had he been *thinking*? Rebellion could be done in smaller, less damaging ways than this: —ordering a vibrator from Amazon, or, or . . . or finding something that interested him, to invest in, like a collection, or even an exhibit or a whole museum. That was something neither his parents nor Hazel could stop him from doing, but it would anger them all the same, since it was still him, nerdy juvenile him, instead of mature and well-thought out, like investing in the stock market or in other "adult" pursuits. It would be a rebellion that would *go* somewhere, let him end up with something all his own.

It wasn't that he thought Kovie had led him in the wrong direction. No, no, he was perfectly aware this little mishap was all his own doing.

Jim threw his hands up and sat back on his heels, his complacent facade cracking. How long had he held it? Seconds? Percy thought it was possibly a record for him.

"Then what did you hire me for?" Jim said, glaring up at him. He still had his sunglasses on, pushed up into his hair and making it temptingly messy. The kind of bedhead Percy's own hair wasn't thick enough to manage. "Maybe you don't know, but this is what I *do*."

And that was the problem. "Then your website is false advertising," Percy said snottily, tone made strident by his irritation. It was leagues better than sounding shaky and uncertain, so he didn't bother correcting himself. Making himself more polite and palatable, like he would do at parties. "Because what you're *supposed* to *do* is a lot more than—" He waved at Jim's position.

"Than what? Than getting on my knees and sucking your dick?" Jim snorted. "Yeah, right. We both know that was how this was going to end up. Don't pretend it's not." Something Percy couldn't identify flashed over his face, some conflicted emotion, and then he bit out, "Look, I really am sorry I'm not—what you were expecting. This isn't what I expected either."

Percy clenched his jaw and felt the ache of it all the way down his spine. "And why's that?"

Jim fumbled visibly, eyes darting down to Percy's hands. Percy tensed, ready for another stumbling apology, for an awkward comment, but instead, Jim said, "You're not *old*."

O . . . kay then. Percy's automatic, defensive anger flickered, then faded out. He stared down at Jim, lost for words. Remembering Jim at the door, asking for his *father*. It was sort of funny, now that Percy wasn't panicked about Hazel seeing him letting Jim in and knee-jerk furious at being treated like a child . . . again. He'd had to schedule this very, very carefully, when his parents were in their respective offices, busy with meetings, and Hazel was doing her morning laundry. By the time the agency's office had opened this morning, Percy had barely been able to give them an hour's warning.

Jim squirmed. "What?"

"I'm not sure," Percy admitted. He leaned away from Jim, pressing into the back of the couch. Jim either didn't realize or didn't care he was still on his knees, despite the fact that Percy was definitely not taking him up on his offer. "Whether you believe me or not, I didn't want it to end up like this. I thought maybe . . ." He gestured helplessly at the TV, at his endless stacks of neatly organized films.

"Uh huh. Sure." Jim looked away, toward the TV.

His casual, flippant distrust got under Percy's skin, rankling him right back up. "I mean it! I hired you for *him*, not for sex."

Jim's blue eyes—the same color as Percy's, but a darker shade—snapped to meet his. The muscles over his square, carbon-copy jaw worked for a long second, and then he said, bitterly, "Well, I'm not him. I'm just a whore who looks like him. And if that's not good enough, then—then fine."

But he didn't get off his knees. Like he couldn't commit to leaving.

If he was trying to get Percy to feel sorry for him, then, well . . . Damn it, it was working.

And Percy knew exactly how it felt to anticipate something and have his chance to do it cut off before he could try. Jim's search result had been new. Did that mean *he* was new, too? New at this? There was no way Percy could send him away if this was one of his first jobs.

He sighed, a nervous twang pulling under his stomach. "Would it . . ." He squirmed. "Would it make you feel better if I . . . if I *let* you? Do your job, I mean?"

Jim darted an assessing look at him. "I dunno, is my job to suck your dick, or is it to watch movies and I'm down here for no reason?"

"It's not like I asked you to get down there," Percy retorted, and then swallowed anything else he could say. He wasn't sure what it was going to be, whether it would be, *"never mind, maybe you should leave after all,"* or . . .

Anyone could see Jim was attractive. And his haughty assertion that he looked *just like* James was true. It was everything else about him that didn't fit, really: his mannerisms, his speech, his bearing. Like someone had taken James's body and put another soul into it.

Did that have to mean this soul was inferior? Wasn't *good enough*?

"Well, sorry. I did."

"Stop apologizing," Percy said, exasperated.

Jim muttered, "Oh my god," under his breath, then shoved forward and put himself between Percy's knees. Percy reared back further into the couch, wheezing. "Have you ever had your dick sucked before, Percival?"

"For God's sake, it's Percy," he admitted, sick of the formalities *he'd* set. "And just because I'm . . . sick or disabled or crippled or whatever it is you're stereotyping me as doesn't *mean* . . . anything."

Jim's mouth dropped open. Then his eyebrows curved into that familiar annoyed ridge. "Fine. Percy. Look. If I'm assuming you're a virgin, it's because of this whole stuck-up rich boy act and your movie collection, okay?"

It was another bucket of cold water on the coals in his belly. Of course it was his luck that Jim would think the movie collection was the sign of someone who was defective or socially incapable. Of course he was judging the one thing Percy had truly wanted to share with him. "Okay," he said. "But if one of us can talk about putting on an *act*, it's certainly you more than me."

"So you admit you really are a stuck-up rich kid?"

"Is this how you treat all your clients, Jim?"

Jim laid his head on Percy's knee, eyes closed. Sighed. Opened his eyes again. "No. Just you."

What the hell was that supposed to mean? Percy's first instinct was to bristle again, thinking Jim was singling him out because of his hands or the obvious dark circles under his eyes or the way he was breathing hard just from having a heated conversation. But Jim sounded more annoyed and weary than anything, and when Percy shifted minutely, his eyes slid closed once more. Percy watched him, then reached out and carefully took his sunglasses off, putting them next to him on the couch.

No, this wasn't the first time he'd had someone this close to him, but last time had been too-fast, fumbling handjobs against the wall, him and the son of one of his father's friends sneaking off during a party and back to an empty, cold sitting room. Percy didn't remember the other boy's name, just that it had been that once, and that he'd flinched the first time Percy touched him, and complained about how cold his hands were.

Jim didn't complain about Percy's hands, not even when Percy gently toyed them in his hair, smoothing back the softly tousled strands. If Jim had been striving for accuracy, he should have had his hair gelled back, but Percy was beginning to see an upside to the anachronism.

They both sighed simultaneously, Percy with relief and Jim like he was on the edge of sleep.

"You're different from the others, Percy. That's what I meant."

"Well, yes. You said as much, didn't you? I'm not *old*." His nose crinkled, a weird laugh escaping him. "Although I do have as much trouble with arthritis as even your most wrinkled client."

"Yeah, but *you* don't smell like mothballs." Jim lifted his head, Percy's fingers still in his hair. "But I didn't mean your age, either. I mean . . . I don't know what I mean. I'm treating you different because you are different, and it's not that you're sick and it's not that you're young. I don't know what it is, exactly. Whatever, I guess." He broke off, full mouth twisting. From snapping off softened insults to brooding to vulnerable in ten seconds flat—maybe he had more resemblance than Percy'd originally thought. And with Percy leaning a little toward him, moved by him sitting up, Percy could smell *him*, and it was all cigarettes.

His flickering arousal returned in full force. His fingers cracked quietly, joints popping when he pushed Jim's hair back, fixing it the way it would sit if he had gelled it. It fell loose almost immediately, as uncooperative as Jim himself. Somehow, that didn't bother Percy as much just then. Probably because he had more important things to focus on.

Like the fact that Jim had apparently sensed the change in atmosphere between them, because now his hand was snaking upward along Percy's thigh, thick fingers splayed. Percy sucked in a sharp breath, stomach going concave under his soft blue shirt, and clung to Jim's hair in one hand and the couch in the other.

Jim's breathing came in deep, slow heaves, his broad rib cage rising and falling, straining his tight T-shirt and pressing his body against the insides of Percy's thighs. He was so warm, and his hand was blazing when it found Percy's waistband and slipped under it, fingertips brushing Percy's stomach. Percy jumped, couldn't help it, and Jim glanced up at him, hand stilled, apparently waiting for some signal. Percy nodded, licking his lips, and Jim leaned forward, fitting himself closer, and, oh, pushed both his hands under Percy's shirt, moving from his stomach to cup his sides, where they cut in under his ribs.

"Jeez, you're skinny," Jim said, but it wasn't derisive or awed or put off. A simple observation.

Percy squeezed him with his knees. "And you're pretty squishy, considering your line of work. I thought I detected the magic of

Photoshop in your profile photos."

Jim laughed, surprising Percy, and muttered, "God, she'd be pissed," before he rucked Percy's shirt up and licked his stomach right above the cut of his jeans. "Don't worry, babe, with these love handles comes a truly epic ass."

Percy couldn't help it. He let out a moan. Both from the wet heat of Jim's tongue and in reply to Jim's bragging, because he'd looked—subtly—and yes, yes, Jim certainly did have a *truly epic ass.*

"Who's 'she'?" he asked, trying to keep his body from turning completely to liquid against the couch cushions as Jim cupped his pec with one hand and palmed his dick with the other.

"Oh," Jim said, nuzzling into Percy's groin now with his mouth and nose. The sensation of his lips and his breathing through the fabric of Percy's trousers was maddening, so maddening Percy barely registered what he said next. "Marilyn Monroe. She's my boss."

"That—" Percy gasped, squirming against Jim's hot damp mouth. For a moment, he was out of it enough to wonder if Jim meant the *real* Marilyn, but obviously not. "That's—really?"

"Really. Well, *Ms.* Monroe, technically. She's way better at this job than I am, too. If you swing that way, you should give her a call."

I don't, Percy could have answered, sweet and to the point, but instead he said, "I'd rather have James Ringer."

Jim's smooth movements hiccupped for a second. Then he came back to life and his eyes went half-lidded. He smirked, unzipping Percy's fly. "Well, you've got him." He cut off anything Percy could say in response—what, Percy wasn't sure—by slipping his clever, capable fingers into Percy's trousers and shoving his briefs down to get his hand around his cock. He could have come just from that. That sure, teasing grip, closing around his shaft.

Percy's head fell back, every single word in his vocabulary vanishing. Jim's hand withdrew for a few seconds, then came back wet, and Percy started, breathing out a shivery noise. He wound his fingers back into Jim's hair just to feel it, then immediately unwound them again, worried he would yank on Jim's hair if he—

And he did: lapped over the head of Percy's cock, tongue just as hot as it had been on Percy's stomach but so, so much better. *This* was new. Having someone else's hand on him, Percy remembered, even if it wasn't the most pleasant of memories, but a *mouth* was brand new and it sent shocks of want up Percy's spine.

Jim definitely knew what he was doing here. While the rest of their interaction . . . conversation . . . appointment?—that was the word—while the rest of their *appointment* had been stilted and Jim had wavered between aggressively defensive and uncertain, here he was on level ground, sure of himself, and Percy was helpless in the face of it. His chest heaved, his hands clutched the cushions of his sofa until the joints ached. He bit his lip to keep from crying out.

They shouldn't be doing this here. They should be in the bedroom, with at least a couple more doors and walls between them and the rest of the house and Hazel.

Fuck, he couldn't be bothered to interrupt.

Still, he glanced over at the clock on his wall, checking the time. Forty minutes until Hazel would be in to check him for lunch. That was enough time. Enough time for this.

Especially the way Jim was going, one hand braced on Percy's thigh and the other wrapped around the shaft of his dick, pumping him in time with his bobbing head. After years and years of jerking off to carefully selected and barely arousing porn, this was pushing Percy right to the edge of orgasm, far faster than he was used to.

And nothing of the sort for Jim.

Should Percy feel bad for that? Did the other clients, the *old* ones? Did Jim even want to get off, or did he prefer to compartmentalize? Or was Percy being selfish, lying here like a prince while Jim worked away?

He gasped. Twisted. Reached out and clutched Jim's jaw with shaking fingers.

"S-stop," he managed to get out. His cock pulsed with need as Jim pulled off.

"You okay? Need to switch positions? Something else? It's okay if you come in my mouth, if that's what you're worried about." Jim said it all so matter-of-factly, like he said it all the time. He probably did; this was his customer service, since he was clearly more talented at this than being James.

Percy felt his face flush, somehow even hotter than it already was just from the exertion. He hadn't even thought of . . . He shook his head mutely, burning up with the shame of how inexperienced and stupid he was. How could a man get a blowjob and not consider where and how he'd be coming? He really *hadn't* been prepared for this to end in sex, and now he wished he'd thought about it a little more, at *all*.

Jim raised his eyebrows. "What, then?"

"I—you're not doing anything," he blurted.

"Well, I *am* sucking you off. You don't like it?" Jim wiped at his swollen mouth peevishly with the back of his hand. "If you want something a little more athletic, I can ride your dick, but you'll need to give me a few minutes to get myself worked open."

Percy's eyes bugged out. He wasn't sure if he was more short-circuited by the way Jim had misinterpreted him, or by the image he'd just put into Percy's head. "N-no! You— This—" He groaned. Wiped his palms on the tops of his thighs. "It's amazing. It's so good." Did that sound overeager? Fake? "It's just, I'm going to get off and I won't have done anything for you. You're just doing all the work."

"Well . . ." Jim drawled, "this *is* my job."

Percy huffed at him. "That's not what I meant."

Realization seemed to dawn on Jim's mean face, which softened considerably. "You're worried that you're not getting me off, too," he announced.

"Yes. That."

"Oh!" He laughed. Tilted his head back and laughed. It was pure joy and relief, and it washed Percy over with warmth. How often did he get to hear laughter like that? "Here I thought I was getting my jaw sore for nothing. That's real sweet, Perce, but it's not necessary."

Perce. The second time in as many days he'd been called that.

"You wouldn't like it?" Percy asked carefully. Was that what Jim was trying to say, in more flattering customer-friendly terms? *This is just a job for you, you don't like me, you don't want me to touch you or give you pleasure. How could you? How could you want these hands touching your dick?*

"What guy doesn't like getting off? No, I just mean, don't feel guilty, okay? You're paying my bills. I can deal with a couple hours of blue balls in exchange. Let me spoil you."

"But you don't *have* to," Percy said, almost cutting him off. *I get spoiled all the time. Spoiled little rich sick kid, that's how you see me, you can admit it.* "That . . ." He ignored the heat that rose on the back of his neck, made his voice firm. "You said it yourself, this is your job. So that's what I want."

"You want me to get off too?" Jim gave him a look on the edge of suspicious.

"Yeah," Percy replied. He licked his lips. "Yeah. Not as some kind of power trip or anything. Just . . . I want to give you pleasure, too."

Now it was Jim who blushed. "Give me pleasure," he echoed. "Can't say I've heard a john put it that way before."

Percy wrinkled his nose at him. No one else Percy had regular contact with mentioned the way he spoke, but then again, everyone he had regular contact with was over forty—with Kovie as the exception now, he supposed. "Are you going to pick apart my vocabulary or are you going to get in my lap?"

That blush darkened, giving Percy a little thrill. "I guess . . . uh, your lap, yeah." Percy gave him a *well?* look when he didn't move, and Jim got up, right back to uncertain. He seemed to stall, his suspicion lingering, but his eyes flicked to Percy's, caught, and held, and he thumbed the button of his jeans open and tugged his fly down before he pushed himself over Percy's lap, legs spread wide, caging Percy in against the couch. "I didn't, um. In the interests of clarity, I didn't mean to criticize your vocabulary. It was just a little more sentimental than I'm used to. I think I like it. That you're sentimental."

"Well, don't get used to it, because I'm not," Percy snapped. Wasn't sure why he said it—because he *was*—but he did.

Jim seemed comforted by his curt reply, at least, like equilibrium had returned between them. "Take my dick out," he said, all business. "If you want to get me off."

It sounded like a challenge, and Percy took him up on it, shifting his shoulders against the sweat-sticky back of the couch until he could get a hand between them. Jim was wearing boxers, and his zipper scraped the back of Percy's hand on the way in. His dick was hot and sweaty inside his boxers, thick enough that Percy had a hard time getting his hand around the shaft. Just touching him like this, that soft, loose skin against his palms, had his own cock leaking.

Jim's eyes had fallen shut. His tongue touched his upper lip. He thrust almost imperceptibly into Percy's hand.

"Y-you like that?" Percy asked. God, why was he trying to dirty talk? What in the world would possess him to try that? Maybe he wanted to prove to Jim his vocabulary wasn't all "sentimental."

Apparently it was working: Jim's tongue slipped out again, wetting his lips, and he nodded. "Hands're nice."

Percy snorted—that *had* to be customer-friendliness—and tightened the curl of his hand, wincing when his fingers twitched from the strain. He held his grip, though, and Jim's hips shifted restlessly toward him. "Go ahead," Percy said, voice throaty, either from their sex or because the smell of Jim's cigarettes was overwhelming.

Jim pumped into his hand experimentally. "While I'm totally hot for you with your hand stuffed in my underwear, don't you think it'd be better if you got me out and I dunno, we knocked cocks a bit?"

Percy snorted so hard he reared back with the force of it, and out popped Jim's substantial cock. "Knocked cocks," he wheezed. "Knocked. Cocks."

"You're laughing now, but . . ." Jim draped his arms over Percy's shoulders and dipped his hips, glancing his cock against Percy's. Just the barest of touches, but Percy moaned aloud. "Take us both in your hand," Jim directed. "It'll feel even better."

Percy's eyes stung with frustration. "I want to, I do, but . . ."

"Your hands?" Jim asked.

Percy nodded, ashamed. He didn't want to draw attention to them. What if Jim looked? What if he put on a brave face, but his boner still faded?

"Don't stress," Jim purred, rolling his hips, rocking their dicks against one another again. "Seriously, you got that little line between your eyebrows." He pouted, tracing it with one finger, then reached down, wrapping his fist as best he could around both their dicks, squeezing them together tight.

Percy shuddered, and knew by the kiss Jim pressed to his forehead that the annoyed crease there had smoothed away.

"We'll do it like this today," Jim said, fucking against him slow and deliberate. "Because we're just getting to know each other. Next time, I want to swallow your cum, rich boy. Or would you rather fuck my ass?"

"Jesus," Percy huffed. "Shut up." No way was he coming this quickly, this much faster than Jim.

"You didn't answer my question. You a top or a bottom?"

"Fuck if I know." Percy thrust his hips, shuddering and making noise and sweating like a damn animal in rut.

"So you *are* a virgin." Jim smirked. Percy was about to snap at him again, but he followed it up with, "Guess we'll have to try both. I'm a switch, personally. Maybe you are too. Either way, I bet we'll both have fun finding out."

"Who says I'm ever going to call you again," Percy gasped, judging himself for how breathless he sounded. It certainly wasn't from the way Jim was talking. It wasn't. And it especially wasn't from the way Jim swept a hand back over his head, brushing his hair back in that way that so resembled the real James Ringer.

Jim shrugged, squeezing them both just that much firmer and sending heat punching low in Percy's stomach, tightening him up in all the right places. "I got a feeling." His tone was unreadable, and the next second he sped up his own fluid thrusting, playing perfect, experienced counter to Percy's unsteady rhythm. He grinned; it was blinding, this close. "I got a feeling you're about to come, too."

"I am *not*," Percy said, and immediately did.

CHAPTER
TWELVE

Percy looked *cute* when he came. Was that a fucked-up thing to think about a guy?

It was just—his eyes scrunched up, that little line between his brows reappearing, and his nose wrinkled, and it looked like he was going to sneeze, and then suddenly Brandon's hand and wrist were both coated in cum.

"Liar, liar," Brandon taunted, keeping a tight grip on his softening dick, using Percy's cum to lubricate his thrusts against it. Percy frowned deeply at him, but it was belied by the quiet moan Brandon worked from him as he kept going, because Percy wanted him to get off, and it was fucking weird, but really good at the same time. Brandon had been freaked out at first, worried about it, but now? Percy was frowning, sure, but his eyes were half-lidded and fixed on where Brandon was thrusting through his fist. "Regretting that whole wanting me to come thing?" he teased, voice husky. Percy's dick had to be one hundred percent oversensitized at this point, but he soldiered on, flattening himself against the couch, concave belly twitching and heaving, as Brandon worked him over. Brandon respected commitment like that. "You can say uncle if you want."

Percy didn't reply, just shook his head hard.

"What if I asked you nice to suck my dick? Would that help you save face?"

No reply, unless you counted Percy licking his lips once, fast. Kid looked like he was in pain now, though, his whole face contorted, sweat beading on his temples. And Brandon wasn't a fucking sadist, so he murmured, "Okay, okay," and shuffled in place, letting Percy go. Percy jumped under him when his cock hit his belly, smearing his cum on his skin, but his shoulders relaxed, so Brandon called good move, even if Percy was frowning up at him again. "Whatever," Brandon told him. "I called uncle for us both."

He rose up on his knees, took his dick in hand, and gently nudged Percy's chin with it. Saw him inhale shakily, lick his lips again, his pupils fat and deep, deep black.

"Please?" Brandon purred, asking nicely, as promised. It felt completely different from saying "please" when he'd been down on his knees, thinking Percy would shove his ass out the door, and different still from begging "please fuck my faggot ass" to Harvey.

Percy opened his pretty pink mouth, and it looked so wet and soft and perfect, and—

And then he closed it again. Turned away. His jaw tightened, and was that his lip curling? Distasteful. Like a toddler refusing a spoonful of mashed carrots.

Right. Of course. Percy was the client. Brandon was the whore, and he'd stepped too far. Why should he be allowed to ask to have his dick sucked? It wasn't like anyone else had wanted that—wasn't like anything had happened that should lead Brandon to thinking it was fine.

Or maybe Percy just didn't like sucking dick, and Brandon shouldn't be an asshole and take it personally. People—clients or not—were allowed to say no, obviously, and it had been his dumb mistake in the first place.

He sat back again, cupping Percy's tense jaw. "You still want me to get off?" he asked, carefully, trying to keep the bitterness and the disappointment out of his voice. He wasn't going to be an asshole about this. He wasn't going to be an asshole about this.

Percy's expression was closed off. He was staring out the sides of his eyes at something. Anything other than Brandon, probably. "Sure. Whatever. If you want. It doesn't matter."

Maybe it only mattered when it was a good visual for Percy to get off to.

"Fine." Brandon had half a mind to just get off, strip his cock and do it fast and dirty to spite Percy, to do *as he'd asked*, but his erection was flagging already, and he was pretty sure there wasn't a single thing in the world he could think of to get it back up. He stuffed himself back into his jeans unceremoniously. "I need a smoke," he snarled, and stalked over to the nearest window.

"Wh—" Percy protested, fumbling to get his own dick back into his pants, and Brandon knew he was about to spout some bullshit about not smoking in the house, but Brandon cranked the window open, hopped up onto the sill, and lit a cigarette before he could get his shit together enough to protest.

He got a few good lungfuls in, had to hook his hand under the sill to lean out and breathe them into the air. Hey, he could see Cyrus's car from here. Fucking great. If he didn't get an earful from Percy, he'd probably get one from Cyrus about "serving clientele" or whatever quip he could come up with today.

It wasn't until Brandon realized he'd yet to hear Percy at all that he glanced back over his shoulder.

Percy stood in the center of the room, stock still, mouth hanging open in dumbfounded silence.

There went Brandon's slim fucking chance of a good review. Brandon took one last drag of his cigarette, then flicked it out the window.

"Maybe it's time for you to leave," Percy finally said.

"Yeah," Brandon replied. "I guess it is." He swung his legs back inside and pushed the window back down, latching it so he didn't have to look at Percy. Now that he was trying, though, it wasn't hard to avoid Percy's eyes. Brandon looked at the clock, the floor, the door—oh, there were his shoes, he stared at those a while, then got them on. He wasn't sure what else there was to say, and Percy wasn't any help.

It wasn't even that Brandon felt like he'd fucked up this appointment. He knew he had. He knew it was him being stupid and assuming and too fucking flippantly playful and intimate that had made Percy back off. But he didn't feel the same rush of guilt and self-consciousness he had after Harvey, or when he got his shitty reviews. He just felt . . . he wasn't sure what it was.

Nothing, maybe.

He wasn't sure he felt anything.

That explained how his voice sounded so hollow when he said, "Bye," and pushed his way out the suite's front door. He only made it a step before Percy grabbed his arm and reeled him back in. He opened his mouth, peeved about being trapped, but Percy held a hand up to his mouth, signaling for silence.

He led Brandon all the way downstairs again, moving like a spooked cat, and opened the door for Brandon—not because he was being chivalrous, but because he obviously felt he needed to open it like half an inch every five goddamn minutes to keep it from creaking.

The second Brandon could fit himself through the gap, he did, jogging down the steps and out to Cyrus's car.

"Don't start," he said, when he was safe in the back seat. "Just fucking *don't*."

And, to his surprise, Cyrus didn't.

He took the equivalent of like five showers when he got home, scrubbing himself down with Dahlia's all-natural sunflower-honey-basil-something-something bath gel. Over and over. He was glad he hadn't let Percy fuck him, because he didn't have the energy or the heart or whatever he would need to finger himself right now, but he also wasn't sure he would've been able to stand Percy's leftover lube inside him.

There was a weird hitch in his breath, and he felt cold despite the scalding hot water running down his back. Pressing his face to the tiles, he sucked in air like he was smoking. Thinking about a cigarette made a craving kick up on the back of his tongue, made his hands start to shake, but it was better than standing here wheezing like—like a scared little kid.

He hadn't felt this bad after Harvey, even. That had been his fault, sure, but at least all along he'd had an idea of what Harvey thought of him, what Harvey hired him for. He had no fucking idea what Percy wanted. And no fucking idea what he'd been *thinking*, trying to ask for shit, trying to get Percy to suck his dick. What the fuck?

Despite the difference in trappings, Percy wasn't any different from any twenty-dollar back-alley blowjob Brandon had given. Wasn't any different from the guys who paid for a filthy, shitty motel room and fucked him on his hands and knees, calling him a jumped-up little tweaker slut. He wasn't any different from Harvey. Harvey wanted James Ringer's face and a hole to fuck, someone to punish, and Percy wanted James Ringer's face and . . . what? Company? It was still a service he'd paid for.

So he really was no different.

Brandon had let himself get carried away, that was all. He was tired, he was on edge, he needed to smoke, he needed caffeine.

Calling up Ms. Monroe and asking her out for coffee didn't seem like such a bad idea now. He couldn't keep flailing from client to client with no fucking idea what to do. If he could go into appointments with some kind of baseline for handling clients, maybe things would fall into place. Maybe he could stop fumbling through every single appointment until he got to the sex. The sex he could do. It was the Jim Ringer part that tripped him.

Fucking Percy. No resemblance, his *ass*.

Brandon had only gotten this job thanks to his face, just like James Ringer had done his whole life. And, same as James Ringer, he had no idea what to do if that face wasn't enough to automatically impress people.

And he couldn't *stand* it.

The water ran cold however long later, and he shook himself out of his daze, going to fire up the coffee pot. He felt guilty, wanting to call her. Felt needy and rudderless and out of his depth. He probably hadn't earned himself a lot of high regard with her at the photoshoot, and his professional attitude hadn't exactly improved in the past few weeks. But she was still his boss, and she'd probably appreciate the chance to set him straight before he permanently damaged her business. Disappointing and inconveniencing her now would be better than letting everything fall apart.

He chugged half a mug of too-hot coffee and picked up his phone . . .

And, shit, he didn't have her number.

Theresa picked up on the second ring, her call queue apparently not as heavy today. "Hey, you!" she gushed. "How did it go this morning?" Her voice lowered conspiratorially. "Was I right about the, you know, the area?"

"You were totally right." He sucked down the rest of his coffee while she apologized for giving him such short notice. "It's no big deal, really. That's what I'm here for, right?" Barreling on before she could comment on that—because Brandon wasn't entirely sure what he meant, either—he said, "So, uh, if I have some kind of . . . If I have questions, for like, Vince, or Ms. Monroe, should I . . ."

"Oh! I'm sorry, I usually send a list of contact numbers out with my introductory email. I must have forgotten." There wasn't one ounce of facetiousness in her voice, but Brandon felt the stab of shame anyway. Yet another email he hadn't read.

A few papers rustled. Then Theresa said, "Just give me one second, Brandon," and he heard her ask someone else to sit down. "New hire," she whispered to him. "We're finally getting an Idris Elba, he's a very hot request right now. Anyway! I have Ms. Monroe's number, are you ready?"

"Yup." Brandon scribbled the digits on Dahlia's whiteboard. Had to ask her to repeat them when he smudged the last two.

She did, patiently. "Are you okay, hon?" she asked afterward. "You sound tired."

"Yeah, I'm only on my first cup of coffee."

"Ohhh, right. Well, I'll do my best not to give you many morning calls like that! It really was unusual, but I thought you could use the business."

Brandon bristled, half-hearted at best. He knew she didn't mean anything by it. "Thanks. Hey, I'll see you around, okay?"

"Of course! Say hi to Ms. Monroe for me."

"I'll do that." Brandon hung up, exhausted again. Didn't let himself rest or even take a breath before he punched Ms. Monroe's number into his phone, because otherwise he was gonna lose what was left of his nerve/motivation. As it was, it felt like it was taking all his worldly power to keep his body solid, like if he let that painful tenseness between his shoulders relax, his bones would crumble and the rest of him would melt into a puddle.

He wasn't entirely sure that would be a bad thing. Not a bad way to go, at least.

Ms. Monroe picked up on the fifth ring. "Mmm, hello?" she murmured into the phone sleepily. Her voice was so sexy so effortlessly that even a hopelessly gay guy like Brandon had to pause.

And how come she could do that cute retro accent in her sleep when Brandon couldn't recreate James Ringer even trying his hardest?

"Uh, hey," he said self-consciously. "It's Brandon. Um, the James Ringer lookalike from Hollywood Doubles."

Brandon heard the sound of shifting blankets through the phone, like Ms. Monroe was rolling over in bed. "Hi sweetie," she purred. "How was your first couple weeks?"

Had it only been two weeks?

"Uh, okay, I guess. I guess that's why I'm calling. I'm starting to realize this isn't exactly a normal sex work job. I could use your advice on the whole *Hollywood* end of things." It came out sounding way steadier than he thought it would, so he swallowed, heartened, and went on. "I just—you said clients buy the whole package, and I'm not exactly, uhh, used to doing the whole before-and-after conversation. And you have that down, obviously, you have all of it down, so—"

"All right, all right, deep breath," she murmured, then yawned. "There's a reason I'm your manager. Of course I can give you some guidance. It's not as easy as it looks, is it?"

"Fuck no." Brandon laughed. "When can you . . .?"

"Actually, could you meet me today? We could do lunch." Her rich tone made the cliché proposition sound luxurious and not at all cheesy.

What Brandon really wanted to was to roll himself up in Dahlia's sweet-smelling blankets and nap, but he was the one who called. And he needed the help. There wasn't one person who would look at him and say he didn't. "Sure, that's great. When?"

"Mmm, what time is it?" He heard her blankets rustle again. "Ahh, I need an hour over here, so let's meet at . . . one-thirty? Canter's Deli?"

"Sure," he said automatically. There was a few awkward seconds' pause before he unstuck his jaw and said, "Thanks, ma'am. Bye." He hung up and leaned on the counter, blowing out a long breath. She hadn't sounded disappointed in him.

Too bad he couldn't shake being disappointed in himself.

CHAPTER
THIRTEEN

"I fucked up."

Percy held his phone tight to his cheek, his whole body curled up in a ball and rocking back and forth in the corner of his sofa.

"Hello to you too," Kovie replied. "You need me to come over? You sound like you need me to come over."

Hazel's voice rang in the back of his head, reminding him how inconvenient it would be for her, how it was a waste of her time . . . Percy shoved it down. "I need you to come over," he agreed. His eyes felt raw and sore and they were red, he was certain—not because he'd been crying, but he'd been rubbing his hands over his face since Brandon left, trying to coax himself out of his quasi-panic before Hazel came in to ask him about lunch and got to lecture him again about how he was ruining himself for social interaction by perpetually facilitating social interactions with "undesirable people" or what have you.

"Well, it *is* my turn to be naked when we meet up, but if you don't feel the need to have your nudity favor returned, you're gonna have to give me a few minutes, here." There was a sudden flood of sound on the other end of the phone, Kovie cursing, the slam of a door. "Guess who just spilled their entire makeup case all over the floor," she groaned. "Guess we can be fuck-ups together. What happened?"

"I—" Percy jerked his head up at the familiar sound of the hallway floor creaking. "The dragon's coming," he hissed, his free hand white-knuckled, fisted in his trousers. "Just—please come over."

"You got it," she promised, all traces of teasing gone from her voice.

Percy hung up on her, shoving his phone under his thigh. He

fumbled to grab the remote just as Hazel bustled in, tsking as usual about something or other. The TV wasn't on, but Percy made a show of holding the remote, like she'd interrupted him.

She moved around behind him, her shoes squeaking on the wooden floors—then stopped abruptly when she reached Percy's bedroom. "What's that?" she asked, and Percy panicked for a moment, panicked about any trace of himself Jim could have left behind, any loose end Percy hadn't covered up. But she went on, "Is that cigarette smoke? *Percy*—"

"It's not from me!" He let the remote thump down on the couch, willing himself not to look at the window, not to think about *that*, not yet. "One of the groundskeepers smokes and he was working on the garden below my window, that's all."

"Hmmph," she grumbled. "I'll have to have a talk with them. Your lungs are too delicate for them to be doing that so close to your window." Then, of course, she turned on him. "Did you have your window *open*? Percy, there's any number of allergens—"

"I just needed some air," he said, a little coolly. He wasn't prepared to have another fight like the one from last Friday, the last time Kovie had tried to come around. "And oh, uh, I'm having a guest this afternoon. Don't want the place stinking of my sickness, now do I?"

Her spine stiffened. "What do you mean, you're having a guest?"

Percy had to quash the bizarre urge to laugh. If only she knew what kind of guest he'd already had. "Kovie," he said firmly. "She was upset I didn't get to go out last week, so she's . . . coming over for a movie marathon today. Just the two of us, here, where you can help if something were to happen. Nothing strenuous." God, even in all his conviction, he was still scrambling to justify himself to her. Why the hell did he need her approval?

He hated that he did. But it was too late now.

She was giving him a flat, unhappy look. "I don't think . . ."

"We're not going out anywhere," he said, which wasn't so much justification as it was, *What will your excuse be this time, if you don't want me to see her?*

There was a stiff, cold silence as she stood there, staring at him and the miserable, defiant ball he'd tucked himself into. Then she made a dismissive gesture and went to collect his laundry. "I don't have time to get the rest of lunch prepared for two people, not with the diet you're on," she said on her way out. The door closed behind her with a snap. She didn't have any of lunch prepared at all yet, Percy knew, and in the quiet loneliness of his room, he let himself be angry with her.

It was easier than being angry at himself.

Suddenly the clothes he was wearing seemed stained somehow. There wasn't cum on them or anything—Jim had been vaguely professional about that, at least—but the scent of his cigarette smoke . . .

For a moment he could see Jim outlined in the window so clearly, the lean cut of his body and the angle of his jaw and wrist, the clean drop of his cigarette from his mouth. He'd made a striking image, as striking as any posed or candid photo of James Ringer. For just that moment, Percy could see the resemblance he'd been sold, and that single, short-lived glimpse was *intoxicating*. After he'd escorted Jim out, he'd stood by the window breathing in the smell of the second hand smoke like it was fresh mountain air.

He'd loved it too much. Hadn't realized that the smoke would be a dead giveaway to Hazel.

And so much else could have been, too. How could he have been so reckless? It wasn't as though he'd ordered a vibrator and was trying to sneak it out of the mail. Jim Ringer was an actual *person*, and one slip-up, one wrinkle in Percy's timing, one slight change in Hazel's schedule, and he would have been caught. It would have unraveled everything. His parents, for as little as they were in his suite, knew about his collection, his fascination. They would recognize Jim. He wouldn't put it past Hazel, if she knew, to personally track Jim down and convince him to blacklist Percy from his life, all for Percy's "own good."

Not that she would have to, now.

No, no, Percy had done that well enough on his own.

He stripped out of his sweet-smelling clothes, threw them viciously in the direction of his hamper. Had a quick hot shower to wash the smell of sex off of him. The smell of being pressed against Jim, wishing to kiss him, wanting him to be everything Percy had hoped for since calling, willing him to pass that magic threshold where he became the person Percy needed him to be.

But was that person James Ringer, or Percy's boyfriend?

Kovie had told him to find someone temporary, and he'd *done* that, relished his small spike of rebellion, but here he was, again, with Hazel passive-aggressively trying to lock his doors. Honestly, though, Percy hadn't even done the rebelling right. If it was a boyfriend he wanted, he'd done a poor job of turning Jim on to the idea—of turning Jim on at all.

He'd been so close to Jim's cock, his mouth had actually watered, but he . . .

He'd choked.

A sweeping wave of *what the holy hell are you doing?* and *can your glass jaw even handle that kind of strain* had enveloped him, and by the time he'd dragged himself out of its riptide, it was too late. Whatever had manifested itself between them was gone. Jim had seemed . . . hurt? Angry?

Unprofessional, Percy reminded himself. Because it was Jim's job. It was a job, and Percy had paid for it. And it was done.

Right?

The knock on his front door said otherwise. "Perce?" Kovie's voice called.

Oh god.

"I—give me a minute!" Percy startled up from where he'd sat on the end of his bed, having gravitated back toward the window. He was still in his towel—what was with the universe and its need to have him naked every time Kovie came to his house?—so he dashed it off and found clothes, just loose jeans and a T-shirt, and raked his fingers through his hair, for once grateful it was thin and straight and only ever dried into one style.

Kovie was grinning when he finally pulled his bedroom door open, and—oh, apparently Hazel's refusal to make food for both of them wasn't going to be a problem, because she carried a big paper bag of something heavenly-smelling. "Hey, you," she said, breezing in. "I didn't know what you liked, so I stopped by the deli and got a bunch of shit." She went right for the couch, setting the food on the coffee table, then spun to face him. She looked as effortlessly put together as she had at the gala, tight jeans and a flowy shirt, winged eye makeup with her short black hair wrapped in a neon blue scarf.

"This is . . . wow. Thanks."

"Did you shower just for me? You sure know how to make a girl feel special." Hands on her hips, she turned to survey his room, letting loose a low whistle at the sight of his movie collection. "Look at *that*." She did what he'd hoped Jim would do—went right up to his shelving units and marveled at the DVD cases, picking through them one by one, her bumblebee-yellow fingernails running reverently over the spines, like she thought his collection was the precious treasure he knew it was.

"How do you even pick? Do you have a lottery?"

"I perform a séance and ask the spirits. The ghost of Adam West keeps suggesting his own movies."

"P...retty sure Adam West is still alive."

Percy knew that, but he grinned. "Are you telling me Adam West has been breaking into my house every movie night?"

"Stranger things have happened," she said, deadpan. Her expression broke a few seconds later, and she waved him over. "C'mon, help me eat all this. And tell me what happened." She started unpacking the food, and lord, she really had brought some of everything: he saw bits of toasted bread, a few containers of soups, myriad sandwiches, some cubed cheese, apples, sliced sausage . . .

"Did you bring the entire deli with you?"

"Nah, they were charging too much for that option." Popping the lid on one of the soup containers, she drank straight from it, then arched a perfectly groomed eyebrow at him. "You're not answering my question. I thought you were going to knock yourself out with how hard you were hyperventilating earlier."

He sighed. Well, he had wanted to talk to her. "Well, you know how . . ." He stuffed his face with a handful of cheese cubes, buying himself some time. Swallowed. "How you told me to . . . rebel?"

"Uh-huh."

"Well I kind of . . . hired an escort."

"A *what*?" Kovie shrieked. "You're joking!"

"I wish I was."

"Shut. Up."

"S-sorry," Percy muttered, feeling ashamed. Should he really be shocked that a woman might be disgusted at the fact that he'd hired someone for sex?

"Not shut up like that, oh my god. I just can't believe *you*—" She hooted and slapped her knee. "How did you even arrange it?"

Percy flushed. He should have been relieved she wasn't angry, but there was no overriding this sense of shame. "I don't . . . I don't know, I found the website and I called the number and they had me fill out some forms and then I just had to pick a time when I knew Hazel wouldn't catch me . . ."

"You already went out with this . . ." She paused. "Girl? Guy? Person?"

There was no judgment of suspicion in her tone, so he answered honestly. "Guy. And I wouldn't really call it *going out*, he kind of just came over. You know, made a house call."

"Oh my God! Okay. When I said you needed some teenage rebellion I meant, I don't know, go wild on your parents' credit card, or like, befriend a crusty hipster or smoke some pot or something."

"He had that one down well enough on his own," Percy muttered, and promptly shoved another handful of cheese into his mouth at the intrigued look Kovie gave him. She made a "come hither" gesture, and he sighed. "He smoked. Not pot, but he smoked, without even asking. In my *bedroom*."

Kovie curled her nose. "Gross."

"Yeah. I mean, at least he opened the window first. God, I should have taken a picture of him up there on the window sill, puffing away like he was . . ."

Like he was James Ringer.

Kovie must have copped to his expression, because she draped herself across the couch, popping a cheese cube into her mouth with a mischievous know-it-all smile. "Mmhmm," she said. "And was that all he did, just came in and had a smoke?"

Percy's face went hot. "W-well no! No."

"Was he good?"

"G-good?"

"You know, in bed? Was he good in bed? I would hope he was. Honestly, if he was, I'd have forgiven the guy a post-coital cigarette."

"He, uh, didn't get off. And it wasn't in bed."

She blinked once, then glanced at the couch they were both

sitting on. "Oh my *god.*" He expected her to move, jump up in disgust, but she didn't, just put a hand on the cushion between them. "Congratulations on your christening," she said—to it, to him? Then her eyes were back on his, narrowed and searching. "Did *you* get off?"

"Kovie!" he stammered, face heating. It was much easier to talk about Jim's orgasms than his own. Was this how other people their age talked? Jesus.

"No, I mean really. If this is your rebellion route, I want it to be good for you. Even if you didn't want to bother getting the other guy off too."

"That's not how it was," he said before he could stop himself. There was a bright, short-lived spark of . . . anger? in his voice, too, there and burning before it cooled and died.

She winced. "Hey man, no judgment, no judgment. I'm not gonna pretend like I never got eaten out and went straight to sleep after."

Wasn't that exactly how it was, though?

"Well it was just, he asked me to . . ." He couldn't believe he was telling her this. "You know. S-suck."

"Oh? And you're not into that?"

"No, I mean, theoretically it sounds fine—" Okay, okay, it sounded fucking *hot*, especially the thought of doing it while Jim smoked, looking the height of James Ringer. "Just, my jaw. My arthritis. I don't think I'm up for it."

"Hmm." She settled back into the couch, hugging her knees to her chest. "That is kind of a bummer. But you know, you can still give a guy a BJ without doing the whole take-the-whole-dick-down-your-throat thing they do in porn. Me, I have a shit gag reflex, so I have all kinds of tricks. Suck the head a little, lick the shaft, use your hands when your mouth gets tired, that kinda thing. I know everybody treats you like you're totally incapable of everything, but there *are* workarounds. Pretty sure there are disabled people around the world getting off every minute of every day."

Percy honestly would not be surprised if someone told him his face was on fire, he was blushing so hard. "I—thank you? Thank you," he repeated, for that last part. Even if every cell of his body was drenched in embarrassment, he appreciated that, at least. Her freedom with calling him disabled instead of afflicted or "different" or "special" was invigorating.

"Nooo problem." She reached out for a piece of pepperoni, picking it apart into delicate little bites. "So when are you going to call him back?"

He frowned at her. Had he made it seem like he was going to? "I'm not," he said. "That . . . was it. My rebellion." He spread his hands, fully aware how pathetic it sounded. "Ta-da."

"Hey, hey, I said no judgment, remember? And I'd let it lie at that, except it kinda sounds like you want him to come back and annoy you with his smoking again."

"I do not!"

"Sure, okay. So what did this guy look like?"

Fucking gorgeous.

"Well, okay. Don't laugh, but well, he works for this company that um, does celebrity lookalikes."

"What!" She reached out, like she was about to slap his shoulder, but stopped herself at the last second, slapping the back of the couch instead. "Do they have a Chris Evans?"

"I, uh, didn't look at that part of the site. Maybe. They kind of have a couple of sections. One for current A-list celebrities and then one for like . . . silver screen stars. So Marilyn Monroe, Elizabeth Taylor, young Clint Eastwood . . ."

"James Ringer?" she guessed with a sly smile.

He hung his head. "Yes, James Ringer. Although he calls himself Jim."

"You have to call him again!" she gushed. "You have to! Is he a close match? Or more like a cheapo Vegas Elvis imitator?"

"He's . . ." Percy's mouth went a little dry remembering. He hadn't been lying when he'd told Jim there was no resemblance in attitude, but in body? In face? "He's a perfect match," he admitted. "The jaw, the eyes . . . everything is the same. Except." He wrinkled his nose and held up a hand, cutting off any romantic ideas Kovie could possibly get about Jim. "He knows *nothing* about James Ringer. When I hired him, I was barely thinking about sex. I thought he could come over, we could watch movies, something. But he wasn't interested, not at all. So maybe he is an imitator, in that respect." He couldn't keep the disappointment from his voice.

Kovie chewed on her lip. "Maybe you could ease him into it," she suggested. "I have this friend Clint who swore up and down he didn't like anything made before 2000, and we took him to this fifties monster movie marathon, and now he can't get enough. Drives his boyfriend nuts."

"I don't think Jim's like that." That casual disinterest was attractive in theory, sure, in movie posters, but Percy just wasn't up for fighting a battle to keep Jim interested in the things he liked. In *him*. It was hard enough accepting Kovie actually *was* interested in him; he didn't think he had the willpower or the self-confidence to strong-arm someone into it. "Plus, that's not his job."

"His job is to smoke out your window?" She arched an eyebrow at him. "Why was he smoking, anyway, if you didn't ask him to?"

"He's got no sense of what's professional," Percy said. "I think he's new at it."

"Or maybe he just doesn't give a shit. Maybe I was wrong to think you should call him again."

"No, he—" Percy cut himself off, clenching his jaw until it hurt. Why was his first instinct to *defend* Jim? He'd thought worse of Jim himself, when he'd been here. Had accused him personally of not giving a shit. "No, you're right." He cracked a lame smile. "I could take up pot-smoking after all."

She snorted, then sobered fast, peering at him over her knees. "Look, if you like him . . ." She shrugged. "Why not go for it? Don't let me tell you what to do or what not to do."

"It was a mistake to hire him in the first place. God knows what Hazel would do if she found out."

"So tell her he's . . . I dunno, a friend?"

Percy shook his head. "She knows I don't have friends. Except you," he added, his little smile brighter this time.

"Sooo tell her he's one of my friends. Someone who was gonna go with us last week."

"Okay, but then how do I explain the credit card charges that just so happen to appear every time he visits?"

She made a face. "So he's not a friend. He's someone you hired for something? Cleaning? Physio? Tutoring?"

"Tutoring," Percy murmured, turning it over. Hazel cleaned—

there would be no point in even pretending that was what Jim was for. And no way a soft-stomached, dour-faced smoker like Jim could be mistaken for a physiotherapist. But tutoring? Percy had brought up the idea of getting a degree in film or history a couple months ago, which had been immediately brushed off by both his parents and Hazel. Of course he wasn't "fit" to attend college in person, but what if he could take courses online? And conceivably, he could have hired a tutor to ensure he wasn't falling behind, ensure he wasn't getting too tired to complete assignments, as Hazel had warned he would.

"I see those wheels turning." Kovie snagged a finger sandwich and ripped it in half, offering part to Percy. "You gonna snap him up?"

Percy picked the sandwich apart just for something to do. If hiring Jim in the first place had been insane, this was . . . what? Insanity with full awareness of what he was doing? "We didn't end on a good note, exactly."

Kovie hummed. "Shit happens. Look." She put her half of the sandwich back on the table and leaned forward, patting his knees. "You do you, babe. If you decide he's not *the one*—to rebel with, that is—I'll find you a crusty hipster or come sneak you out of your bedroom in the middle of the night to go to a hookah bar or something. Okay?"

The out felt good, even if ninety-seven percent of him had already made up his mind to hire Jim again. "Okay."

"Good deal," she said, stealing a slice of cheese from his deconstructed sandwich. Grinning, she waved a hand at the racks of DVDs. "Now that that's settled, how about you introduce me to the Holy Grail?"

CHAPTER
FOURTEEN

The only thing that had changed about Canter's in the nineteen years Brandon had known it was the prices. Seriously, even the *salads* were fifteen bucks now, and though Brandon was arguably better off thanks to Hollywood Doubles, he wasn't exactly rolling in dough, here.

He paged through the menu, keeping an eye on the door. He'd gotten here fifteen minutes early, leery of making his lateness tally two for two. If he was gonna be asking Ms. Monroe for help, he needed to have his best face on. On time, paying for lunch, listening to her, the whole nine. It helped that he actually trusted her advice, unlike, say, Vince's. God, he couldn't even imagine what Vince would've said if Brandon had called *him*. "Suck it up," probably, if not, "I'm firing you." And both of those were more desirable than, "Well how about we give my plan a shot, huh? Marketing gig, commercials, we could donate some tissue samples to that celebrity salami-producing company . . ."

And Brandon was extensively used to sucking it up by now, so he would've, if it didn't keep ending in him just plain *sucking* every time. Every damn time.

Fuck. He needed to get out of this misery spiral before Ms. Monroe got here. The last thing he needed was to be looking all sullen and moody (in the unattractive way) about asking her a favor. He flagged down the waitress when she passed—he'd told her to hold off on her first round—and asked for the biggest cup of coffee she had, black so he could have an excuse to rub a packet of sugar between his fingertips while he waited for it to get here. He was still itching for a cigarette, for a whole *pack* of cigarettes. Something in his veins that wasn't self-pity.

Because that was exactly what he was stewing in. What was he even going to say to Ms. Monroe? She'd want to know what made him ask today, of all days. *Oh, I got pissy because some kid wouldn't suck my dick.* Yeah, that would go over well.

"Shit," he muttered, startling the waitress, who hesitated a second, then put his coffee down. He ducked his head. "Sorry. That—uh, sorry. That wasn't for you."

"Well, I'd hope not. I already threw out two guys this morning. Don't make it a third, kiddo." She gave him a rough pat on the shoulder and went on her way.

He was still reeling from that—just the thought of getting kicked out of the diner before Ms. Monroe had even arrived to meet up with him—when the woman herself walked in.

Off-duty, but still dressed head-to-toe in vintage, with perfectly curled hair, mascara, red lips, a little blue sundress, and white peep-toe pumps. How she could look so put-together with an hour's notice, he had no idea. By comparison, he probably looked like a hobo who'd crawled out of a cardboard box.

He almost sent his coffee flying in his effort to get up to greet her, and she was the one to reach out and steady his cup with perfectly manicured nails. "You are a bundle of nerves today, aren't you?" she teased, sliding into the other side of the booth. She lifted a hand in greeting to someone behind the deli counter, motioning with two fingers. Then Brandon had her full attention, and it was just as intimidating as it had been during the photoshoot.

"Thanks, uh, thanks." Real smooth. "I mean thanks for coming out to see me, especially on short notice."

"It's no problem. So what's up? Should we talk now, or after you've put some food into you? You look like you could use some calories."

"What happened to slimming me down?" he asked, mouth on automatic. He grimaced at himself, but she laughed.

"I said *tone*. And I'm still saying it. But you look exhausted." Her tone went from throaty teasing to warm concern in a second flat. "Have you eaten at all this morning?"

He shook his head. His stomach had been in knots since he left Percy's house; he wasn't sure he *could* eat.

Ms. Monroe pursed her lips. "I know you come from a kind of

rough background, Brandon. So do I, honestly, though I can't imagine what it must have been like for you to grow up so closely related to such a prominent celebrity." She didn't have to say *one you look just like*. He saw it in her face. "But this is a different kind of business. We're still customer service, and the customer is always right, and you can't take care of your clients if you don't take care of yourself. You understand?"

"... Yeah."

"I could loan you my personal trainer, if you like. He can come up with a workout and a meal plan for you. I think treating your body right would be a great start to improving everything else."

"Thanks, but I, uh." Fuck, how were you supposed to say "I'm not making enough to afford things" to your *boss*?

As always, she saw right through him. "Vince covers it as long as the service is rendered under my suggestion. I'll set you up a consultation." Her eyes flicked away and she smiled. "Akanksha!" she said to the waitress from before. "Darling, how are you?"

"Same old, same old." Akanksha put a glass of water down in front of Ms. Monroe, iced and with lime instead of lemon. Her smile was a little stiffer than Ms. Monroe's, not so excited. "How are you?"

"Busy, as always. But life's treating me well." She gestured at Brandon. "This is Brandon, one of my coworkers. Brandon, Akanksha. We went to high school together in Pasadena."

It was weird to be called Ms. Monroe's coworker, as if they were peers, as if they were anywhere near on the same level. Which they weren't. At all.

"Nice to meet you," Brandon mumbled.

"We're going to camp out here for a little bit," Ms. Monroe said, not letting the awkward silence linger. "Can you bring me my usual? And Brandon, did you decide on what you want?"

"Just a salad, I guess," he said. "The, uh, garden one. No dressing." Would that be healthy enough to make a good impression?

"Extra protein on that salad," Ms. Monroe added. "Oh! Are you a vegetarian, Brandon?"

Brandon shook his head.

"Lots of grilled chicken, then?" Akanksha said, scribbling on her notepad.

"Yes. And turkey bacon, if you have it?"

"Yep. Got it. Anything else?"

Ms. Monroe shook her head. "That's it. You've covered it all, as usual." She seemed oblivious to the lingering plastic in Akanksha's smile—or she was willfully ignoring it and blasting her own charisma to counter, which was way more likely.

Either way, Brandon gave Akanksha a quick thanks and gulped a few mouthfuls of coffee, preparing himself for the rest of this conversation.

It was a good thing he did, too.

As soon as Akanksha had gone, Ms. Monroe leaned forward, crossing her arms delicately in front of her. "So," she said. "Does this have anything to do with your last-minute appointment this morning?"

Well, fuck.

"Sorta. I mean . . . that's part of it, yeah, but I really just don't know . . . how to do this." He buried the face he made at himself in his coffee cup. Ms. Monroe raised a pale, sculpted eyebrow and waited for him to go on. *How* to go on, though? Or: how to go on without sounding like an idiot? "You know I've done the sex part of it," he said finally, lowering his voice. "And I basically won the genetic lottery, when it comes to this kind of work. But like I said, the actual impersonation part isn't something I'm used to. And obviously you . . ." He gestured broadly to her.

"Mmm." She tilted her head, resting her cheek on one hand. "Realizing just your face isn't enough to get by?"

Ouch.

But he had to agree. "Something like that. I mean, yes. I mean, I don't *want* to get by on just my face. I had this one client—is it okay to talk to you about this? I mean, we work together, so it's not like . . . breaking confidentiality or anything, is it?"

"It's fine. Just don't use names, since we're in public."

"Okay, I had this one client last—uh, recently, and he seemed kind of lukewarm on me, but he still . . . y'know. And then afterward he said, 'You look like him, at least.' And I know he must have been talking about James Ringer. But he sounded so *disappointed*. And I don't know how to fix that."

Ms. Monroe put a finger up. "Question, do you think I roll out of bed looking like Marilyn Monroe?"

"Kinda." Brandon laughed.

"Well, I don't, babycakes. But don't you dare tell anyone else that." She winked, but then her face turned serious, her lively grey eyes roving over him for a long second before she went on. "I want to tell you something really personal. Can you be cool?"

"I won't be an asshole, if that's what you mean. But *cool*? I don't think I'm capable of cool around you."

Her answering smile was sweet and patient. "I appreciate the honesty. And . . . I think I can trust you." She stirred her straw through her glass of water a moment, her plump lower lip pinched gently between her teeth, and was she . . . was she *stalling*? "I don't know if you poked around the Hollywood Doubles website, much, but if you went on my profile page you'd see a few . . . Let's call them code words. Not the most flattering language, if I'm honest, but it's what sells."

Brandon shook his head, lost. "What kind of code words?"

"Well, I'll just come right out with it. Becoming Marilyn Monroe wasn't nearly as drastic transformation as the one I went through to be my plain old everyday self. If you'd have met me ten years ago, it would have been as a pimply, greasy-haired, teenage *boy*." She gave Brandon a pointed, expectant look, not quite wincing in anticipation of his response, but guarded all the same.

"O-oh!" Brandon sputtered. "Oh. Oh."

"I guess the point I'm making is, to truly *become*, sometimes we have to put in more effort than we think we should have to. It wasn't enough for me to just acknowledge and accept the fact that yes, despite everyone saying otherwise, I was a woman. That was just my first step. Recognizing what was within me was only the first step. Is it fair? No. Is it hard? Yes."

"I . . . I don't want to insult you, but I don't understand exactly what this has to do with *me*."

"It took me years of hard work to be the woman sitting in front of you. And you know, Queen Bee, she only really looks like Beyoncé because she's a magician with a contouring brush. King dyes his hair black, which is funny, because so did the real Elvis. You may have the right face and the right hair, but you still have to put the work in, too.

If you want this, if you really *want* this, you have to undergo your own transformation." She smiled. "Even if it's just to confirm something you knew and believed about yourself all along."

And . . . he wasn't following. Brandon had already had everything he knew about himself at this job confirmed by everyone around him growing up. As for what he *believed* about himself? Yeah, that was an empty list.

He couldn't handle disappointing Ms. Monroe, though. Especially not after she'd told him something so personal. "I'm willing to do the work," he said. "I swear to God. I'm not . . . I'm a prick, but I'm not *lazy*." How many times had he heard that from bosses? That had been their confirmation: that he was lazy, spoiled, didn't want to put in hard work. The truth—did this count for what he believed about himself?—was he just never had any reason to care. He brushed them all off—bosses, customers, everyone. They didn't think anything of him, so why bother giving a shit? It never mattered whether he did or not.

Until, well, *now*. With Ms. Monroe staring him down, pep-talking him like she thought he'd actually be able to do better, he cared.

"Like, I'll go to this trainer. I'll eat healthier. I'll work out. Whatever."

But somehow he didn't think that was what it was going to take. Being fitter wouldn't change that lack of resemblance. The thing standing between him and the real James Ringer wasn't a six pack of abs. It was, as always, his attitude. Because for Ms. Monroe, this was her whole life—her whole transformation. This was all part of her. And for Brandon . . . this was a *job*. Just another job. A means to preserving what little of Dahlia he had left. It wasn't the end all be all.

Ms. Monroe's lips twitched into a half-smile. "Working out would be enough at a lot of other escort agencies, but something about the look on your face tells me you know that's not gonna cut it when it comes to this particular problem." She leaned closer, her perfectly curled hair sweeping down around her cheeks. "Do you know what your problem *is*, Brandon?"

Yeah. For the first time in my life, people are saying I'm not enough like James Ringer.

"It's the impersonation thing. I can get fit or whatever, I can be friendly, but I can't be *him*."

"Why not?"

Because I'm not him. Because I hate him. Because I have spent the last decade of my life fighting not to become him when everyone said I would, and I'm doing it anyway. This whole job was the antithesis of everything Brandon had been fighting for, and had he been stupid to think he'd be able to be himself while still making money off not-being James Ringer? "Because . . . because I'm *me*, dammit."

"Ah," Ms. Monroe said, leaning back in her seat. She crossed her legs and her arms, giving him a studious look. "Now that's . . . that's a do or die kind of question. There are some people, they can't do this job. They feel like they're losing their grip on themselves. Like method actors. They live the job. They forget who they were, don't know how to go back. Sometimes they don't want to or are afraid to. It's an escape, a sanctuary, and a poison, all at the same time. If all anyone loves about me is how I look like Marilyn Monroe, is my true self even worth a damn?"

"Is that why you dress like this even when you're off duty?" Brandon asked.

"Because my only value is in being Marilyn Monroe?" Ms. Monroe countered. "Maybe because that's the only way I can see myself as a woman?"

Hot shame bit into Brandon's lungs. "I didn't—"

"I know you didn't mean it that way, sweetie. But I'd be lying if I said there weren't a few mean, bitter men who tried those lines on me. And you know, it's true, I do love looking like a bombshell, and the looks people give me when I look like a bombshell. I like borrowing Marilyn's celebrity. But my *name* is Judy. Not Marilyn Monroe, not my birth name. Judy."

"Judy," Brandon echoed, trying out the feel of it in his mouth.

"Right. After Judy Garland, because I always did love musicals."

"So Marilyn Monroe is . . . a costume? An act?"

"Marilyn Monroe is a *lifestyle*."

"You lost me again." And he wasn't going to say it to her, but no way *in hell* could he think about transforming James Ringer into his *lifestyle*.

"Sexy Mermaid is a costume. You pay a ridiculous amount of

money to buy it off some skeezy lingerie website, you wear it one night, it gets you laid, and you never wear it again. And calling it 'an act' just sounds so . . . fake and resentful. And it's not. I'm committed and I'm happy and I'm getting paid fat stacks of cash. And like any other job you care about and are proud of, you put time and effort and study into it. If I were teaching a high school math class after going to teaching school and learning how to treat students, wearing a buttoned-up blouse and a pantsuit, would you call that a costume or an act?"

Brandon shook his head, because he figured that was the answer she wanted to hear.

"No, you'd call it dedication to a career. And it wouldn't make me any less Judy. I wouldn't stop wearing silk nightgowns after I got home. I wouldn't stop having a martini and a cigarette."

"So, what, I need to . . ." Fuck, he didn't know.

"Study, Brandon. Study. Figure out what the job requires of you, and be that."

He took a long sip of his coffee to give himself a few seconds to scrape together something to say. It didn't matter—he sounded just as bad as he had in his head. "But I can't figure out what the clients want. It's like they want a different me every time. I'm too slutty or not sultry enough or I'm selfish or I'm withdrawn or I drink too much and they talk about how they're going to get kicked out of hotels because it's obvious I'm a hooker, and—"

"Breathe," Ms. Monroe said. "Brandon, you're missing the point. Willfully, I think. I didn't mean study the clients. I meant study James Ringer. Have you watched anything he's been in?" She took Brandon's silence for the answer it was. "I understand this must be harder for you, because I can see your relationship with him is . . ." *Fucked up? Twisted? The stuff of terrible coming-of-age movies?* " . . . complicated," she went with. "But if you want to do this job, you're going to have to own up a little. If you actually want to do what you told me and rely on skills rather than your looks, you need to build up your skills."

Brandon chewed on the inside of his cheek. He wasn't going to say James Ringer had been a no-talent wreck of a person to her face, either. "Okay. Do you have, like . . . basics? A starter kit?"

She ticked off on her fingers. "Watch him, like I said. Watch how he moves, how he speaks. Not that your accent isn't charming, but it's not James Ringer's. I sound like Marilyn because I learned her speech patterns. Do that. And dress like you expect success. I saw a few of the comments about your attire, and that can easily be fixed if you find some period clothing, or even period-style clothing. Believe me, I would know, you can put together fabulous period outfits from thrift stores. That's all there is to it, really. Most of our clientele isn't actually looking for Daniel Day-Lewis's levels of skill and dedication. But a little bit of effort and thoughtfulness goes a long way. All you have to do is *try*, Brandon."

"But what if . . ." He twisted his fingers together, out of coffee to fiddle with. "What if this isn't what I want for a career? What if I just . . ." He didn't want to say this, either. Not to her.

What if I can't do it?

"Then work it to the fullest you can until the financial stress lets up, and plan an exit strategy. Look, I'm a very happy whore. But women like me, we wind up in sex work a lot more than most other demographics, and a lot of the time it's not because the work's so great and pays so well and makes us all so happy. Sometimes people work a job out of desperation, or coercion, or whatever else. Sometimes you just do it because that's the only choice the world gives you. If it's anything other than because it makes you happy on one level or another, then I always say . . . plan to get out if you can. No shame in that."

"But if I'm just gonna leave, then why bother? Why bother working so hard? Why bother transforming?"

"Because you *want* to. You want to do your best at it while you're here. You're smart, and you're driven. I've seen your stubborn streak." She seemed to be inviting him in on the joke, but when he couldn't get himself to laugh, too busy wondering if he *did* want to, if she'd seen right through him again, before he even knew it himself, she pressed her lips together, her eyes softening. "Sweetie, if you *don't* want to your best, then just try to be well-behaved and enthusiastic enough that you don't get any more really scathing reviews."

His face burned. "You saw all of them, huh."

"Yeah. You're new, though. I'm willing to cut you a little slack, especially since you calling me to arrange this meeting means you're trying. But honestly, as long as I'm not hearing complaints about you, I'm not going to take you to task on your dedication. Do what works for you and what doesn't get me in shit with Vince. After that . . ." She shrugged. "But if you do want to get on *my* level, if you want to be more than 'at least you look like him,' then now you know what to do. I've seen everything Marilyn's been in. Multiple times. I've studied every photoshoot. I've commissioned replicas of her dresses. Why, this little number I've got on now was based on something she wore in a 1957 photoshoot with Sam Shaw."

"Wow," Brandon said, quite honestly.

"Uh-huh. I'm not saying you have to go out and do all *that*, but buying a nice leather jacket and a pair of vintage blue jeans wouldn't hurt. When I said you needed to dress the part, I didn't mean wear things you'd wear when you did this before. This is a different level, with a different, more selective clientele. People notice those minute touches because they paid for them—and those touches are what result in good reviews."

"Isn't that still just . . . looking like him?"

"No." She shifted in her seat, not an ounce of impatience in her expression. "It's *caring*. It's being good at your job. Just looking like him, that's your genetics. It's passive. Dressing like him, that's active. It's knowing what to buy because you know *him*."

But I don't want to know him.

No way could he say that. No way *would* he say that.

He was saved from having to think of anything to say by Akanksha setting a stand down at their table side and passing them food—salad for him, drowning in strips of grilled chicken, and a salad for Ms. Monroe, too, hers rich with oranges and drenched with fruity-looking dressing. Brandon dug a fork into his, surprisingly hungry. Or maybe he wanted something to focus on that wasn't all Ms. Monroe's good advice, all the good tactics and suggestions and help that just didn't seem to be sinking in for Brandon.

All because of who James Ringer had been to Dahlia, and because of who he still was to Brandon.

A wraith, dogging Brandon everywhere he went.

If he was just a normal guy, just some other random dude out there who managed to mysteriously look like James Ringer, he was sure he could've done this job, easy. It would've been cash, steady work. It would've been impersonal, exactly the same as the shit he used to pull in bars and motels, with married dudes who wanted to call his asshole a pussy or pretend he liked being tied to headboards.

For Ms. Monroe, this career, this *transformation*, had been freedom. For Brandon, it was walking down those dark steps in Dahlia's house to that crypt of a basement filled with rotting memorabilia.

"You all right there?" Ms. Monroe asked, startling him. Her eyes were slightly wide, her lips curved up. "That chicken didn't last long."

"I—oh." No, it hadn't. Jesus. All he had left was a pile of greens and some shredded carrots. Still all tasted better than the shit he was living off at home.

"Eat your veggies too," she said gently. "I don't want you dying of scurvy."

"Yeah," Brandon mumbled.

She sighed. "I feel like you're understanding what I'm saying, but there's still something holding you back."

"You have no idea."

Her eyebrows lifted. "It's okay if you're still conflicted or emotional about all this, you know. It is a business, and you are selling a service, but it's still personal, too. Just try your best, that's all."

Brandon pushed his shredded carrots around. "What if that's not enough?"

"Your best will get better," she said. "Trust me. Mine did."

"I can't even imagine you ever being bad at this."

"Oh, I never said I was ever *bad*." Her eyes twinkled. "I came into this job with a passion for it. You've got to find that. Even if that passion might not necessarily come from a place of love." She speared a forkful of oranges and passed them onto his plate. "You ought to eat more fruit, too. I'm going to give Marco a call the second I get home, get a nutritional plan drawn up for you."

"Thanks," Brandon said, then looked up from his salad and looked her in the eye. "I mean it. Thank you for all of this. It's true I've got a couple hang-ups, but what you're saying is totally right, and I'm just gonna have to work around them."

She gave him a gentle smile, the same one she'd let him go with the day of the photoshoot. "You're a good kid, Brandon. You know?"

He was silent for long enough that she sighed quietly and passed him another forkful of oranges. "I'll give your client schedule to Marco so he can work around your appointments. And why don't you and I meet for lunch again soon? Say two weeks from today?"

Brandon nodded, maybe a little eagerly.

"You can do this, sweetie."

God, he wanted to believe her.

He really, really did.

CHAPTER
FIFTEEN

Ms. Monroe paid for lunch, calling it a business expense and charging it to a card emblazoned with Hollywood Doubles' logo. Brandon would've felt bad taking money out of her pocket, but out of Vince's? Something told him Vince could afford to lose money out of his tacky suits and even tackier jewelry budget.

Which gave Brandon an idea. A way to start on his list—he was considering it homework—that didn't involve having to put himself face to face with his grandfather. Yet.

This side of town had a lot of vintage places, stores that chipped in to attract the old Hollywood crowd who ate at Canter's. There was a chain of thrift stores close by, close enough to walk to, and after Brandon saw Ms. Monroe to her white Cadillac, he hiked over to look. The least he could do to put Ms. Monroe's advice into effect was to spruce up his wardrobe. Looking like a hooker he could do. Looking like James Ringer dressed like a hooker—that he could do, too. But looking like James Ringer dressed like James Ringer...

Well, he just hoped "Hepcat Vintage" or one of its sister stores would be up to the challenge.

The shop smelled like old perfume and dust and a little like Dahlia's basement, actually. It was dark inside, the racks of clothing making it feel smaller than it was. "Can I help you?" the clerk called from behind her checkout counter, which was stacked with handmade displays, holding rings, cigarette lighters, baggies full of (fake as hell) gemstones, you name it.

"No," Brandon said automatically, then, "Actually, yeah. You got any leather jackets?"

She shrugged, popping her gum, then looked him up and down.

"Something to fit you?"

"That's the idea."

"Don't think we do. We've got mostly women's." She pointed him toward the back with a limp, unenthusiastic wave. "Far right. Check it out yourself, if you want."

Jesus. What great fucking service.

Brandon headed through the racks and to the very back of the shop, where a vertical rack was stacked with leather jackets. The clerk was right; none of them looked like they'd fit Brandon's shoulders, much less have sleeves his size. "Fuck," he muttered, thumbing over one that had some ribbing on the front he liked. Then he checked the price tag swinging near his wrist and winced. Almost two hundred dollars.

Okay, there had to be *something* else in here he could get. He doubled back, getting his shitty phone out and googling "James Ringer photoshoot." There were a few things that looked easier—AKA, less expensive—than a leather jacket, so, with the results page pulled up on his phone, he went hunting.

By the time he surfaced and brought everything to the bored clerk, he'd picked out six shirts, one of them wide-collared with stripes, a worn denim jacket with leather farmer's patches on the elbows, and a pair of black slacks way looser around the ankle than he was used to. On the way to checking out, he found a large-faced, patinaed watch on a pleather strap for ten bucks and added that to the pile, too.

He'd need some white T-shirts as well, but he sure as hell wasn't going to be paying these vintage store prices for them. All of this was going to be— "Ninety-eight forty-nine," the clerk said, holding out a hand.

Yeah. $98.49. That was enough financial effort for now—he'd buy a ten pack of Hanes T-shirts at Walmart.

Brandon paid with cash, earning him a look from the clerk, and then stood there until she raised an eyebrow and said, "You want it bagged, then?"

"Uh, yeah." He stuffed his hands in his pockets, thrown. For a strip with this kind of reputation, he would've expected someone who at least *pretended* to give a shit about pretending they were happy to be here.

Oh.

. . . That was probably exactly what Hollywood Doubles' clients expected, too. The kind of personal, warm experience Brandon had never bothered to try giving them.

Well, he was bothering now. Ms. Monroe thought he was stubborn, thought he could do it? He'd show her just how far that stubborn streak could take him.

He took the fat bag the clerk handed him and held it to his chest. "Have a good one," he said, and, as predicted, got no response. Outside, it was getting dark, and the neons were lighting up. There was a snap in the air, and he stopped on the sidewalk to fish the denim jacket out and slide it on. It fit just right. Didn't feel too bad, either. It almost made up for how many PB&J's he was going to be eating for the next month to cover the cost.

Almost.

Didn't take too long for a call to come in that would test his newfound resolve. His very first client, Alfred, had finally booked a long-in-coming second appointment—probably because the agency's Cary Grant or whoever had to take a sick day.

Oh well, his loss and Brandon's gain. He ditched the tight pleather hooker pants from last time, picking a more subtle outfit out of his new wardrobe. Slicked his hair back like John Travolta in *Grease*. The people making that movie must have done their homework, right?

Either way, it had been almost slicked back by the time he'd left rich kid Percy's place, and he half-remembered Percy running his hands through it, fixing it. So that had to be a point in the "be realistic" column.

He brushed his teeth and gargled mouthwash. Flashed his reflection a cheesy late night TV guest smile. Then he thought of what Ms. Monroe would say, seeing that, and tried to soften it into something a little more genuine, more real, with a sort of wryness to it. Not like he was bored or anything, but like you had to work to get him to *really* smile. And that when you managed it, it felt like a reward instead of a begrudging surrender. Like something you'd waited for your whole life.

You look like him, at least.

He wondered what Alfred would have to say about him this time.

All good things, he told himself.

He was working so hard on a good attitude that when Cyrus pulled up, he actually greeted the guy with a smile and a, "How's it going?"

Cyrus gave him a dead-eyed, unimpressed look. "How d'you think it's going?" he grunted. "I'm here. Get in the damn car."

Brandon sighed, but hey, this was sort of like on-the-job training, right? He was going to have difficult clients, that much he already knew, and he was going to have clients who were shitty to him and expected him to be a ray of fucking social sunshine in return. He almost asked if Cyrus was married before he figured he should stick to questions he could actually ask his clients and said instead, "So how long've you been a driver?"

"Kid," Cyrus said flatly, "I don't know what you're hopped up on, but I'll do you a favor and won't tell the boss if you spend the next twenty minutes being quiet."

"We can't talk a little?"

"Didn't think talking was your specialty," Cyrus said nastily. "Considering you're doing this job."

"Hey," Brandon said, determined to be unruffled. "Gotta put your cards on the table where you can count best."

Cyrus snorted. "Look. Maybe this's the only job you're qualified for, but me? I gotta degree and I'd've ended up somewhere way fuckin' better than this if—" He waved a hand. "Never mind. Ain't none of your business anyway."

Brandon was so not the type who could handle playing therapist, but he couldn't resist pressing. "If what? Do you need money?" Cyrus's gaze snapped to his in the rearview. "I just mean I know what that's like, you know."

"Oh yeah, I'm sure you do. Nice big house like yours, I'm sure you know what it's like to live in a one-bedroom and try to feed five kids." He shook his head, muttering to himself, and took a turn when the next light was green. "Just let it the fuck go. If you're so interested, all's you gotta know is I wouldn't be driving cocksucking queers around for a living if I didn't have to, got it?"

God damn. The old Brandon would have snapped, maybe told Cyrus to fuck off and let him out of the car, but new Brandon thought about what Ms. Monroe would think and instead just smiled again, saying "Got it, bud."

Cyrus's eyes lingered on him in the rearview, narrowed and suspicious. Brandon settled back in the seat and ignored him all the way to the hotel, the same mid-century they'd met in the first time. "Get in, get out," Cyrus grumped at him. "Got places to be today."

"Me too," Brandon said mildly. "But that's for the *paying customer* to decide." He shrugged his denim jacket all the way up over his shoulders, pulling the collar to straighten it, and headed in, less slouch this time. Found himself a perch at the bar and ordered a soda water.

Alfred was right on time.

Brandon pulled his sunglasses down his nose, peering over the tops of them in flirtatious appraisal. He cocked a smile, eyebrows lifting. Alfred was dressed in the same sort of old dude clothes as last time, and he didn't look exactly *thrilled* to see Brandon, but that just meant Brandon had to work harder for it.

Just like he'd promised Ms. Monroe.

"Hey," he said, sliding off his stool to greet Alfred instead of just waiting for him to sit. "Nice to see you again. Can I get you a drink?"

A quick flash of surprise crossed Alfred's face, followed by a cautious smile. He shook Brandon's hand, like they were friendly business acquaintances. "Nice to see you again too, Jim."

Brandon kept it subtle, but made sure to brush his hand across Alfred's lower back as he climbed up onto his stool.

Was that a little bit of redness showing at the tops of Alfred's ears? "I'll have a rum and coke. What're you drinking, there?"

"Just soda," Brandon replied. "Keeping on my toes."

"Are you, now? Not turned teetotaler, have you?"

"Me? Never. Just figured there were better ways to have fun today."

Those ears were definitely blushing now.

Brandon had to admit it was super charming.

Despite Cyrus's demand he "get in, get out," Brandon and Alfred spent ages at the bar, talking about baseball, mostly. Neutral territory, something they could both address. Something two guys from any point in time could talk about. The conversation was . . . surprisingly easy, and Brandon felt himself laughing easier than he had in ages. Alfred, when Brandon wasn't hurrying him along, had more than a few great stories. Having season passes to Dodger Stadium in the sport's golden age could do that for a guy. At one point, Brandon even caught himself actually sitting rapt with his chin in his hand, elbow on the bar, listening to Alfred talk about a girl who'd somersaulted over three empty rows of seats to catch a fly ball and got the whole team to sign it.

It was then that Alfred cleared his throat. "You care to take this elsewhere?"

"Thought you'd never ask," Brandon said, and sure it was cliché and cheesy, but Alfred seemed to like it fine. He actually put his hand on Brandon's back on the way out of the bar, and got them both into the elevator and upstairs, keeping Brandon casually close to him the whole time.

Inside the room, Brandon made the first move, gently spinning him so his back was to the door and giving him that kiss he'd assumed he couldn't have the first time around.

It was the right choice: Alfred melted in his arms, kissing back like a lovestruck teenager.

Maybe he'd been one, once, gazing up at James Ringer on the big screen, in the dark where he could feel safe to let his feelings show on his freckled face.

They kissed for almost as long as they'd talked at the bar. Alfred's hands wandered, pressing but not groping, and he leaned into Brandon sometimes, like he was trusting Brandon to hold them both up. He was also unabashedly eager in a way Brandon would never have expected—not just because Alfred was the age he was, but because Brandon had assumed his stiffness last time was stodgy primness instead of discomfort.

The sex, after that, seemed like almost a footnote to the main attraction. This time Alfred had him on his back, Brandon's legs wrapped around his waist, and they only stopped kissing long enough for Alfred to catch his breath.

"Thank you, thank you," Alfred gasped when they'd both spent. "Oh, thank you."

He collapsed on Brandon's chest, and Brandon wrapped an arm around his shoulders, wishing he had a cigarette, for once not out of anxiety or irritation. "No thanks needed," he said gently, and kissed the top of Alfred's head.

When he didn't get up and dress right away, Brandon found himself speaking. "You loved him, huh?" *My grandfather.* "James Ringer."

"Hated him too, sometimes. He was . . . the first man I couldn't lie to myself about."

"But not the last?" Brandon asked.

Alfred chuckled. "No, no, that would have to be Tony. We were together for forty years."

The thought warmed Brandon right to his bones. "Sounds like he was the one."

"He was. Still is, at least in here." He patted his chest, over his heart. Sweet grief overcame him as plain as day, but he shook it off with practiced practicality. "How about you, Jim? You have a special someone?"

"Nah," Brandon replied.

"You will. Keep that chip off your shoulder, be open to life like you just were with me, and you will."

"Chip on my shoulder, huh?" Brandon chuckled. "That's a nice way of putting it."

"How would you put it?"

"Hmm. Disrespectful, selfish little prick sound okay to you?"

Alfred laughed, warm and genuine. "I wouldn't put it like that."

"It would be okay if you did. I'd deserve it."

"Maybe the first time we met up."

"I'm sorry for that. I hope I made it up to you."

"And then some," Alfred said, patting Brandon's hip. "You warm up okay, Jim."

"Well thanks." Probably for the first time Brandon could remember, there was no sarcasm in the phrase. "I tried," he said, which came out pathetic.

But Alfred just patted him again. "Obviously."

Brandon preened quietly, then caught sight of the thick watch he'd strapped around his wrist and saw it was almost two hours past the time he was supposed to be done. He was surprised Cyrus hadn't come storming in to demand Brandon free up his precious time.

Because he definitely wouldn't come storming in to make sure Brandon hadn't been, like, strangled in the bathtub or dumped out the window by an unhappy customer. Hell, that would be a *good* day at work for him.

Alfred stirred next to him. "Oh," he said, squinting at Brandon's watch. "Sorry to take up so much of your time."

"Nah, don't worry about it," Brandon hurried to assure him. "I don't have any o—uhh . . ." Was that rude? That was rude.

"You don't worry either," Alfred chuckled. "Go on. And thanks."

"Thank *you*." Brandon hopped off the bed to find his clothes, which were scattered around like he'd had normal romping desperate-to-get-your-clothes off sex instead of put in one neat pile like they'd been for the rest of his appointments. When he was dressed, he paused, rubbing his fingertips together. Alfred had pulled the sheet over him and was watching him dozily, not leering or anything. "Hey," Brandon said quietly. He cleared his throat. "This is probably unprofessional, but I uh, I hope you hire me again. Not for the money, just . . ." *You're way better than lots of the others.*

Unless Brandon's shit attitude had affected all of them, too. Which was entirely probable.

Alfred's smile was soft. "You betcha."

The warm feeling it gave Brandon carried him all the way downstairs and to the car, where Cyrus's snarled, "You know you don't get *overtime*, right? And neither do *I*?" wasn't even enough to dim it.

That feeling lasted all through the next couple of hours. Right up until he remembered the second part of Ms. Monroe's advice: watch James Ringer. Watch everything he'd been in.

Brandon sat down with the last of the untouched—and probably old and disgusting—beers from the back of Dahlia's fridge and opened his laptop. Loaded YouTube. He could make it through just an interview, right? Watching a whole movie would be too much, and anyway, he'd only be sitting through secondhand embarrassment, not learning anything. It wouldn't even be James Ringer, really, it'd be whatever typecast bad boy character he was.

Of course, full pirated copies of *Break of Dawn* and *Call Me, Callie* were the first things that popped up in the search.

But below them was an interview he'd done for a TV talk show in 1950, and the thumbnail was James Ringer grinning at the laughing host, both of them backlit by a marquee sign.

Brandon cracked open the beer and gulped half of it. Yep, disgusting. Enough liquid courage for him to fire up the interview, though.

And then close the tab two seconds later.

Shit. His fucking hands were shaking.

What was he so afraid of? What? That he'd like the public persona his grandfather wore? That he'd see himself there more than he did now?

"Suck it the fuck up," he told himself, and reopened the tab.

He skipped to halfway through the video so he didn't have to hear the host's no doubt glowing intro. "—hangin' around with a bunch of classy ladies like that?" the host was saying when he let it play. "You gotta have girls hanging off your arm every time you walk around that place, huh? What's it like being a star mixing with a bunch of startups?"

"Well," James Ringer said, and Brandon paused it again.

Took another swig.

Hit play.

Hit pause.

Switched it to mute.

There. *This* he could do. He could work on the accent and voice tics later. Sometime.

For now he sat through the entire interview, watching the way his grandfather leaned forward rarely, letting the host know he had his full attention, before slouching back and shrugging his way through every answer, like he had all the time in the world and didn't give a hoot about time slots or the fact that the host wasn't doing a lot of talking. The guy sure was laughing, though. Every time James Ringer stopped talking, the host was slapping his knee and damn near giggling his way through his next question.

"Come *on*," Brandon muttered. "He's not that funny."

As if on cue, the host sobered and put a hand on his chest, moving closer to ask his next question. To Brandon's surprise, his grandfather's body language changed completely: he straightened up, lifted his chin, and his smile turned from easy charm to something genuine.

"You wanna see?" Brandon read on his lips, plain as day. Then watched as he stood and pulled a leather wallet from his back pocket, opening it up to reveal—

Dahlia.

The camera zoomed in on the little square photo of Dahlia, from the very same photoshoot Brandon saw on the Internet. Except this one was her solo, not her and James Ringer. She was lying back amidst tall grasses and waving wildflowers, a hat shading her eyes, and was looking right into the lens. Brandon didn't need color to see the way her eyes were sparkling, to see her red, red lipstick and the faint flush on her cheeks.

She looked so happy.

He closed the tab.

Drank the rest of his second beer.

She looked so happy. So genuinely happy to be where she was. With James Ringer.

But, well.

She'd been an actor, too.

He spent the rest of the night on the couch in a mild buzz, then watched another couple interviews the next day on mute, keeping his eyes on his grandfather's shoulders and hands instead of his mouth. He took note of expressions when he could, but was careful to keep himself from making out anything the man said. Turned out his body language was a lot simpler than what Brandon had been going for—simpler and subtly expressive, and not so much flirty as intensely focused.

At least, when he was talking to a show host. Brandon was sure he was flirty plenty of other times.

He was still watching the tail end of a third interview when

Theresa called to say, "You remember the Saturday client? He wants to hire you again!"

She was so cheerful Brandon didn't want to bring her down, so he just coughed a lot and said "thank you" over and over until she released him from her friendly clutches.

Then he sat down on his couch and breathed for a while, staring at the frozen interview before he closed his laptop lid.

Because fuck.

He remembered being on his knees with his mouth on Percy's dick telling him he was *different*, that Brandon was treating him different because he was *different*. And he didn't think his attitude adjustment would be enough to sway Percy from his . . . different-ness. Whatever that particular difference was. Brandon hadn't figured it out yet, apart from just that Percy was young and a rich little shit.

Maybe it was that Percy *knew* James Ringer. Or seemed to, with his library of videos and his pretentious authoritativeness, telling Brandon he was nothing like him.

As if Percy knew him personally.

He did know him better than Brandon did, though. Better than most people, if his rampant fanboy act was how he was all the time. Brandon could imagine him memorizing all James Ringer's movies, and watching those very same interviews over and over, and collecting biographies and posters and who knew what. The kid probably knew all the trivia facts and then some. Things Brandon had never cared to learn.

So watching his grandfather onscreen was hard for Brandon. But what if . . . what if meeting Percy again could be like on-the-job training?

He was pretty sure Percy would perk right up if Brandon asked him to tell him obscure facts and talk about what *he* liked to see in someone pretending to be James Ringer. What he'd been expecting to see the first time he hired Brandon. Even if he wanted to watch movies with Brandon, it'd be easier for Brandon to sit through it if he could laugh at the outdated cheesiness with someone. Plus Percy could lecture him about this and that and this stunt man and that day James Ringer was on set . . . It'd probably play right into his ego, which had Brandon seeing dollar signs.

Or maybe it would end up making Percy feel good, and useful, and needed, like being warm to Alfred had done for *him*. Why did Brandon have to assume the worst of people? Why did he always have look at the world like it was such a cold, callous place?

It had been cold to him, sure. His parents. His schools. His jobs. But now that he'd seen the difference in Alfred, he couldn't help but wonder if his *fuck you* attitude had been the whole reason for everything. If even the gay thing would've gone over better with his parents if he'd just been less of a pain in the ass about it.

Well.

He gritted his teeth and squeezed his fingers tight around his phone. He was changing all that, right? He couldn't do anything about what had happened before. All he could do was fix what was happening now.

Which meant fixing his epic fuck-up with Percy.

Step one: no more asking clients for sexual favors, you dumbass, and definitely no more getting all put out because they say no to something.

His laptop chimed with an email notification—the briefing for Percy's next appointment, this coming Saturday morning, same time as last.

Step two: make sure his socks matched for when he had to take off his shoes.

That, at least, he was *sure* he could do.

CHAPTER
SIXTEEN

He could do this. He'd come up with a convincing alibi in case Hazel got wise. He'd gotten a good pep talk from a wholly supportive Kovie. He'd come prepared with a selection of movies for them to watch together, hoping a solid plan would help him be more firm about what he wanted out of this.

Because Jim would inevitably ask why Percy had hired him again, after how badly last time had ended. And Percy wasn't sure how to tell him it was because he'd seen a tempting slice of James Ringer, because that would sound like he wanted to change Jim, which he didn't. Honestly.

But if Jim just wanted to watch a few of James's movies, *see* him, see what Percy meant by resemblance . . .

Well, Percy could provide.

He'd also considered simply coming out with it—ha—and telling Jim about Kovie and her wild suggestions. Seemed like a character like Jim would have all sorts of ideas on how to rebel. Maybe even more than Kovie's greasy-haired drug dealer ex.

. . . And that thought should *not* be exciting Percy this much. Wow.

He was in the middle of trying to get his shit together when an unobtrusive knock sounded at the door.

Discreet. Much better. Maybe Jim's agency had forwarded his list of requests.

He opened the door, and Jim—

He . . . oh. Wow.

He was wearing soft pale blue jeans and a tight white and black striped T-shirt underneath a denim jacket. There was a packet of cigarettes in the chest pocket. And his hair! His hair, he'd slicked back into a perfect pompadour, like every photo Percy had ever slavishly studied.

And he was *smiling.*

"Can I come in?" he asked quietly.

Percy opened his mouth, managed an embarrassing, faint noise, and nodded vigorously, stepping aside to let Jim in.

Jim, who was already taking off his shoes without being asked. "Look at that," he whispered, scooping them up and giving Percy a lopsided grin. "Matching socks, eh?"

Suddenly Percy was glad for the harrowing trek back to his suite, because the silent handful of minutes gave him time to collect himself.

Also to watch.

Jim struck out ahead of him, just by sheer difference in height and his naturally quicker stride. Percy watched. All of him. Watched him move, the casual assurance, since he knew where he was going. The way he left his hands in his pockets, not sullenly, but honestly relaxed. And was that a vintage Omega watch around his wrist?

Never mind Jim, was *Percy* going to be able to stick to his plan to only watch movies?

Some rebellion that was, anyway. *Yes, this is Jim, we just watch old movies same as I do with Kovie, but I'm paying him so that makes it clandestine.*

"So," Jim said after Percy had closed and locked the door.

Percy was worried there was going to be some kind of serious talk—that Jim was going to take him to task for refusing to suck his dick last time or being a superior, stuck-up piece of shit—but then Jim said, "I think we got off on the wrong foot last time I came. So let's try it again. Hi, I'm Jim. What would *you* like to do today?"

There was no fakeness there. No plastic customer service voice. Jim's blue eyes were warm and sincere, and so was everything else.

"I, uhm." Percy fumbled for something to say. Anything. "I'm— sorry, I'm not, ah. Prepared for this?"

Not that.

Smooth, Perce, said a voice that sounded suspiciously like Kovie's.

Jim laughed. "Yeah, I've been getting that a lot." He shifted—not much, just enough to pop a hip and slide a little more into Percy's space. He seemed to hesitate for a second, then said, "I took what you told me to heart. About not knowing James Ringer."

Was this actually happening?

Percy feverishly pinched the inside of his arm behind his back, making sure he wasn't asleep. He hadn't written this in his review, right? He hadn't put this in his requirements?

"Uhh, you okay?" Jim reached for him, then hesitated again. Suddenly he seemed as uncertain as Percy, his fingers stalled a few inches from Percy's shoulder.

Clearing his throat, Percy shuffled into his touch. "I . . . didn't expect this. Honestly."

Jim's full mouth quirked. "What, you thought I'd come back here and be a little shit again?"

"Honestly?" Percy repeated. "Yes." Jim's grin invited him to tease—or at least tempted him to—so he added, "I thought being a brat was hard-coded in your DNA."

Something sparked in Jim's eyes. Whether it was interest or anger, Percy didn't know. Either way, it softened away after a bare second, and Jim's fingers moved over Percy's shoulder. "Well, I thought it could make room for other stuff hard-coded in my DNA. And I thought maybe you're the best one to help me with that, actually."

Damn it, Percy was *not* going to melt because Jim had suddenly developed the ability to flirt. "M-me?"

"Mmhmm," Jim murmured. "You have—" He looked away toward Percy's movie collection, and then paused, and was that Percy's imagination, or did he go a touch pale?

Oh, he'd seen the movies Percy had laid out.

Before Percy could defend himself or explain or babble uselessly, Jim collected himself, and grin brightened, morphing back into genuine. His fingers shifted on Percy's shoulder again. "Are those for me?"

Percy nodded. "I thought . . . I'm not sure what I thought." How rude was it to say *I thought maybe you were worth it?* because that was not something you said to a person. That was what people had said to Percy all his life: *"I think this treatment might be worth it," "I think the effort of bringing him home and tutoring him will be worth it," "I think skipping vacation this year to tend to his eye issues will be worth it."* "If you don't want to . . ."

"No! No, I mean, yes, I do." Jim laughed, rubbing his free hand over his face. "I guess this isn't something I should ask, but you've seen me be way more unprofessional, so, did you hire me to do this, or . . . ?" He waved a hand toward Percy's bedroom.

"Smoke?" Percy challenged, raising an eyebrow. "In my bedroom? Without permission?" *After you brushed him off in the middle of sex.*

He winced.

Jim startled, releasing his shoulder. "Sorry, fuck, did I hurt—?"

"No."

The tense worry went out of Jim's expression instantly, but he didn't put his hand back. "Anyway. Sorry about that. But no, I meant . . . sex. And I guess I'm sorry about that, too. You know. The way it went last time." His voice got gruffer as he went on, and there was a little of the stubbornness Percy had seen last time. It was relieving to see it now, really. "I shouldn't have tried to make you, you know." He gave Percy a look Percy didn't think was meant to be pleading, but very much was.

"I know," Percy said, letting him off the hook.

Jim's shoulders slumped with a long exhale. "So yeah. Anyway, so did you . . ."

Percy gave him a smile. "Hire you for sex? Or did I . . ."

". . . just wanna invite me to your own personal drive-in?"

"Actually, yes," Percy said, and it didn't slip by that Jim's shoulders slumped at that too—with relief. "I wasn't sure you would be interested in that."

"No, I am." Jim's hand lit back on Percy's shoulder. His palm was broad and warm. Percy couldn't help leaning right back into it. "I just . . . after we did this last time, I talked to my boss, and she . . . she *is* the person she impersonates, you know? She's so good at this, and I'm . . . not."

"So you really want to be better at it?" Percy couldn't help the slight hint of skepticism. As charmed as he was by Jim's apparent shift in perspective, it was hard to believe he'd changed this much in a couple weeks. But this could be the start of his change, Percy reasoned. The beginning, for him. "You really want to do this?"

Jim raised his eyebrows. "You really want to pay three hundred bucks an hour to watch movies with me?"

Percy shrugged. "I'm not doing anything else with my money." He hoped he didn't sound bitter; it wasn't Jim's fault he couldn't do anything worthwhile without his parents bustling in. But while they were on the subject . . . "I did need to talk to you about that, however. I have a caretaker."

He wrinkled his nose automatically, waiting for Jim's inevitable pitying "oh," but Jim just nodded and said, "Uh huh?"

"Sooo I sort of told her you're my tutor," Percy said. "For online college courses I'm taking."

Jim blinked. Blinked again.

Then, "Ha! College, that's rich. Ha! Ha ha!"

Percy recoiled like he'd been slapped.

Jim threw his hands out. "Oh, God, Percy, no. I didn't mean you. Oh my god, no, you are totally smart enough for college. It's me. Me, tutoring college? Me, *in* college? Ha! I was too much of a loser to finish high school. *Remedial* high school."

It took a few long seconds for Percy to unwind all the defensive tension from his body, and Jim watched him do it, looking more nervous by the second.

"Aw Perce," he said. "I really didn't mean you. Seriously, you shoulda seen me in high school. Disaster central."

"Right." Percy shrugged jerkily.

"Do you really think people would consider you not good enough for college?" Jim asked softly, reaching out to cup Percy's shoulder.

"Well, look at me."

"You're wearing a sweater vest right now. If that doesn't scream Ivy League, I don't know what does."

"I don't mean my clothes, I just . . ."

Did Jim really not see? Did Jim really not understand? Was he that fucking clueless about how sick Percy was? How little he was capable of?

Or did Jim just not look down on him the way Hazel and his parents and all their rich friends all did?

"It's not that I'm not *good* enough," Percy gritted out, still torn. "It's that I'm not *capable.*"

Jim squinted at him. "You think you're not? Or is that something other people *tell* you?"

Percy hitched one shoulder in another shrug.

"Well." Jim patted him on the other shoulder. "Listen, if you wanna teach me all about James Ringer, that's fucking awesome. And I'll pretend to be your tutor if that's what you want. But one thing I know I'm really really good at already is telling other people to go fuck themselves. So maybe you need to try that too. A life lesson worth your three hundred bucks for today." He winked despite the slight doubt lingering on his face. Was he worried about what Percy would think of him? What he would say?

Time to put those fears to rest, then—Percy hoped.

"Maybe I do," he said, carefully neutral. "But if you could just tell people . . . I mean, if anyone sees us. My parents will have an explanation for the charges, and you won't have to scramble to leave." Now it was his turn to hesitate. It was inconsiderate of him to assume he could eat up all of Jim's day, right? And on a weekend, too! "Unless you have other things to do. I know it's Saturday."

"Perce. I'm an escort. It's not like I have your typical nine-to-five, Monday-to-Friday kind of job."

"Oh. Obviously, since you're here. Sorry."

Jim waved off his apology. "Look, I don't wanna shove this into, like, business territory, but you get me for however long you want."

Right. This was Jim's job. And if Percy wanted to spend $1,500 to have him around for an afternoon, he could. "Of course," he said. Cleared his throat.

"Easy," Jim said, patting his shoulder. He didn't let go right away, not when Percy expected him to. His hand just sat there, cupping the round of Percy's shoulder, his fingertips pressing in gently.

Was he . . . did Jim want a *hug*?

Maybe not consciously, Percy recognized, but he was already stepping in for one anyway.

And Jim enfolded him like it was the most natural thing in the world, like they weren't on shaky terms after a disastrous first meeting. He was gentle, but not overly considerately so, and he let Percy rest his forehead on his shoulder, face against the soft, worn denim of his jacket. He smelled like Old Spice, and he didn't fidget when Percy expected him to—right away—and not even when Percy laid his hands on his sides to alleviate the awkwardness of simply having them at his own sides.

He did finally fidget, and cleared his throat, right before he said, "Do you want to talk about it? You not being capable, I mean?"

Percy laughed, strained. "Let's not," he said, letting Jim squeeze him one last time before he pulled back. He fiddled with the edge of Jim's jacket, then touched the Omega around his wrist. "Let's talk about this instead."

Jim's face pinched. "Is it not good?"

"No, it's perfect." Percy towed Jim farther into the room, back to the couch. Jim only balked for a second before dropping down and spreading himself out, fanning his hand with interest over the films Percy had picked. "Did your boss put it together for you?"

"Nope. I did it myself."

That was pure sheer pride, so Percy was careful to say, "It really is perfect."

"Thanks." Jim picked at the jeans. "These feel like I'm wearing bags on my legs." He frowned, looking guiltily over at Percy. "I mean, uhhh . . . they're period-style. . . . Right?"

"You can relax," Percy told him, pulling his legs up so he was sitting cross-legged, facing Jim. "You want me to be your fifties guru, right? Any guru knows their padawan needs guidance."

"I'm . . . pretty sure 'padawan' isn't a real word."

Percy stared at him. "Star Wars?"

"Huh?"

"*Star Wars*," Percy enunciated. "Padawan is from Star Wars. Forget James Ringer's, do you watch *any* movies?"

"Ehh."

"'Ehh'? What's 'ehh'?" Belatedly Percy thought "ehh" could mean no, or yes, or it could mean Jim had any other hobby, literally any other hobby that anyone not sequestered away in a giant lonely house could have at their leisure.

But Jim said, "Not really my thing."

Too curious not to, Percy asked, "What *is* your thing?"

"Ehhhhhh." And *that* was definitely a hint of mischief.

Percy smacked him lightly on the shoulder. The shock ricochet up his hand was worth it. "I'm serious!"

"Me too!" Jim smacked him back, on his thigh. "'Ehh' *is* sort of my thing, man. I'm just 'ehh' all around."

"Hmmmmmmm," Percy hummed, for long enough that Jim looked sideways at him. "Everyone has a thing. Even me." *Even me, shut up in this house. Even I have a thing.*

Jim shrugged. Then he lifted the movies and spread them out in front of his face, hiding it from Percy. "Which one first?"

"Subtle."

"I know, right?" Jim lowered the movies and narrowed his eyes at Percy over the tops of their cases.

Percy couldn't tell if he was daring him to press more, or if he was telling Percy to back off. And even more, he couldn't tell what *he* wanted to do: let Jim have the space, or push and find out what he was really about, since it clearly wasn't the '50s.

More than either option, he knew he didn't want to scare Jim off. Again.

So he cleared his throat and reached out, skimming his fingers over the covers before picking *Falls Lake*, one of James's first—and most quotable—movies. "This one." He turned it around to show Jim, who blinked at it with nothing—no recognition, not even the cursory amount most people possessed.

Percy sighed and cracked the case open carefully, gentle so as not to ruin the outer packaging. "You really don't know anything, do you?"

"I thought we covered this," Jim said testily, lowering the rest of the DVDs. "And yeah, I guess that's pretty apparent from my high school record, huh."

"That . . . isn't what I meant." Percy's voice softened with his surprise, and he looked up from the glossy DVD to see the familiar defensiveness plastered across Jim's face. Familiar on him . . . and familiar because Percy knew exactly what it was like, throwing up self-protection at the first hint of judgment. It was an odd flip of conversation from a few minutes ago. "I meant about James Ringer."

Jim softened too. Not by much. "No." He looked away, and God, there was that jawline. It really was uncanny, because anyone could have a thick, sharp jawline, of course, but the slight crookedness, the prominent rise of bone at the back . . .

It was an exact match.

Jim swayed, jerking Percy's attention upward, to his re-narrowed eyes.

"What?" Jim snapped, looking a little sick. "Do I have something on my—my face?"

"No! Nothing." Percy reached out a hand, trying to placate him. Maybe he had been a little too judgmental. Jim was here to *learn*, and he'd come willingly, with that as his plan. He wasn't only doing this because Percy asked. "I'm sorry. I shouldn't have said that." Percy jiggled the DVD in his lap. "Do you . . . would you rather . . . watch something else? Like, with a different actor? Paul Newman's always a hit."

He felt more than saw Jim take a deep breath and let it out. "Nah," Jim said finally, the irritation bled out of his voice. "That's really nice of you, but no. I really should try watching one of . . . *Ringer's* movies. I've been putting it off for way too long." He winced and added, "You know, since I, um, since I started the job."

"Mmhmm." Percy jiggled the DVD again, wondering if Jim would say something else—he seemed about to—but he didn't. So, "Grab that," Percy told him, gesturing at the universal remote sitting on the coffee table. He went to put the DVD in, and took the remote from Jim when he sat down again, pressing the buttons to dim the lights in front of the TV and turn the surround sound on.

"*Whoa*. This setup is fucking amazing, dude."

Percy grinned. The rest of the furniture and adornments in his room were standard, chosen by his parents or by Hazel to match and complete the set of a room no guest would ever see. But this? This was *his*.

And more than just pride, it made him incandescently happy that the one true reflection of himself in this space was what had caused Jim to drop his guard like that.

They were silent as the movie opened on credits, but at the first scene, Jim made a quiet noise.

"Huh?"

"Nothing, I sort of . . ." Jim was squinting at the screen. "Sort of expected it to be in black and white."

Percy kept a careful leash on his tone and tried not to sound too enthusiastic when he said, "The first color movie was in 1939. *Gone With the Wind.*"

"Wait, seriously?"

"Yeah!" Jim kept looking at him instead of the movie, and Percy honestly could have gone on for a while about the changing technologies of film, but he wanted Jim to pay attention, so he, before he could think about it, reached over and gently pressed at Jim's cheek, turning his head. "Now pay attention."

Jim coughed a little and nodded, shuffling into a more comfortable position. Percy did the same, arranging himself automatically so he wouldn't be putting too much pressure on his hips or shoulders.

He kept glancing at Jim, expecting to see him looking bored with the beginning of the movie, but Jim was watching with sharp eyes and rapt attention, taking in all the details.

Then James Ringer came on screen.

CHAPTER
SEVENTEEN

JAMES_RINGER_LIVES. Brandon's rejected camwhoring screen name popped crystal-clear into his mind as he watched its namesake stride confidently onto the screen. Living, breathing, his hands in his pockets and his eyes squinting as the title cards played over his image.

Brandon had grown up surrounded and bombarded by iconic images of his grandfather, staged and posed and framed just so, each of them compelling in their own way.

He'd never seen the man just . . . breathe. Or see his pupils dilate, or the way his frowning mouth hesitantly crumbled into a reluctant smile.

If you'd have asked him before this moment what James Ringer in motion was like—his smile, his walk, his brow—before the interviews, Brandon would have pointed to himself, to the man he saw in the mirror every day. After, he would've described the lenient shoulder slouch and left it at that. James Ringer's defining mark. He would've thrown out a half-assed answer that showed just how little he'd paid attention to the whole picture of his grandfather.

Because he'd been wrong.

He suddenly understood why Percy had said he didn't resemble James Ringer at all.

His own grandfather. The genetic link between them couldn't be more obvious, but that was all there was. Brandon may have had a chip on his shoulder, but James Ringer's brooding was a part of his presence, as compelling and charming as a smile or a laugh could be on someone else. The way he moved wasn't stiff or staged at all. If he weren't so attention-grabbing when he was working—there was a distinct difference between him in an interview and *this*—then he would've blended into the set, as natural and easy as anything.

The movie itself was a cheesy, dated melodrama, with men beating each other up over blown out of proportion slights and hysterical women getting slapped in the face before throwing themselves, wailing, onto the nearest horizontal surface.

Brandon couldn't get enough of it. Sure, the secondhand embarrassment nibbled on him a few times, but it was never about his grandfather. All the wasted air time Brandon had assumed he would be, all the talentless space-taking... He'd been *so wrong*.

James Ringer could fucking act. Could act all goddamn day, and yet Brandon could still see him under his character. The way he stumbled and mumbled through scenes wasn't just *not* sloppy and disaffected, it was goddamn *masterful*. The camera wasn't even on his face half the time. The moneymaker Brandon had assumed was the reason his grandfather managed to keep a job was only a fraction of the acting James did. Of the way he staked out the screen and then dragged every bit of the movie toward him with giant gobs of pure natural magnetism.

And yet every time Brandon glanced at Percy, seeking silent connection in how deeply this bullshit was getting to him, Percy wasn't even watching the film. He was looking at Brandon.

He was looking at Brandon like Brandon was the one affecting *him*. And Brandon almost couldn't be self-conscious about it because his focus kept getting pulled back to the screen, where James's sheer presence ate up every shot he was in. What Brandon had all his life taken for sullen disconnection from everyone and everything around him was more James observing people—and then when he spoke to them, he already knew what they were about.

Like it was that goddamn easy to look at everyone and *care* and—and genuinely connect to them. He talked about *them*. Or his character did, but fuck, it was *him*, and he never talked about himself, Brandon realized however long later. He talked about the people he was talking to, but he never offered stuff about himself. And boy was that a familiar thing.

James never looked at the camera—duh, even Brandon knew that was film 101—but somehow it was like he was drawing not only the set and his costars to him, but also the camera, like he was talking directly to Brandon, telling him to his face how wrong he'd been.

Brandon and Percy both.

Brandon was white-knuckled all the way through a terse fight between James and his onscreen parents, chest aching as James stole his father's car and went screaming down the too-quiet suburban street and to an old abandoned warehouse. James held himself stiffly when he was upset, keeping his shoulders hunched, and he sulked his way up the grungy warehouse stairs to the top floor, where the camera panned over the city skyline, then hovered over James's shoulder as he propped himself in the huge industrial-sized window and lit up a cigarette.

Suddenly Brandon remembered the almost stricken look on Percy's face when he'd lit up in Percy's room, sat . . .

Sat just like that.

Somehow, though, for the very first time, he didn't feel quite so bothered to know he was following in his grandfather's footsteps.

He chanced looking over at Percy again, and this time Percy wasn't just watching. He was leaning closer in that kind of unconscious way people do when they're interested. Not like he was expecting anything or trying to push his way into Brandon's space, but like he was magnetized, like they were drawing together the same way James was drawing Brandon in.

Brandon felt his mouth drop open slightly, felt himself listing sideways too. Putting down a hand to steady himself on the couch, he accidentally covered Percy's hand instead.

Percy flexed it underneath his own, letting out a little gasp. Not pain, he didn't think, but Brandon forced himself not to ask if he'd hurt him anyway. Trusted Percy to speak up for himself if he needed to . . . which he didn't. His expression had gone glazed, as dewy and romantic as James' leading lady's.

"Is it—" Brandon started, voice coming out gravelly. "Can I—"

Percy lunged forward and kissed him.

Brandon's eyes dropped closed and he reached his free hand out to gather Percy by the small of his back, drawing him in close.

His kiss was hungry and youthful and sweet, not the least bit guarded or restrained.

How had Brandon thought he was stuck up? Sure, he was prim

and he acted about ninety years old sometimes, but all the forced awkwardness from last time had to've been Brandon, just like it had been with Alfred.

Percy was nothing like Brandon had assumed. He wasn't some spoiled kid. Wasn't some older than his age bitter shut-in, either. Unlike Brandon, he didn't seem like he actually *wanted* to avoid people. Maybe he'd just never been given the chance to hang out with someone. Now that he'd found his footing, he was a guy with a bangin' home theater system and a delightfully sloppy kiss and wandering hands—currently wedging themselves under the waistband of Brandon's vintage jeans to clutch his ass.

Maybe even more well-adjusted and *normal* than Brandon himself.

Percy shifted closer, one hand moving up Brandon's chest under his jacket as he tilted his head, teeth scraping a little on Brandon's bottom lip. *That* was more than enough to keep Brandon's attention exactly where he wanted it to be. He finally got his hands with the program too, and even though he couldn't get them under Percy's shirt—which was *tucked into his pants*, there was that ninety-year-old man tendency—he could fit them along Percy's sides, bringing him in even more.

Percy shuddered, leaning into his hands, and this was way better than sucking him off—not that that hadn't been nice, but getting to feel him react in his totally shameless way made it feel like the stiffness of an appointment and expected sex had melted away and it was just *them*, making out like kids because they wanted to, not because Percy was paying him three hundred bucks an hour and he felt guilty the customer wasn't getting his money's worth.

Now, at least, Brandon knew Percy was getting what he *wanted*, even if other people would've considered it a waste of his time. Maybe considered Brandon a waste of his time.

But Percy didn't.

He got as close as Brandon let him, and didn't pull back until Brandon's side started to cramp and he had to push Percy away a little. Percy's expression flashed from concern to suspicion and back.

Brandon bumped their foreheads together. "My side's cramping, dude."

"Oh. Oh!" Percy jerked back, letting Brandon straighten up from the slouch he'd slipped into. "Sorry," he said with an awkward laugh.

"Worth it," Brandon assured him.

"Honestly my hands were starting to hurt, too," Percy admitted with a smile. He flexed them in illustration, and Brandon reached up to catch hold of one before he could think better of it. He let his thumb press into the center of Percy's palm, where his hand drew in sharply. The muscles were tensed, but Percy wasn't.

"Jeez." Brandon rubbed his thumb back and forth a little. "Are they, uhh." Fuck. That was a dumb question. *Are they always like this?* Of fucking course they were. "Do they always hurt?" he tried instead.

"Everything always hurts," Percy said. "Except for the first day after an infusion, which is when I feel like God. I'm like *Look at me going up and down stairs!* like it's a superpower." He laughed, a sound which started out genuine but quickly turned self-conscious. "I know it probably sounds kind of crazy or pathetic or whatever, but until you've been in pain all the time, you just don't get it."

"You don't have to explain yourself to me, man. I don't think that sounds pathetic at all. It's not exactly the same or anything, but I get being excited about stuff nobody else does. After living rough a couple months my first hot shower made me feel like a supermodel. Shifts your perspective."

Percy nodded, relief washing over his features. "Yeah."

Brandon hesitated at asking another question, not because it was weird for him or anything, but because he didn't want to make Percy uncomfortable all over again by prying, and ruin the easy camaraderie that had bloomed today. "Does the pain make it really hard for you to go out?" he asked. It was only after he did that he realized he was looking for the reason someone as completely deceptively normal as Percy was shut up in this room all by himself, since all his old explanations had been upended. "I only ask because you're my only— you're the only one who has me doing house calls."

Percy's face fell. "Y . . . es and no. I mean, if I can get a ride and there's not too much walking or standing involved, I can definitely go out places okay. I go to parties with my parents all the time. The problem is more convincing them I'm *capable* of going out."

Capable. That same word from before. Brandon suddenly understood how heavy a word like that could be.

"But they're such hypocrites about it. Like, if they need me to make an appearance somewhere then my limitations don't or shouldn't matter, but if I wanna go to a movie suddenly I'm too crippled to function." Brandon made a face, and Percy laughed, not really amused, just wry and frustrated. "I know I shouldn't complain. Here you are talking about difficult living situations and I'm . . ." He waved a hand at their surroundings. "Here. I must seem silly or selfish or—"

"No." Brandon hadn't meant it to come out that sharp. "You have a sweet theater system and a fucking amazing house, and you can afford to go to college, but that doesn't make your problems stop mattering. I'm not the kind of person to think like that, and I don't want you thinking like that about yourself, either."

"For someone who thinks he's not smart enough for college, that sounds well damn thought out."

"I said I wasn't smart enough for *college*, not that I couldn't, I dunno, think about things."

Think about things like you and me, and how we fit together.

Percy looked like he was turning that over in his head, which was good, because Brandon wasn't sure what the hell he was gonna say if Percy pushed him for further reasoning. He just knew he didn't want Percy to be locked away up here. He *liked* people. He'd be better at being out there, hanging around Ms. Monroe, than Brandon was.

The TV screen suddenly flickered and went dark, and then the DVD restarted on the menu. Brandon blinked. Had it really been that long? "Anyway," he said, shrugging. He reached for the pile of DVDs. "Another one?"

"Sure." Percy took the DVD Brandon picked at random and stood to change them out. He had his back to the door when the knob rattled, then opened, and Brandon saw him draw up stiff, so painfully straight-backed he looked like he'd stopped breathing.

Brandon twisted around on the couch to see a middle-aged woman holding a silver tray. She froze just like Percy, except instead of looking scared, her dark eyes narrowed and she said with no pretense of friendliness in her voice, "Who exactly are you?"

Brandon glanced at Percy for permission to answer, and Percy took the opening, though his hand was white-knuckled on the DVD case. "He's my tutor," he said crisply. "I enrolled in online film studies courses, like I discussed with my parents, and he's helping me with my homework."

Her nostrils flared.

"Yo," Brandon said.

"Yes, hello," she replied, disgusted, in the same tone of voice Brandon had heard from countless of the *"get a job"*-types he'd met panhandling. "I do hope you're very good at your job, young man, because Percival here will need all the help he can get to even hope to pass his courses, what with his condition." She said it salaciously, like just the mention of it should have had Brandon recoiling in disgust, as if Percy were AIDS on a toilet seat. "He *did* tell you about his condition, didn't he?"

Brandon's jaw dropped.

He heard Percy's upset, wheezy inhale.

Holy *shit*.

"I," he stammered, telling himself *don't get mad don't get kicked out don't don't don't.* "I-I, uh, yes, yeah, he did, and I think he's totally *capable* of everything he needs to do to succeed."

She scoffed unsubtly. "Well, you certainly have your work cut out for you. I suppose this explains the charge on your credit card from last week?" she said to Percy, her eyebrows raised. "Your parents were curious about your spending habits, especially with the type of company you've decided to keep lately." Okay, Brandon had no idea what *that* meant, but it seemed like she was talking about someone who wasn't him, and he wasn't sure if he was glad about that or not. "He's pricey for a tutor, isn't he?"

You have a fucking hell of a habit of talking about people like they don't exist, don't you, lady.

"He's worth it," Percy said. Then, more blandly, he said, "And very good at his job, just like you said."

"I and your parents will be the judge of that. We'll be keeping a very close eye on your transcripts."

God, Brandon hoped to fucking hell Percy had actually enrolled in the courses he'd specified in his alibi.

"Of course," Percy said, in the same bland, lifeless voice.

Couldn't she *see* how much he shut down? Shut *off*? Did she even care?

"Here." She slammed the tray down on the coffee table, making Brandon jump. Not Percy, though. Used to it? "Take your medication." She raked a disapproving gaze over Brandon, who was doubly glad—and not for authenticity purposes—that he'd dressed like a stodgy old '50s dude today and not like a hooker. She stomped off, coming back not twenty seconds later with another tray, this one full of hospital-esque food: a watery thin soup, a limp-looking sandwich with pale sliced turkey, and a few crackers next to a fruit cup. Brandon had eaten some pretty questionable shit in his life, but he'd take that stuff over this any day—and Percy ate this *every* day.

After she left, slamming the door and taking all the air in the room with her, Brandon, shaken, looked from the tray up to an equally shell-shocked Percy, still standing there like a mannequin with the DVD hooked on one of his fingers. "Maybe for our next *tutoring session* we should go somewhere that serves cheeseburgers, huh?"

Percy flashed him a tight smile. "Yeah. Maybe." He put the DVD in with quick, jerky movements and came back to the couch, skirting the food entirely but swallowing down the pills on the first tray with a couple practiced movements.

Brandon said "hey" quietly when Percy made to sit down at the other end of the couch. He shifted his arm up, laying it along the back of the couch, inviting Percy over to him. For a second he thought Percy was going to refuse, and wasn't sure if he should apologize, or try to explain it was just because Percy's caretaker scared the hell out of him and he couldn't imagine being forced to interact with her every day. No wonder Percy stood so straight; he had to have a backbone made of steel to withstand her.

But then Percy smiled, for real this time, and sank down against Brandon's side, tucking into him. As the movie started, he put his fingers on Brandon's jaw again, turning him to face the TV. "Pay attention," he said softly, and rested his head on Brandon's shoulder.

CHAPTER
EIGHTEEN

Five stars. That was what the subject line of the email said.

Actually, it said FIVE STARS!!!!!!!!!!! ;) :) :0) !!!!!!

Brandon had just gotten home from a long, sleepy afternoon at Percy's place, takeout in hand, and gone straight to his laptop to try and distract himself from the fact that he hadn't had a cigarette in six hours and it was starting to make his skin itch. Normally he would've had one right away, but Percy's irritation with it last time made him wonder if he couldn't cut back altogether.

Also, the fact that James Ringer could act and Brandon's nineteen-years-in-the-making idea that he was a no-talent loser who only had a cult following because he'd died young and pretty was . . . wrong.

No, not just *wrong*.

It had been *obliterated*.

Fuck.

He put it aside for now—he wasn't thinking about it, seriously, not at all—and concentrated on the review . . . of him impersonating James Ringer . . .

Stop it. Now he wished he'd focused on wanting a cigarette instead. At least this review was a thousand times more satisfying than lighting up.

Theresa had prefaced it with more exclamation points and LOOK! LOOK! I'M SO PROUD OF YOU, which, like always, came through wholly sincere even through text. As he scrolled, he made a mental promise to himself to send her a fruit basket or a big bouquet of flowers as soon as he had expendable income to spare. Or tea, to repay her for the probably expensive stuff she gave him. Whatever it was, a gift for her, just for being so damn good at her job and so damn nice besides.

Speaking of nice, this review had it in spades, and what's more, it was from Alfred, who'd once called Brandon cold and unenthusiastic, but now referred to him as passionate, kind, and charming, "the kind of person who will make a repeat customer of everyone he meets."

Brandon sat back on the couch, containers of Chinese food cooling, ignored, on the table.

It was true.

Wasn't it?

He'd made a repeat customer of Alfred, and of Percy, too. And both appointments, he'd left feeling great, and both of them had been just as happy.

He had known he was working toward making a change in himself, but working toward it and seeing it right in front of him— his first fucking well-earned five-star review—were two completely different things.

It felt good. It felt so good. Now he understood why Ms. Monroe took so much pride in her job, why she was so enthralled with the person she'd made a career of. Brandon could have been all along. Even that appointment with Harvey. If he had just fucking *cared* and taken the time to pride himself in his work, then that job would've gone smoothly as well. Hell, Brandon would have been *glad* to take that appointment, and every other one after it.

Oh well. He could make it up with all the appointments after today.

The prospect of getting *more* five-star reviews was dizzyingly good. The prospect of feeling this awesome after every day of work was even better. He'd started this job on the luck of his genetics, but he was going to *own* it through pure skill and dedication.

He could be good at something. He could really, honestly, be good. And really, honestly like it.

And he couldn't help his mind wandering back to the movies he'd watched today. He saw people who loved their jobs all the time, who fit into them, but seeing his grandfather in action had proved just how much of a natural he'd been in front of the camera. And not with slick, barely passable skill. With real talent, and real love. Brandon had been right about one thing: the typecasting. He could see why James Ringer had been typecast, but had seen too how he changed with every role, still keeping the thread of himself in each film. He didn't give up who he was depending on the job he was working.

How fucking weird was it that Brandon was almost finding the guy he'd spent years resenting . . . sort of inspiring?

Well, not exactly the *whole* man. Just his attitude toward his work. Watching a couple movies and realizing James had been able to back up the good looks didn't change the fact that he hadn't been able to back up his relationship with Dahlia. Unlike with Brandon's opinion of his acting abilities, there had been rumors to back up James's infidelity—paparazzi photos of him sneaking around, people calling in to say they'd spotted him at a hotel. Brandon had heard his mother talking about them his entire childhood, and though his parents were the last people he wanted to listen to when it came to who was worthy of approval and who wasn't, he had to give them one single point there. After all, he hadn't listened to anything else they'd said, but when it came to James Ringer, he was happy to swallow all their distaste like they'd spoon-fed it to him.

They kind of had, he thought.

And he *had* swallowed it.

All along, though, he'd assumed being told he was like his grandfather was some kind of insult—and people had meant it as one, yeah. But if Brandon ignored James's personal life and thought about the guy in the movies from today? The one stuffed to the gills with talent? Being compared to him wasn't so bad. How could it be, when it impressed someone like Percy? And when being impressed by skill would help Brandon get better at his job. Ms. Monroe was, well, *Ms. Monroe*, because she loved Marilyn Monroe. Brandon sure as hell didn't *love* James Ringer . . . but he wasn't all bogged down with blind hatred anymore, either. Now all his quaffles with his grandfather were backed up with proof.

He never thought he'd see the day where he'd thank the paparazzi for something, but here it was.

He reached for his food finally, digging into cold schezwan chicken. Percy hadn't said outright he would hire Brandon again, but Brandon was almost positive he would, and he was embarrassingly excited to be able to see more of James's stuff.

He didn't have to wait, though, did he?

His email always pulled up advertising on the sidebar, most of it relevant to his camguy job, but there were a couple YouTube links for James Ringer thanks to him watching the interviews earlier. Brandon clicked on one at random and sat back when he saw it was a six-minute clip from a movie he hadn't seen yet. He almost felt bad, going ahead without Percy. Hell, though, he wouldn't mind watching everything again *with* Percy.

He'd just watch a couple, he decided.

Four hours later, he peeled himself, crusty-eyed and stiff, off the couch and down the hall to bed. And this time when he passed the basement door, he didn't ignore it. He let himself look at it, at the shadow of it, and then grazed his fingers over the doorknob and unlocked it. Left it open.

Just for tonight.

He had three appointments that week, and every single one of them went swimmingly. Monday's guy bought him a nice steak dinner and then asked to bottom—Brandon's first time on top with a client—, left him a fat tip, and personally called Hollywood Doubles's office to rave about him.

On Tuesday, he got his ass eaten out then well-fucked by a fit Vietnam veteran who'd booked an extra hour just to talk. And he ordered room service for them, to boot. Brandon rubbed his feet and played the rapt listener in between French fries. It wasn't hard; the guy had a good sense of humor and a lot of stories about stuff him and his buddies had done. "Cook never did manage to clean those eggs up all the way," he said fondly, and Brandon laughed, finishing off the last of the fruit they were splitting.

Appointment three was on a Friday night. He met the guy at a country and Western gay bar, borrowed a cowboy hat off a hot shirtless dude, and learned to line dance. There was a little bit of heavy petting in the backseat of his client's car, right up until Cyrus knocked on the window and told him off for violating company safety policy.

Cyrus was the only part of his job that didn't improve at all, but

Brandon couldn't find it in himself to give one flying fuck about that. Especially not when his reviews from all three appointments were five-stars, and *especially* not when he got an email from Ms. Monroe that Sunday telling him he was "doing splendidly" and she was thinking they should meet up soon and redo his photoshoot now that he had a better handle on things.

By "things," he was pretty sure he meant "himself," and somehow it was a compliment.

She'd also gotten him an appointment with her trainer Marco, which he was actually looking forward to. He still thought his body was okay, it could just use some fine-tuning. Which was actually his philosophy on the whole thing, kinda. The more he let himself indulge in liking his job, the more he realized all it took were small changes, a little extra effort, and "passable" turned into five stars. Everything he'd accused James Ringer of doing—getting by on his face, relying on bare-minimum talent—he'd been doing, and now he wasn't, and it was *great*.

Saturday came and went with no appointment from Percy, which was worrying but not altogether unexpected. Judging by his caretaker's reaction, he would need some time to ease them into the idea of Brandon hanging around all the time.

Well, not *all* the time. Just Saturdays.

But he wondered if eventually Percy would hire him for more days. Tutors did multiple appointments a week, right? That was plausible.

Plausible and *totally* not up for Brandon to decide. Not even worth thinking about. It wasn't as simple as saying, "Hey, let's hang out." It was, "Hey, let me come over and sit on your couch while you pay me crazy amounts of money."

The next week, he woke up early on Tuesday with water all over the first-floor bathroom, and, thanks to the money he'd stashed away, he got a repairman in and had it fixed and paid for before lunch. Even made the repairman coffee and got a ten percent discount because "Jeez, thanks, man, you've got no idea how hard it is to do back-to-backs all day when I don't have time for coffee."

On a roll, he called about the property taxes on the place to explain what had happened with Dahlia, explain his financial situation (which he fudged somewhat by saying he was saving money to attend college, but it turned out being emancipated from his parents held more weight than "potentially going to be crushed by student loan"), and see if he could start a payment plan. Then, to top it all off, he paid the electric and water bills early. The woman at the water company even offered to cut him a deal since he'd had a leak—some kind of customer protection thing he would never have known about if he hadn't asked.

Wednesday was his appointment with Marco. He sweated and grunted and coughed his way through an hour and a half of crunches, push-ups, and bicep curls, trying not to look like he was on the verge of puking and dying.

"Stop smoking!" Marco clamped a meaty hand down on Brandon's shoulder as he finished his last rep of sit-ups. "I tell Judy all the time already, don't you pick up on her bad habits!"

"Don't blame her, man," Brandon puffed back, but that was all he said in protest. Even a couple of months back, anyone telling him to quit smoking would have gotten the finger or worse, but now he was kind of starting to understand the appeal of quitting. On the one hand, his smoking had brought him closer to his grandfather's image—maybe inspiring that precious callback from Percy—but on the other hand, Percy was sick, and smoking around him seemed like a dick fucking move.

Obvious solution would be to just not smoke around Percy anymore since they only saw each other once a week, but somehow that just didn't seem to go far enough. Was Brandon thinking of quitting smoking altogether in the hopes that that one day a week might turn into more?

How *much* more?

The kind of more where Percy hung out with him and didn't pay him to do it?

"Stop being such a dope," he growled at himself, then wheezed.

"What was that?" Marco asked.

Brandon gave his head a shake. "Nothing, nothing."

He left the gym with noodly arms, a sore back, instructions for daily at-home workouts, and an appointment for the following week at the same time. At home, he slurped down as much water as his stomach could handle and sat down to check his email.

The very first one had a subject line that read "Appointment Saturday!!! You-know-who!"

He grinned like an idiot, clicking through to see the usual client brief for Perce. It was all the same as last time, except under the "special comments" section, he'd put, *"This is not mandatory, but I suggest you bring yourself lunch this time. Also not mandatory, but In-N-Out is good. I like animal-style fries and 3x3s."*

Brandon felt his stupid smile getting wide. "Not mandatory my ass," he said, rolling his eyes. He emailed Theresa back thanking her for passing the appointment along, and had a response back before he closed his laptop.

Brandon,

Always a pleasure!!! You seem to have gotten yourself your first regular, huh?! Congrats!

P.S. Judy said you might be redoing your photo shoot, so let me know when you're stopping in! I have some tea-related presents for you!

Love,
T

Brandon sent back a quick *I don't deserve you* and went to take a shower. Funny, but suddenly his muscles weren't aching *quite* so bad anymore.

CHAPTER
NINETEEN

"**J**ust because your parents have agreed to this venture doesn't mean I'm going to be happy about it," Hazel sniffed, yanking Percy's curtains open.

Not good morning, not hello, not even "here are your pills." That was the opener.

And what the hell time was it? Percy reached for his phone, squinting at the screen. *6am*? What was *up* with her? Hazel never woke him up this early. He didn't even think *she* was usually up this early. Normally she didn't start work until 8 a.m., unless she'd decided he'd had a "bad night" and needed extra round-the-clock care. Percy had long since trained his body not to wake up too early lest he need help getting out of bed and wind up lying on his back bored out of his skull and needing to piss until she showed up for her regular start time. Staying up late on "good" nights to make it happen was hardly a burden, since it gave him some much-needed alone time where he could be pretty much positive she wouldn't "pop in."

But it certainly didn't help him now, waking up at the crack of dawn for no discernable reason and without warning. And talking to him, for once, like he was an adult. An adult who needed to be chastised.

"—and don't expect me to clean up after him," Hazel was saying, bustling around and straightening things with stiff, angry shoves. "Don't expect me to cook for him, or let him in, or act at all like I approve of you straining yourself to maintain some kind of social connection that you thought would be acceptable—since I don't see any other purpose for a degree in *Film Studies*. But you ought to be focusing on your classwork, if you really think you're capable of getting—and using—this degree. Not playing host to some . . . whatever he is. Nor host to that girl. I don't know what's gotten into you lately."

Percy forced himself upright in bed, making a point of straightening his back. "Nothing's gotten into me. He's a tutor, and having him here *is* focusing on my classwork. Why else would my parents agree to my hiring him? And my parents know Kovie Mittelstaedt as well, so you're the only one who seems to have a problem with her."

"Yes, well, your parents aren't exactly involved in your life the way I am, now are they? As for Miss Mittelstaedt, I can assure you they know more than enough about her. And your new guest . . . apparently they have no reason to suspect their son's tutor is anything other than what he says. I, however, *do*."

"What are you implying?" Percy asked tightly.

She can't prove anything.

But she *could*, if she really wanted to. He didn't think it would be this much of a problem. Couldn't believe how aggressive she was being. Where were the baby-talking, sweet little lectures about how he needed to take better care of his glass bones? He swallowed against his sudden shortness of breath and glared at her.

"Absolutely nothing," she said, glaring back. "I'm to be completely supportive of your studies, which is why I'm here, making sure you're getting an early morning start. No more lazing about if you intend on following through with this."

"Which I do." Percy had originally *mostly* enrolled in the courses to provide an alibi, figuring he could drop them once he and Jim stopped seeing each other or when the pressure of them got to be too much, but the more Hazel pushed him, the more determined he was to actually see this thing through. And the more determined he got, the more optimistic he felt, too. Because if he could actually accomplish this despite her saying he couldn't, what else could he do? How much of his "helplessness" was nothing but a fabrication?

He was scared out of his mind, sure, but still interested to find out.

Maybe with a degree he wouldn't have to settle for just buying a collection and letting it laze around. Maybe he could curate one himself, or even curate for a museum. Maybe he could be an archivist, or a collectibles appraiser and dealer, or any number of other incredibly nerdy jobs that would fit right into his obsession.

Hazel sniffed. "Well. We'll see how it goes." She came to his bedside and peeled back his covers with her usual lack of regard for his state of dress or undress, though with an unusual roughness to her touch. He hadn't had much privacy since he got sick, but his parents had at least looked away when his doctors poked and prodded him, or when he dressed himself. Hazel showed none of the same concern, reaching right in and sweeping his legs off the bed.

He stiffened and shifted backward, frowning at her and fighting the urge to cover himself, or squirm away. "I'm getting up. I can do it myself."

"Nonsense," she said, putting an arm around him to lever him up to his feet. His skin crawled. "You're already going to be straining yourself enough today."

Something in him snapped. "I'm *not*," he said—almost gasped it. But he wasn't short of breath from moving. He was *furious*. Suddenly and overwhelmingly. He was furious and he wanted *out* and *away from her*, and he was *done*. "When will you stop saying that? I know myself enough to know when something will strain me, and sitting on a couch and talking to someone isn't *strain*. If that was too much for me, don't you think I would need to miss all the parties you shuttle me to?" He stepped away from her, crossing his arms. "I handle those just fine, *like I'm expected to*, but the moment *I* want to do something, it's too much."

"It is too much! Your parents and I carefully monitor—"

"My parents," Percy said quietly, "don't monitor anything."

"*Hmph.* Well, *I* monitor your activity, which is why I'm the one who's qualified to decide what does and doesn't push you too far."

Percy stared at her for a long moment, and she stared back, her stern frown not wavering in the least. Finally, he asked, "Why?"

"Why what?"

"Why are *you* the one qualified to decide what isn't good for me when it's my body? You don't know how I feel. You didn't know I was fine to get myself out of bed today." Percy took a shallow breath and barreled on, everything spilling out of him. "You didn't think I could go out with Kovie, but I could have. I would have liked it, too. You didn't think I could go to college, but I *am*. You didn't think I could have friends because I inconvenience people. I don't."

"What do you call making them come all the way out here to see you, Percy?" Hazel waved out at the front lawn. "Do you think it's convenient for them to drive half an hour out of the city to see you?"

"No," Percy had to admit. "But if they want to see me, that's an accommodation they have to make. And they're okay with it. Because I'm worth it."

Her frown deepened. "Do you know that for sure? Do you know how time-consuming and annoying accommodations can be for people who aren't doing it for a job the way I am? Have you *asked* them?"

Well no, he hadn't.

But that was because the way they treated him made him feel like he didn't *have* to ask.

He didn't have to ask. He could just trust.

"I know you put a lot of effort into making me feel like a burden, like I have to feel sorry for who I am and for how much I put people out, but Kovie and Jim have made me realize that *you're* the only one who feels like I do that. So no, I haven't asked if they're okay with it, with *me*. If I'm worth the effort, because unlike with you, with them I already know that yes, yes I am. Now if you'll excuse me, I'm going to dress myself today, thanks."

Hazel's hands balled into fists. "Very well then. Clearly *you* know best. And since you're feeling so independent, I won't bother with *burdening* myself making you any meals today." She turned on her heel, stomping toward the door, but when she reached it, paused. "And don't think this means I'm about to let go of my suspicions regarding this *tutor* of yours, Percival. Whether you believe it or not, you are still a dependent, you do not sign my paychecks, and you are not my boss. I answer to your *parents*, and if I get even the barest hint that you are using their money fraudulently . . ." She let that one hang, and slipped out the door.

Percy sucked in a breath and fumbled his way to the bed to sit, just in case the shakiness in his hands spread down to the rest of his body. If he fell, he had no doubt she would simply leave him there until she felt like he'd learned his lesson.

She clearly intended on him going hungry today already. Something she'd never done.

Something he'd never *imagined* her doing.

What with her practically finger-feeding him when she was concerned he wasn't maintaining a proper diet, or wasn't enjoying something she made him, he'd never expected her to mistreat him like this.

That was what it was. Mistreatment. Far from the cotton-wrapped coddling she always handled him with.

Thank God he'd left that note about In-N-Out for Jim. He just had to hope the guy would actually *bring* some.

And if not?

God. He wasn't going to think about that. He was going to take a nice hot shower, take his pills, get dressed, and wait for his appointment time.

Now that he and Jim had a plan of action and Percy wasn't left wondering whether or not his film offerings would be spurned, Percy put himself to work, filling his extended morning before Jim arrived.

Having something to do with his hands, something he loved, made his lingering irritation fade and helped him forget his growling stomach, and by the time he heard Jim's car rolling up his driveway, he'd spread a selection of movies over the coffee table—not only the James Ringer films they hadn't watched last time, but some Paul Newman, even a Marilyn Monroe or two, since Jim had mentioned his boss was a Monroe lookalike. And beside the films, he'd put out his prized collectibles: three expansive James Ringer photobooks containing, yes, the photoshoots that were readily available on the internet now, but also rarer gems, like behind-the-scenes candids and interviews with people who had been on set.

He went downstairs to open the door for Jim, who had his back to the door when Percy opened it, yelling, "Nice fuckin' day to you too!"

Percy burst into startled laughter and Jim whipped around, holding—

Oh, thank God.

The bags of takeout were in Percy's hands before he could think about how rude it was to snatch them away. But Jim was already saying, "Thanks, man," and bending down to untie his shoes. "Uh, sorry about that. My driver's kind of a dick."

"Mmm," Percy hummed absently, picking at the bags.

Jim took one back, tucking it under his arm and turning to lock the door, jamming the tricky deadbolt just right. "So how goes it?" he asked, making no effort to keep his voice down.

Good, Percy thought bitterly. Let Hazel hear them having a real conversation, like real people. "It goes. I have more things for us to watch."

"Awesome." Jim sounded genuine, like last time. "Hey, I went home that night and watched a bunch of stuff on YouTube, you know. Some interviews, too." He shot Percy a nervous grin. "You've probably seen all that stuff, huh? You probably know it front and back."

"Yeah, probably," Percy said, hugging the In-N-Out bag to his chest. He hesitated before he mentioned it, because he'd never told anyone about it before, and hadn't planned on telling Jim about the crown jewel in his collection. It was his one most prized thing, the one thing that was his alone. Something he'd never planned to include in a collection or donate to a museum. Something he watched late at night, when he needed to. "I . . . actually own a hard copy VHS of an interview he gave the year he died. It took me seven months to hunt it down, because there were only two copies made." He thought it would be gauche to mention the price tag, so he kept it to himself.

That didn't stop Jim's curiosity, though. "Why only a couple? I mean, he was pretty big. Uh, right? In that time?"

"Well, yes." Percy led Jim past Hazel's suite—its door resolutely shut and probably locked for good measure—and into his, leaving Jim to shut the door while he situated himself on the couch with his coveted food. Normally he may have hesitated discussing the interview, but "normally" meant he would be around his parents' friends or Hazel, all of whom would disapprove. He didn't think a gay escort would be particularly sensitive to the fact that— "It was for a queer magazine. An underground one, run by some beatnik offshoots. There were rumors on the old Yahoo Group forums saying he'd agreed to give one interview about his sexuality, but it never surfaced, so people let it die. Assumed it didn't exist."

Jim had an odd look on his face. Curiosity, still. Something else, too. "But you found it."

"Mmhmm." Percy dug into the bag, pulling out a container of animal-style fries. "I just . . . want to know. You know? I wanted to be able to . . ." He ducked his head, wondering if this was too sentimental for Jim's tastes. Wondering why he felt so comfortable baring this part of himself, which felt a thousand times more intimate than having sex did. "I wanted to be able to see something of him no one else had. Not to brag about it or show it off, but just to have it, for me. For my own."

Whatever he was saying, it didn't seem to actually make it past Jim's ears, because he burst out with, "So what did he say? Like, not that it matters, obviously . . ."

Percy wasn't sure what made him say, "Well, obviously it does matter."

Jim flinched, his hands crinkling his bag. "I mean . . . I, well, I mean. I'm supposed to be learning about him, right?" The slight tremulousness faded from his voice as he built up steam. "What better way is there to learn about him and to be the best at my job than to know shit about him no one else does? Right?"

"Ah, right," Percy murmured, staring at him. Jim looked a little . . . manic, honestly, with his jaw clenched tight and his eyes full of wild fever. Percy cleared his throat, able to picture every second of the interview in crystal clarity thanks to nearly wearing out the tape with so many rewatches. "Well, he was vague, of course. If you came out then, there were no two ways about it. You weren't an actor *and* were gay. You were a gay actor. That's why the interview was kept hush-hush—by James's PR people, I assume." He took a bite of his fries and made an altogether embarrassing noise, sinking back into the couch cushions.

"And? And what did he say?"

"Well, he said he wasn't gay." Percy expected surprise at that, but Jim just nodded and leaned forward like a little kid begging for story time. "But that's to be expected. He was bisexual. The interviewer outright asked him if he was gay, and he sort of did that . . . actually, you do it. That head-tilt almost-no."

Jim squinted at him. "I do what now?"

"That!" Percy pointed at him. "That squinty head-tilt. Very enigmatic. You *have* been catching up on his videos! So anyway, he did that and looked away, and then the interviewer asked about Dahlia Delair—that's James's late wife—"

"Uh huh."

"—and James did the same thing, and made an aside about how he and Dahlia had an 'understanding.'"

Jim paled. " . . . What kind of understanding?"

"I'm assuming that she would keep his confidence? I've seen interviews with both of them and I don't think she was his beard or anything, if that's what you're concerned about." *Although, why is that concerning?* "I don't know," Percy sighed. "He never outright *said* anything. Maybe I'm not explaining it right. He had this air about him, this look of, *You know it and I know it.* Like he and the interviewer had a secret."

"I guess . . . I guess in those days it'd have to be a secret."

"Well . . . yeah." Percy smiled a little, not with any mirth. "Like I said, it would have been career suicide. All the swooning girls his studio was selling his image to, and all the straight men his studio was telling to be like him? Back then, 'bisexual' wasn't something people recognized. He would've lost everything."

Jim rubbed a hand over his face, blinking at the coffee table. He looked kind of dazed. "But I mean. Are you sure? What if it's just something you're reading into it? I mean, not *you* you." He reached for Percy's knee, but didn't touch. "Just people. Reading into it. Are you sure it was like that? Are you *sure*?"

The urge to back down from the intensity was almost overwhelming, a deep pulling current that called for Percy to capitulate and shrug, mumble a wishy-washy answer, say he maybe didn't know what he was talking about. But Percy didn't want to back down anymore. Not for Hazel, and not here.

"Yes," he said. "*Yes*, I'm sure."

CHAPTER
TWENTY

It couldn't be true.

All the bitterness Brandon had left said it couldn't be true.

James Ringer had been a playboy. He'd cheated on Dahlia repeatedly. Stayed out all night partying. He'd been fucking *photographed* doing it. He'd been talented, okay, yes, but he'd also used that talent to get away with being a charismatic scumbag. He hadn't been some tragic closet case with a sympathetic wife and an "understanding."

But if anyone would have been open enough and giving enough and just plain cool enough to have such an understanding back in the '50s, it would have been Dahlia. She would've loved James anyway and fuck what everyone thought about it, fuck what she could have had if she hadn't glued herself to him. She'd never given up on Brandon, either. It was just the kind of woman she'd been.

So what kind of man had James Ringer been?

After being so sure all his life, Brandon suddenly didn't know.

Was he the only one?

It snapped into nauseating clarity: the sheer and total hatred his mom had spat out every time James's name came up. Damn near the same tone she used when she was telling Brandon he needed to grow up and stop being a rebellious, ungrateful little (gay) shit.

She knew.

She knew. She knew, and that was why . . .

The nausea deepened, and Brandon shoved the bag of food away, getting the thick greasy smell of good French fries as far away as possible. His whole life he'd hated James Ringer because his parents said he was good for nothing, probably a drug addict, useless, shitty to Dahlia. His whole life he'd thought Dahlia wanted to bury her memories of a man she'd ended up bound to for the rest of his life thanks to the media and James's fans. His whole life he'd thought James had made Dahlia miserable because he couldn't get enough of other women.

But what if none of that was *true*?

He heard Percy say his name, heard the rustle of paper bag. His name again, louder. Only he was too dizzy to respond, and worried if he opened his mouth, he'd throw up. This was a thousand times worse than being a dumbass kid who went along with what his parents said. He'd never *bothered* to look deeper, never cared why his mom forbade him from asking questions about the guy. Never actually asked Dahlia. Just assumed. Just bought it all.

What if all those photos—what if they'd been staged to protect James? To protect them both? If he and Dahlia *had* had an agreement, it would've been smart for James to be photographed running around with other women. It would've sated the paparazzi and given James the chance to . . .

To cheat on her with men?

But if there was an agreement . . .

What if Dahlia hadn't been sad because she'd been tied to James? What if she'd been sad she had to keep his secret for all those years? What if she'd wanted to tell people about it, let them know the real James, make them stop thinking he was inconsiderate and ungrateful and unloving? What if she'd wanted Brandon to know he and his grandfather had more than looks in common, but she'd promised James she wouldn't tell?

He turned to Percy, his mouth working faster than his mind. "I need to see the video," he said. Shook his head. "*No.* I need to see it and then I need for us to upload it online."

Percy's eyes widened. "You *what*?"

"This video of yours. It's rare. You said only a few people have ever seen it. That they tried to suppress it. You and me are going to upload it for the whole world."

Dismay flashed across Percy's face; he shook his head and it vanished. "Why is this so important to you?" he asked quietly, earnestly. "For . . . for your job? Wouldn't seeing it be enough? Why do you want to upload it?"

Shit. Brandon swallowed hard. Reached for the fast food bag and yanked out a handful of fries, stuffing them all into his mouth. He'd said way too fucking much. Acted like a certifiable crazy person. If Percy hadn't already caught on, he was gonna, if Brandon said anything else. And then what?

Hell, he probably would have caught on by now if he wasn't staring at his hands, looking all hangdog. Shit, right. That video was precious to him. What was it he'd said? *"I wanted something of him no one else had."* And Brandon had just tried to make him give it to everyone.

Still wanted to do it.

"I dunno why I said that. It was stupid. Sorry. I guess I just have a little bit of a rebel streak in me, huh? I just . . ." He stuffed his face again to buy himself time. *If it is true, I just want other people to know the truth. If I can think differently about him, me, of all people, I want other people to be able to, too.*

"You hear *they* wanted to keep it hush-hush, so you automatically want it spread far and wide," Percy filled in.

Actually? Yeah.

But Brandon couldn't tell him just how deep the need to do it went. The real reason why his heart was still racing a thousand miles an hour.

"Yeah, well . . . They say left, I go right." He nodded at Percy's bag. "You should eat before that gets cold."

Percy blinked, then looked at the bag like it was a miracle right before his eyes. "Right. Yes. Food." He tore the bag open and spread it out on the table, reverently unwrapping his 3x3s and taking the plastic off his fork to dig into his fries. "Thank you, by the way. This is perfect."

"Uh . . . huh," Brandon said, watching him wolf down three huge bites of fries and then half his first 3x3 in like thirty seconds. "Do you always eat like you're starving?"

Percy's expression soured, and he set his burger down. "No."

A faint stab of guilt wormed its way into Brandon's stomach. That was the second time today he'd upset Percy—and this time at least, he was being a genuine asshole. "Sorry. That was rude. Eat however you want, Perce. Obviously. Ignore me."

"It's fine. I actually am kind of starving, honestly. I didn't get breakfast this morning." He curled a lip and managed to look contrite at the same time. "Not that that's your problem."

Brandon frowned at him. "I'm your 'tutor,'" he said flatly. "So I'm supposed to make sure you're eating, you know, balanced public school 'meals'" he finger-quoted "every day and keeping up with your homework." He reached over and put a hand on Percy's wrist. "Tell me what happened."

"Hazel," Percy sighed.

Fucking knew it.

"What did she do?"

"She doesn't like our . . . situation. Obviously." Percy gave him a weak smile and turned his arm over so Brandon was almost holding his hand. "She woke me up early and tried to tell me I need to stop doing things that 'strain me,' and I . . . well, I went off on her."

Brandon wrapped his fingers around Percy's hand. "*Good.* She deserves it." Then he frowned again. "Wait, so you guys got into an argument and that's why you didn't eat today? Did she— Is she— She withheld food from you? She wouldn't give you *food* because you stood up for yourself? What the fuck?"

"It was just breakfast," Percy mumbled with a shrug and a duck of his head.

"Sure, okay. You probably won't starve to death without breakfast, but that's not the *point*, Perce."

"Then do tell me what the point *is*, Jim."

"She can't just decide not to feed you just because she's pissed off at you. That's the point. It's wrong. It doesn't matter if it's just breakfast, it's *wrong*. What if it's not just breakfast, huh?"

Percy's gaze broke with his own.

"It's more than just breakfast," Brandon said. "Isn't it."

"She said today. Just today."

"Stop saying 'just'!" Brandon squeezed Percy's hand, tugging him to make sure he had Percy's full attention. "Stop acting like if she's only *this* shitty or she only does this *one* thing, that's okay. I don't care what bullshit she's been spoon-feeding you forever, it's all fucking lies anyway! Don't let them tell you who you are. Don't let them tell you who you—when you can fucking *eat*, Jesus Christ, Percy. You should be able to eat whenever you want. Do whatever you want in general. Fuck!" He slumped back against the couch cushions, breathing as hard as he had been when Marco got done with him.

Percy was silent beside him. Brandon could feel his hand shaking.

"Can't you tell your parents?" Brandon tried. He hated suggesting it, but if his parents really didn't pay enough attention to notice when Hazel was *starving* him, then something had to change.

"They'll say I'm making trouble. Causing friction for lack of anything better to do." The words sounded rehearsed, and Percy's tone was dull, all his excitement over the food sucked away. "Look," Percy said, taking his hand back from Brandon. "I know this seems . . . It must seem unfathomably cruel to you, or, or just odd, but—"

"Please don't tell me she's done this before." Brandon gaped at him. "Has she? *Percy.*"

"No! No, of course not. But . . ." Percy wouldn't look at him, just stared down into his lap. He was quiet for a long time. "I'm used to it," he whispered finally. "The whole of it, all of it. I'm used to having my schedule primed for me, to having people make my meals and clean my rooms and drive me to my appointments. I know you want me to buck the system and tell everyone to fuck off, but Jim, I c—" He swallowed audibly and shook his head. "I'll work on it. No," he said, when Brandon opened his mouth. "I'll work on it. Myself."

He didn't sound very convinced of success, but Brandon knew how fucking frustrating it was to be told what to do, and he knew how much it could cost to rebel, so he shut up and ate his food.

Mostly.

"It's not right." He picked apart his last burger. "People see this big fancy house and big fancy cars and parties and whatever and they assume you're some spoiled rich kid."

"Like you did?" Percy murmured, voice not quite light.

"Yeah. Yeah I did. Like, okay." Brandon turned to face him, sitting cross-legged. "Look. I know a lot about your shitty family, so here. I came out when I was fourteen and the first thing my dad did was try to get on the horn with some of those nutso conversion therapy people. And my mom vetoed that. But her solution was to kick me out. I guess she assumed I'd come crawling back once I realized no one was going to take care of me. Like if the choice became being who she wanted me to be or being hungry, then I'd come to her side on my own." Brandon scratched at his jaw, wondering if it was fucked up or insensitive to compare their situations. But he barreled on anyway. "So I was on the streets for a long time. Starving. So I know how it feels, okay? And it's not fair, and it's especially not fair for people who are supposed to give a shit to do that to us."

Percy scoffed. "So what, you want me to just live on the street too? Not to make this into a competition, because I don't doubt what happened to you sucked, but the risk for me is a lot worse than it ever was for you. If I'm cut off, it's not just food and shelter, it's my meds. It's the ability to walk, to talk—Jim, if I don't have my drugs, I'm going to go *blind*. It could even attack my heart. So yeah, it means I have to play along with some stuff, be the doormat, whatever. I don't let her walk all over me all the time, but sometimes—sometimes, yes. Sometimes I have to."

That edge of panic squirmed back into Brandon's chest and hung there, like he'd smoked a pack too many. "I didn't know that."

"Of course you didn't," Percy said crisply. He made a face and softened. "I don't expect you to. But you have to understand these things are different. I'm sorry about what happened to you, but I can't just shove my middle finger in my parents' faces and walk away clean. It doesn't work like that for me, Jim."

"Brandon." It slipped out before Brandon could bite it back, pretend he'd been trying to say something else. He wasn't even sure why it was suddenly so important he *did* say it. Why he didn't want to take it back once it was out there. Why he was sure it was okay for Percy to know, to have this piece of him none of his other clients did.

Percy looked up at him. "What?"

"My name. It's not Jim. It's Brandon."

CHAPTER
TWENTY-ONE

I t was difficult for Percy not to feel torn in two.

The one side of him was frustrated with Jim—with *Brandon*, almost blindingly so, but the other half was lit up inside with an unexpected happiness at being trusted. Not only with Jim's name, but with his story as well. And with his bald reaction to James's interview. He was a full one-eighty from how locked up he'd been their first appointment, glazing himself over with irreverent slutty grins and anger in turns.

And Percy wouldn't be hard-pressed to admit he was mostly angry at himself. Not at Brandon. Not at someone who wanted him to have better things not because "oh poor Percy," but because Brandon saw him as an equal, someone who didn't need pity so much as a basic standard of living.

Which Percy did have, always.

Almost always.

"Thank you," he said when he realized Brandon was starting to look nervous at his lack of reaction. "No, I mean it!" He reached and took Brandon's hands in his, seeing flashes of the cigarette stains on the inside of his thumb and forefinger as he folded Brandon's fingers in his. Odd, but he hadn't smelled fresh smoke on Brandon the last two times he'd been here. Disappointing aesthetically, but best for his lungs in the long run. "I mean it, I promise. Thank you.

"But that doesn't change what I said before." He gave Brandon a little smile and brought one of his hands up to kiss the knuckles, trying to soften what he knew was a response to Brandon's purely good intentions. Brandon wasn't ignorant, or rude—he was a dick, but he'd never looked down on Percy, and Percy, though he knew he didn't *owe* Brandon anything in return, was warmer toward him for it and wanted him to know that.

Brandon flushed. "Yeah? Yeah. I know."

"Do you? I have another friend who told me to get my teenage rebellion in, even if I was late." What would Kovie think, seeing the two of them together? She'd be proud of him, Percy thought, which made him go on, his voice ruthlessly steady. "That's actually why I hired you. I mean. I saw the ad and I just . . ."

"Wanted a piece of him," Brandon finished quietly. "Is that right?"

"Not necessarily. I told you I wanted someone to watch films with me. That really was it. *Is* it."

Brandon tilted his head. "Why movies? Why him?"

Percy let go of one of his hands and waved to indicate the room around them. "This is going to sound pretentious and rich-kid and—"

"Stop it." Brandon pushed at Percy's knee. "Don't try to apologize or whatever, you got your problems just like anyone else, I said that. And you know I'm not gonna be an asshole and think you're some whiny pompous rich kid." One side of his mouth curled with a mischievous smile. "Not *anymore*."

"Hush, you." But Percy felt the tension seeping out of his shoulders as the tension eased. He reached for his—now cold, damn it—food and talked between the last bites of his burger. "I've just always loved it. Have you ever found something, or seen something, or tried something and you just *knew*? Like there was some part of you that was always unsatisfied, and that was *it*?"

Brandon looked outright uncomfortable, but he nodded. "Sure."

"This is it for me. I spent a lot of time in hospitals as a kid. In doctors' offices, in homeschooling. I only went somewhere when my parents felt it was necessary to make a social appearance. Probably to show I wasn't wasting away to nothing. And when I found movies, it was like . . . suddenly I could live that. Vicariously. Obviously." Percy shrugged and ducked his head.

"Why *him*?" Brandon repeated. "Why James?"

Percy rolled his bottom lip between his teeth. Now it was his turn to flush. "Brandon, come on." He waved a hand at Brandon's unclassically handsome everything.

Brandon snorted. "Yeah. Fair. How'd you find him?"

"He was in the first movie I saw, actually. *Matchstick*. And I never let it go. He was just so . . . You know. Just *so*. Once my parents started giving me an allowance and let me on the Internet—" he tried hard to ignore how childish that sounded, and certainly didn't tell Brandon he'd been well into his teens when that happened, "—I found books, movies, the collectibles, all of it, and it . . . was a way for me to connect to people, I suppose. That was really it." *A way out of this dreary room.* "And then when I found out he was queer . . . It was like I was meant to find him. Like all along I'd *known*, like he'd been preserved on film just for me. Which sounds ridiculous, and selfish, I know, but—"

"No, no it doesn't. No." Brandon blew out a long breath and stared at Percy, wide-eyed. "No, I know how you feel. I get it."

Which brought Percy back to why James being bisexual was so important for *Brandon*. Maybe it was just for his job, but maybe . . . "Why him?" Percy parroted back.

Brandon raised an eyebrow and parroted right back. "Perce, come on."

"Well, why escorting, then? You obviously hated it when you started."

"Well. I mean, I started because I thought I was good at it. I know how to, uh." He wrinkled his nose. "You know, I know how to suck dick. So I figured, why not."

"Maybe because you hated it?" Percy said, bringing it out as gently as he could.

"Mmmm." Brandon picked at his jeans. They were Levi's boot-cut, wide-legged, light-washed.

Percy touched them too; the denim was buttery-soft from age.

Brandon nudged their fingertips together playfully, then shrugged and tossed his arm along the back of the couch. Somehow on him it looked relaxed and easy, not at all like a teenager on a bad date. "I don't hate it anymore. I think I can be good at it. Especially now." He cut himself off sharply, but before Percy could ask why, he closed his hand over Percy's and said, "Which you're supposed to be helping me with. We're slacking off on school today, Percival."

Percy almost choked. "Don't you *ever* call me that," he sputtered, half laughing and half horrified. "God." He put his trash on the coffee table and reached over Brandon to pick a DVD. "You don't get a choice today," he told Brandon primly. "My lessons, my rules, my pick."

"Yes sir."

Make that almost choked twice.

Brandon licked his lips, shot him a shit-eating grin. "Somethin' wrong, Perce?"

Percy pointed at him, flustered. "Stop that. You. Stop."

"Got a little authority kink?"

"*No.*" Percy fumbled with the DVD case and hooked the disk on his finger, leaving the case on the coffee table. He wasn't sure what he'd grabbed, but he shoved it in the player anyway and lowered the lights with the universal remote. He recognized the standard DVD data when it came on—it was *The Easy.*

"Ohhh," Brandon said, picking up the case. "I know this one. I saw a clip, like, when he goes to the bar? And . . ." He was off and running, waving his hands as he talked about a scene Percy knew by heart: James Ringer going to a bar and hitting on the waitress in his subtle sultry way, then getting kicked out by her husband.

And Brandon knew it just as well as he did.

"Move your arm," Percy demanded, cutting Brandon off midsentence.

"Uh . . .?"

"Your arm, put it back where it was."

Stalled, Brandon laid his left arm along the back of the couch. Percy shoved himself under it and along Brandon's side, settling in against him.

He felt Brandon take a breath.

"So anyway," Brandon said a second later. "Yeah. Good movie."

"It is," Percy agreed. He smothered a smile in the side of Brandon's chest and turned the volume up. "Now—"

"Yeah, yeah, I got it. Pay attention."

Neither of them moved until they'd finished the rest of James's filmography. Brandon couldn't lie, as the last one closed and faded to black, he slumped down and thick disappointment descended over him.

It was done. It was over.

No more.

Except there *was* more.

Percy had photobooks—giant things that cost more money than Brandon had ever held in his hand at once, big and leather-bound with copies of black and white and color photos. The kind of books collectors killed each other over on eBay. The kind of books Sleazeball Harry had been salivating to get his hands on. The kind of books Dahlia had been given for free.

Which made Brandon wonder. He still hadn't gone down into the basement again, but if he did, would he find shit like this? Stuff that wasn't mass-produced cheap novelty crap? Stuff Percy would like? It would be better here than in Dahlia's dusty basement. Appreciated more.

Well, maybe.

The idea of being able to give it to Percy was only slightly more exciting than getting to look at it himself.

" . . . and this was actually a family vacation," Percy was saying, one of his hands curled on a spread of James in those stupid old person swim trunks, lying on his back in the sand with Dahlia next to him, her stomach round. She was mid-laugh, head thrown back unselfconsciously. Just as happy as she'd been in the picture from the wildflowers shoot. "On the forums, someone who knew the photographer said she just happened to be there, and James asked her to take a picture of Dahlia for him because she was so beautiful."

Brandon's eyes stung. "He loved her a lot, huh."

"God, yes. He talked about her all the time." Percy turned the page. There was another one of Dahlia, drop-dead gorgeous in her effortless way with her hair blown wildly this way and that.

"It's called artful disorder, Brandon."

"S-so you don't think," Brandon managed, and stopped to clear his throat before his voice could crack. "You don't think he was just with her for . . ." He'd asked before, or insinuated at least, but he needed to know now, for sure, and Percy would know. Percy would know.

"Definitely not," Percy said gently. He touched Brandon's jaw, almost turned his head before Brandon cleared his throat again and shrugged him off. "Brandon?"

"It's fine, just. You know, she just died. I dunno, maybe I'm sensitive or something today, stupid shit."

Percy laughed under his breath. "You're *always* sensitive."

"Pfffff. Yeah, right."

"No, you are." Percy touched him again, and this time Brandon let him angle his face, press his thumb down on the middle of Brandon's bottom lip. "That's why you get so upset. Or why you're so touched by this, and by the movies. You connect. Like I tried to."

"With James?"

"With *people*," Percy sighed. Apparently Brandon wasn't keeping up with him. "You're good with people, you just don't let yourself be."

"Puh-lease. Any boss I've ever had can tell you I suck with people." *Any boss except Judy.*

Percy rolled his eyes and patted him on the chest. "Sure you do, tough guy," he said, and leaned over to press a kiss to Brandon's jaw.

He made like he was going to go back to the book, but Brandon wrapped a hand around one of his wrists. Kept him close.

He didn't get this way with clients. Not like he didn't get hard or he didn't come or he didn't like what happened, because mostly he did, but he didn't get like *this*. Warm and interested—interested beyond "hey here's a dick I can suck/a guy I can fuck and make money off it."

He'd told Percy his name.

"Perce . . ."

Percy kissed him.

Just like last time.

And fuck no, Brandon didn't *want* him to stop. Pretty much not ever. But— "Hey," he said, pressing Percy back carefully. Percy's face tensed, and Brandon hurried to shake his head, shift closer. "No, I just—give me a turn at starting? Maybe?" He grinned. "Or I'm *really* not gonna believe you when you say you don't have a thing for being in charge."

"Maybe I didn't expect you to believe me," Percy said, which was such a bold-faced lie. Brandon had seen the way he twitched, the sudden shy interest.

"Sure you didn't." Brandon took the book from Percy's lap, laid it out on the coffee table, open to their place, and leaned over Percy, pressing him back. Percy was breathing fast, but not shallowly, not with a strain or a rasp or anything, and he went back eagerly, holding onto Brandon's shoulders until he was flat on the couch, his eyes wide. "This okay?" Brandon checked, arranging himself so he had a knee against the back of the couch and one between Percy's legs, not anywhere dangerous yet.

Yet.

Percy nodded vigorously. "Yes. Yes." He slipped his fingers under the collar of Brandon's shirt, dragged them over the back of his neck.

Fuck. Brandon dropped his head and Percy squeezed, making Brandon outright shiver.

"Maybe *you* have an authority kink," Percy whispered. He pressed his lips together, but it didn't hide how fucking obviously he was laughing at Brandon.

And this—this was what Brandon meant when he said Percy was different, all the way back at their first appointment. What he meant when he said he wasn't the same way with anyone else.

Because Percy didn't mean for it to hurt, and it didn't.

"Maybe I do." He pulled Percy's shirt collar down and lowered himself down, snuck a kiss and then a lingering bite—but no hickeys, he was pretty sure Perce couldn't pass that off as a tutoring extra—that had Percy whining in the back of his throat. Brandon pushed himself back up and smirked down at Percy. "Whatcha gonna do about it?"

Percy's eyes narrowed.

Uh oh, Brandon thought, and then he was being tilted and—

They were on the floor.

"Ow fuck," he wheezed, Percy's weight pinning him in the uncomfortably narrow place between the couch and the legs of the coffee table.

"I am *so sorry*," Percy said, trying to untangle himself and squashing Brandon even more. "That was not what I was trying to do, I swear, I forgot—" He cupped Brandon's face in his hands, peering down into his eyes. "Did you hit your head? Is anything hurt?"

"Mmphhgnh." Brandon batted at Percy's hands with the one of his that wasn't jackknifed under him. "Fine, I'm fine. You weigh a lot, you know that?"

"Right!" Percy moved to get off him again and almost slipped on the way up—it was only Brandon twisting to the side—ow *fuck fuck*—

that saved him from smacking his face on the coffee table. "Well all right," Percy said, staring at the table, a few inches from his eyes. "Let's try this . . . differently. Somehow."

Brandon made an executive decision. "I'm gonna scoot back. It's me that's the problem anyway." He took up all the space next to the frankly ridiculously huge table, and he didn't think either of them could find a place to put their feet until he was out of the way. "Okay, can you just . . . there you go," he said, watching Percy shuffle up on his knees with a soft wince. "Is that okay?"

"Fine. Not for long, though."

Brandon grabbed for the coffee table and pulled back. He maybe needed to talk to Marco about lifting more weights, because his bicep felt about as useful as a wet noodle.

Then Percy moved, putting his shoulder against the table, and said, "Just move the table, that has to be easier than you."

"There are nicer ways to tell me I gotta lose weight, Perce," Brandon grunted, shoving the leg of the table. Together they moved it a few inches—enough to get Brandon's other arm free. "Thank *god*." He wriggled back and sat up, and . . .

And then Percy was in his lap.

He must've been staring. Percy squinted at him, turning red. "What? What?"

"Nothing." He looped an arm behind Percy's back. "You have freckles."

"Well yeah." Percy fluttered his hands for a second, then put them both on Brandon's shoulders. "You do too."

"I do not."

"You *do*. Why are you so contrary?"

"Part of the charm."

"Hmmmm. Maybe." Percy slid one hand down to Brandon's stomach. "For the record, I like this."

"My boss doesn't," Brandon said, shooing his hand away. He wasn't self-conscious or anything, but Percy's hand was too close to moving lower and Brandon needed a second to breathe before Percy took that away again. "She has me working with her personal trainer."

Percy's eyebrows rose. He touched Brandon's bicep. Squeezed consideringly. "Hmmmmmmm. I could agree with that."

"For my stomach, not that."

"I like both," Percy said. "But some more here wouldn't hurt."

True. But Brandon wasn't about to admit that. Especially not after selling his stubbornness. "You don't think I have enough?"

"It's not what you have."

"Oh no?"

Percy barely managed to hold back his giggles before he got out, "It's how you use it."

Brandon groaned and shoved Percy off his lap. "You—I can't believe you. C'mon, you spent *how* many years watching cheesy old movies? You gotta have better lines than that, man."

"You'd laugh at those too." Percy grabbed hold of the couch and the table and eased himself to his feet, using Brandon's shoulder for balance when he was upright. He hesitated, then said, "Maybe we . . . shouldn't try repeating that experience. Just in case."

"Oh. Uh—yeah, sure." An uneasy swoop in Brandon's stomach made him go a little cold, made him wonder if he'd been trying to get Percy to do something he didn't want to do. *Again.* "I'm sorry if I—"

"I mean not on the couch," Percy interrupted. "Not on the couch, and definitely not on the floor. I do have a bed, you know."

"Uh. Oh."

"Yes. *Oh.* I do sleep occasionally."

"I assumed you had a nest in your movie collection."

"Funny." Percy knocked their shoulders together and stepped past him, half turned toward the bedroom and half looking at Brandon. "Do you want to?"

Brandon wasn't all the way sure what he was asking—did he want to fuck? Sleep together? Make out?

Did it even matter?

No, it didn't.

Because yeah—whatever Percy wanted, Brandon wanted that too.

CHAPTER
TWENTY-TWO

Percy had the brief thought that he hadn't made his bed this morning, but obviously Brandon didn't care. He came in and didn't so much poke around Percy's things as he *looked*—not the cursory glance he'd given it the first time, picking out the right place to smoke, but a look that was evaluating, examining. Curious.

"What's that?" he asked, detouring from his path to Percy's bed and heading for the door at the far end of Percy's room.

"My library." Percy moved around him, taking the key from its hiding place in his dresser and unlocking it to show him. It was twice the size of his bedroom, easily, and showed off its size thanks to shelving that was chest-height. "Mostly history books. I'm sure you're stunned beyond belief."

"Oh yeah." Brandon leaned inside. "Anything else about James in here?"

"That row."

"Of books?"

Percy felt himself puff up. "Of *shelves*."

"Man." Brandon took a step inside. Shook his head and turned back around. Purred, "Later."

Maybe Percy was reading too much into it, but to him, "later" meant Brandon would be around later today. Much later.

After . . . ?

He let Brandon back him out of the library and toward the bed, one of Brandon's hands hovering at his back and a slow smile playing on Brandon's mouth. "You look permanently smug now," Percy said, letting his library key drop to the floor at the side of the bed.

"Don't mean to." Brandon reversed them at the last second and dropped onto Percy's bed back-first, spreading out. His shirt rode up, showing off the belly his boss so wanted him to get rid of. Percy thought it was charming—as contrary to the typical specificities of Brandon's profession as Brandon himself was contrary to . . . everything.

"Well, you do." Percy touched the strip of exposed skin, the thick trail of hair that disappeared under his jeans. "Like a cat in the sun."

"Pretty sure cats are always smug no matter if it's rainy or sunny or whatever."

"Then calling you a cat fits well," Percy said, pinching him lightly. Brandon jumped, then licked his lips, breathing out hard. He didn't move away.

Percy *burned* with sudden and absolutely unrestrained want.

Oh, really?

They could test that theory of Brandon's, he decided.

"Put your arms up over your head." He gripped Brandon's thighs in his hands as tightly as he was able, holding on to him. He waited until Brandon, whose pupils were fat enough there was only a thin ring of blue around the edge of his irises, had obeyed, wrists crossed above him. Then he moved his own hands a few inches up Brandon's thighs, teasing.

He was dizzy from, yes, being so attracted to Brandon it was hard to think about anything else, but also from how relaxed Brandon was, how private this particular obedience and happiness was.

Just for Percy.

He wanted to see what else he could wring from Brandon.

And he knew now—*trusted*—Brandon wouldn't storm out or think less of him if he tried and couldn't finish, so he said, "Are you okay with me trying a blowjob? Um, on you?"

Brandon lifted his head. "I'm kinda tied up at the moment, Perce."

Percy couldn't help it: he laughed. Okay, it was very nearly bordering on a snort. "You do realize you are just holding on to your own arms, right? No 'tying' involved whatsoever."

Brandon blushed straight to the tips of his ears. "Oh! Uh! Right!" He squirmed, still not moving out of the position Percy had put him in. "Does that mean I can, uh, you know, put my arms down now?"

"No," Percy replied cheerfully. He used his grip on Brandon's thighs and pushed them further apart, until the seams of his jeans strained. "Shimmy up."

Brandon did, never letting go of his grip on his own wrists.

With newly freed mattress space to claim, Percy lowered himself onto the bed between Brandon's legs and slithered close to him as best as he was able. Halfway, he realized he had no idea what curled positioning was going to allow him to both suck dick but also keep his joints from staging a full on rebellion. Maybe next time he sent Brandon home, he could ask him to do some research on arthritic sex positions, a million miles away from possible keyloggers. With the side bonus being that Brandon would have to be the one looking at stock photos and illustrations of elderly people getting it on.

For now, though, Percy propped himself up on one elbow—getting an eyeful of Brandon's very full jeans bulge—and then immediately regretted it when pain shot through every inch of bone in his arm as if he'd jumped off a ten story building and landed elbow-first. He hissed, clutching himself, and Brandon shot straight up to sitting, eyes wide with concern.

But still with his arms held over his damn head.

It was so funny and cute and also kind of hot that Percy completely forgot to be frustrated by his physical limitations.

"Hey," Brandon said, softly. "How about we both lay on our sides?"

That might work. No propping or kneeling necessary. Percy nodded, and Brandon fell back again, waited for Percy to get out from between his spread legs, and then rolled onto one side facing him. Percy laid down too . . . except lower.

Now he really *did* have a face full of Brandon's bulge.

Could feel the heat of it on his face. Could smell it. And god, it smelled good. He shivered, eyes sliding shut as he breathed in deeper.

"Okay?" Brandon asked.

"Better than," Percy groaned. He reached out with both hands, framing Brandon's groin with them, pulling the denim taut to reveal the shape of him underneath. Under the scrutiny, Brandon's dick *twitched*. "Good lord."

"You're getting me all worked up." Brandon muttered, with a little squirm that suggested he was trying hard to be polite. He sounded surprised, but not in a sharp way; not in a way that was directed at

Percy specifically. Maybe he wasn't used to being turned on with clients.

Maybe he wasn't used to it not feeling like he was with a client at all.

At least, that was what Percy hoped he felt like right now, because Percy sure didn't feel like he was with hired help.

He moved his thumbs closer to the line of Brandon's dick and murmured, "Is there something else you want me to do?"

Brandon groaned, and Percy looked up to see him twisting to push his face into the side of one of his arms, his eyes squeezed shut. "You're killing me," he said, voice muffled. "Jesus, Percy."

There was a tacit "come on" underneath that. He was still being so polite.

Percy figured that deserved some rewarding.

He nuzzled forward, pressing his mouth and nose against the rigid line of Brandon's erection, hot breath flooding the fabric of Brandon's jeans. "Undo your zipper," he instructed, not quite sure if his own hands were up to the task just then.

Or maybe because he just wanted to order Brandon around some more.

It seemed to be working for Brandon as much as it was working for him. His face was flushed and his eyes were glazed, and it took him a couple seconds to work his arms free and stretch them down to thumb clumsily at the button of his jeans. He worked it open and got the zipper down. Licked his lips and said, "Anything else?"

Oh, Percy could get used to this.

"No, that's all." Percy nudged his hands away and shifted, easing the strain on his shoulder. He wouldn't be able to lie like this for too long, but he was going to take full advantage of the time he did have. And that started with tugging the open vee of Brandon's jeans wider until that hard cock popped right out into his face.

No underwear? *Hell.* Percy shot a quick glance up at Brandon, expecting to see some kind of smugly satisfied expression at the success of his play, but found no such thing. Instead, his eyes were slitted, his breath coming in laboured huffs. Concentrating hard. Maybe even a little pained by it. Fighting to keep himself under control?

Just the thought had Percy losing a little control of his own. He lunged forward, pressing wet open-mouthed kisses to Brandon's shaft, barely able to stop himself from trying to swallow the whole thing down.

He wanted to. Fuck, he wanted to. That smell he'd noticed before was mind-blowing now, consuming his senses, and the little bitten back noises Brandon made at every touch filled him with an obscene sense of power. As strong as the urge to deepthroat him was, though, Percy knew now that there was more than one way to get the results he sought. There were no joints in his tongue, and no joints meant no pain meant all the freedom and flexibility in the world. Keeping close, he used the flat of his tongue to wet Brandon's entire length from root to tip, paying no mind to how sloppily he did it, or how his own spit was coating his lips and nose from the clumsy attention.

Who cared if it was clumsy? Not Brandon, who was biting the side of his hand now in a sweet bid to keep quiet.

Surprisingly considerate for a guy who'd once nearly given away their whole game by lighting up a damn cigarette right in Percy's bedroom without even attempting to ask first.

When dragging the flat of his tongue all over Brandon's dick started to get a little repetitive, he alternated it with little sucking kisses. He never opened his mouth wide enough for it to hurt, but turned out he didn't need to. Especially not once he found the spot right at the crown of Brandon's dick, that little V where shaft and head met on the underside. Sucking on that produced some truly gratifying—and bordering funny—high pitched noises from Brandon that had Percy returning there again and again just to repeat that reaction.

Tonguing the guy's slit didn't quite produce the same response, but it tasted so good, so salty-bitter and earthy and unlike anything Percy had ever tasted before, that he stayed there a long while, pursing his lips and just sucking up whatever moisture that slit produced.

And the whole time, Brandon smothered his whines and moans and little tortured laughs. Kept his hands to himself, held obediently above his head, but couldn't quite stop himself from doing those little aborted hip thrusts whenever Percy's teasing went on for too long.

"You're very good when you want to be," Percy murmured, using a fingernail now to scrape across the slight impression of Brandon's sensitive slit. "When it suits you."

Brandon whimpered, then scoffed. "Huh, guess I am. Not gonna lie though, you make it easy."

"The power of positive reinforcement," Percy affirmed. He sucked that little V again and gave Brandon a couple of careful pumps with his hand. His balls had drawn up tight, and he pulsed against Percy's loose fist, the head slick and shiny and dark red. "But will I let you come?"

"You could, but you shouldn't."

Percy's eyebrows lifted. "Oh?" He propped himself up, trying to get a handle on Brandon's expression, make sure he was still okay.

Brandon still had that dignified pained holding himself back look. Not exactly comfortable, no, but not upset or frightened or withdrawn, either. Just . . . too close to orgasm for comfort, maybe.

"And why is that?" Percy asked, just to be sure.

One corner of Brandon's mouth twitched and he bared his teeth in a grin. "Because you don't want to miss out on how good it feels when I pop with your dick in my ass."

For someone who'd just spent the last several minutes sucking and licking another man's cock, Percy still found it in himself to blush like a virgin.

Brandon could barely stop himself from throwing Percy down onto the bed and dry humping his leg until he shot. Instead, he forced himself to take a deep breath, to sit up and cup Percy's face in his hands, and press the slowest, least demanding kiss onto Percy's mouth that he could manage. He wanted this to be good, wanted Percy to feel like he was worth taking time on, worth all the time in the world, wanted him to have no question that Brandon was here for so much more than just the chance to get off.

Maybe it was weird to go from off-color joking straight to tenderness—about as weird as how chaste this kiss felt even at the same time as Percy's lips and tongue still tasted like dick.

At least Percy didn't seem to mind the change in pace, maybe because keeping his mouth busy gave him a convenient excuse to not respond to Brandon's bluntness. That look he'd made after Brandon had said it—wide eyed, gasping, high pink in the cheeks—seemed to suggest he didn't have a comeback at the ready. Or forget anything as complex as comeback, more like the poor guy's brain had shorted out entirely.

Brandon didn't blame him. He was almost there himself.

And he tripped closer when Percy's hands lit on his wrists, stiff fingers curling there to hold him. The tying—well, not really, the fake-tying—had been good, and the echo of the sensation made Brandon wonder just what other demands Percy was hiding under his prim exterior. What else he'd ask Brandon to do, someday.

Percy shifted in his hands, blinking up at him. "Is something wrong?"

Oh, shit, he'd just been sitting there staring at the guy. Like an idiot. "N-no," he said, kissing Percy again, firmer. "You look really good." He ran a thumb over Percy's swollen bottom lip, leering.

There was that nice little flush. "So do you."

Brandon's eyelids dropped, a predatory growl working into his voice. "I *could* be even better."

"Could you?"

The clear challenge made Brandon grin. He liked that—liked that they could play with each other and not have it be weird. "Hell yeah I could." He moved his hands to Percy's shoulders and pressed him down, bracing himself on the mattress once Percy was laid out flat under him, his knees planted on either side of Percy's hips. With Percy like that it was tempting to rub down against him, but that wasn't what Brandon *really* wanted.

He tugged the hem of Percy's shirt up, getting all the way up to his chest before he saw Percy's slight grimace. He paused. "You okay?"

Percy squirmed, then nodded.

Brandon frowned at him. "Dude, I guarantee nothing you can tell me right now is something I haven't heard before."

Percy's expression pulled in, a slice of dark frustration in his eyes—but Brandon could tell it was aimed at himself, not Brandon. "I've never done this before."

"Well, I've got enough experience for the both of us." Brandon left his shirt where it was, rucked up to just under his pecs, and spread his hands open on either side of Percy's ribcage. He was really skinny, like

Brandon already knew, but it was starker with his bones right there, curving into Brandon's palms. "You have trouble putting on weight?" he asked, rubbing his knuckles down toward Percy's navel.

Percy's stomach heaved with a breath. "Yes."

"Heh." Brandon licked his lips, then shuffled down and bent to press a kiss above the waist of Percy's sweatpants. "I got enough of that for the both of us, too." He peeled his T-shirt up and off his body, tossing it onto the floor. "See?" He pinched at his stomach. It was a little flatter, he guessed, but every time he took his shirt off Marco still made a face, so he wasn't there yet, obviously.

Percy laughed and pushed his hand away. Reverently stroked where Brandon had just pinched. When Brandon didn't stop him, both of his hands rose to touch Brandon's skin, flat palms and curled fingers tracing Brandon's shape, from his belly and love handles up to his ribcage and pecs, which Percy cupped, his thumbs sweeping over Brandon's nipples.

"Ah!" Brandon squirmed, then laughed. Then moaned when Percy tipped his hands and pressed the very edges of his fingernails in. "Jeez, Perce." He licked his lips, suddenly way interested in rolling them both over and letting Percy do more of that. But no, he had a plan.

He scooped Percy's hands into his and nudged them back to rest up by Percy's head. "Your turn to stay still." He shuffled farther back, trying to bend down, and his jeans trapped his thighs, pulling where they were half-open. He hopped off the bed and shoved them down out of sheer frustration, letting them go wherever they wanted so he could back on Percy as fast as possible.

"Turn around this time?" Percy asked, his voice soft but somehow still completely irresistible.

"Sure, kid," Brandon said, affecting a pitch-perfect imitation of his grandfather's old Hollywood accent. If that play didn't have Percy wide eyed and gawping, what he did next would: he climbed back over Percy's body, but this time instead of straddling his hips, he sat right down, bare ass to Percy's clothed pelvis.

He heard Percy's breath stutter out of him, and then his cool hands brushed the small of Brandon's back. Brandon rocked his hips gently and heard Percy gasp again, right before he grabbed Brandon's waist in a surprisingly firm hold and held him right where he was. He hissed and let go a second later, but Brandon got the message just fine and let his weight sink down deeper into the cradle of Percy's hips, right down to the point where Percy's clothed erection settled into the cleft of his ass.

"Good?" he asked, voice deep in his chest.

Percy didn't answer. He kept touching, first at Brandon's shoulder blades and down his back and then to his waist and then lower, fingertips pressing into his ass and, fuck, pulling him open a little.

Brandon shifted, squeezing his fingers in the bedsheets so he wouldn't touch himself. He didn't think Percy would care if he did, but *he* cared. For some reason.

He ran his hands up Percy's thighs instead. Listened to him be weirdly quiet for another couple minutes, his hands flitting all over Brandon's back, before he said, "You like what you see, Perce?"

Percy's voice was shaky, broken, but somehow still keeping with the dry snark as he said, "Even when I thought you were a complete sullen shithead phoning in on your job, I still liked *this*." He gave both cheeks of Brandon's ass an illustrative squeeze.

"Well, you weren't wrong." Brandon glanced over his shoulder. Percy was flushed all the way down his chest, his eyes half-lidded and his pupils blown. Brandon pushed into his hands. "Glad you like this, though."

Percy stared at him for a long second, chewing on the inside of his cheek. Then his fingers flexed, pulling Brandon open wider, and he said, "I like you, too."

The sense of relief Brandon felt at that was massive, immeasurable, profound. "I—"

And then followed by a touch of doubt, like fingers down his spine: *Do you like me or him?*

"No, shh." Percy cutting off his thoughts was downright merciful. "Can I touch you, Brandon?" The pad of his thumb skimmed over Brandon's hole lightly. "Here?"

Brandon closed his hands tighter, his knuckles cracking quietly. "You just did."

"*Brandon.*"

"Yeah," Brandon said, ducking his head. He leaned his weight forward enough to tilt his hips better, for Percy to see him. It hit him suddenly: the memory of bending over in front of his laptop, miserable and angry, watching his viewer counter drop. Only this didn't feel like he was putting on a show for Percy. More like . . . opening himself up, offering himself, giving himself to Percy's pleasure.

"Fuck," Percy murmured. It sounded filthy coming from him. He got a handful of Brandon's ass with his other hand, making Brandon present himself how he wanted. Then he was touching Brandon's hole again, a slow, firmer press, like he was testing how much Brandon would give for him.

And it was a lot.

He breathed, "Fuck," again when Brandon tightened his muscles. "I want . . . do you have . . . ?"

It took a few seconds for Brandon to muddle through what he meant. "I—yeah. Yep."

" . . . Are you going to go get it?"

Brandon blinked. Shook his head. Right. Fuck. "Yeah. Uh huh." He extracted himself from Percy's lap and his hands, stumbling out of his room and heading for his backpack. The DVD they'd left on was cycling through the menu over and over, James Ringer in black and white, shadows falling over his face and eyes shining.

This is all thanks to you.

He'd thought that before. Lots of times.

When he got kicked out. Every time someone said he'd end up no good. *This is all thanks to you, fucker.*

But this? Percy?

"It's all thanks to you," he said under his breath, as sincerely as he'd ever said anything. *For better or worse.* And he went to grab his pack.

CHAPTER
TWENTY-THREE

Percy was so pale he almost blended into his cream sheets.

And Brandon knew that because he'd *taken all his clothes off*.

He almost felt cheated at the fact that he hadn't gotten to unwrap Percy like a Christmas present, but on the other hand, after the way he'd hurt Percy a little just by taking his shirt partway off, maybe it was right to let Percy have some privacy to undress himself. Maybe eventually they'd be close enough that Percy would trust Brandon to help and to listen, trust him enough to ask for what he needed and not be ashamed, but for now this was fine too. Better than fine, actually, because here Brandon was, thinking about them together in some distant, trusting future and not feeling the slightest bit insecure or worried that that eventuality would come to pass.

They were going to be together for a while. Long *enough*, even. Brandon could trust in that.

"Hey you," he said, coming right up to the side of the bed.

Percy wasn't flushed anymore, but his smile was a little faint. "Hey."

Brandon dropped his handful of lube and condoms—three, just in case, who knew—and propped one hip on the bed, sweeping his eyes down Percy's prone body. The starkness of his ribs carried lots of other places: his shoulders, where the socket was outlined under his skin, and his hipbones looked like someone had drawn them on with white marker.

Brandon thought for the first time that Percy looked frail. Like Brandon had to take extra care with him. And he knew Percy wouldn't want him to think like that, even if Brandon was well-meaning. Sure, Percy needed extra consideration, but didn't every guy he'd been with? Did Percy's pain really make sex with him any more precarious than with, say, Alfred, who had told Brandon last time he had two hip replacements? Or Eddie, whose ego required a degree of slavering worship in every act? Or Brandon himself, who couldn't stand being talked to or looked down on, even when his job and his orientation and the rest of it all predisposed people to doing exactly that? Was Percy frail, or did he just have specific needs to be met in order for sex to be good and fun and hot? Or was he both at the same time?

"How do you want me?" Brandon asked, knowing already he'd waited too awkwardly long to say something. Percy didn't look at him. "Perce. Hey."

"Are you going to get tired of this?" Percy said to the wall. It was like he knew exactly what was going on in Brandon's head. "Making concessions?"

"Are *you*?" Brandon asked right back.

Percy startled and turned his head to blink at him. "Maybe," he said eventually. "Maybe I already am. What then?"

"Well, we can figure out how to do this in a way that's good for the both of us, or we can go back and watch some more movies."

"I'm *tired* of movies," Percy said, his eyes narrowed in a way that looked suspiciously like he was trying to keep tears from escaping them. "I'm tired of just watching other people live."

Brandon's chest squeezed. He pushed up to sit on the bed at Percy's side, moving in until they were pressed together. "Is that why you called me back?" He'd never really gotten up the guts to ask, had just taken the break and run with it.

"I—no, I . . . No. No. I called you back because, I dunno. Because you were exciting. Because you made me mad and you made me horny and you made me into one hell of a rebel. Why did you *come* back?"

"Because you gave me a second chance. You didn't write me off altogether. Not many people I can say that about."

Dahlia. Judy.

Brandon twisted and bent, kissing Percy softly just beside his mouth.

"And be honest. You're not tired of movies. You fucking love movies, you colossal nerd. You're tired of watching them *alone*." Brandon ran a hand over Percy's brow, brushing his downy-soft hair back and letting it fall back into place. "But you're *not* alone anymore." *And neither am I.* "So it's okay. You know? We can find out how to have sex together, or we can watch movies. Doesn't matter to me which, because as long as we're together, we're both living."

Percy's throat clicked on a hard swallow. "You're impossible," he sniffed. He ran his bottom lip between his teeth, eyes on Brandon's, then shook his head. "Impossible."

"You have no idea," Brandon replied with a laugh. "I mean, you think I was an asshole the first time we met? That was me on my best behavior, then. You shoulda seen what my *grandmother* had to put up with—"

Shit. That was close. Brandon shook his head, forced his brain to switch tracks.

Because he couldn't . . . could he?

Percy was pretty level-headed, but on the other hand, he was also, if not as creepy as some of the other superfans Brandon was aware of, still very dedicated, and what if he decided Brandon was like the real life version of the queer interview he'd hunted down? What if telling him shot any chance Percy would see Brandon as his own person in the face?

What if telling him would make Brandon lose him?

"Brandon?" Percy said, touching a couple fingertips to his lips.

Brandon shook his head again, dismissing the idea. *Later.* If ever. But definitely *later.*

"Anyway," he said, letting his voice go syrupy. "What's the verdict, babe? You wanna go cuddle under some blankets in your private movie theatre? Or will I . . ." His hand reached out, swept over Percy's bare thigh, fingers barely brushing the base of Percy's half-hard cock.

Percy's eyes squeezed shut, his hands balling up in his bedsheets. "The second one, god. The second one. Fuck it."

"Me," Brandon murmured.

"Huh?"

Brandon circled his hand around Percy's cock and gave it a couple light pulls. Didn't take much to have him hard again. "Fuck *me.*"

"Oh. *Oh.*" Percy cracked an eye open and promptly rolled it at him. "That was terrible."

Brandon laughed. "It was, wasn't it? Sorry. You make me into this cheesy monster."

"Something to put on your resume," Percy said lightly. The rest of the tension bled from his slim shoulders and he reached out to drag a palm over Brandon's closest thigh. "I want you like before. In my lap."

Brandon was moving before Percy even clarified. Some part of him was probably hardwired by now to just do what Percy said, since it usually ended up amazing.

He settled in Percy's lap, this time with nothing between them. Percy's hands fell right back to where they'd been, confidently probing at Brandon's ass. But this time, Brandon wasn't going to let himself be so passive in the show. He grabbed his bottle of lube and drizzled it all over the fingers of one hand, waiting until Percy had him spread open before he reached back.

"Brandon!" Percy gasped, his grip on Brandon's ass tightening deliciously.

Brandon stroked his wet fingertips over his hole, tracing and circling. "Can I?" he asked.

"*May* I?" Percy corrected, so fast Brandon knew it had to be automatic.

For some reason, that turned him on all the more.

He glanced over his shoulder. "*May* I, Percival?"

Percy's straight face cracked immediately. "You're *horrid*. That was—just, yes, go." He pushed Brandon's wrist, mock exasperated. "Go."

Brandon knew this wasn't a performance like the others when the minute he pushed that first finger into himself, he couldn't help but let out a long, guttural moan, like no voluntary sound he'd ever made on cam.

Percy moaned too. Kneaded at Brandon's ass while Brandon fingered himself in slow, teasing plunges. One finger, and then two. It was a thousand times better than doing it by himself, cursorily before an appointment who requested "no gross stuff," or just to get himself off. He could feel Percy watching him, devouring every move he made.

He felt sweat slip down his spine.

And then felt Percy's fingertips tracing the same path.

He buckled forward, catching himself on his free hand. "You can too, you know." He turned his wrist and widened his fingers what little he was able to, opening himself up for Percy to touch. "I can take a couple of yours too. Sound good?"

Percy swore, his thighs tensing under Brandon. He swept his hand down Brandon's spine and then there his fingers were, pressing in next to Brandon's curled ones. "It doesn't hurt?" he asked. His fingers were pointier than Brandon's own, narrower and more bony, and the difference in sensation had Brandon arching his back and whimpering.

"N-no," Brandon replied, quickly, before Percy misunderstood. "God no. It *can* hurt, but not now. Not when I want it so bad. Want *you.*"

"There you go being cheesy again," Percy chuckled.

"Hey, that's *science.*"

"Mmmmhmm."

"It is." Brandon thought so, at least. With as much capacity as he had left to think right now, anyway.

Said capacity swiftly collapsed to zero as soon as Percy pressed his fingers deeper. Then it was two of Brandon's and two of his, and his were pushing Brandon's up at a fucking great angle, making Brandon want to arch his back and try for more, maybe.

He *had* more, waiting and ready.

"This is great 'n all," he said, "but can I—*may* I have your dick now?"

"Hmm."

"Perce, c'mon. *Please.*"

Percy laughed quietly and slid his fingers free with a teasing graze of his thumb around the rim of Brandon's stretched hole. "Since you asked so nicely . . . Face me, though?"

"God yes. Please." Brandon reluctantly withdrew his fingers, reached for a condom with his dry hand, then switched positions so that he was straddling Percy in the opposite direction.

Percy's face and lips were flushed a healthy red, and his long dick was so hard it had fallen backward onto his belly. Brandon reached forward and took it in his lube-slick hand, teasing it, teasing Percy, gently working him over as slowly as Percy had done to Brandon earlier. "Now it's your turn to say please," he said with a smirk, holding up the condom package.

"Which I can do with no problems whatsoever," Percy said, tipping his chin up.

Brandon tilted his head and grinned, rocking in Percy's lap. Not too much. Just enough. "Oh yeah? So go ahead."

Percy cupped Brandon's hips, but said nothing.

Brandon rolled his hips again, shimmying a little. "I can do this alllll day, Perce."

"If that's what does it for you." Percy's smile was small and devious. He pressed his thumbs in under Brandon's hipbones; it felt like they were tangling straight in his nerves. "I'm in no rush." His dick said otherwise, smearing precum on his pale belly.

Brandon gave in anyway. Ripped the condom packet open with his teeth and pulled it out to roll it down over Percy's length. He looked up to find the lube, only to see it in Percy's open hand—and see Percy's smug smile beyond that. "Yeah yeah," he muttered, grabbing the lube and squeezing some onto his fingers to slick up Percy's dick. "Live it up while you can. Someday I'll win."

"Mmhmm."

"I mean it." Brandon shifted forward on his knees and took Percy's dick in hand, lining them up. "Someday."

"Mmmhmmm." Percy's eyes dropped to where Brandon's legs were spread and stayed there, hazy with want. When the blunt head of his cock pressed to Brandon's hole, his eyes fluttered closed, and his lips parted, slick and still red. Veins stood out on his wrists when he gripped the sheets. "Good," he murmured, sounding delirious, as the head of his cock breached Brandon's body. "That's good. Good."

Brandon shuddered and sank down more, until Percy was as deep in him as they could manage. "Fuck." His thighs were trembling; he reached and grabbed Percy's hands, put them there so he could feel what he was doing to Brandon.

"Y-you're okay?" Percy asked. "I'm not hurting you?"

Brandon huffed out a laugh at his concern. "I swear on the soul of James Ringer you are not hurting me in the slightest. I swear on *my* soul that even if you did hurt me now, I'd probably like it."

"You're not supposed to say that kind of thing to people," Percy murmured.

"Yeah, probably not." Brandon flexed his hips, then tried for a slow thrust, long and slick. Percy tossed his head back with a low groan.

"Brandon." Percy's hips shifted underneath him, his cock circling with the movement and tracing Brandon from the inside. "Brandon, Brandon."

"Feel good?" Brandon taunted, rolling his hips and arching his back. He fell back onto his palms and rode Percy with such delicious, perfect smoothness his whole body felt like melting. Percy fit so well between his thighs, they fit so well, the two of them, they fit so well *together*, like this—all the time, really. "You never did say please, y'know."

He meant to stop then, try to tease Percy again, but he didn't have the self-control to. Not when their movements—working in sync, working in opposition, it didn't matter—together had every nerve of his body glowing. Not when Percy was starting to really fall apart under him, making little punched-out noises with every one of Brandon's thrusts.

"Yeah, it feels good," Brandon answered himself. It probably would have sounded insufferably smug, if not for the way he was huffing and puffing, his voice broken up by exertion and just plain pleasure. He shifted forward on his knees, bringing his hands down to brace on the mattress, and Percy's feverish eyes dropped down to where he was buried in Brandon. Brandon grinned, on the edge of saying something filthy when Percy reached out. He half-thought (half-hoped?) Perce was going for his cock, but he wasn't—he found Brandon's hand and clasped his on top of it, pulling it closer to his heaving chest.

So Brandon leaned in the rest of the way, sliding their sweaty chests together, and kissed him. Kissed him slow and deep, tongue needy and stretched, breath coming out in short pants across Percy's lips.

Under his palm, Percy's heart pounded, strong and sure.

"I'm really—" Percy said it into his mouth, like he couldn't bear to pull away from Brandon even an inch. He didn't give Brandon time to answer, just dove back at him, his other hand finding the back of Brandon's neck and sliding into the short hair there to grip.

Brandon was right there too, but he wanted Percy there first, wanted to watch it this time, so he squeezed down around Percy's cock and kissed him harder, clumsily turning his hand over to slide their fingers together. "C'mon," he panted. "C'mon, come for me, Perce. Lemme see you."

He felt Percy seize up, said, "Yeah, like that," but Percy wasn't coming—he was untangling their hands and reaching for Brandon's cock, fingers skating over his thigh and then his stomach before he found it and wrapped his hand around it tight, making Brandon buckle.

Percy's voice was full of the smugness Brandon hadn't been able to manage. He squeezed the back of Brandon's neck and demanded, "You first."

In another, kinder-to-his-ego universe, Brandon would have tried one last time with the whole *say please* taunt.

But here, he just did exactly as he was told.

Percy couldn't help murmuring, "Lovely," as Brandon shuddered through his orgasm. Maybe he wasn't lovely from an outside perspective—he sort of screwed his face up like he was in pain, and there was sweat dripping off his jaw and sticking his hair to his forehead, and he came a *lot*, all over Percy's stomach—but to Percy it was exactly what he wanted, and exactly what he expected, knowing Brandon.

He kept his hand on Brandon's neck and tentatively pushed his hips up, mindful of the pressure. But Brandon moved for him right away, rocking up on his knees to take the weight off his hips and give him room to thrust. Percy didn't last long, not when Brandon did indeed feel fucking *amazing* around Percy's dick as he came, but especially not with Brandon staring down at him, fascinated and flushed, his lush mouth open so he could say Percy's name.

The second he spread his hand open on Percy's cum-covered stomach, Percy was done for. His hips snapped up, his hands crashed to Brandon's hips, and sweet tension pinned him still under Brandon as all his muscles tightened and then released, the buzz of orgasm sweeping from his hips up to his head, washing the pain out of his every nerve.

He blinked at the ceiling, feeling a little stunned.

Brandon squirmed on top of him and then—*squeezed* around him again with a lazy, curly grin before he pushed up and off and collapsed at Percy's side.

"You're a shit," Percy told him. Then he had to clear his throat, because his voice was hoarse and fond. He reached down to tug the condom off, only to find Brandon's hand already there, rolling it off and tossing it away and then wiping him clean with a corner of the sheet. Then he moved closer and buried his face in the side of Percy's chest, draping over him with his arm resting on Percy's stomach— carefully off all his joints. Percy brought his hand up to touch the back of Brandon's neck. Lightly this time, not gripping.

Until Brandon leaned into his palm like a satisfied cat, humming deep in his chest.

It was on the tip of Percy's tongue to ask *do you do this for all your clients?*

But he didn't. Because this didn't feel like client and escort. It felt . . . deeper, wider, skating the breadth of something he wasn't certain of.

His breath hitched.

Brandon lifted his head up, peering at him with red eyes and mussed hair. "S'up? You okay?"

"I think all my bones have been replaced with Jell-O," he quipped, because he couldn't say any of this aloud, couldn't let himself voice it, not when the allure of Schrödinger's Relationship was so much better. Not when Brandon could cut it all off with one quick word, one brusque joke about Percy getting in over his head or expecting too much.

"Mmmm." Brandon dropped his head again and settled over Percy's side, a hot stretch of skin that soothed the swiftly growing ache in his hips.

Percy rubbed his knuckles up and down the back of Brandon's neck, turning the possibilities of them over in his head and listening to Brandon breathe until he realized he was dozing off, and Brandon already had. Half of him wanted to let it happen, let them both sleep as long as they needed to. But the other half knew Hazel had every chance of getting bored of ignoring him and barging in on this.

And then . . .

He didn't want to think about what then.

"Brandon." He roused himself and tapped on the back of Brandon's shoulder. "*Brandon*. Up."

"Mmmno."

"Mmm, yes," Percy responded, tapping him harder. "You promised to feed me, remember?" He had been doing his level best not to seem like he *wanted* it, because the idea of being dependent on Brandon to feed him was ridiculous, but the exercise of sex had made his hunger all the more apparent.

"Oh!" Brandon snapped awake and pushed up on his hands, his hair flat on one side and sticking out on the other in haphazard tufts. "Right. Right, yeah. I . . ." He turned and glanced at the clock, then the window, then groaned. "Aw, fuck. I have my driver with me."

Ah. His company driver. Who . . . probably would not think it was professional for them to be going out to dinner together. Because it wasn't.

Percy chewed on his lip until he was sure he wouldn't sound too disappointed. "That's all right. I'll work it out."

"No, no, dude, I promised you dinner." Brandon leaned over and smacked a quick kiss off Percy's cheek, then scrambled off the bed to scoop up his clothes. And wasn't *that* a lovely view. Brandon caught him looking and shook his hips with a shit-eating grin. "Here, let's do this," he said, tugging his jeans up over his bare hips. "I'm gonna go home and, uh, shower, you know, and then I'll come pick you up myself. How's that?"

Percy blinked at him. "Off the clock?"

Brandon paused in the middle of buttoning up his shirt. "Uh . . . yeah. I guess so." He bit his lip, wariness creeping into his bright eyes. "That okay?"

"Yes!" Now he sounded overeager, but Percy couldn't bring himself to care. The chance to go *out*, not on the clock . . . Just the two of them going out because they wanted to . . .

He would get a stern talking-to from Hazel, he knew.

If she noticed.

If she even cared.

He could say they'd gone to LAPL's main branch. It was open on Saturdays, and Percy had browsed its catalogue enough that he could

tell her what they'd looked at that was relevant to his film degree. Yes .
. . the library and then dinner, of course, because they had been out so
long. It was only sensible.

Brandon dropped down on the mattress in front of him. Bounced
a couple times. "Percy? You with me?"

Percy smiled, barely holding back a laugh at his puppyish
excitement. Was he really that eager to tote Percy around town? "Yes,
I'm here." He leaned forward and kissed Brandon briefly. "Do you
really want to do this? I can take care of myself."

"I know. But if I go home, I'm just gonna watch . . ." He shrugged
and flushed. "To be honest, I'll probably watch more of James Ringer's
stuff and drink shitty beer until I fall asleep on the couch again."

Again?

"So I'd rather go out with you."

Percy smothered another smile. "Go out?" Brandon shrugged,
jerkily this time. Percy knew the telltale signs of his embarrassment by
now and needled him a little more. "*Out* out? Should I wear a suit?
Tie? Dress like your best guy?"

"You *are* my best guy," Brandon muttered. He kissed Percy on the
mouth—presumably to keep him from responding, which was better
for the both of them, all things considered—and stood, patting his
pockets down. "Seriously, let me go home and get stuff taken care of
and then I'm all yours. An hour at most."

He kissed Percy again, a chaste, sweet "off to work" kiss straight
from TV sitcoms, and practically fled the bedroom. Percy heard him
pick his backpack up and call, "Bye!" and then he was out, the suite
door thumping closed behind him.

Percy lay still for a moment, listening to him thud down the
stairs and then outside, leaving a trail of life and noise through the
cavernous house.

A car motor rumbled. Gravel crunched all the way down the
drive.

Silence descended, except for the faint hissing spit of the
automatic lawn sprinklers outside.

Percy stared at his window sill, his heart pounding wildly, like
it was trying to fill in the spaces Brandon left empty every time he
walked out.

"I'm in trouble," he murmured to himself. So, so much trouble.

If Kovie had been surprised by him hiring an escort . . . what would she think of him starting to fall in love with one?

CHAPTER
TWENTY-FOUR

his?

Percy sent a snapshot of himself in a black and gray vest and a dark gray sweater—the fifth sweater he'd tried—over a pair of dark jeans.

Kovie's text came back almost immediately. *Find a shirt lighter and not so heavy but keep the vest, it's sharp*, with a thumbs-up emoticon. *No bowtie!!!* she sent a second later. *He's seen you naked you don't need a bowtie*

Percy glanced guiltily at the hanger full of them he'd laid on his freshly made bed. *Okay.*

He swapped out his sweater for a forest green, long-sleeved collared shirt and rolled the sleeves up, examining his reflection before buttoning the vest again. This time, his picture was met with *five* thumbs-up emoticons.

And then, just to be a shit and because Brandon wasn't here yet, he took another picture adding a green and black plaid bowtie to the ensemble.

The text back was nearly instantaneous.

Percy I swear to god I will come over there

Two seconds later: *And I am totally naked right now so it will not be pretty for either of us*

Percy laughed as he texted her back. *Okay, okay.*

You nervous? About tonight?

He gave himself a once-over in his mirror, trying to pick out any signs of unease in his features. His stomach was rumbling, but that was hunger, not nerves. *No? Should I be?*

Nah. We already know you can handle him ;)

Be honest. Do you think it's . . . weird that I'm seeing him like this?

Off the clock?

Don't take this the wrong way but I'm not all that familiar with the etiquette of seeing escorts. But hey, if he's cool with it and you're cool with it, then that's what matters.

Are you regretting not putting me in contact with a pot dealer now?

Hell no. This is way cooler

I think I might like him, like like him, Percy typed, and then deleted it, replacing it with, *Never thought in a million years someone would call me or anything I do cool.*

I come from a pretty high standard of cool too so take it as a real compliment

I do, he sent, just as he heard gravel crunching on the driveway. He nearly dropped his phone in his haste to get around the bed and look out, make sure it was Brandon.

And he . . . thought it was. He would have pegged Brandon as the type to own a beat-up nineties car, or even a motorbike, but the car rolling up the drive was vintage and sky blue. A Mercedes?

He stood by the window until the car reached the head of the driveway, and then—oh, yes, it was Brandon. Still wearing the same jeans from their appointment, but was wearing aviators and he'd swapped out his old denim jacket for a more modern one over a light T-shirt. Percy waved, and Brandon waved back, making a *come on* gesture.

Percy grabbed his phone and his shiny house key—had he ever had to take it anywhere with him before?—and hurried out the door. Hazel was nowhere in sight, the door to her suite tightly closed. Once upon a time, he'd have felt obligated to knock and ask for her permission to leave—not that he'd left without his parents in a very long time—but now? He brushed past it and downstairs, his leather shoes squeaking on the clean floors, every step echoing uninterrupted into the depths of the house.

Brandon was waiting outside, leaning on the driver's side flank of the car with his aviators pushed up into his hair. "Hey," he called, peeling away from the car and coming . . . was he coming to open Percy's *door* for him? "Nice bowtie."

"Bow . . .?" Oh *god,* he'd left it on. He felt himself flushing as he reached up to undo it. "I didn't mean to—"

"No, I like it!" Brandon closed his hands over Percy's, then jerked a look at the house and let go of him. "Uh, leave it on." He laid a hand in the small of Percy's back, guiding him to the car's open passenger side door. "C'mon."

"R-right," Percy agreed, and accepted Brandon's help into the low seat of the car. It was all clean navy blue leather inside, and he saw with relish that none of it had been restored or swapped out for newer technology. The radio was dilapidated and two of its buttons were permanently pushed in, but its silver knobs were shiny and Percy was reaching for them before he could stop himself.

"Like that?" Brandon asked, dropping into the driver's seat.

Percy hummed an absent response. "This is yours?"

"Yep." Brandon twisted the keys and started it up; it rumbled around them, grinding a little. "It was, uh. It was my grandmother's."

"O-oh," Percy replied. Brandon hadn't said much about his family, but what he *had* said had sounded sad and guarded, so Percy forced himself not to pry. Which was easier said than done, because a car like this came with a story.

Brandon, in the driver's seat, jiggled his leg and drummed his fingers on the steering wheel.

"Are you okay? I, um, look, I'm really happy to be doing this with you but I have this feeling it's not . . . usual and maybe it's kind of crossing some boundaries for you so if you're having second thoughts—"

"No!" Brandon squeaked. "No. No. Perce, no. I *want* this."

Relief hit Percy so hard it nearly blanked out everything else.

Brandon chewed his lip. "I really, really want this. Maybe too much for my own good." He swallowed. When he went on, his voice was thick. "As soon as I got home I thought about calling my boss and asking her what she thought because you're right I don't think this *is* normal and actually I think it's downright unprofessional, but you know I had my phone in my hand ready to call her and I just put it back down again because I don't even want to hear her answer." He sucked in a breath, his fingers curling around the thin steering wheel. "Which basically means I already know her answer, but fuck it. Because that's how much I wanna do this."

"I'll try and not make you regret it," Percy said gently, touching his shoulder. Suddenly he felt like taking a deep breath, too, overwhelmed by the shift from the lazy, playful Brandon he knew to this. He had to give something back—not because it was obligated, but because he *wanted* to. He wanted to keep whatever he could of Brandon.

"Look, can I just say? I want this too." He let his fingers brush against the side of Brandon's neck, where his hair curled a little. "I don't know what's going to happen, or how this is going to change things, or *if* it's going to change things, but I don't care. I'm willing to risk it. For you. With you."

Brandon looked up at him, and his expression was awed and watery. His smile trembled, but then he gave his head a shake. "All right, my newly minted risk-taker. Let's get out of here before we wind up making out in your parents' driveway. Not that making out doesn't sound like a great time, but I think you're really gonna dig the restaurant I'm taking you to."

Brandon had planned and agonized over every detail of this evening: how to groom himself, what to wear, whether he ought to spend some time super cleaning Dahlia's car, whether to call Judy, whether to call Percy and cancel because this whole thing was completely goddamn crazy and *what the fuck was he thinking getting this personal with a goddamn customer*. But the one thing he hadn't had to agonize over, was where to take Percy on their totally inappropriate date.

They didn't talk much on the way there, but it wasn't an awkward silence. Percy kept touching the car—the console, the seats, the radio. Brandon didn't even bother pulling the "stop changing stations, it's my car" asshole move because he was too fascinated watching Percy be entranced.

And trying not to crash the car while he did.

Percy straightened up as soon as he noticed what part of town they were rolling into. Brandon swung Dahlia's car into a parking space in front of Canter's and reached for the handful of quarters he'd stuffed in his pocket to cover parking. It was a trip to think that last time he'd been here he'd had to take the bus because he didn't have the cash to pay the month's insurance for the Mercedes, not to mention gas. And, well, he'd done that pretty much every time he had to go somewhere before that, too. As a teenager, he'd just walked or hitchhiked everywhere, or caught a ride with a guy who looked at him a little too long. Back then, getting twenty bucks *and* a ride for a BJ was almost a goddamn miracle.

Now he had more than enough from work to park *and* treat Percy to dinner, and not even worry one bit about it.

He twisted the keys out of the ignition and eyed the road so he wouldn't get his door knocked off, then slipped out and hurried around to get Percy's open. Percy emerged with a wry smile and gave Brandon a little half-bow, half-curtsy. "Thanks for your services, Jeeves."

"Any time, sir."

Percy's eyes widened and his cheeks turned ruddy. Brandon grinned at him, and he looked away, coughing into his sleeve.

Brandon laughed, patting him on the back. "Anything else I can do for you, *sir*?" he drawled, feeding quarters into the meter to give Percy time to recover. Or maybe both of them—he was feeling hot under the collar himself.

Percy gave him an arch look. "Take me inside," he ordered. After a second, he offered his arm.

Aw, hell.

There was no reason to pretend anything here. No reason to pretend they were tutor and student, or just friends, or client and hooker.

He leaned in and kissed Percy's cheek, cupping the other side of his face because he looked so goddamn sweet standing there in the reflection of the neon light and offering to escort Brandon inside. Sweet and sharp, in his tight vest and tight jeans and his dorky but somehow stupidly hot bowtie.

Percy blinked at him. "What was that for?"

"'Cause I wanted to." Brandon kissed him on the corner of his mouth. "That okay with you?"

"I suppose. It's a terrible burden, but I can bear it." Percy's smarmy little smirk made Brandon want to pin him against the car and lick it off him. But instead he skipped linking arms with Percy in favor of wrapping an arm around his lower back . . . and then, on a whim, slipping his hand into Percy's back pocket.

"C'mon, kid," he said, steering Percy toward the deli's polished doors. "I'm about to give you a nerdgasm."

And give Percy one he did.

"This place!" he nearly shouted, eyes huge, head swiveling in every direction trying to take it all in. Brandon had never seen him this animated before. He was practically a puppy. "This place! Brandon!" He slapped Brandon's shoulder. "Look at this bakery case!" He rushed forward, and Brandon could see in his body language how much effort it was taking him not to smoosh his hands and face against the glass. "Look at this!"

"It's been open since the 1930s," Brandon said, recalling Judy's own spiel. "Marilyn Monroe used to eat here all the time. And you know who else?"

Percy stared at him, holding his breath.

"James Ringer. Believe it."

Percy slapped him again, this time with both hands, peppering his shoulders and chest with excited little blows that didn't hurt a bit. "And we get to eat here? Do you think he had a favorite booth? Can we *ask*?"

Brandon's heart felt full to bursting with a kind of happiness he'd never felt before, except for maybe in happy childhood memories of Dahlia. He knocked Percy on the chin with a loosely curled knuckle. "For you? Anything."

Percy's attempts to ask a waitress about James Ringer's favorite booth sadly didn't turn up any concrete leads, but after she seated them in a not-quite-so-significant booth, Percy still bounced in his seat and petted the red vinyl appreciatively, announcing, "I've communed with the Reuben sandwich spirits and they say this is *definitely* James Ringer's booth."

With that decided, Percy resumed a running narration of what he saw in the restaurant's features, sharing his appreciation for every little vintage touch in the decor or the service. Brandon, chin in his hand, just sat there rapt and hanging onto every word, the two of them so engrossed with each other that they didn't even notice the waitress's arrival.

Percy startled when he finally noticed she was there, and Brandon ducked his head in embarrassment when he realized that was *not* her first time saying, "What can I get for you boys?"

"Oh! Um," Percy gave the menu another quick once over. "You know what? A Reuben, please. And a pint of Guinness." He winked at Brandon. "For strength."

Brandon ordered a three egg omelet with spinach and extra chicken and a black coffee.

"C'mon, get a beer with me," Percy cajoled him as soon as he'd ordered. "Don't make a guy drink alone. I won't tell your personal trainer."

Brandon felt the blush come up hot and humiliating. "I . . . Perce, I can't."

Percy's face fell. "Oh. Oh god, I'm sorry, are you—did you—no, I shouldn't pry. I'm sorry for pressuring you." He gave the waitress a pained look as she took their menus.

He wouldn't have thought it was possible to blush harder than he already was, but he did. "Oh Perce, jeez. I'm not a recovering alcoholic or anything. I just . . ." He chewed his lip, getting hotter and hotter by the second. He had to spill it, though, embarrassed or not. Couldn't stand the sorry look on Percy's face for one second longer. "I'm not legal. Yet. I'm nineteen."

"You have got to be kidding." Percy stared at him. "You're not kidding. Oh my God, Brandon, I'm a cradle robber!"

"Shhh! Oh my God, no you're not," he hissed back. "Not unless you're, like, thirty-five." He gave Percy a level look. "You're not thirty-five, are you?"

Percy made a face with about three different expressions in one before his shoulders slumped. "I was going to try to tease you, but I don't think I can hold it. I'm twenty-one. I honestly figured you were older than me."

Brandon leaned back to look at him. " . . . Really?" He wondered half a second if that came out wrong and added, "I mean, that'd be a first for me. Usually people think I'm younger."

"It's the . . ." Percy gestured to his jaw.

"Oh." Brandon rubbed it absently. Fought through the sudden urge to tell Percy who he was, why he had a jaw like this, why he *felt* older than nineteen, why he'd dreaded for so long being the same age Percy was now . . . But the potential consequences listed off in the back of his head, clicking and clattering like an old film reel, and the urge faded fast. "Yeah, I guess. So why didn't *you* think I was younger?"

Percy stared down into his lap for a solid thirty seconds, ignoring his drink when the waitress set it down. "Your eyes," he finally replied, so soft Brandon had to strain to hear.

Brandon swirled his straw and guessed, "They're the same as his?"

Percy looked up suddenly. Shook his head. "They just seem . . . experienced. I wouldn't have called them 'wise', not after our first meeting at least, but I look at you and I can tell your eyes have seen a lot of things."

How could Brandon go from being insulted Percy didn't think he resembled his grandfather enough to being touched for the same reason? Maybe because this time there was no sense of judgment or disappointment, only recognition.

Recognition that he was his own man, his own person with his own past and his own future. Recognition he could have the same face as someone and not *be* him.

Recognition which he'd been waiting and hoping his whole life for.

And if he revealed who he really was, that his name wasn't just Brandon, that it was Brandon Ringer, as in *the* Ringer?

Would Percy still see him the same way?

Now he was almost sure Percy wouldn't, and it ached, but not as much as it could have. Not as much as it would have if he'd given in and told him, and lost him.

He needed a distraction for them both, so he nodded at a poster for one of James's films, tacked on the wall a few booths down from theirs. "Wonder if people said that about him."

"Oh, I'm sure." And then Percy was running again, talking about James's rise to fame and pausing every once in a while to say, "I'm sure you know this already, but . . ." and then keeping right on anyway.

Brandon just . . . watched him.

He was so different here, now, from the Percy who had called him that first day. Out here there was no Hazel to worry about, no strict time and noise constraints. It was just them, and Percy, ruthlessly loving the things he loved.

Tell him. Just get it over with, find out now if you could be one of those things.

Or if it's only James.

God, he really couldn't go two weeks without trying to self-destruct, huh?

"So . . ." Percy trailed off however long later. He shrugged and took a sip of his beer. "You know."

He was hyperaware that he was five words from finding out exactly what Percy would think of him, what Percy would do, if he knew.

And there was the slight, fractional, miniscule possibility he hadn't let himself consider: that Percy would take James Ringer as part of Brandon, instead of Brandon as a novelty, and as a small, touchable, ownable part of James Ringer.

He licked his lips. "Hey Perce?"

"Hmmm?"

"My las—"

"Which one of you had the omelet?" a waiter interrupted, shoving a plate under Brandon's nose.

"That's him," Percy replied cheerfully. "Although wow, I wish it was me, that looks amazing! What's on it?"

Brandon put all his effort into not thunking his head down on the table.

"Thanks," he mumbled when the waiter set his omelet down in front of him.

Percy reached across the table to touch his hand. "You all right, Brandon?"

My last name is Ringer.

He could just open his mouth and do it now. Say it.

But the moment was gone.

For better or worse.

"A-OK," he said, picking his fork up and gently tapping the back of Percy's wrist with it. "Your sandwich everything you dreamed about?"

"*So* good," Percy replied through a comically full mouth.

Brandon had never seen him use such bad manners before, and the sight had him forgetting all the disappointment of his failed confession. He reached out across the table, laying a hand on Percy's. "I'm really happy we did this," he said.

Percy nodded, chewed, swallowed. "Yeah. Me too. This place is amazing."

"Yeah," Brandon agreed.

This place, and you.

CHAPTER
TWENTY-FIVE

He dropped off Percy with a reckless, lingering kiss. Tried to offer to help the guy to his door—he was looking especially stiff after their outing, walking like his knees wouldn't bend—but Percy turned him down with a smile and a ruffle of his hair. "You're a gentleman, babe," he said by way of goodbye, and then, "See you later?"

"I'll have my people call your people," Brandon joked back, because it was easier than trying to clarify whether that *see you later* involved the exchange of money. It would happen how it happened, and he wouldn't ruin their day *or* their night by worrying about it too much.

Already he was dreading a week without Percy's company, his days and nights off spent alone doing various fix-up work in Dahlia's house or watching James Ringer movies on his laptop in bed.

At least his paying customers didn't leave him lonely. Harvey had booked him for the following Friday night and Brandon was feeling cautiously optimistic about the possibility of actually pleasing the man's . . . particular tastes. He read Theresa's email thoroughly; again, she noted Harvey had admitted to liking rough sex, but this time she'd put a note of her own telling Brandon that Harvey expected manners.

Okay. Okay. He'd fucked it up once, but that was like a completely different Brandon. This time, he was ready. He knew what to expect, *and* he had a better attitude about the whole thing, not to mention a new appreciation for the role he was playing, thanks to Percy. Though it would be harder now to grovel and apologize to Harvey, since he knew about the interview, and about James's sexuality. It had been easy to tell himself James deserved to be punished when he'd held the memory of all those cheating rumors and the taste of Dahlia's sadness on the back of his tongue, but until he was *sure* that wasn't as false as James Ringer's supposed lack of talent . . .

Well, he'd just have to pull out all his acting stops. He had to have at least a *sliver* of talent.

He could do this. And he had five days to psych himself up.

Five days in which he had three sessions with Judy's—and his own, now—trainer, as well as a Wednesday appointment with a new client. New to Brandon and to the agency, which . . . no pressure. God damn.

He wasn't letting his nerves get the best of him or anything, but it helped that as he was getting ready to leave on Wednesday night, Theresa emailed him Percy's latest review. Five stars and politely vague, but there were a few choice phrases that Brandon could tell were for him. He emailed Theresa back a quick thanks.

You're really racking them up!! she sent back. *What are you doing this weekend? I was thinking of having a lunch on Saturday.*

As much as he liked her, no way could he cancel on Percy. He stuck his house key between his teeth and slung his backpack over his shoulder, tapping out his reply on his phone. *I could make it for dinner probably?*

Mmmmm, I can't do dinner. I have a hot date. ;)

Brandon blinked at his phone. He'd sort of assumed she was married already. *With who?*

It's a secret. <3

He'd bribe her with tea next time he saw her in person, he decided. Then he stopped short, because . . . he actually *cared*. He wasn't just mmhmm-ing at a coworker's anecdote or halfheartedly listening to someone talk about their kid or their wife or the guy down the street who parked like an asshole every day or the ex-girlfriend who was dating someone. He actually gave a shit about Theresa's personal life, enough that he would email her on Sunday to see how her date went. Enough that he really did feel sorry about not being able to see her Saturday.

Hey, good luck, he sent back. *Let's do something though. Lunch.*

OK! Have fun at your appt tonight. :)

And you on your hot date Saturday ;););)

He jogged outside to meet Cyrus. He reread Percy's review on his phone all the way there to combat Cyrus's usual silence.

It was a new hotel, one Brandon had never been to or seen before. It was probably fifteen stories, huge and square, with a big neon sign out front and a movie theatre-style announcement board under it. Now the block letters advertised Easter specials and their special "room with a view AND a pool!!!"

The lights from it glinted off Cyrus's window as he pulled the car away, heading toward temporary parking. Good riddance. Brandon hiked his backpack higher and adjusted the collar of his jacket.

The restaurant and bar was a floor under the lobby, down a set of wide wooden steps. It didn't have any windows, but there were a bunch of Tiffany lamps scattered around, keeping the place well-lit. Brandon bypassed the hostess's stand and headed for the bar as usual, letting his backpack drop to lean against the bar under his stool.

"Help you?" a bartender drawled, popping his gum.

"Just Coke." Brandon passed a five across to him.

"That's it?"

"That's it."

The bartender raised his eyebrows. "Whatever, man, your drink." He slid an icy glass across and Brandon leaned over it, settling in to wait.

And wait.

And wait.

Twenty minutes in, he checked his phone for a cancellation email from Theresa.

Half an hour: two teenage girls having dinner a few tables down kept whispering to each other and looking at him in clear pity. Something sour curdled in his stomach.

By the end of an hour, even the bartender seemed sorry for him. "On the house, bro." He handed Brandon a shot of whiskey.

Brandon tossed it back, because why the hell not?

He couldn't think of *one time* this had happened before. Not even when he was tricking out of hotels or groping guys in cabs. Not once had anyone left him hanging or decided you know what, nah, they'd rather not.

It was stupid, he told himself, letting his shot glass clink to the bar. Maybe the guy had been delayed at work, or his wife had found his appointment confirmation—or hell, his husband, Brandon didn't know his life. A million little things could have happened to him, and none of them had anything to do with Brandon himself.

So why did Brandon feel so weird about it?

After an hour and a half, he cleaned his sorry ass up and left, trudging his way sullenly back to Cyrus's car.

Cyrus already knew what had happened.

Because of course he did.

Had probably been hoping and praying for this moment since the day they'd met.

Didn't keep him from being his usual charming self, though. "What the fuck?" he said, getting out of the car. "You made me wait out here for an hour and a half for *nothing*."

"I—"

"The guy doesn't show up in half an hour, you book it," Cyrus snarled, throwing his half-smoked cigarette to the asphalt. "I got other things to do, other places to be, other jobs I could work. Newsflash: if you don't get paid, I don't get paid. You're costing me money just having me sit around all these fucking places lately, wasting gas. If you wanna piss your time away, do it when you don't have my car waiting. I never have this problem with the girls. They're in, out, done. But you fucking queers think it's your damn job to *cuddle* or whatever afterward, and baby your 'clients,' and I'm supposed to wait on you hand and foot and look after you like you're fucking Madonna." He jabbed Brandon in the chest with one finger. "Don't you ever fool yourself into thinking you're anything other than a piece of ass. You're not like one of the girls who can flash their tits and get a job anywhere she wants, college degree or not. You're going to be stuck in this job *forever*," he snarled, with renewed vigor roiling. But his tone broke, too, and he whipped around to face the windshield, hiding his face. "You're going to be stuck in this job forever because no one's ever going to buy you as anything other than a whore."

"What the fuck is your problem?" Brandon burst out. "If you don't like us, then why the fuck do you drive us around? Why do you drive me around at all if you think I'm just a washed-up going-nowhere *fag*?" He expected Cyrus to flinch at the slur, but he didn't.

If anything, it seemed to strengthen his resolve. He jerked the car through a hard left turn and said, "I have something to tell you, just you wait and see."

Brandon scowled at the back of his seat. He wanted to pretend he wasn't intimidated or worried by Cyrus's steely silence, but it made him squirm.

And when Cyrus pulled up in front of Dahlia's house and turned the engine off, Brandon knew he'd been right to be anxious.

Cyrus twisted around in his seat to glare at Brandon, his eyes dark. "You listen to me," he said. "I'm not stupid."

"I never said you—"

"I know whose house this is."

Brandon froze.

Cyrus's smile was nasty. "You thought you could have me come pick you up here every week and I wouldn't know? You think I'm some ignorant dumbass like your cushy clients? That I'd see this address and your face and not put two and two together? I notice. I notice things, *Brandon Ringer*."

Fuck. *Fuck fuck fuck.*

All he could think for a long second was: *thank god I didn't tell Perce, too.*

Which wasn't fair to Percy.

But life wasn't fair.

"So what," Brandon said flatly. "What do you want?"

Cyrus shrugged. "It depends what *you* want. Either I can go to the press and tell them the Ringer boy is selling his ass and pretending to be his granddad to get his rocks off, or you can compensate me a little for all the time you make me spend waiting."

Brandon gritted his teeth. The shock faded fast, replaced by a twisting knot of *you knew this would happen*. He'd known from the beginning this was a risk, putting his face out there. That someone, somewhere along the line would make the connection and turn to blackmail—or go to the press directly and let *them* pay for the scoop. And now it had gotten him in exactly the trouble he'd wondered if it would.

That didn't mean he had to lie down and take it.

"Fuck that," he said. "And fuck *you*. If you're so bored of sitting around doing your job, ask Vince to get someone else to drive me."

Cyrus scoffed. "That's not how this business works, kiddo. I know you're used to being chauffeured around by anyone and everyone who thinks it's a privilege to kiss your ass, but I'm not like that. You can't always get what you want."

Brandon's vision fuzzed at the edges. At first he thought it was because he was going to *cry*, but no—he was just so angry it was making him dizzy. He grabbed for the car door handle and wrenched it open, spilling out onto the driveway with his bag dangling from one hand. He slammed the door behind him and lit out for the front steps because he really didn't want to punch Cyrus. He really didn't want to yell "I quit, fuck you!" and take his shirt off and storm out. He would do just about anything to keep this job from being like all his others.

He'd already done so much.

He came to a stop on the bottom step and clenched his hands, staring at the white cement.

Then he took a deep breath, tossed his pack up on the porch, and went back to the car.

Cyrus rolled his window down, looking smarmy as all get out. "Well?"

"Well nothing." Brandon rested a hand on the roof of the car and bent down to look Cyrus in the face. "I totally get it. You're right. If you don't want to wait around for me, that's fine. See ya, bud. I'll drive myself to my own appointments from now on. Thanks for *everything*."

Cyrus's stunned silence was almost, *almost* enough to make up for this shitshow of a day. It would have been if Cyrus hadn't opened his mouth a few seconds later and said, "Don't think you're firing me."

Brandon curled his fingers on top of the car, fingernails scraping metal. "Then what."

"You drive yourself, but I keep my job. And my paycheck," Cyrus said, perfectly calm now. "I'm still going to have to go through the trouble of taking Theresa's calls, so I think it's only fair I get what I'm supposed to get."

Without actually doing the work.

And conscript Brandon into the whole scheme.

"No," he said. "No way. You hate your job? Fine. I get that. I've been there. But I'm not gonna lie for you."

Cyrus shrugged. "Sure then. You know, Hollywood Doubles keeps very thorough record books. I get all my appointments listed on my invoices for my checks. I wonder what TMZ would think of all 'Jim Ringer's' appointments?"

"No one would care," Brandon bit out. "James Ringer died sixty years ago. It'd be a day's news and then gone."

"You and I both know that's not true, *bud*. You want me to keep quiet, then you keep quiet, too."

Brandon stared down at him. Any ounce of sympathy he may have once had for the guy—had a family to provide for, hated the job he was overqualified and probably underappreciated for—was gone now. "You know," he said, "maybe if you gave enough of a shit to get to know us, you'd think different. Your life's hard? So's mine."

As soon as it was out of his mouth, he knew he'd said the wrong thing.

Cyrus barked out a laugh. "Wow. You're really a lot more stupid than you look, aren't you? You think you know what a hard life is? Living here? Getting driven around and getting fat tips from rich faggots—" oh, there it was "—who have nothing better to do with their money? You think *your life is hard*?" The sheer venom in his words made Brandon stumble back.

"You wouldn't know hard if it smacked you across the face," Cyrus finished. "I ought to take everything I have to the press right now just for that."

So go ahead. I don't care. Look how much of a shit I don't give.

That was the old Brandon.

"Don't," new Brandon said, clenching his fists at his sides.

Cyrus's nasty smile came back. "So we've got a deal."

No.

Fuck you.

I quit.

I don't care.

But he did care. He'd let himself care.

He didn't *want* to quit.

Not this time.

This time, he didn't want to walk away from any of it.

His job. Dahlia's house. James Ringer's legacy.

Percy.

"Yeah," he said. "We've got a deal."

CHAPTER
TWENTY-SIX

Hazel's cooking strike lasted four days.

Percy was sure she intended on him being miserable and hungry enough to beg for mercy by Sunday, and maybe he would have . . . before the glorious invention of online takeout orders. As it was, the worst inconvenience she'd caused him was the bloating he was getting from eating so much fatty food. He'd barely resisted the urge to text Brandon a photo of his newly rounded belly, just to see if he got a sexier one back.

He hadn't texted Brandon at all, actually. Nor Kovie. Brandon because he was paranoid, Kovie because he knew she would ask in an instant what was wrong, why he was "off."

Having finally given up on her fruitless efforts to break him—and probably worrying about job security, considering she'd never done anything like this before and Percy finally had something "real" to take to his parents if he wanted to—Hazel stomped in with breakfast on Tuesday, hardly sparing a word for Percy between setting the tray down and scooping up the bag he'd used to collect all his takeout containers. Breakfast was small: one soft-boiled egg, two pieces of toast, and half an orange. Nothing like the spreads she used to put together, which, though he couldn't finish them most of the time, left him with something to pick at over the course of the mornings.

He'd only be able to pick at this, too; his stomach was still too tender to handle much at one time. He certainly wasn't about to credit Hazel with predicting that might be the result of his diet the last few days, not when it was so much more *likely* that she'd intended the portion and plating to be prison-esque, a continuation of his punishment.

It wasn't the breakfast that got to him, though; it was what was missing from his tray.

"Where are my pills?" he asked when she came back in with a glass of water, trying to keep his voice light.

Even when she hadn't been cooking for him, she'd still come in twice a day with his pills and a tall glass of lukewarm water to take them with.

"Oh, you still need those?" she asked, her voice as artificially friendly as his own. She set the glass down without looking at him, didn't give him a hint of her expression, just busied herself with tidying his room.

His hands started to shake. "Of course I need them." He watched her move around. Watched her *ignore* him. And suddenly he knew this was her next move, her next tactic. If food didn't work . . . He swallowed with a dry throat. "Hazel. *Hazel.* Look at me."

She didn't.

"Hazel, I need my pills. You're a nurse. You know that."

She slapped down the armful of clothes she had. "I thought you'd found *better* pain management."

The *fuck*? "Excuse me?"

She braced her hands on her hips and stared him down. "I told you. You may have fooled your parents into believing this farce about hiring a tutor, but that boy you've been seeing is no academic, and the money you're giving him—"

Oh, God. The keylogger. Had she found out about Brandon's real job?

Percy's mouth moved soundlessly. His hands trembled. "It's my money, and I can pay him whatever I want. He's good at his job."

"Oh, I'm *sure* he is. Quite good, actually. He's obviously bringing you some alternative medication, or as those of us in the real adult world like to call it, *illegal drugs.*"

Illegal . . .

She thought Brandon was a *drug dealer*?

Relief hit him first, at the fact that she hadn't discovered Brandon's real identity, followed quickly by dread, because thinking him to be a drug dealer wasn't, in fact, any better than him being a sex worker.

Although Kovie would get a kick out of it, if the accusation hadn't come with trying to withhold his meds.

"I'm not doing drugs," Percy said, and his teeth were chattering he was so terrified and furious. "I swear to you, I'm not. And I'm sorry you're angry with me, but you can't withhold my meds."

"Oh yes I can. I talked with your parents, and they agree this is the only logical explanation for your erratic behavior lately. I'm sorry, Percy, but until you come clean about this visitor of yours and the drugs he's selling you, I cannot responsibly give you your medications." Her voice was icy. Not one bit of the syrupy hovering over-care from before remained. Percy didn't want it back, but he'd take that over this any day. "Did you even stop to consider that whatever this boy has been giving you could be toxic with your pills? That you're upsetting the chemical balance of your body? I won't be held responsible if your own carelessness puts you in a bad situation."

"He's not *giving me anything*!" Percy shoved his tray away and stumbled out of his bed, shaking all over now. He didn't know how to convince her otherwise without telling the truth. His mind was blank. "He's not giving me anything," he repeated, flatly. Uselessly. "And you can't keep my medication from me, not legally."

Hazel shrugged and went back to rearranging. "It's perfectly legal. I'm your caretaker, and withholding something I think may be a threat to your health is not only legal, it's part of my job. There's nothing I can do to help you if you won't confess what it is you've been doing."

"You have no proof. My parents—"

"Your parents trust my judgment."

"This isn't okay. Even I know it isn't. Even if I was doing drugs—which I'm *not*—you can't take away my pills as punishment. You *can't do that*. I'll get them myself." He glared her down. "Do you understand that? I got food myself, I cleaned my rooms myself, and I could get my own medication myself."

"How? Do you know where I keep them? No. And even if you did, I've moved them, and they're under lock and key now. Listen to me. I'm not taking away your pills as punishment, Percival. I'm taking them away for your own safety. I've I already explained that." Her mouth twisted into something that—somewhere horrible and dank and cruel—might be described as a motherly smile. "But, for your own good, your *punishment* is me taking away your privileges of leaving this house, with . . . *him* or anyone else, as well as your phone and computer access. It's obvious all this stemmed from me not keeping a constant eye on you, so I'll have to rectify that, won't I?"

"B—*Jim* is coming on Saturday. He's already booked."

"Well, far be it from me to tamper with his schedule. You can use your appointed time together as an opportunity to tell him in person to never come here again, or your parents will have him arrested. And that girl, too. Don't think I didn't notice all this started when you met her."

Percy couldn't breathe. "No," he managed to get out. "No, I—I. No, you can't. Kovie's my friend."

"Which proves you have very, *very* questionable taste in friends. I looked into your *tutor*, too." Percy's stomach dropped to the floor. He must have paled, too, because Hazel gave him a grim nod. "Funny how I couldn't find any advertisement for his services in any school postings, or even any advertisement for film studies tutors, period." Hazel turned on her heel, heading for the door. "I think I've adequately made my point. I won't argue about this anymore." She slammed the door behind her.

Percy's eyes watered. He felt like he was walking through mud, struggling to reach a point of clarity beyond thinking *this isn't happening* over and over. *That didn't just happen. This isn't true.*

Any slight trace of relief had been wiped away, because this was worse, this was a thousand times worse. If she'd found out Brandon was a sex worker, she might have just barred him from the house—and Percy knew by now they could find ways around that. But withholding Percy's pills for an indeterminate amount of time for a reason Percy couldn't even disprove, and cutting him off from everyone, everything . . .

There went his easy solution to his lack of food as well.

And his parents were leaving it all up to her. Of course. Complaining wouldn't get him anywhere except taken to the doctor, maybe, so they could leave him there for the specialists to poke and prod at, trying to sniff out the imaginary damage he'd done to his body. Sure, a drug test would prove his innocence, but only for that brief moment before Hazel whispered in his parents' ears about all the ways drug tests could be fooled or foiled.

And even if they *did* believe Percy wasn't doing drugs, what would their explanation for Brandon be then?

He sank back on the edge of his bed and put his head between his knees to stop his vision from swimming. He kept his eyes wide open, though, because suddenly he remembered what he'd said to Brandon: *I could go blind.*

All of his terrible symptoms that his meds only barely kept at bay; they'd be left completely unchecked for however long Hazel chose. No pain relievers to even keep the edge off as his disease returned to full force, maybe even worsened, causing him pain and further crippling his body.

It was torture, and what was worse, Percy had no way of making it stop.

No way to contact anyone.

Except now. Right now.

He pushed up to stand, only to sway in place and nearly collapse, so dizzy from hyperventilating he couldn't walk straight. Bracing a hand on his night table, he frantically struggled to even his breathing out before Hazel came in, so he could—so he could do *something*, tell *anyone*.

Get *out of here.*

And go where?

He'd told Brandon that, too. If he left, where would he go? Where would he get his medications? How would he pay for the undoubtedly astronomical cost of his everyday care when he wasn't on his parents' medical insurance? Trust fund or not, he'd seen the bills for his infusions and his medications. He'd be able to afford them for a little while, but not for long. And what would he do if there was an emergency? Pay a hospital bill that would easily reach into six digits? He couldn't live on his own. He couldn't even manage to get himself food without ordering it in, which got expensive quickly, even for people who *didn't* have thousands of dollars in prescriptions every month.

The thick well of frustration in his throat made it hard to breathe again. He hated feeling helpless like this. He hated having things taken away because people—especially the people who were supposed to know the ins and outs of his life—didn't *understand.*

Or they just didn't care.

Before he could gather himself any better, Hazel came back into his suite, leaving the door open behind her. She stopped short at the sight of him, and then looked at his untouched breakfast. "Eat," she ordered, then softened, sitting down beside him. "I'm trying to do what's best for you, Percy, and I assure you I don't enjoy it, so try not to make it harder on me?" She rubbed his shoulder affectionately. He shrugged her off hard. She tsked, taking her hand back. "Come on now. And don't fret. Once this visitor of yours is gone for good, I'll know for sure you're safe to have your medications back, and maybe, in time, we can consider allowing you to make some friends again— with better supervision against bad influences this time. All right?"

He didn't reply.

"All right?" she repeated. "Come now, don't make it worse. After all, I did say you could tell this friend of yours in person, didn't I? I didn't have to do that, but I did. Because I understand, Percy. You're lonely and not very good at making friends. Desperate to fit in. Of course you'd succumb to peer pressure from that . . . girl. And I'm sure this dealer of yours feels less like a pusher than like a friend, but Percy, it's all an act. You think it's not because you don't know better and you want approval so badly, but he's not your friend. He doesn't like you. He just wants your money. That's all he wants, and he'll do anything he has to in order to get it. He doesn't want *you*."

The sob ripped out of him so painfully he gasped after. It wasn't all sadness. It was sadness and anger that once it was out, was so white-hot he couldn't feel anything else.

Hazel wrapped her arm around his shoulder, and that was all it took. He pushed away from her and stumbled to his library room. Slammed the door behind him and twisted the lock closed with shaking fingers. Fell back against the door and stared out over his books.

He heard his bed creak, and then Hazel's footsteps coming closer. She knocked gently on the door, once, then once again, but he ignored her, arms wrapped around his middle, and eventually she went away, the distant slam of his suite's front door echoing back to him.

In the quiet, all he could hear was his staggered breathing.

What the fuck.

What the fuck?

He clung to the anger, to the desperation, to knowing he had to *do* something. To knowing he *was* an adult, with people who cared about him, and that Brandon was coming on Saturday, and it would be okay. It would be okay.

He clung to that, he had to think that, because if he didn't, he was worried he'd listen to the little voice at the back of his mind that had whispered to him from the moment he was old enough to understand his diagnosis and what it meant for his life.

It said: *You'll never get out of here.*

CHAPTER
TWENTY-SEVEN

Instead of letting himself waste all his time being pissed at Cyrus, Brandon put his energy into cleaning up the Mercedes. He'd felt kinda bad when he brought it to Percy, no matter how fascinated Percy was, so he called up the impound place to see what shops their mechanic recommended and finally got that rust spot fixed, along with some of the nicks and dings. Then it looked so damn good he figured he really would drive himself to meet Harvey instead of calling a cab like he'd planned to.

He did himself up just as nice as the car, hoping it would cover how weirdly shitty he'd felt the past week. It was like after the brilliant high of Saturday night, the universe had *had* to send Cyrus and his shitty blackmailing attitude to bring him crashing right back down.

So he'd just have to pretend he felt awesome.

Fake it until he made it. That had gotten him this far, after all.

The hotel wasn't the same one as last time, which was a good thing, Brandon thought. A fresh start for the two of them. Hell, if he could get through tonight with five stars from Harvey, that would make his week better. Maybe his whole damn month, and his minor setback with the no-show would be a thing of the past.

He checked himself in his rearview one last time, nervous. Which he refused to feel bad about or question, because this was a big deal. A chance to redeem himself, to prove how much he'd changed. Of course he had sweaty palms over it.

He locked the car and hiked his backpack up over his old denim jacket. Today his outfit was that—since it had impressed Percy so much with how vintage it was—over his usual white T-shirt and his jeans.

The bar was dimly lit and just behind the elevator bank, off to the right. It was pretty busy, but Brandon found a stool by the bar and claimed it and the one next to it by casually resting the heel of his shoe on its rungs. Harvey had wanted to drink together last time, and Brandon was going to start this off just right.

Just when he was starting to get paranoid and wonder if Harvey wouldn't show up either, the man himself strolled in the door, hands in his pockets, clearly looking for Brandon.

Brandon stood and waved a little, and when Harvey got close enough, he ushered him in, grinning lopsidedly. "Hey, you. Nice to see you again." Harvey seemed surprised, which Brandon took as a good sign and plowed on ahead, remembering to keep a friendly, indolent affectation in his James-accented voice. It was amazing how easily James Ringer came to him now, even as nervous as he was. "Want a drink?"

Harvey stopped short of letting Brandon guide him to sit. "No," he said, shaking his head. His shoulders were relaxed his hands still in his pockets. "I thought we could get started now."

"Sure, that's just fine with me." Brandon ducked to get his bag. He was almost disappointed he wouldn't get to wow Harvey with his new skills with small talk, but he could do this, too. He could do whatever Harvey wanted him to do. Be whoever Harvey wanted him to be. "Where we headed?" he asked on the way out, mouth close to Harvey's ear.

Harvey shrugged him off as they got to the elevators, but there were people milling around. Brandon got that. He settled at the guy's side, taking up the same loose posture. "So how's it been?" he asked, perfectly normal. Any two guys having a conversation.

But Harvey shrugged again and didn't answer. Shit, had he fucked it up already? Again? He was sure he'd done everything right.

He shuffled his feet, following Harvey into the elevator and sticking by him when a bunch of other people joined them. He didn't know what else to do—or what *not* to do. Harvey had been pretty clear about what he wanted last time.

Well, Brandon would just have to up his game. He couldn't just expect everyone to be predictable all the time.

"S'a nice place," he said when they got off on the floor. Now it was just him and Harvey alone in the velvety hallway, walking down the long stretch of red floor.

Harvey shrugged, which was better than no response at all, Brandon guessed, and took a sharp left, almost running Brandon into the wall. Their room was all the way at the end of that one, on the right. Harvey slipped the keycard through and unlocked it . . . then held it open for Brandon.

Some of the nervous tension in Brandon's stomach unknotted itself. Okay, maybe all the guy wanted was some more privacy today. "Thanks," he said with a slow, curling smile, and slipped in first, giving his ass a little extra shift as he did. He dropped his backpack in the closet off to the right of the entryway and toed his shoes off, trying to anticipate what Harvey would want this time.

But it'd be better to hear it from the man himself, wouldn't it?

He smoothed a hand back through his hair and went to close the curtains, since they were on a low floor and the last thing he needed was to ruin this with someone squawking about indecent exposure outside. "So, what d'you want to do tonight?" he asked, turning on the nightstand lamp.

"Well," Harvey said coldly, "you could've started with apologizing."

"Wh—"

"Your behavior. On our last meeting. It was completely unacceptable, and then I meet with you today and you try to pretend it never happened?"

"I thought we could have a fresh start," Brandon said. When had Harvey gotten so close, so close he was looming . . . and Brandon was shrinking, lowering himself timidly onto the edge of the bed?

"Any fresh start comes from me. My choice. My call. You presumptuous . . ." He reached forward, grabbing a fistful of hair at the back of Brandon's head. Then he kissed him. Hard. Brutal. Brandon held himself still only because the very second he wanted to pull away, he remembered Harvey's shitty review, Theresa telling him what Harvey liked. Ms. Monroe's disappointment. He held himself still because this was his job, and for once in his life he wanted to be good at it.

Harvey pulled them apart, his fingers painfully tight in Brandon's hair. "Do you understand? Do you even understand what you do enough to feel sorry for it?"

"No," Brandon gritted out, forcing himself to uncurl his fists, let the fight leave him, just give in to what was happening and for once in his fucking right just do it right. He struggled for the words, even though his throat was thick, even though his voice came out small and scared and none of it was acting. "No, I don't understand." He squeezed his eyes shut; somehow he couldn't say the words that came next with them open. "Teach me. Please, teach me."

Nothing. For a long, horrible moment, all Brandon could do was flinch, and wait.

Harvey's voice, when he finally spoke, was too calm, too measured, too cold. Close to Brandon's ear, but the effect was far from sexy. "You can't learn, James," he spat, taking Brandon by the shoulders and spinning him, then shoving him facedown onto the bed. Brandon went limp on top of the covers, face buried in the fake-perfumey smell of hotel detergent. "But I can demonstrate anyway."

The hiss of a belt being pulled loose made Brandon stiffen. Made him want to get up and *run*, get the fuck out of there. A week ago he could've yelled for Cyrus if he got really fucking desperate, but he'd ended that, so here he was, alone, facing down the kind of childhood nightmare a kid like him never, *ever* outgrew.

"You think just because you're handsome, just because everyone wants a piece of you, that means you can walk around ignoring all the broken hearts and lives you leave in your wake. You think you can move on to your pretty wife and forget the rest of us?" Then the sound of leather hissing again, like Harvey was running the belt through his hand.

Brandon gripped handfuls of the comforter, swallowing down nausea. It was a game. It was a game. He'd been warned about this. It was just a game, and all he had to do was play along, do a good job, get his good review.

"I was good enough for you to sell a movie ticket to, good enough to buy a membership to your fan club and a forged autograph, but not good enough to look twice at, to feel even an inch of concern for." He thrust his hand under Brandon's hips, yanking at his button and fly. Brandon was thankful for his faceful of blankets, because it meant Harvey couldn't see how badly he winced. "And all the while you got richer and more spoiled—" Harvey was yanking his jeans down his ass now, down to hobble his thighs "—more people sucking up to you and giving you everything you wanted, all on *my* back, but did you care about the things I sacrificed for you? The things you took from me? My money, my life, my marriage. You took it all from me, James Ringer. You selfish, narcissistic *queer*."

He had a sudden memory of Alfred at their second session.

"You loved him, huh? James Ringer."

"Hated him too, sometimes."

How many men had loved and hated James Ringer? Wanted him, lusted after him, all while wishing they could stop? Living their lives in fear and misery and bitterness when they couldn't? Alfred had accepted his desires, fell in love, found someone to love him back.

Had Harvey been the same, once? So where had he gone wrong, that his hatred and resentment were still so potent, so unlike the bittersweet memory they were for Alfred?

Brandon was starting to question whether any of this was an act, like he'd first suspected. This wasn't kinky sex, this was catharsis. Revenge. Years in the making.

"Don't you even have anything to say for yourself?" The folded belt touched the lower curve of his ass. Didn't strike, more caressed.

Brandon still sweated and quaked as if he'd taken fifty blows with it.

"I—I—" Brandon cut himself off before he could say *I'm not him, I'm not James.* He yanked an arm underneath him and bit down on his wrist to remind himself why he was here. That this was *agreed upon.* This was in his fucking prep email. Sex game or not, this was his job.

If Harvey wanted him to be James, then he was James.

"I'm sorry," he said. "I'm sorry. I was selfish. I didn't think about the . . . the effect I was having. On—on my fans. On you."

"How could you be this selfish? Did you even think about what this would do your mother and I, Brandon? Did you think about what we'll have to deal with after this little stunt? Your mother has enough problems staying out of the spotlight and now you have to go and do something dramatic. Just like him. Always just like him."

"That's right," Harvey purred, petting Brandon with the loop of the belt. "You only thought of yourself. How you could use your body to use me. To ruin me. All for fame."

No.

But wasn't it true, at least a little? James had gone on to have Dahlia. If not for the accident, he would've been acting until he died, Brandon just knew it, and he would've been spoiled for roles, everyone begging him to act in this and that and make an appearance here and there. He would've been fine, and people like Harvey, like Dahlia . . .

People like *Brandon*.

They didn't get to be fine.

For a second Brandon wanted to laugh at the idea that he'd thought this could be fine—any of this. This job, this life. Him. How could he have thought everything was fine?

Then he remembered Percy, and thought, *well.*

At least there was Percy.

For now.

Because everything—even their date together—had been about James. Brandon had taken him somewhere off the clock, just the two of them, and all Percy wanted to do was look for James. James was the only reason Percy had hired him.

This is all thanks to you.

So it would collapse if James was taken out of the equation.

Percy was in love with James now, as starry-eyed as Alfred or Harvey had once been, but would he stay that way?

Or would he become disillusioned and embittered too, whether Percy knew his who he was or not?

What would happen to *Brandon* if Percy's love for James turned to hate?

Harvey trailed the loop of the belt down Brandon's spine and then lifted it away with a whoosh of air that had Brandon's skin prickling with goosebumps.

Even though he knew it was coming, even though it didn't even hurt as bad as he knew it could have, the first blow of the belt brought him to tears.

CHAPTER
TWENTY-EIGHT

I t was just like last time.

Brandon surfaced slowly from wherever he'd gone, muzzy and disoriented. Only this time his whole back was alight with hot stripes of pain and he was cold. He swallowed and pushed himself up on his hands. His jacket was half off, looped around one wrist, and he shrugged it off—then froze when he saw the back was crusty with spattered, dried cum. He recoiled, shoving it off the bed and just— just *away*.

And to think he'd been so proud of wearing that today.

He forced himself off the bed and yanked his jeans up, zipped and buttoned them with clumsy, shaking hands. The scrape of the denim on his tender, bare ass made him want to cry all over again, but he wasn't sure he even had the tears left for it.

He felt raw and numb and wrung out. Going through the motions of getting his shit together and not really feeling anything his hands touched. Watching himself from a million miles away, some thick slice of fogginess between him and his body. He fixed the covers. Made sure everything was in the trash. Found his shoes. Picked his backpack up.

Looked at his jacket. He half-reached for it, then stopped because he couldn't. He just. Couldn't.

No amount of washing would ever let him look at it without thinking of this room. It was ruined. He didn't even want to try bringing it with him, as if he was hoping that by leaving it here he would leave everything else that had gone down in this room here, too. He picked it up with the toe of his shoe and dropped it into the trashcan, on top of the balled up tissues Harvey had left.

He took the stairs out, head down. He didn't want to look at anyone, have anyone see him. Suddenly he was glad he was driving himself. Or he was until he climbed in the car, which still smelled like Dahlia's perfume, and then he wanted to throw up.

He cranked the windows down and drove home, trying to ignore that the numbness was melting into a weird buzzing that filled his whole body, spreading out from his back. It was a twenty-minute drive, and it felt enormously long and quick at the same time, like time was oozing by in weird stops and starts.

One second he was in the hotel parking lot; then he was in Dahlia's driveway, staring up at the house with his door open. He was reaching for his backpack; then he was inside, his shoes still on, the front door letting the breeze in.

He dropped the backpack and pushed the door shut. Leaned his forehead against it.

All this time you were just pretending it would be okay.

The thought caught and held and he couldn't push it away, not as worn down as he was. He sank to his knees, palms against the inside of his door, and huddled against its surface just to keep himself upright. His breathing was harsh over the roar in his ears, cutting through the silence of the house. This big fucking house.

This big fucking house that James Ringer had purchased outright, all in order to play straight and narrow while his closeted fans were left to suffer with nothing.

Harvey, who carried so much hate and resentment he'd turned to violence. Even Alfred's memories, fond as they were, had been bittersweet. Dahlia's, too. She'd talked about James sometimes, not often, and always with that same off note in her voice. And what had Percy called their marriage? An "arrangement"? Had she ever gotten what she really wanted from James?

Had anyone?

And here was Brandon, profiting off that just as much as James Ringer ever had.

No one was just happy to have known him.

No one who had lived with James *or* Brandon Ringer talked about them with uncomplicated fondness.

Except Percy.

Brandon was dragging his backpack closer, fishing his cell phone out, and dialing Percy's number before he could really process it. He just wanted to hear Percy's voice. Wanted to reach for him, so he could be the tether to keep Brandon here, keep him from totally losing it.

Whether they talked about what happened today or Brandon just listened to Percy nerd out about a seventy year old movie, didn't matter.

He cupped the phone to his cheek and listened to it—

Go to voicemail.

"Perce?" Brandon cut the call and dialed again, hands shaking. "Perce, c'mon."

Voicemail again.

"Hello, you've reached the voicemail of—" crackle crackle *"Percival Charles. Please leave a voicemail and your call will be returned promptly."*

Brandon cut the call again before it could record him. What would he even say?

What had he been planning to say if Percy *had* picked up? *Hey, I'm a disaster, talk to me.*

I thought I could handle my job but I really, really can't, please tell me it's okay that I suck.

Please tell me you don't just want James.

Please tell me I don't have to be him.

So maybe it was better Percy hadn't picked up after all.

A night of restless sleep didn't leave him feeling any better. He tossed and turned to keep the weight off his back had weird dark dreams. He couldn't remember any of them after he made coffee, just felt off and restless. Even the thought of getting to see Percy couldn't cheer him up all the way.

He wanted a cigarette. A lot. But he wasn't going to slip *that* far backward.

First cup of coffee finished, he poured himself another, looking out over the pool. It was strewn with leaves, and a couple of the deck chairs were knocked over. The place needed maintenance, like Dahlia's car. And getting Dahlia's car fixed had stretched his budget, what with the mortgage payments he'd been managing to keep up on. And taxes would be due sometime soon, and Brandon was shit at math, so he'd have to hire someone . . .

Shaking his head, he downed half the second cup. He needed to fucking *do* something, get out of his head for a while so he could stop cycling back on the same old shit.

Coffee in hand, he headed for the living room to check his email, then detoured when he remembered Harvey was prompt with his reviews, and that was just one more thing Brandon didn't want to think about.

The basement door was right there.

Brandon stared at it. He hadn't gone down there since . . . since he'd moved in. Months ago. He'd left it to rot like the neglected dump he'd thought it was.

Dahlia hadn't seen it like that, to have kept it preserved all these years, organized and well cared for. To her, it had been a memorial, not just dusty mass-produced junk. Somewhere she could go when she wanted to remember those good times, maybe, even if they had been rare. Somewhere she could go and feel a little bit of James still there, like Brandon felt when he was watching James's movies with Percy.

Brandon could see himself doing something like that for Percy. Keeping good things close. Remembering.

He squinted at the door.

He could muster up some of that feeling for Percy right now. And for himself, too. To remember there *had* been good times, for Dahlia and for Brandon both. Watching James onscreen and in his interviews proved him as someone so totally different from the person Brandon's parents—and Harvey—made him out to be. If Brandon could just remember that until he got over this dark point, if he could stop thinking about what Harvey had said to him, it would be fine.

Hell, maybe he'd ask Ms. Monroe to go to lunch again. That would fix him right up. Maybe he'd introduce her to Percy. They'd probably *both* get a kick out of that. The sheer amount of potential nerdery there could flatten a couple buildings, he was sure.

Mind made up, he set his coffee on the hall table and pulled the basement door open.

He knew exactly what he was looking for.

CHAPTER
TWENTY-NINE

Saturday. Percy was almost—almost—excited by the thought, before the first twinges of his morning pain hit him and he remembered. No pills, not for days now. No phone. No computer. Nothing but his movies, and even those seemed less vibrant, less funny, less clever, less engrossing. And not just because the pain made it hard to focus on anything else.

Because Brandon was right: he did love movies, but he didn't want to watch them alone anymore.

But he was going to have to, because after today, he was never going to see Brandon, or Kovie, or any friend Hazel hadn't personally vetted, ever again.

Hazel was in and out what seemed like every half hour, bringing him glasses of water and meals he didn't want to eat and encouraging him to "get it out of his system." The pain was making him sweat, making him lose his appetite, keeping him practically bedridden. It probably did look like withdrawal, and even if it didn't, Hazel would have done mental backflips in order to see withdrawal symptoms in him anyway.

He didn't have any time alone to himself, not even when he was sleeping—he'd woken up three times the past night to Hazel standing in his doorway. And the last time she'd come in and smoothed his hair back and told him it would be over soon.

It would be over soon.

And then what?

It was true Percy was desperate for some measure of relief from this pain, but at what cost?

He wished he could be normal. He'd wished it before, but never this viscerally. He'd never wanted so badly to be different. To be able to take care of himself, and never need to depend on anyone, so no one could do this to him. If not for his illness, he could have been out of here months ago. *Years* ago. He could have escaped to college like a normal teen. He could have found an apartment of his own. Had friends, maybe a boyfriend he didn't have to pay to fuck him. Had a medicine cabinet with a bottle of Advil and some Tums instead of the double-wide, extra deep standing cabinet with a refrigerator compartment that held all of his supplies. Had his own laptop and cell phone with no one to take it from him like he was a five-year-old. Went to the doctor once every six months because he sprained something or had strep throat instead of his monthly visits to specialists and therapists and infusion clinics.

And the worst thing was he couldn't find it in himself to stay angry. He was just frustrated and lonely and lost, and the brief flickers of upset that rose up every time Hazel came in to see him vanished quickly. He kept telling himself he was playing the good boy, that he'd be back to himself as soon as all his *privileges* were restored, but that small hope was bleak in the face of an entire life lived in this suite, by himself, with his every move and his every visitor forever monitored by Hazel.

He pinched the crust of his dry toast between his fingers and watched it crumble to nothing.

A shadow darkened his open door. He didn't even look up. "Percy, your . . . visitor is here. I'll give you a half hour." She left without another word, and after a minute or so, Percy heard his suite door creak open.

"Perce?"

He looked a mess, he knew, and could barely gather up the effort to set his tray aside and sweep his hand back through his hair. "In here."

Brandon came to the door, and he looked . . . honestly, just as bad as Percy felt. There were dark circles under his eyes, and his shoulders were slumped in a way that was from his usual purposefully sexy languor. "Hey," he said, eyebrows furrowed. "What's wrong? You sick?" He jerked a thumb over his shoulder. "What's her problem now?"

Percy huffed a sardonic little laugh. "I don't know where to start," he mumbled.

"Yeah, me neither." Brandon eased in, but didn't sit down until Percy moved over to make room for him, which left him breathing hard, with bright flares of pain radiating up from his hips and pulling every muscle in his back tight. Brandon frowned at him. "You really don't look good, Percy."

Percy shrugged and swept his eyes down Brandon's body so he could have an opening to say *neither do you*, but his gaze caught on the jacket Brandon was wearing, and then he couldn't say anything at all.

A Schott Perfecto motorcycle jacket, supple black leather worn and scarred in places, vintage, and absolutely *not* a reproduction or rip-off.

It was an absolute stunner, even better than Brandon's other vintage clothing finds. But the jacket itself wasn't what really caught his eye.

No, that was a particular gash on the right arm of the sleeve.

Just two inches long, a clean split. Scored by a knife in a stunt that very nearly went wrong.

A dramatic knife-fight scene that had an entire chapter to itself in one the biographies in Percy's library.

A knife-fight James Ringer had done his own stunts in.

A jacket that had never been on the market, never sold at auction, had never been featured in any costuming exhibition or public collection.

Because Ringer had brought it home with him off the set after the costuming department had replaced it, and it had never been seen since.

Until now.

Until right now, worn with the casual air of someone who had no idea of its true significance. No idea what it was doing to Percy to have it so close, *right there*. In his room. On his bed.

On Brandon, who looked so much like James Ringer he'd made a clandestine career of it.

"You must think I'm the stupidest person you've ever met," Percy whispered.

Brandon Ringer's brow furrowed. "N-no?" he stuttered.

"Seeing me all this time, and me such a huge fucking nerd, as you so kindly put it, for James Ringer, and I *still* never put two and two together. Not all this time. Not after seeing your face, not after seeing you dress like him, not after watching his movies with you, not even after fucking you. Did you wear the jacket just to see how far you could take it without me figuring you out?"

"Wh—" Brandon sputtered, plucking at his jacket. "No, I—I thought—"

Percy cut him off on a hard laugh that made his ribs ache. "For fuck's sake, I was online not two weeks before we met, trying to find James Ringer's mysterious grandson because I heard he was trying to sell off Dahlia Delair's collection, and what do you know, he's been under my fucking nose this whole damn time!"

Brandon's eyes were wide. The same blue. The same damn color as James's. Not coincidence. God, had Percy just been willfully ignorant? Had Brandon thought it was fun, seeing how long he could go without Percy finding out? "You were looking into my grandmother's collection?"

His grandmother. Because *Dahlia Delair was his grandmother*.

Percy shook his head, refusing to let the wonder at that thought distract him from the point. The point being that Brandon had been James Ringer's grandson this whole time and never told, and what was more, he'd callously tried to sell off his grandfather's memory—that precious jacket included—the same way as he'd sold his inherited famous face and his body. "Well, yes. I figured it ought to go to someone who'd actually *value* it and care for it properly. Actually, I think my searching for it was what brought me to your stupid website in the first place."

He saw the instant Brandon closed up, his expression souring. "I don't know what you think," Brandon said. His voice was shaking. "I don't know what you think, Percy, but I wasn't *doing* anything—I wasn't trying to play some game or—or hurt you, I. It was just a job."

Percy's voice came out blank. "It was just a job."

"Not like that. Percy, *listen*—"

"*I* was just a job," Percy repeated, louder. "So that's it then."

"*No*, not . . ." Brandon breathed out hard and jerked away to stand. Percy felt like he was being strangled from the inside of his chest. *"He's not your friend. He doesn't like you. He just wants your money."*

"I was just a job," he whispered. Then he was shouting. "And that jacket, and whatever else was in Dahlia Delair's collection, all of that was just junk to you too, wasn't it? Just old worthless junk, taking up space and waiting to be sold for the best price you could get? You never cared at all. You never cared about anyone but yourself. You didn't even care about James until not knowing enough about him was hurting your wallet. As long as you made your money, got ahead, who cared how many people you *used*?"

Now Brandon's face turned mottled red. "And what about you, huh? You trying to say you never used me? You didn't use me for how much I looked like your vintage wet dream when I was sucking you off? You didn't use me by seeking me out *in the first place* all so you could own the things I had? All because you wanted what was left of my grandfather all for your spoiled self, the same way you hid that interview where he admitted he was bi?" The look of disgust and hurt on his face was unbearable, more unbearable than Percy's physical pain without pills.

But not as unbearable as the sight of tears shining in Brandon's eyes. The way his voice faltered and broke. "Do you know how much that could have changed my life if you and your asshole nerd friends hadn't hidden it and hoarded it? Did you ever think that maybe someone else might need to know the truth about James Ringer, someone who was more to him than just some pathetic shut-in fanboy?" The tears rolled down his face and he let them without acknowledgment, his jaw clenched.

That day. The *second* Percy had told him about the rare interview video, Brandon had begged that he put it online, get it out there, and Percy hadn't understood. Had guarded it jealously, questioned Brandon's motives.

And now it all made horrible sense.

And it all ached so much.

"This pathetic shut-in fanboy doesn't want to see you anymore," Percy bit out, prim and even, because their half hour was coming to a close and if Hazel wasn't outside the door right now, she soon would be, and there was nothing else he could say, anyway. The damage had been done.

"That's fine, because James Ringer's whore grandson doesn't want to see *you* anymore, either." Brandon took a jerky step toward the door, then stopped and unzipped the jacket with one furious tug. He balled it up like it was trash and tossed it into Percy's face. "Here," he snarled. "Since it matters so fucking much to you."

Then it was over. Just like Hazel had said it would be.

CHAPTER
THIRTY

The moping fest Brandon held for himself over the next few days was pathetic. Completely pathetic.

And he didn't care one bit. He only dragged himself out of bed to piss and get coffee and sometimes a bagel from the rapidly staling bag in the pantry. Other than that, he sacked out and stared at the ceiling, ignoring his email and his phone and the fact that the world existed outside the house.

Apparently he ignored it a little too well, because on Thursday— he thought it was Thursday—Theresa called the house phone, which was the last contact on his list for Hollywood Doubles.

The ringing woke him up, and he rolled over to grab for the ancient off-white wall phone next to his bed. "H'lo?"

"Brandon?" Theresa's usually cheerful voice was high with worry. "Is that you? Are you okay?"

Not even close. "Uh, yeah," he said, coughing to get the gravelly sleep out of his voice. He sat up and rubbed a hand over his eyes. Maybe if he did it long enough the piles of dirty clothes around his bed would disappear. "What's up?"

"You haven't been answering your email or your cell phone. What's going on?"

"Uhh. Been sick."

She made a sound like she didn't believe him, but let him slip on the lie. "Well, I was calling because I've been emailing you to ask you about a schedule conflict at the beginning of next week. I have two clients asking to be booked on the same day, and we don't usually do that unless the escort is comfortable with it. And I know you've never done that before . . ."

A week ago, Brandon would have leaped at the chance to see two people in one day.

Because it would have made you more money, Percy's voice taunted in the back of his head.

Yeah. Exactly.

Now he didn't know if he could even handle seeing *one* person a day. "Is it anyone I know?"

"Mmhmm. One of them is Harvey. Then there's . . ."

Her voice was drowned out by the pounding in Brandon's ears. "I-I'm sorry, what?"

"Oh, did I cut out? This darn phone, all day it's been like this. I said Harvey, one of your regulars, I think? I sent along his last review, it seems like you're developing a good rapport with him. And then the other is Nolan, which . . . my system says this is his second appointment, but I don't remember seeing a review from him. Hmm."

Nolan. Brandon's no-show. "He skipped out on our last appointment. I don't know if you guys have a list or something for that, but yeah. He stood me up."

"Oh," Theresa said, her frown evident. "Yes, I'll make a note of that. We have a two-strike rule, so if you want . . ."

If he wanted, he could choose Nolan over Harvey. He needed to choose one or the other, because money was drying up and God dammit, he was not going to let this whole thing with Percy destroy his entire life.

He didn't want to see Harvey, he really, really didn't. Even when he was in a great mood, Harvey brought him down to nothing. What would he do to Brandon now that he was worn down and weak and heartbroken?

But he couldn't risk Nolan not showing up again.

And fuck, if he was going to get up the energy to dress himself and go out and be James fucking Ringer, then he wanted to get paid for it. It didn't matter if Percy thought he was a scum-sucking selfish leech or whatever. He had bills to pay, and unlike Percy, he didn't have parents giving him a thousand-dollar allowance and a personal caretaker there to cater to his every whim.

Which was . . . totally not fucking fair for Brandon to think. Sure Percy was an asshole, but Hazel was still a bigger one. And she was abusing and controlling him, not catering to him. Jesus. One bad fight and he was sinking that low.

"Brandon?"

"Yeah, I'm here. Sorry." Brandon sighed. "I'll, uh. I'll take Harvey."

"Okay." He heard Theresa typing and waited for her to say goodbye. But she didn't. Instead he heard her shuffle the phone before her voice came through lower. "Brandon, are you really okay? I know we had a rough start, but you've been one of our best lately, and even Vince has been asking why you've stopped taking appointments. This isn't like you."

Brandon scoffed before he could stop himself and said, "This is *exactly* like me."

Theresa didn't say anything.

"I'll talk to you later," he muttered. "Thanks for calling."

"Don't you—" she said right as he went to push the end call button. He hesitated and heard her finish, "—want to know how my date went?"

He ended the call.

The split lip smarted. Brandon dabbed at it with an ice cube wrapped in paper towel, wincing at his reflection in the mirror. Cried-red eyes with black circles under them. A bruise coming up on his cheekbone, where he'd been backhanded.

How long could he go on like this?

Today's appointment had been less than an hour, but it felt ten times longer. He'd make $180 from it. That was it. For *this*.

Sure, he could call Theresa and tell her "one of his regulars" or no, "good rapport" or no, he didn't want to see Harvey anymore. But if not Harvey, how long until another trick like him arose? And even if one didn't, it wasn't like Brandon had been doing much better with any of his other clients lately, either. How long until Brandon ignored his phone often enough, rejected enough paying customers, that Vince started calling him difficult and choosy and self-centered? Until Ms. Monroe called him to say he wasn't worth her effort after all? Until Hollywood Doubles sent him packing and he became desperate and hungry and homeless again?

How long would it take him to come crawling back to Harvey and others like him—maybe even worse than him, without Hollywood Doubles doing the pre-screening—just to make ends meet?

Alfred didn't see him often enough to keep him afloat. Percy had, but Percy was *gone*.

Harvey was his only regular left.

What else could he do, but put up with the put-downs and the pain?

So that was what he did.

Oh, sure, his other clients didn't kick him while he was down *quite* like Harvey, but the more regularly Harvey booked him, the harder it became to warm up to even his most benign tricks.

As hard as he tried to recapture that feeling of pride in his work he'd had not two weeks ago, he just couldn't. Not when even the gentlest little kisses had him thinking of Harvey's biting teeth, not even when Harvey's hateful words seemed to echo in Alfred's James Ringer stories, making them seem more bitter than sweet. He'd been so sure after Percy told him about James's long-lost interview tape that his parents had just been wrong, that everyone had been wrong, that being twisted up in the Ringer legacy maybe wasn't the end of him he'd always thought it would be.

But where the fuck was Percy and his rosy vision of James Ringer now? Now that Harvey's dark truth of him had been revealed?

Nowhere, that was where.

Gone.

Harvey's hatred and resentment fed his own, until he carried it in his stomach like stone.

He wished he'd sold the stupid fucking collection when he had the chance. Gotten rid of Ringer when he was still capable of it, before Ms. Monroe and Percy had gotten under his skin, undermined his lifelong resentment until he could barely grasp it anymore. He'd be sorry for being a shit to everything that was left of Dahlia, selling her stuff off, but at least it would've been gone instead of feeding him hope and then poison in turn.

Now he hated James Ringer *and* himself. Again. And this time he knew exactly what trying to find a path out got him.

A split lip and bruised hips.

One more wrong move away from losing this cushy job, losing Dahlia's house, and hitting rock bottom all over again.

He was *exactly* who everyone said he was: a complete fuckup, just like James Ringer. He'd probably end up like they said he would, too. The looming deadline of turning twenty-one—a year and a half away—didn't seem as awful as he'd once thought. It'd just be the last predictable strike in his book. Enough for everyone to say they'd always known.

A worthless piece of shit. No good for anyone who really knew him. Born to die.

And once he got to that point, once he really let the truth of that settle into him, it was easy to be the punching bag Harvey paid him to be.

Harvey even tipped him for the privilege. Which was almost enough to make up for the fact that he didn't pull in repeat customers anymore. He was back to how he'd been: scoring one or two or, rarely, three stars, all forwarded to him with no notes from Theresa. She sent him the usual HD booking emails, too, but she didn't call or text him anymore outside of work. He skipped a week, then two weeks of sessions with Judy's trainer. Picked up a pack of smokes "just in case," and smoked four of them in quick succession right in the hotel room where Harvey left him next.

He remembered wanting to clean up the room that one time, the one last time before Percy. He'd wanted to pick it up, make it look neater. Maybe to make himself feel neater. But mostly because he didn't want to leave a bunch of shit laying around for the housekeeper. He'd done that at other appointments, too. But not anymore. What was the point? Everyone who saw him come in and go out and walked down the fucking hallway while it was happening knew what he was and what he did.

They were just lucky he hadn't stooped low enough to be picking up his tricks in the hotel bar in his trashiest clothes. He didn't wear anything he'd bought from Hepcat Vintage—*that* he'd shoved in one of Dahlia's closets and done his best to forget which one—but he came in mostly clean jeans and a clean shirt every time, mostly because he hadn't run out of shirts and had to do laundry yet.

It wasn't just picking up the rooms. It was like every bump in a task, no matter how small, took him forever to convince himself to get over: needing to find an accountant to do the taxes on the house, having to fill up the Mercedes's gas tank to go out for an appointment, getting a voicemail when he called a dealer, ready to take whatever price the guy would give him to just gut and empty the fucking basement. A chair blocking the pantry door getting in the way of breakfast—so he had coffee instead and skipped out and didn't realize until he came home at eight that night that he hadn't eaten all day. A trick who couldn't wear latex condoms. A front desk clerk who'd caught a whiff of why he was in the hotel and gave him the stinkeye for it. Every single bad or lukewarm review he received.

The fact that Theresa never prefaced his emails with any kind of personal chatter anymore, just forwarded the relevant info with her official signature. Not an emoticon to be seen.

He had the feeling that if he weren't pulling in so much money from Harvey's weekly visits, they probably would have fired his ass by now.

The minute they got a new Paul Newman or Humphrey Bogart, Brandon was toast.

His life was back to being a waiting game. A countdown.

Scant months—maybe even weeks—left working this job. One year to live.

A month later, and he still hadn't been fired. He also hadn't seen Alfred in all that time or gained any new regulars, but Harvey had upped his sessions to twice a week so nobody at Hollywood Doubles was riding his ass too hard.

Of course, nobody was talking to him, either.

But he had five figures sitting in his bank account.

He wondered how long before Harvey got bored of him or ran out of cash. Wondered which would come first. Not that it actually mattered to Brandon, because the outcome would be the same regardless.

Would it happen before or after Brandon completely self-destructed? Because the past few weeks had brought into focus just why so many people in this line of work turned to drugs. For Brandon, it was a steady path through the rest of Dahlia's liquor cabinet every night he came home from an appointment, and a few-or-a-pack of cigarettes out by the pool, which was souring and turning green, the trees potted at either end dropping their dead leaves into the murky water. Cigarettes he could always get, but once he ran out of booze, he didn't know how he'd sleep, how he'd function on a semi-normal schedule enough to feed himself, much less do appointments.

Whatever. He'd figure something out.

That was assuming Harvey didn't destroy him, first.

Every session saw him escalate in tiny terrifying ways, and Brandon just let him do it, just checked out and took what he was given until it was over and he came to on the bed or the floor with aches and pains and sticky tears—or worse—dried on his face.

Of course, maybe Harvey wouldn't get the chance to take things that one step too far, because when Brandon arrived home—sore and exhausted and disoriented and *alone*—from their latest appointment, there was a strange man standing on Dahlia's doorstep.

Sure, a normal person would have assumed door to door salesman or Jehovah's Witness, but Brandon wasn't a normal person, he was a used-up whore on a serious down-spiral.

He cut the engine. Licked his chapped lips. Considered backing right out again, or calling 911, then decided fuck it, he had nothing to live for anymore anyway. Maybe this would be a mercy. So he gathered his apathy, lit a cigarette, and climbed out of the car, ready to face his fate.

A year early. The thought of that final fuck you to James Ringer's hold over him actually made him smile.

And then the stranger at his door turned. He was black and clean-shaven and bald, and in his arms, he held a bouquet of fresh daffodils.

The longing look on the old man's face made something queasy worm into Brandon's stomach. He took a long drag of his cigarette and raised his eyebrows at the guy. "What the fuck are you doing here?"

"I had to see you," the stranger replied, coming down the white steps to meet Brandon in the driveway. He paused at the edge of the gravel and gathered his flowers to his chest. "And your agency wouldn't let me."

Was this the no-show? Or someone who hadn't even passed the background check?

Did it fucking matter, now? "Who told you I lived here?"

"Nobody," the stranger said, shifting from foot to foot, the toes of his shoes carving through the gravel of the driveway. "This is Dahlia Delair's house."

Okay, Brandon had been maintaining his apathy, right up until this moment. Now, his heart pounded. "It's *my* house," he corrected. When he lifted his cigarette to his mouth, his hands were trembling.

"You're his grandson, aren't you? I thought you might be."

"What the fuck," Brandon sputtered, backing away. "Who the fuck are you, coming here? This is *my house*—this—it doesn't *matter* who I am."

The man's shoulders stiffened even as his expression softened. He clutched the flowers tighter, so tight that a few yellow petals fell to the ground at his feet. "It matters to me."

"You're freaking me out, man. You're freaking me out bad."

"I'm sorry. I'm really sorry. I had to see you and I didn't know how else to go about it. The first time I booked you I couldn't go through with it. And then after that, it was too late. They wouldn't let me make another appointment. I couldn't leave it be."

So the no-show, then. Yeah, that wasn't much of a comfort.

"How did you find me." Brandon rushed it out so fast it didn't even sound like a question. He backed up, toward the car. If Harvey booked appointments to do what he wanted, what kind of person skipped out of actual appointments and came to someone's *fucking house* to do whatever *they* wanted? "Leave. Right now."

"Please let me say what I came here to say. I'm not here to hurt you." He held out the crushed flowers. He may as well have been holding a grenade.

"Tell me how you fucking found me. Did it . . . Was it in the tabloids?" Had Cyrus gone through with the reveal?

Had *Percy*?

Brandon balled his hands into fists. If this fucker wanted a piece of James Ringer, he'd have to fight for it.

"Wouldn't know. Don't read 'em. *Never* did. Never touched one of those damn things."

That . . . sounded more invested than the average Joe on the street who thought paparazzo were shit for, say, hounding Britney Spears to the point of a mental breakdown.

More like someone who'd lived with them.

"Look, son. I'm not . . . I'm not some reporter, or, or a stalker, I swear. I came here because this is Dahlia Delair's house and I saw your face on the website, and I thought maybe . . ."

"Not exactly talking me out of the whole stalker conclusion." Brandon fumbled behind him, hand closing on the driver's side door handle of Dahlia's car. The fucking thing was locked. He'd have to turn his back on this guy if he wanted to get it open.

"Please, son," the man rasped. "Please, I'm dying, and I don't want to take what I've come here to say to the grave with me. It'd be like him dying all over again."

A shudder crawled down Brandon's spine. Not cold, not dread, just there, like a phantom touch. "Who are you."

"Nolan Crawford, although I expect that name will mean nothing to you."

"You're right. It doesn't."

"They worked hard to keep my name out of the papers. To keep it from being connected in any way to . . . him. And that's why I had to come. Because if I let them win, and I die without making myself known, it'll be like I never existed, and what's worse, it'll be like parts of James Ringer never existed, either. I can't let that happen." He shook his head. A few more crushed petals dropped to the gravel. "Please. I can't let that keep happening to him."

Brandon *knew* what he meant by that before he knew. Could feel it in him, the enormity of that truth, slowly dawning on him, lighting him up from the inside. "You were his . . . " he said, softly. He didn't know how to finish it. *Lover? Boyfriend?* "His . . ."

"Yes," Nolan said, his face somber and sincere. "I was his. Now can we go inside and talk? There's more I need to say."

CHAPTER
THIRTY-ONE

T he house was a goddamn mess.

Brandon guessed polite people were supposed to ignore it, and Nolan did all the way through the entranceway and the living room, where Brandon's clothes were piled here and there. And into the kitchen, where Brandon moved to put the island between them so he could have some room to breathe.

Nolan took one of the stools on the other side and glanced at the counter, which was covered in dishes and takeout boxes and empty booze bottles.

Then he looked at Brandon with a semi-disturbed, pinched look on his face and said, "Son, are you okay?"

"The name's Brandon, and no, I'm really not, but never mind that. Time's a-wastin'."

"I suppose any young man posing as his own grandfather to make money a call-boy would have to have a few demons to contend with." The words were harsh, but Nolan's expression wasn't judgmental, and Brandon was too damn curious to make a big deal out of it, in any case. "Not that I don't."

"Which brings us to why you're here," Brandon reminded.

"Yes. That. Well. You already figured out my relationship with your grandfather. Jim and I were *together*. In a way men weren't supposed to be, back in those days. We met before he was a household name. I was working construction on the set of his first movie."

"Break of Dawn," Percy's excited voice recited in Brandon's mind.

"He didn't dismiss me like a lot of the others did. It was different days then, you understand. We became good friends. And, well. It wasn't long before we were finding private corners on set, if you catch my meaning. He was gorgeous, electric, larger than life right from the start. And then he got big and Hollywood closed in and private corners became harder and harder to find. But he never put me out or sold me out, not even when Dahlia came along."

"Dahlia. My grandmother. Tell me, did he love her?" Even though Percy had reassured him on that front, once, Nolan had *been* there, and Brandon needed to know, even if just asking made him sick.

But Nolan smiled. "Of course, son. Dahlia was a looker, and she was brilliant and had a wicked sense of humor and she didn't fall for Jimmy's celebrity status the way other dames did." Nolan huffed a little breath at himself and touched the flowers he'd laid carefully on the counter, in one of the few open spaces. "Not even the way *I* did. Your grandfather and I were lovers, and I never felt second best, or used. But your grandmother . . . she and Jimmy were best friends."

"So she *was* his beard."

Nolan laughed, slapping the counter. "Not in a million damn years! Dahlia was understanding and accepting, but she was no fake bride, and she didn't turn a blind eye to him or to us. Your grandfather loved her, passionately. The baby and his agent pushed the marriage to the press, but that didn't mean he loved her any less. And what was more, she was never jealous. To be honest, I think she got a bit of a kick out of the whole thing. If I went for girls, I think the three of us could have even made a go at it. But either way, we were happy. As happy as we could be, in those days."

Brandon heard himself snort, "You're telling me he *really* made you happy? And that he made *Dahlia* happy?"

"Now what's that tone for?" Nolan frowned at him. "You think I'd still be on his doorstep like a lovesick puppy after all these years if I didn't feel for him?"

Brandon wrung his hands. "Let's just say, in my line of work, I've met a few men holding a torch for my grandfather who aren't so . . . charitable."

"That who gave you those bruises?" Nolan asked, touching the side of his neck in illustration, where, mirrored, Brandon's skin was tender and swollen.

"Never mind."

Nolan's frown deepened. Then he sighed. "Your grandfather

got his fair share of abuse, too. All men like us did, but people in the public eye, especially. It was one of Dahlia's people that finally ordered him to cut me out of his life. Put all sorts of stories in his head about how the truth would come out and it would ruin her career, have paparazzi dogging her, destroy her reputation until she was no better than a whore. A freak, for loving him as he was, especially since he was the way he was with a black man." Nolan swallowed audibly. He no longer met Brandon's eyes. "Who knew if any of it was true, but it was enough. And I understood, of course I understood. I loved Dahlia too, in my own way. I didn't want to see her hurt on my behalf. To go on like we were was just selfish. But I didn't understand what Jimmy was really giving up when he made that choice. I thought it was just me, but it was *himself*, too."

He smiled wistfully, staring somewhere past Brandon's shoulder. "I found myself a new squeeze—a boy out of costuming—and I thought, Jimmy had Dahlia, he'd be okay, too. But I didn't realize. It wasn't about not being alone, it was about being who he was. And Dahlia wasn't enough—couldn't be enough—to heal the hurt of that being taken away from him. He could have gone on without me or any other man in his life, been happy with Dahlia alone . . . if he'd have chosen it for himself. If we'd have had a blowup fight and never spoken to each other again, he'd have swaggered off just fine. But to be *forced*, and to hear his lifestyle put *Dahlia* in danger . . ." Nolan shrugged. "He couldn't just shrug that off. He was dead not long after the birth of the baby. Maybe he couldn't stand the thought of ruining a child's life, too."

This time Brandon's shudder was *all* dread. "What do you mean by that? James Ringer died in a motorcycle accident." Every word of it suddenly sounded false and hollow, echoing up inside all the places Nolan was cutting out of him.

Nolan shook his head. "Now you understand why I couldn't bring this secret to the grave with me. They covered up who he brought to his bed, who he *was*. I can't let them cover up why he died, too. I can't let them take that from him. There was no motorcycle accident, Brandon. He used his motorcycle to commit suicide. He made it *look* like an accident because it was the only way he could protect Dahlia and their child."

Those softly spoken words pelted him like stones. Seemed to find every bruise on his aching body, until the pain sank right through skin and muscle and bone down to his very soul.

He couldn't process any of it, so he did the only thing he could: He screamed.

Screamed and screamed and screamed, a horrible primitive sound, the only one capable of communicating the soul-deep anguish that was washing over him. He pulled on his hair. Kicked the counter stool over. Swept the entire cluttered counter free, toppling takeout containers and breaking glass and filling the room with the stink of old alcohol and rotten food.

He only realized he was crying, too, when Nolan's arms had enclosed him tight, and Nolan's weight had pulled him to the floor.

"Why me?" he sobbed, and he pounded Nolan's chest with the heels of his palms until his arms were too numb and tired to lift anymore. He slumped forward, burying his face into Nolan's pressed shirt, until the smell of his cologne drowned out every other sense. "Why are you telling me this? Why me, why me, why me . . ."

Nolan didn't speak, not at first. Just petted and shushed him, keeping him anchored, keeping him close enough that he couldn't lash out anymore, even if he had the energy to. But he didn't. He felt like he was sinking, being pulled down and down. Right down through the floor and into Dahlia's basement, her shrine to her dead husband, and then down deeper, down into the dirt where they'd buried him, where the earth had digested everything he'd once been.

When his sobbing subsided, he heard Nolan's voice, soft and sure by his ear. "I wanted to make sure his story—his secrets—didn't die with me. But not by making a public spectacle of him. Not like that. I'm sorry, Brandon, but it *had to be you*. I think later you'll appreciate why."

Brandon couldn't picture this "later" ever coming to pass. It was as impossible as his twenty-second birthday, as impossible as getting to hold Percy again, as impossible as getting his parents to love and accept him, as impossible as having Dahlia back, as impossible as preventing the desperate, inevitable tragedy James Ringer's life had become.

So he stayed in the now, here, with Nolan, the man who had

accepted and loved James Ringer once, and begged the universe that someone would accept and love him, one day, too.

He woke up in his bed. The smell of bacon very nearly prevented last night from being his first thought upon waking. Not for long, though, because he rolled over and thought *who the hell is making bacon?* and then tried to open his eyes, which were sore and aching, just like the rest of his face. And his hands, too—he coaxed his eyes open and squinted at them, curled his fingers some to work the stiffness out.

The blankets had been tucked around him. His room hadn't been cleaned, but all of his dirty laundry had been gathered into one tremendous pile, and the garbage that had littered every surface as of last night had disappeared.

For a moment, he remembered his first morning waking up here, after he'd moved in with Dahlia. She'd cooked him breakfast, too. Washed his clothes. Bought him new shoes. She hadn't asked any questions. Not, *Do you want to try going back?* Not even, *Do you want to call them?* She'd just taken him in, taken him on.

He had a weird second of wondering if maybe having him around had eased the ache of losing James, either because he reminded her of him, or because he gave her a second chance to do right.

Then he decided he should get the hell out of bed.

Nolan was in the kitchen. The clean kitchen. A middle-aged white woman was there with him, mopping the floor.

"Morning," Nolan greeted. "Hope you don't mind I invited Maggie over. The chemo means I don't have nearly the kind of energy I used to, but I still didn't want you to wake up to any kind of mess. She's my housekeeper. Don't worry, she's discreet."

Maggie tapped her nose and gave Brandon a wink that weirdly, immediately put him at ease.

Nolan gestured toward one of the counter stools, righted and polished to a shine. "Sit. Eat."

"Why are you doing this?" Brandon asked, his voice raw. More than his voice, really.

"I thought we could talk more now that you've gotten a good

twelve hours' sleep. Also, you really didn't look okay last night, even before I dropped my bombshell. And I got to thinking, had things gone different, maybe I would have been like a second grandpa to you. Had a hand in raising you, caring for you. Maybe I'm making up for lost time."

Dahlia had said the same, when he'd ask why she even fucking bothered with a hooker runaway who wasn't even her problem.

They'd fought about it a bit. Their only fight.

The only time she'd *ever* expressed disapproval about Brandon's behaviour: because he'd been putting himself down, questioning his worth.

He didn't go down the same path this time.

"Thanks," he said. Maggie set a plate in front of him while Nolan made one up for her and himself.

They all tucked in, eating in strangely peaceful silence.

"Do you want to see the basement?" he asked, with a mouthful of hashbrowns. He had no idea what made him say it, but he didn't regret it once he did. "I've been too chickenshit to really go down there since I moved in myself, but I figure I owe you an invitation. And maybe having you there will help."

Nolan glanced at him once, then swallowed a bite of eggs and looked back, holding Brandon's gaze. "Help?"

"Help me face him. Look, before tonight I wasn't exactly . . . I wasn't exactly charitable with him. Probably hated him more than my worst clients, at times."

"Neither was I," Nolan admitted. "Especially not after he up and left me. You can love someone with all your heart and still feel . . . complicated about them. Especially if they've hurt you in some way. We don't *have* to be charitable all the time. But open to understanding's another matter entirely, and by that invitation of yours, I'd say you are. So yes, let's go down. But no guilt."

Brandon barked out a bitter laugh. No *guilt*. He caught Nolan and Maggie's stares and shrugged. "Never tried that before when it comes to him. Unless you count rest periods for hating him and being a little shit, I guess."

"He was often a little shit himself. You should have seen the list of demands he had on set once he made it big." Nolan braced his hands on the counter and stood up, a slight wheeze evident under his breathing. He seemed to have trouble straightening, and Brandon moved in automatically, reaching for him. Nolan caught his arm and smiled at him. "But he had a heart of gold, too, that kid," he said quietly.

Brandon had no idea what to say to that.

Nolan patted his arm. "Take me downstairs, Brandon."

They descended into the darkness of the basement, and of their respective pasts, together.

When Brandon flipped the light on, Nolan gasped.

"I thought you knew about the basement," he said, watching Nolan soaking it in.

"Knew about. Never seen for myself. Kinda thought the rumors were exaggerations. Now I'm thinking they were underestimating. Wow. Dahlia kept everything, huh?"

Nolan shook his head, setting his hands on his hips and sighing. "Boy, if you didn't believe *me* when I said she loved the hell outta him, you can tell by this, can't you?"

Brandon glanced out over the trove. Which was what it really was, in Nolan and Dahlia's eyes. Not a crypt or a hoard or a ghost. It was like a folded picture in someone's wallet, a postcard taped above a deployed soldier's bed. Or rather, a love letter home from a soldier who'd never made it, to the girl he'd gone to die for. Kept close for all these years.

It hadn't haunted Dahlia—no more than it was haunting Nolan, who shook his head again and wandered out into the shelves, huffing and puffing from the single flight of stairs.

He limped, too. Shuffled along, touching things here and there with knobby fingers. He'd said he was dying. That he needed chemo.

Then he'd said he could've been like a grandfather to Brandon.

And damn if it didn't hurt, watching him like this.

Brandon was glad he'd let him in. Glad he'd listened.

"Brandon?" he heard Nolan call.

"Yeah?" He headed along the back wall until he found Nolan looking up at the hook in the framing where James's leather jacket had hung. There was a plaque built into the side, showing a photo of the stunt wreck and James grinning, arm around the pale film director's shoulders, the picture signed by both of them. "What's up?"

"This . . ." Nolan glanced at him. He cleared his throat. "Where is it?"

Brandon was probably imagining the slight accusatory note in his voice. Hopefully. But he also didn't have one good answer that didn't make him sound like a skeeze. "I, um. I gave it away. To a superfan."

Out of spite, he didn't add.

Nolan raised his bushy eyebrows. "Son . . ."

"He'll take care of it." Brandon pushed his toes into the carpet, rubbing at the back of his neck. "Trust me."

There was a moment of silence. Then, "Sounds like you *know* this, er, 'superfan.'"

"I, uh. A little, yeah. Met him through work." *Lost him through work, too.*

"Hmm." Nolan looked back at the plaque. "He was so proud that day," he said quietly. "Came to see me grinning like an idiot, said he scared off one of his lives but it was gonna look great on the screen."

Brandon looked, too. James looked incandescent, elated. "It did."

"Yeah."

Silence fell between them. Brandon kept staring at James's face, wondering if that was why he died the way he did. If he wanted to reach for that happiness again and couldn't think of any other way to do it but self-destruct.

"It was a client," he blurted out.

Nolan jumped. "What? What was?"

"My—the fan. He's young. Older than me, but young." Brandon watched the plaque instead of Nolan. "He knows everything about James. *Everything.* He has all this stuff. Not like this place, like, he doesn't collect commemoratives, and obviously every prop or costume there is to be had is down here, out of reach. But he has a lot of stuff, like one-of-a-kind things and books and interviews. James made him happy." Brandon's voice hitched. He coughed and turned away, shoving his hands in the pockets of his sweatpants. "I guess. So yeah."

Nolan's shuffling footsteps followed him. "I know this isn't any of my business, Brandon, but it sounds like this boy of yours—"

"He's not my *boy.*" Brandon winced at the harshness in his voice. "Sorry. Sorry. I'm not yelling at you."

Nolan touched his shoulder. Turned him around when Brandon

let him. "What happened?" he asked. "With the boy who's not your boy?"

Brandon opened his mouth to tell him "nothing." Which was why it was surprising when, ten minutes later, he was finishing with, "—so I told him I didn't want to see him again, either. And, you know. The jacket. I gave it, uh. Threw it. At him." He licked his lips and chanced a look at Nolan, who seemed torn between sympathizing him and judging him, if his expression was anything to go by. "I know, I know. I'm not giving anything else away, I promise. Unless . . . I mean, unless *you* want it."

Nolan was already shaking his head. "I don't need this." He took Brandon by the shoulders and squeezed him. "All I've needed for a long time was for someone else to know about James. And I'm sorry I didn't reach out to you earlier, son, I am. I never knew how to come and talk to you, and I think seeing me after James died was hard on Dahlia, no matter what she pretended. I didn't want to cause her more pain. And I don't want to cause *you* more pain." He shook Brandon gently. "And I don't want you causing yourself any more pain. You hear?"

"Yeah," Brandon mumbled.

"Eh?"

"*Yeah*." Nolan made a disapproving face. For someone Brandon didn't know until yesterday, he really did feel like he was being scolded by a family member. "I mean, yeah. I just don't know if I know how anymore."

"Don't say that. That boy of—that boy who's not yours sounded like he was plenty good for you."

Brandon shook his head. "He only wanted James. That was the point of everything I just told you. *James* was the one who made him happy. Like you and Dahlia. It was all for James."

Nolan sighed. "Brandon."

"What."

"I spent," Nolan said, "a long, long while regretting a lot of things. That brief time I had with him . . . Everyone likes to say they're glad they had those moments, however short. But for me it wasn't enough." His eyes grew watery. "It wasn't enough to carry me forever, Brandon. And I'm sorry I let him go. I'm sorry I didn't try harder. Dahlia was too."

"It wasn't your *fault*," Brandon said immediately.

"No, it wasn't. But I can still wish it went differently. Can't stop wishing, really. And *that* . . ." He squeezed Brandon's shoulders again, weaker. "That's something I wouldn't want anyone else to have to go through."

"There's nothing to wish for, though. Whatever I thought there was between us . . . it was never there." Brandon closed his eyes against remembering Percy grinning at him, remembering Percy touching his jaw and whispering for Brandon to watch because he wanted Brandon to see the same magic he did. Wanted to share it with him.

"Maybe." Nolan patted him, smoothing his shirt down over his shoulders. "Maybe you could give the boy a call, though. Give him a chance to explain himself. Obviously he left quite an impression on you." He held Brandon still, watching him with his still-wet eyes, until Brandon shrugged jerkily and nodded vague agreement. "Good." He let Brandon go at last and moved past him, toward the stairs. "Maggie wants you out of the house for a while today, anyhow. Let her do her work. A lot of it, by the looks of things."

"Yeah." Brandon's face heated. He hadn't exactly planned on anyone else seeing the hovel he'd turned Dahlia's main floor into. "I'll, uh, thank her."

"And she'll appreciate your manners," Maggie said from the doorway. She was grinning, leaning on a squeegee. "Nolan, Dominic is here to take you to your appointment."

Brandon stuck close behind Nolan as he heaved himself carefully up each step, breathing growing more and more labored. He never complained once, though, or asked for help, just kissed Maggie's cheek on the way past and went to collect his coat and hat from the hooks by the front door.

"I'll come by tomorrow," he said, retrieving a cane from where it was leaning on the wall. "You call that boy, understand?"

"Yessir." Brandon hovered there awkwardly until Nolan reached out and pulled him into a firm hug. He smelled sweet and sick underneath his liberal spray of old man cologne. "Thanks," Brandon muttered into his shoulder.

"Don't thank me yet." Nolan rubbed Brandon's back. "I'm leaving the car so Maggie can see herself home. I'll see you later." He pulled the front door open and made his way slowly down the stairs to a black Lincoln, where a guy around Brandon's age was waiting for him. The guy waved at Brandon, then hurried to open the back door for Nolan.

"He's been talking about you since his diagnosis."

Brandon startled and swung around to look at Maggie, who'd tied her curly red hair up and was leaning on her squeegee again. "Yeah?"

"Mmhmm. He wrote a letter before his first biopsy, but he always said he wanted to come see you himself." She nudged their shoulders together, then went on, a gentle note of warning in her voice. "You'll probably see a lot of him, until he dies."

Brandon looked out after the car, watching as it turned smoothly out of the driveway and headed toward the city. "That's fine," he said, and meant it. "That's just fine with me."

CHAPTER
THIRTY-TWO

Percy woke at three in the morning to a face wet with tears. The dream had been in black and white, accompanied by the swell of string instruments and a romantic, hazy lens.

Dreaming in noir was sad, on the surface, but considering his only other human contact in the past month other than his movies had been Hazel, he was glad to be dreaming about them and not her.

Funny thing was, he couldn't tell if his co-star in this particular flick had been James Ringer . . . or Brandon.

He hated that he didn't know. Made him feel like the exact piece of shit Brandon had accused him of being, using Brandon like he wasn't his own person, and all to satisfy his urge to own a piece of his grandfather. He'd been too startled and angry to really process when he and Brandon had been fighting, but what Brandon had said about him had held a kernel of truth, buried under all the defensive mud-slinging. Percy had hired Brandon for James; he'd gotten upset when Brandon wasn't *enough* of James. And they'd bonded over Brandon learning how to be more like James.

But it wasn't *just* that. Percy knew himself enough to know what had happened between them wasn't because of the remnants of a ghost. At first all he'd been able to see was James, like Brandon was wearing his skin, but as they'd spent more time together, Percy noticed the differences more than the similarities, and not in a way that disappointed or frustrated him like it had that first meeting.

He'd seen Brandon as his own person. Someone Percy loved spending time with. Someone he hadn't meant to push away.

Maybe it was stupid, the way he'd reacted. He didn't honestly think Brandon had been waving his family history in front of Percy, laughing at his inability to see it. Maybe Brandon had reacted so badly because he'd expected Percy to be happy he and James were related. Or maybe he hadn't been trying to reveal himself at all. Maybe he didn't know the jacket was legendary. Maybe he had good reason to keep his identity a secret. How much would a story like that—famous cult star's doppelganger grandson whores himself out as a lookalike—sell for? And how would the news getting out affect Brandon?

And Percy had been angry at him for keeping it a secret?

Maybe he hadn't been angry. Maybe he'd just been looking for a way to break them up permanently, a way to do it without admitting to anyone—even himself—that if not for Hazel's ultimatum, they might have been together a long, long while, maybe even after the money ran out.

He'd never know now. He'd never know what they could have been, but what was worse, he'd never know who *he* could have been. Had he stuck it out with Brandon, remained friends with Kovie, learned how to socialize within his limitations, gone to college. Maybe he could have even moved out of his parents' house, one day. Gotten his own medical insurance and paid for his own pills. Left Hazel behind for good.

He could have.

But not anymore.

He wrapped his arms around himself and shivered. He had a pile of blankets on, was curled up on himself as best as his knees and hips would let him, but he was still cold. Cold from the inside out. And, like everything else lately, he had no idea how to make it better.

Hazel had taken to casually punishing him so easily, now that his parents had given her free rein. It wasn't anywhere near as bad as depriving him of his medications for a week, but if he got smart with her or, once, when she caught him watching movies at four in the morning, she would shuffle his meal times back or not come in and clean for a day or two. She also hadn't given his laptop or phone back. The phone hardly mattered anymore, but the laptop . . . Percy had wanted to continue his classes. And after missing five weeks of them, he had no idea if he would even be able to catch up, or if he could retake them without completely destroying his GPA.

Or if he should try at all. It would just be another thing he couldn't use. What was he going to do with a degree, anyway? He couldn't work most archivist positions from here, and if he were to find a job online, he would have to limit his work hours spent typing, thanks to his hands.

His hands were aching now. His knuckles were red, the skin around them bloodless because he'd been gripping his blankets, trying futilely to make them warmer.

He just wanted to be warm again.

As warm as he'd once been resting against Brandon's side, Brandon's arm draped casually around his shoulders.

In a trance, not sure where he was going or what he was doing, he rose from the bed, padded across his room to his closet, where, tucked at the very back behind his sweaters and vests and dress shirts, hung James Ringer's—no, *Brandon's* leather jacket. Percy'd been planning on getting it preserved in a shadowbox, next time he got ahold of his computer to search for a trustworthy framing company. Just because it represented a bittersweet memory for him didn't mean it wasn't still pricelessly valuable and worth preserving. Now, he pulled it off its hanger and draped it around his shoulders. Breathed in its unnamable smell as its warmth enveloped him.

Collapsed with it back into bed.

Brandon, he thought, as his eyes slipped closed and he returned to his restless dreams.

"Hello, you've reached . . . Percival Charles . . . Please leave a message after the tone."

Brandon yanked the phone down and ended the call before he could leave a voicemail—another voicemail. Two seemed okay, three seemed like it was pushing the edge of bad ex territory. Not that they were exes. But, yeah.

He tried to tell himself that at least he'd tried, could tell Nolan as much and get the guy off his case, but the truth was, this wasn't just about Nolan. Brandon was disappointed. He'd . . . wanted this.

Wanted to tell Percy what he'd learned, about finding James Ringer, the real James Ringer, buried under all the bullshit again.

Extend his forgiveness and acceptance of James to forgiveness and acceptance of Percy, too. Heal both relationships together.

They could have apologized to each other. Worked this out. Moved forward.

But if Percy wasn't ready for that, then he wasn't. Not like it never took Brandon time to come around after he'd been hurt. Time, like, a lifetime.

He just felt like he couldn't really push on, couldn't *really* do this, until he talked it out with Percy, who had been the only thing anchoring him to a positive idea of James for so long.

He sighed and scrubbed his hands over his face, groaning, only to jump when Maggie cleared her throat right behind him.

She gave him an impish little smile that made all her many freckles stand out. "I'm all set here," she said. "Think you can last a few days without letting it become a hellhole again?"

"I'll try."

"You do that." She tugged her tiny cleaning cart out behind her. "Nolan asked me to come on Tuesdays," she said on her way out the door. "So you won't have to last long. Just remember, takeout containers go in the trash. Clothes go in the hamper. Cigarettes go . . ."

"Actually, I, uh." Brandon leaned in the doorway, shrugging. "I'm not really much of a smoker anymore. Just a bad week. Er, month."

She smiled again. "We all have 'em. Also, I didn't see the booze bottles I cleaned up, because a certain someone told me you're nineteen. Just make sure I don't see them again next time, either, got it?"

"What're you gonna do about it?" Brandon asked, toothlessly.

"It's not what *I'm* gonna do. It's Nolan."

Maybe all his talk about being a second grandfather wasn't just talk, after all.

The thought warmed Brandon from the inside.

"Anything else my new Pops plans on making off limits?"

"Yeah. Giving away any more of your grandfather's things until you're in a better place emotionally. In fact, don't do *anything* right now you can't take back, because feeling like this? Isn't gonna last forever."

Brandon stuffed his hands into his pockets, raising an eyebrow at her. "He said all that?"

Maggie just smiled. "See you Tuesday, Brandon."

Not long after she left, his phone rang.

For a perfect, heartbreaking second, he hoped it was Percy.

But it was Hollywood Doubles.

Don't do anything you can't take back, Maggie's voice echoed in his mind. So he answered the call with a smile. "Hey sunshine," he greeted.

"O-oh! Brandon! Hello!" Theresa sounded surprised, but pleased. "You're sounding well today sweetie! Just calling because you've got a new booking for Saturday—oh! Tomorrow's Saturday, tomorrow morning, I mean. Sorry, I'm all over the place today. I thought . . ." Bless her, she didn't say it. *I thought you had a regular, but I guess you lost him.* Yeah, he did. She coughed delicately. "Anyway, sorry, this appointment is different than your usual, though, so I wanted to double check with you before I said yes."

"Shoot," Brandon said. He'd do it. Whatever it was, he'd do it.

"The client is a woman," Theresa said.

Oh. "Oh. Uh."

"I normally wouldn't book a woman for you, but she says it's for a gay friend of hers who's having a bachelor party. You've never done a party before, so I said I'd ask. She says you'd just be there to mingle and flirt and have a good time, maybe do a little teasing, but no group sex whatsoever. And tomorrow's meeting is just supposed to be pre-party planning, so you'll be able to get a feel for what she wants and see if the two of you will get along."

"So be charming?"

"Y-yes," Theresa replied, and bless her heart, she tried to hide the note of doubt in her voice.

"No problem, Theresa. Look. I'm sorry for the way I've been acting lately. I haven't been myself, or . . . maybe I *have* been myself, but myself isn't that great of a person to be. So I'm sorry."

"Thank you for the apology, Brandon. I . . . I hope that it's not too late for it." She paused. "With your clients, I mean. It's never too late with me. You know that, right?"

Brandon couldn't help but feel a little choked up. "You're way too good for me," he told her.

"No such thing."

"Um, Theresa? While . . . while I've got you . . ." He worried his lip between his teeth. "There's kind of a bit of an explanation for my downswing. Not an excuse! A lot of it is still on me, but . . . Harvey hasn't helped with my mood. He hasn't done anything illegal or anything I haven't agreed to, but he's . . . he's been pretty rough." But rough wasn't the word. "Rough" was what he'd been using all along to convince himself that what Harvey was doing was perfectly fine. All part of the job. "To be honest? He's been more than rough. Abusive, really. And I'm sorry, but I don't want to see him anymore, and I don't know if you should let anyone else at the agency see him, either. God, I'm so sorry for springing this on you, I should have told you about this earlier, I should have—"

"Brandon? Not another word."

He shut up immediately, heart dropping into his stomach.

"You're right, I wish you would have told me this earlier. But you have *nothing* to be sorry for, and if you're honestly calling him abusive right now—which that tone in your voice and your behavior lately tells me you're not using the word lightly—then it doesn't matter whether it's illegal or not, or whether you 'agreed' to it or not. Agreeing to a bit of rough from a client isn't a carte blanche, baby, and there's a difference between someone who's kinky and someone who's an *abuser*. Sadly, men like Harvey count on people not recognizing the difference. But we *do* recognize it, Brandon, and we'll absolutely blacklist him. I'm just sorry I didn't ask you about it earlier. I should have realized."

Brandon didn't realize until right this moment that he almost hadn't expected Theresa to believe him. That he had expected her to blame him, or say—in gentler terms than most people before her— that it couldn't be helped. That he'd agreed, or had it coming.

But she hadn't. She'd taken him at his word.

And suddenly, he felt like a complete and total ass for not just coming to her in the first place. His talent for assuming the worst had already cost him Percy. Nearly cost him Nolan last night. And he'd almost let it cost him Theresa, too.

"So yeah," he said. "Bachelor party. Flirting. No problem at all. You can email me the details. But first, tell me, how did that date go?"

On Saturday morning, Percy's breakfast was late.

Who knew what it was for this time. Hazel could have come in and seen him sleeping in the jacket and been angry he'd mussed his bed, or she could have just been peeved he'd left his remote on the couch yesterday.

Either way, Percy's stomach was gnawing and his hands were shaking and stiff. And he was still wearing the jacket.

It was warm enough to wear outside.

He could go outside.

The mocking little voice that told him he couldn't was patronizing and sweet, gentle and even, just like Hazel was after she yelled at him, or told him how much of a worthless burden he was. Percy was sick of it.

He was sick of so much. And he kept thinking back to telling Brandon he was tired of seeing other people live their lives. The dream from last night was haunting him, nagging at the back of his mind. He'd been an actor, he remembered clearly, but the terrible thing was that it hadn't felt different from how he was every day. Acting fine with Hazel, even when she was starving him. Acting polite to his parents when he happened to see them, which was nearly never, now, as opposed to rarely before.

He was sick of thinking *why bother*?

So he wanted a film degree. He shouldn't wonder why. He shouldn't have to think it was useless to try to do something for himself.

He shouldn't be *starved in his own house*.

But it wasn't his house. The older he got, the more he got to know the confines of this tiny suite, the more he thought of it as his parents' house, the divide clear and laminated. Even in an alternate universe or far flung future where Hazel was gone from here, her control over his life ended, he'd *still* never have real responsibility or freedom. He'd never get to live his life, make a try at being independent, have friends or fall in love or graduate college. He'd always be at his parents' beck and call, always beholden to their demands of him, never allowed to explore who he was and what kind of life he was really capable of living. He would forever be making appearances at parties as "that poor Charles boy." He would forever be that image people had of him—the poor little shut-in with his silly movie daydreams—instead of the person he *was*.

They'd clipped his wings without even letting him *try* to fly.

But maybe he didn't need their permission to try.

It was time he stopped thinking of *himself* as the poor little shut-in, helpless and alone.

Maybe it was time for him to rebel, just like Kovie had said.

Except this time, he wouldn't just play disobedient son like it was a game. He'd rebel in a way that counted.

CHAPTER
THIRTY-THREE

With his denim jacket ruined and thrown out, and James's with Percy, Brandon was relegated back to the modern motorcycle jacket he'd worn to the first few appointments. He felt sorta guilty for it, but he consoled himself by wearing his nicest vintage jeans, boots, and one of the watches he'd bought at Hepcat. Plus he promised himself he'd buy a new jacket as soon as he had the time.

Normally he'd worry he wasn't looking authentic enough, that his clients would think he was dropping his standards lower and lower and rate him accordingly. But for a bachelor party? He had a feeling leather anything would go just fine.

He combed his hair back, brushed his teeth, sprayed on some of the old cologne he found lurking in one of Dahlia's guest bathrooms. Practiced smiling and winking in the mirror. He'd watched a couple of behind the scenes clips of James on YouTube today, just to refresh himself. Not just on James's charm and mannerisms, but on how he newly felt about the man, too. The admiration and love that Percy and Nolan had woken in him, that let him see James in a new light. It wasn't quite back to the level it had been, watching his movies with Percy, curled up together on the couch and falling in love, but it would get there again. He would get there again, with or without Percy. He couldn't let his sense of self, his heritage, hinge on one relationship with one guy, no matter how special and life changing that relationship had been.

He had to be able to do this on his own, too.

The party was that night in a restaurant by the 310, some place with a wine-tasting bar and its own cheesemaker and a water sommelier, and he'd be meeting the client at the same place that morning. Apparently the raunch factor was gonna be toned way, way down. It felt a little weird, being thought of as somebody's classy, upscale version of a stripper. If only they really knew. Who he was. Where he came from.

But it was good money, and Brandon wanted to get back into Hollywood Doubles' good books.

The hostess looked up as soon as he came through the doors. "Jim?" she asked, which, okay, that was a little weird.

"Uh, yep." Shit, no, he was supposed to be charming and flirtatious. Not with the hostess, though. He could still save this.

He spent the short walk back past the wine bar telling himself to get his goddamn head together, but that was all blown out the window when he saw they weren't headed to a half-decorated back room or a loft with party planners bustling around, but instead just to a single table, where a black girl around Brandon's age was sitting, typing furiously on an iPhone.

"Kovie, he's here." The hostess upturned the water glass across from Kovie and vanished, leaving Brandon alone with his client.

Brandon blinked at her.

Kovie narrowed her eyes. "You'd better be who I think you are."

"I, uh," he said, taken aback. "I'm B—um, Jim, Jim Ringer. I'm here for . . . the party? Planning the party?"

She sighed with relief and set her cell phone down. "I *am* the party. Siddown, would you? We need to talk."

Brandon didn't sit. "Sorry but this is . . . this is really . . . It's really weird. I'm not even sure I should stay. I don't actually take on girls as clients."

"I know. Which is why I said all that stuff about the bachelor party."

He thought of Nolan, and how he'd jumped to all the wrong conclusions.

But also of Harvey, and how he'd ignored all his instincts.

"Okay, I can tell you're pretty spooked, and I get it, but can you just sit down? I'm here to talk to you about a friend of mine. Percy Charles." She stuck her hand out. "My name's Kovie Mittelstaedt."

Brandon's stomach jumped, then sank to the floor. Her expression said this wasn't going to be a cheery chat. He scraped out a chair and threw himself into it before his knees gave out. "What about him? Is he okay? What's going on?" Belatedly, he added, "I'm Brandon."

"I know. What I *don't* know is what's going on with Percy, but I do know enough to be worried. He hasn't been answering my calls. That housekeeper of his won't let me in to see him. My dad says his parents have him on lockdown. Everybody in their circle is talking about it. I was hoping..."

"That I'd know what's up?" Brandon shook his head. "He stopped talking to me, too. One minute we were fine, and the next he was telling me he never wanted to see me again. Since then he's been screening my calls."

"I don't think he's screening them," Kovie said, ominously. "Whatever happened with you two happened, but he wouldn't just ignore my calls and texts, not when we haven't fought or anything. And it's been *weeks*. His housekeeper..." She rapped her fingers on the rim of her water glass. "I don't like it."

"Me neither," Brandon admitted to his lap. "You know she actually starved him once, just because she was mad?"

Kovie's water glass tipped from the force of her hand. Brandon reached out for it, but water still splashed all over the table.

Kovie ignored it. "She *what*? Are you *fucking* kidding me? She—" She closed both her hands on the edge of her side of the table. "Whoa. Okay. That's way more than taking away his phone. That's way more than anyone knows. And you didn't do anything about it?"

"Well, I mean, I made sure he got food, but there's not much else I can do. I'm a hooker, for fuck's sake."

"*Well*," she parroted back, "now you're the hooker who's gonna help me bust him out."

"I am?" Brandon squeaked.

"Yeah. I thought about calling the cops, but . . ." She shook her head. "I'm pretty sure his parents' and his caregiver's combined powers of old money and bullshittery would keep anyone from actually doing anything, and then they'd know we're onto them and do who knows what. Fly him off to some island for 'his own good.'"

Brandon nodded, turning it all over in his head. Busting Percy out, looking after him, taking care of him, it sounded like a fucking fantasy. A fantasy Brandon had definitely had, but a fantasy just the same. And no way was Brandon anywhere near the heroic ideal a fantasy like that required. He was a loser. A drop-out. Still a depressed piece of shit. Yes, a hooker.

And he also loved Percy.

You're the hooker who's gonna help me bust him out. "I'm the hooker who's gonna help you bust him out," he said.

"Good." Kovie leaned toward him. "That's good."

He nodded. No going back now. He didn't know what would happen after—how he'd help Percy with his medical needs, how they would manage anything at all—but he had to do *something*. He was sick of telling himself he was worthless and helpless, especially now that he knew Percy was suffering for it. "Okay. Now what?"

"Now?" Kovie twisted her phone around to show him a Google maps aerial of Percy's house. "Now we plan."

Kovie had made it seem like they were gonna go all secret agent, what with all her talk of "busting Percy out" and the satellite images of his house, but in the end her plan largely consisted of the two of them confronting Percy's parents with the truth about Hazel.

"I called ahead and asked for an appointment with them, but I think we'll have more of a chance if it's both of us there," she explained as she drove. "Like, I'm his friend, but Percy's fucking nightmare caregiver knows some shit about me from when I was younger, so she doesn't like me. And as far as they know, you're his tutor, so obviously you're more objective, and an actual professional."

"Supposedly a professional."

"Supposedly," she agreed. "You could put the screws to them and say you're a mandated reporter through the school or something too, if you think it'll help. Say his teachers are concerned because he's missing work."

"Are you sure they really believe I'm a tutor? I kind of got the feeling that Hazel never bought that."

She gripped the steering wheel tighter. "Doesn't matter if Hazel bought it or not. Once we reveal the truth about her, they're gonna have good reason to doubt everything that comes from her mouth, including her suspicions about you."

"So basically I'm just here to play your credible backup."

"Basically, yeah."

Brandon felt himself holding his breath. Knew it was because he was on the precipice of saying something he couldn't take back. "In that case, I think I might have a better card to play than just tutor."

"Oh?"

"I'm kind of old Hollywood royalty. My grandfather was one of the biggest stars of the fifties, before he died. My grandmother was a famous philanthropist. She was a little weird, but I think her celebrity name and her checkbook still count for a lot."

"You're James Ringer's grandson," Kovie blurted out, screeching to a stop at the next red light and whipping her head around to stare at him. "Oh my fucking God. You're actually him. The one who called my dad looking to sell the Ringer collection. That was you."

"That was *your dad*?"

"I promise his sliminess does not run in the family." She laughed.

"Thank God." He couldn't see the resemblance at all—and not because Harry was a white guy. "Hey, uh. Just so you know, I'm not planning on selling, anymore."

"Good to hear. My dad would have tried to rip you off."

"Yeah, I kinda got that impression. Does that normally work for him, talking to people like their precious stuff is all trash?"

"It's a good way to preface a lowball offer. Also a good way to piss off the heir to a legend, apparently."

"I never really thought of him as a legend. More of a bogeyman." Brandon smiled sadly. "Percy was the first one to convince me of anything different."

"He definitely has a way of making people fall in love with the things he loves."

"Has a way of making people fall in love period," Brandon murmured, earning himself a long look from Kovie. He squirmed the longer she held it, her sharp brown eyes dissecting him, checking for his honesty. "Yeah, so. I do. I love him. Also, please watch the road and try not to kill us."

"*You* watch the road." But Kovie turned back to look, steadying Brandon's panicked heartbeat. A little. Not much. "So you really got it bad, huh? I'd like to be credited with that, for full disclosure."

"Credited with . . . what?"

She slowed to take a turn, heading into Percy's parents' neighborhood. "I mean, I told him he needed to *rebel* a little, but I just wanted him to get out. You know, live a little. Groove to a new groove. Our parents are all the same. Money, appearances, reputation, yadda yadda yadda. Point is, I was lonely and isolated too until I put myself out there. Stopped worrying about my family reputation so much. Which is why, once all this is behind us, I'm . . ." She took a deep breath. "I'm finally gonna stop being my family's dirty secret and train as a Planned Parenthood clinic escort. This whole thing with Percy made me realize rebellions don't come without risks, and it was kind of hypocritical of me to push *him* that way when here I am, too afraid to stand up to my dad when he tries to dictate how I'm supposed to feel and act about one of the defining moments of *my* life." She gave her head a little shake, half-laughed. "For the record, though, by 'rebel a little' I did not mean 'buy a boyfriend'. That was all his idea."

"He didn't—I'm not—"

"Yeah, yeah." Her smile was fond. She reached over and patted him briskly on the shoulder. "At least he bought a decent one."

Brandon flushed.

And then paled, because that was Percy's house. All the downstairs lights were on. Percy's *parents* were there. Hazel, too. Not to mention Percy, who maybe didn't ever want to see him again.

"I can't do this," he blurted.

She scoffed. "Of course you can. You know how to act, right? You must, it's in your blood. Just follow my lead, and nobody will know what shady website I got you from. But I will warn you. These old-money rich types can smell fear. So don't apologize for anything. Walk in there like you own the place. I mean, you fucked their kid, so you kinda do."

"He fucked *me*, actually." Brandon's mouth quirked.

She slapped her hand down on the console with an answering grin. "*Well.* I think I'll keep you. Now c'mon." She gave him a push. "Let's *do this.*"

His stab of bravery at her confidence held out until they got to the front door and Kovie stepped up to bang on it four times, as loud as she possibly could. "Oh my God," he muttered.

"Shut up," she said out of the corner of her mouth. "You're Hollywood royalty. You belong here. And straighten up, you look like you're about to fall over."

"I *am* about to fall over, Kovie."

"Shhhhhh."

The door swung open, and they were face to face with . . . not Hazel, or Percy's parents. A maid. "Hello, yes?"

Kovie lifted her chin. "Kovie Mittelstaedt and Brandon Ringer. We have a meeting with Mr. and Mrs. Charles."

"Of course, Miss Mittelstaedt, they're expecting you." The woman darted her eyes at Brandon, but masked her uncertainty with politeness. "And Mr. Ringer. This way please."

There was a moment of confusion for Brandon as he stooped automatically to pull off his shoes . . . and realized Kovie was doing no such thing. He stopped. Stood straight again. Followed Kovie and the maid into the house. Except this time, rather than going to the left like he always did with Percy, the maid led them right. It was like an entire other house, all dark-paneled wood with ridiculously high ceilings and chandeliers and a fancy kitchen and like *five* sitting rooms. It was silent and sterile, with no family photos, no hint of Percy's omnipresent medical supplies, and no indication there was a second upstairs wing across the way.

It was like Percy didn't even exist.

Brandon kept his mouth shut, which was surprisingly easy because it was hard to multitask at talking *and* forcing himself not to gawk at how incredibly rich and over the top this place was at the same time.

So he was silent, and he faced straight forward, walking like a man going to his execution.

No, wait, that was showing fear.

He walked like a man about to *perform* an execution.

Or, at least, getting Hazel fired, which had to be the next best thing.

The sitting room the maid led them into was prim and sterile and quiet, with beige carpet and beige furniture and beige walls, and two people sitting stiffly on the beige couch.

"Sit," the man said, not bothering with pleasantries. He looked impatient and annoyed; his wife, anxious but faux gracious.

"Thank you for taking the time to see us," Kovie said as she sat.

She spoke differently around them. The words she used. How she pronounced them. Brandon, even after only knowing her this long, picked up on it right away.

He followed her lead, remembering Dahlia's practiced poise at art shows and galas. "Yes, thank you," he said.

"You, I know through your family," Percy's father said, pointing to Kovie dismissively. "But *you*, I'm not sure we've been introduced." He narrowed his eyes at Brandon. "How do you know my son?"

Brandon extended a hand and made sure to shake firmly. "Brandon Ringer, sir. My grandparents were James Ringer and Dahlia Delair. I've been tutoring Percy in film studies, since his project work centers around my grandfather's films."

"O-oh!" Percy's mother squeaked. "*You're* the tutor?"

"Yes ma'am. Or, you know, I *was*." He gave them both a pointed, insulted look.

Percy's mother folded her manicured hands together and looked him up and down, her lips pursed. "Percy's caretaker had . . . doubts. About . . . about your qualifications."

Brandon scoffed, like that was the most ridiculous thing he'd ever heard. "Well, *she* didn't know who I was. I try not to broadcast it, you understand."

Percy's father coughed, and it was obvious he didn't understand at all—but also didn't want to reveal that fact. "Of course, of course. I can see why one wouldn't. I'm sure now that that *misunderstanding* has been cleared up, Mr. Ringer, we can hire you back at your usual rate."

"We're not here about Brandon's job," Kovie put in, forcefully. "We're here about his so-called caregiver."

Percy's parents turned to Brandon expectantly, like they couldn't care less what Kovie had to say about any of it. He stumbled for a second, his plan to play second to Kovie dissolving from under him. Then he gathered himself up, because this was *important*. And if they thought they didn't have to listen to Kovie too, he'd just make them.

"*Kovie* and I have reason to believe she's abusing him," Brandon announced. "Percy's being forcibly isolated." No response on his parents' blank faces. "And she's withheld food from him in the past. To the point where I had to bring it to him myself because he was starving up there by himself."

The fact that that revelation had them looking relieved was not a comfort.

And then, to add insult to injury, Percy's father piped up with, "Is that all?"

Beside him, Kovie's nostrils flared. She didn't speak.

Brandon tried his very best not to scoff. "Is that not enough?"

"Percy has a very delicate stomach," Percy's mother said. "With his condition, you know. He's on a carefully controlled diet."

Kovie reached over and squeezed Brandon's knee hard, digging her fingernails in. Presumably to keep him from yelling, which was a good fucking idea, because he was on the verge of losing it.

"I'm not talking about watching his portions or the ingredients of what he's eating," he gritted out. "I mean, not serving him food at all on a given day. *Starving* him. As *punishment.*"

"Well, she is responsible for his discipline. Have you ever cared for a disabled child, Brandon?"

"No, but I know enough to know that refusing to feed someone who depends on you for food isn't exactly like taking their cell phone privileges away. And Percy *isn't* a child anymore."

"Well, that's your opinion."

Were they seriously . . . ? Brandon's chest heaved. God, maybe they *should* have called the cops.

"Mr. and Mrs. Charles, please," Kovie pleaded. "I'm Percy's friend. We met at one of your parties and I liked him right away. Percy is disabled, but he's more capable than you think. He needs care, yes, but he also needs *freedom to live his life.* That woman you've hired has no idea how to care for him properly. He's lonely, and he's unhappy. You have the power to change that. With the right support, he could lead a really full life—"

Percy's father put up a hand. "Thank you, Miss Mittelstaedt, for your opinion."

He wasn't thanking her at all. He was shutting her down. Shutting her up.

"Please just consider what we're saying," she tried, and it was obvious it was taking all her power to remain polite and respectful. "Or . . . or ask Percy himself. See what *he* says. Please."

"Yes, *thank you*, Miss Mittelstaedt. We'll be sure to do that and handle this issue appropriately as a family."

A family that doesn't include you or your opinion, Brandon could just hear him adding.

"Mr. and Mrs. Charles," Brandon put in desperately. "If you'd just ask—"

Percy's father got out his checkbook, slapping it onto the coffee table and folding it open. "Do you have a cancellation fee, young man? For your services? Name a price. How does an additional two months' pay sound?"

"You are fucking kidding me," Brandon burst out. He couldn't play nice anymore. Not in the face of *this*. This callous fucking lack of love or attention or interest in Percy's life.

And all this time he'd thought it was just Hazel keeping him down?

"Excuse me?" Percy's mother cried, hand flying to her chest.

Percy's father shut his checkbook violently. "I think this conversation is over," he snarled. "And it's time for you both to leave."

"Time for *all of us* to leave," a new voice added.

They all spun in their seats to find Percy standing in the doorway, fucking fuming.

Percy, with a suitcase at his feet.

Percy, wearing James Ringer's famous leather jacket, with his shoulders thrown back and his expression radiantly defiant.

"Percival!" his mother cried. "What in God's name are you doing out here?"

"I tried to stop him!" Hazel wailed, pushing Percy out of the way in order to get herself through the doors. "He's having some kind of psychotic break! I found him out of his rooms, on the phones—" And then she spotted Brandon. "*You!*"

"Yeah, *me*. And lady, the only psychotic one in this house is *you*," Brandon shot back, standing up. Kovie surged up beside him, her hands clenched at her sides.

"Will someone please tell me what is going on here!" Percy's father roared.

Kovie blew out a breath and moved a little closer to Percy. "Boy is it good to see you, Perce." She shot a dark look at Percy's parents. "And apparently what's *going on here* is two separately planned and yet extremely well-coordinated escape attempts."

"*Escape*," Percy's mother sputtered. "My!"

Percy spared a nod at Kovie—and maybe Brandon too?—then lifted his chin, tugging at the collar of the leather jacket. "I think Brandon and Kovie have already told you what's going on here, or at least, as much as they know. Which was all information you intended on ignoring, I see. Doesn't matter. You won't ignore what I have to say."

"Percival!" Hazel said through her teeth.

Percy ignored her. Didn't even glance in her direction. "Mother, Father, I've given it a lot of thought, and I've decided to move out."

His father laughed. "You?"

"Yes, me. I made some calls, once I found where *she* hid the phones," he curled a lip in Hazel's direction, "and I have space in a shelter arranged until next semester when I can move into the disabled suite in my university's residence. The disability worker there was surprisingly helpful, actually. The school has a health insurance plan for students, too. Seems that despite everything you two and Hazel have spent years convincing me of, there's all *sorts* of supports for someone like me, especially when there's an unhealthy home environment."

Percy's mother spread her hands open. "You call *this* unhealthy? Our home?" she said. "Percival, *please*. You can't possibly think we've provided anything less than comfort and stability and—*look* at where you live! You would rather live in some filthy homeless shelter than *here*?"

"He doesn't have to," Brandon burst out. Suddenly the idea of Percy living with him, filling up all the empty space where Brandon— well, and Nolan and Maggie, now—weren't was something Brandon wanted more than anything. "He's going to live with me. I just happen to have a very nice family home with a pile of guest rooms that I think he'll find very comfortable." He looked to Percy. "If you'll have it. Me."

Percy's eyes widened.

His father cut the silence between them. "This is a rash decision,

Percival. Even if your school has a health plan, do you think it'll even begin to cover the costs of your medication? You can't leave. You won't be able to manage."

Percy's small chest puffed up. Brandon saw a glimpse of the confident, assertive person he was when they made love. "The costs of my medication, hmm? You mean the medication Hazel's been withholding from me?"

"She *what*?" Brandon barked. He heard Kovie cry out, too. All the things Percy had told Brandon swirled up: that he would be in pain all the time, that he could go blind. Hazel knew all that shit and she'd *kept it from him anyway*.

Percy put a hand up to quiet them both. "Maybe I won't be able to afford my medications for too long," he said with a wicked little smile. "I know my trust fund won't keep me forever. But you know, I've been thinking. If you two refuse to let me leave, I hear there's people who'd probably pay decent money for a dirty story about a 'good' family. You've toted me around for years as your poor sick son. What do you think people will offer me to get a glimpse of what happened behind closed doors? What kind of people you hire?"

"That's blackmail!" his father shouted.

"That's survival." Percy shrugged, wrapping his hand around his suitcase handle. "Don't pretend you two have never wished I were more independent and resourceful. Well, surprise! I am."

"I told you he needed a firm hand! I told you these two were bad influences!" Hazel babbled.

Percy whirled on her with his focused, confident rage. "It's not them," he said. "Believe it or not, I am an adult who can form an opinion about something by myself. And my opinion is that there's not a single person in the world who's mastered the ability to be condescending and cruel as well as you have. You know," he said, his voice lowering, "I never would have thought you'd stoop so low as to actually *abuse* me. But you did. And you can't couch it in lies. Not to me. Unlike *them*—" he threw out a hand, gesturing to his parents "—I was *there*."

"That is ridiculous," Hazel stammered. "I was only doing what's best for you."

But no one was paying her any attention anymore. They were all looking at Percy.

Because he was smiling. "Well then," he said, "that's something we have in common. Only I know what's best for me is to get the *fuck* out of here."

Brandon moved to Percy, standing with him by the door. He picked up the suitcase. "Well, that's settled, then. Say, I'll do you a deal, Mr. Charles. Just this once, I'll waive my cancellation fee. C'mon, Perce."

"C'mon, sweetie," Kovie added, coming to Percy's other side, and threw her arm around his shoulders. "Proud of you."

"I'll be by with a moving van to pick up his DVD collection and his books," Brandon added, totally unable to keep the smirk out of his voice and not the least bit sorry about it. "Get them boxed up for me, wouldja?"

"This is ridiculous," Percy's father sputtered. "*Ridiculous.*"

They made it to the front entrance hall before Percy's mother caught up with them. Her cheeks were wet and she was twisting her wedding ring nervously around her finger. "Don't worry about paying for your medications, sweetheart. And . . . You can always come back," she said to Percy tremulously. "You can come back, I know you'll need to. Don't listen to your father."

"I haven't for a long time," Percy said. He seemed torn for a second, about to say something, then just shook his head and turned away again. Brandon and Kovie turned with him, and together they walked out the front door, leaving Hazel and Percy's parents and all of it behind them.

CHAPTER
THIRTY-FOUR

"**S**o this can be your room," Brandon said, a little awkwardly, swinging the door open and stepping aside.

They'd parted ways with Kovie after going with her to pick up Brandon's car, but only after promising her they'd meet her for dinner later, once Percy was settled.

Percy peered into the room. A huge bed. Nice—*real*—art on the walls, in heavy frames. A mirror on the ceiling, which very nearly had him laughing. He only stopped because he knew the line between that and crying was paper thin just then. For more than the fact that he was standing in Dahlia Delair's former home. *James Ringer's* former home.

Brandon's home, now.

And his own?

"And, uh. Don't worry about rent or anything, obviously." Brandon stuffed his hands in his pockets, his shoulders hunched. "The house is paid for. And like, utilities are a set thing anyway, and it's covered with my job. I think I have a cleaner now, too? There's that."

Percy's lower lip trembled. "I don't deserve this," he said, softly.

"What! Of course you do. Of *course* you do. Don't let them get in your head, okay? It's not—"

"After how I treated you," Percy amended.

"Oh." Brandon quieted. "It's fine. You didn't mean any of it . . . right?"

Percy shook his head. "That's still not an excuse, though. What I said about you, and your job, it was uncalled for. I wasn't happy, I was scared and angry and in pain, and I took it out on you. I treated you like you were holding things in front of me, teasing me, taunting me with something I couldn't have or didn't realize I already had, and it wasn't . . . none of that was true. And the idea of telling me must have been so hard for you, since you didn't." He took a breath, stemming the rush of words. "And, oh, speaking of which, here. This is yours. I *really* shouldn't be wearing it." He pulled the jacket from his shoulders. Held it out, smiling sheepishly. "I only had it on for strength, mostly. Figure I don't need it for that anymore anyway."

"It *is* pretty much priceless," Brandon said with a smile, taking it. "But here. We'll trade." He pulled the modern leather jacket off his own back and draped it around Percy's shoulders. "Doesn't fit, but living with me for a bit should fatten even you up."

Percy couldn't help it. He lifted the collar to his face and breathed in deep.

The intertwined smells of Brandon and of leather combined to make his eyes roll back with pure contentment.

Brandon folded James's jacket over his arm, shuffling his feet. "And look, just to be totally clear, you don't owe me anything for this. I know that was kind of a boyfriend thing to do, asking you to live with me, giving you the jacket off my back, but it doesn't have to be like that. You don't owe me money, and you don't owe me a relationship or even just sex. Okay? This doesn't have to *mean* anything. You can even leave once you've got that room in university residence you mentioned, or a better roommate comes along or whatever. Or if you just wanna live together as friends, in the meantime or long term, that's cool too. Heck, you don't even have to be my friend, although I think that would be nice." He trailed off, blushing. It was rare Brandon talked that damn much.

Percy bit his lip, considering all of it. "That's really sweet, Brandon, it really is, but before you say anything else, you should know. Some of the things my parents said are true. I'll need things from you that someone who's able-bodied wouldn't. Are you sure you're okay with that?"

"Are you sure you're okay with *me*?" Brandon parroted back. "I'm a high school dropout, I'm still pretty much a dick most of the time, and I'm not exactly working my way up to corporate CEO. Probably won't ever."

"I never asked for a corporate CEO. I don't need you to be rich— or famous," he added, because he wanted Brandon to know for sure that even here, in James Ringer's house surrounded by things he'd touched, things that had belonged to him, that Percy wanted Brandon for *Brandon*, and not for his grandfather. Yes, the house was exciting, and Brandon turning out to be related to James was something Percy would never have dreamt of at his wildest, but when it came down to it, Brandon was here, in front of him, offering him support and space all at once. Offering him everything he needed. "I came here with you because of you. Because we connect. Because I like *you*. Not because of anything else."

Brandon blinked at him, looking suspiciously wet-eyed. "Um. Well, that's good to know." He licked his lips and looked down at the jacket, then perked up and grinned. "Hey, howsabout you come see where this belongs?"

As far as distractions went, it was irresistible. Percy's heart gave an excited little squeeze. "The collection?"

"Yup. It's in the basement. Where it's always been."

So he hadn't sold it. One of Percy's fever dreams had been Brandon showing up with a fistful of receipts and telling Percy he'd sold off the rest of it, too, since Percy clearly didn't think he deserved to have it, just like the jacket. And Percy hadn't had any way to check to see if it had been listed, sold . . .

He hadn't *really* thought Brandon would do that out of spite, but . . .

Well, it was easy to think a lot of things, the way Percy had been.

"Hey," Brandon said, nudging Percy's chin with his knuckle in a way that despite his whole speech was *decidedly* boyfriend-like. His eyes glittered. "You didn't answer my question. You wanna go down and see it?"

"*Is* that even a question?" Percy abandoned his suitcase, following Brandon down the hall and back into the living room. There was a huge pool outside, visible through the back doors, and it was glittering orange in the light of the setting sun—and downtown LA was lit up behind it, only a few miles away.

Percy could see the Hollywood sign from here.

He didn't realize he'd stopped until Brandon cleared his throat and showed up in front of him, a gentle little smile on his face. "You okay, Perce?"

Percy shook his head. "I am, I just . . . I can't believe this is my life. It's not a dream. It's not . . . a movie."

Brandon brushed his fingers through Percy's bangs. "I can't believe this is *my* life, either." He withdrew his hand with a nervous smile.

"You're allowed to, you know," Percy said.

"Huh?"

"You're allowed to kiss me. You're allowed to make it—" He touched the chest of Brandon's jacket, *Brandon's* jacket, this time, "—a boyfriend thing. If you want."

Brandon sighed. Leaned into Percy like he was exhausted, like he couldn't hold up his own body anymore. "I want that," he said. "But—" He cupped a hand on the back of Percy's head and neck. Didn't kiss him. "But, listen, speaking of me not being a CEO . . . I'm not ready to quit my job. There was another guy at Hollywood Doubles—their Paul Newman, actually—who fell for a client and left the agency, but I don't think I can follow in his footsteps. I want to save up some money to fix up the house. I've got some overdue bills to settle, too. And to be honest, I like the work. Mostly. Is that . . . is that okay with you?"

"It was okay with me when I was hiring you," Percy said. He cupped the back of Brandon's head in return, fingertips sifting through his hair. It was grown out some now. "It was okay when we went to that diner and I *wasn't* paying you. I don't see why it wouldn't be okay now. As long as I'm the exception on the 'falling for clients' front, I guess I should say."

Brandon chuckled. "I like a few of my clients, Perce, I'm not gonna pretend I don't, but they're, ah, they're *old*. Still fun to be around 'n all, and I don't mind having sex with them as long as I get paid, but yeah. Old. Too old for me to *fall for*, that's for damn sure. Also, one of them turned out to kind of be my unofficial grandfather?"

Percy gave him a quizzical look, drawing his head back slightly. "How? Like, as a fetish thing?"

Now, Brandon burst out laughing. "No! No! God no! Like, as in he was James's boyfriend back in the day. Wanted to be a part of his family when the baby came along. Oh, shit, there's so much I have to tell you about him. There are actually things even *you* don't know. He's—"

Percy kissed him.

Brandon's hands fell to his shoulders. Then moved again, slipping under his jacket and then under his shirt to rest on his skin, thumbs curving over his collarbones. It always amazed Percy how Brandon just went liquid when Percy made a move on him. Liquid and pliant and—yes, letting Percy move him a step back with the slightest push. Then another push, and another, until Brandon's back was against the back of the couch. His eyes were lit up like the swimming pool and his skin was bathed yellow-orange when Percy leaned back to look at him.

And all Percy saw was *him*, in bright, living color.

He sniffed, and the warm look on Brandon's face fell away. "Perce? You okay? Hey, don't cry." Brandon cupped his cheek.

Percy blinked hard to clear the blur from his eyes. "I'm not! I didn't mean to."

Brandon gave him a lopsided grin. "Uh huh. You gonna cry when we go to the basement, too?"

"It's been an emotional day," Percy huffed, brushing his hands away. He kissed Brandon's jaw to soften it and wandered toward the kitchen, because if they stayed there any longer, he was *really* going to cry. "Now come on and show me."

"You betcha." Brandon opened the door just past the kitchen and flipped the lights on, going down ahead of Percy.

Which was a good thing, because when Percy got close to the bottom of the stairs and Brandon turned the lights on, he stumbled over the next step and caught himself on Brandon's shoulders, too busy gaping at the trove laid out in front of him to care.

This was like seeing Canter's and buying his first limited edition signed book and getting rare old laserdiscs and finding James's buried interview all at once. Percy had never seen *this much*, had never even dreamed—had never even *considered* . . .

"Can I touch," he breathed, practically in Brandon's ear. "Oh my god, can I touch it?"

"Yeah, Perce." Brandon offered his arm for Percy to balance on, and Percy scrambled down the last two steps and froze, with no idea which direction to go in. Then he went right—no, left. Yes, left, where there was a boxed-up pair of sunglasses.

"Oh my god. Oh my god. These are from *Break of Dawn*." Percy skated his fingers over the clear case. "And these!" The pair next to them were branded and old, so old the glaze on the lenses was corroding. There were mass-produced things here and there, but they were few in number compared to the priceless items organized on every shelf. Percy passed up the lighters and plates for a pair of cowboy boots, a stunt knife, a messy postcard signed *-JR*. "That's his handwriting!" he trilled. "Look how ridiculously over the top he is about crossing his T's!"

"You should see the deed to the house," Brandon said, coming up behind him and looping his arms around Percy's waist. His chin came down to rest on Percy's shoulder.

"He did circles over his I's too."

"Oh, Brandon." Percy felt the tears welling up again.

Brandon pressed a quick, happy kiss to Percy's shoulder. "C'mon, kid. You haven't even seen the family photo albums yet."

They stayed downstairs for *hours*. Percy only realized how long it had been when he tried to stand from sitting on the hard floor and his legs simply refused to cooperate. Brandon was there to help him up, though, with a smile and another kiss.

They'd gone through several photo albums, then found a box of personal correspondence, which they'd pored over.

They'd hung the jacket back up together in its lit frame, and Percy had almost pressed his face to the attached plaque, with the stunt coordinator and James's familiar signatures, to read the tiny script describing the knife-fight accident.

And Brandon had told him about Nolan, James's one-time lover.

"He's gonna want to meet you," Brandon said, locking the basement door behind them. "He's the one who convinced me to try calling you back. Before Kovie came and found me, I mean. Actually, hell, probably a lot of people want to meet you. Nolan, Maggie, Theresa . . . Ms. Monroe . . ." He frowned at nothing, then went to rummage around in the refrigerator. "God, I should really meet with Judy—uh, that's Ms. Monroe, my boss. I have a lot of explaining to do."

Percy stuffed his hands in the pockets of Brandon's coat. "So close the fridge and call her up. See if she wants to meet us at Canter's. I could go for a Reuben."

"You'd do that? Come along with me? It . . . might not be pretty. For me."

"Worried about ruining my perfect fantasy image of you, Brandon? I wouldn't be. It's only a matter of time before you fart in front of me, after all."

Brandon stuffed his face into the fridge, wailing dramatically, "Oh my goddddddddd."

Percy moved in close, drawing Brandon back into his arms and nudging the fridge shut with a toe. "I wanna live in the real world, Brandon. And that includes knowing my boyfriend is a little less than perfect sometimes. So go on, call her. Whatever conversation you have to have with her, it's not going to make me love you any less."

Brandon's jaw dropped. "I—uhh. Yeah. I—yeah." He fumbled in his pocket for his phone and headed for the kitchen door, almost walking himself into the wall in the process. He stepped out into the hall, then immediately turned back around and said, "You too! I mean, I love you too. You know."

Percy felt himself smile. "I kinda figured." He made a *shoo* motion, sending Brandon off to call his boss.

Then he explored the fridge, the contents of which were pathetic, to be honest. The cabinets weren't much better. They would have to shop. Percy would have to shop for his own groceries.

If his father took his threat seriously—and he should, since Percy hadn't been lying—then Percy's credit card and bank accounts, including his sizeable inheritance and trust fund, would remain untouched. His was the primary name on them, so all he would have to do was swing by the main branch downtown and tell the clerks he'd moved out and was independent. He could have their names removed. Could have his own money, his own *everything*.

The cash wouldn't last forever, not with his expenses, but it should be enough to get him through university, until he found a job with health insurance. He could even hire his own caregiver down the line, if he needed one. A caregiver he was in charge of, who he could set boundaries with and reprimand or fire if they overstepped them.

He could do this.

He knew he could do this.

By the time Brandon came back to find him, he was in his room, fitting his things into the chest of drawers there. "Heyyy," Brandon said, knocking lightly on the door frame. He looked a little pale. "You're gonna keep this one?"

Percy nodded. He and Brandon were good, solid, but Percy had a feeling it would take some time to transition into being used to someone living in his space all the time. If he had to share his bedroom permanently with Brandon, with nowhere else to go, he would probably drive himself or both of them nuts. "What did your boss say?"

"She seemed . . . not pleased." Brandon flipped his phone in his hand. "Stiff, I guess. Not like her." He scuffed his feet over the carpet. "But I mean, if I get fired, I'll find another job. Another job I like."

Percy hummed his agreement and closed the last drawer. "When does she want to meet?"

Brandon paled some more. "Tomorrow. For lunch."

"Okay." Percy padded up to him and cupped either side of his face. "Say it with me: if Percy can tell his parents to go fuck themselves, then I can talk to my boss."

Brandon made a face. "Yeah, you're right." But he still looked worried, so Percy prodded him toward the kitchen. "Kovie said dinner in an hour or so, but after that I have literally no food," Brandon muttered, glancing in the fridge. "Unless you wanna eat bagged cheese and moldy grapes."

Percy pulled a face.

"We could head down to the grocery store after dinner. Get some essentials. Some junk food, maybe? Microwave popcorn and a movie night?"

Which sounded amazing, but— "Honestly, after sitting on your hard floor all day I don't know if I'm up for that much walking." Percy winced, hating that he had to say it. Hating that he couldn't just go along and go shopping with his boyfriend on a whim like a normal couple.

But Brandon didn't seem put off in the slightest. "That's cool. We can order in, give Kovie a raincheck, or we can still meet with her, and when we're done she can drop you off while I run out and grab a couple things. Or, hey, I could call ahead and see if any stores nearby have a courtesy wheelchair I can push you around in. If you're up for it, of course. But I'd hate to buy you the wrong cereal or one percent milk when you only drink whole . . ."

"They have those?" Percy asked, blinking.

" . . . different percents of milk?"

Percy snorted. "No. Courtesy wheelchairs."

"Uh, yeah. Not everybody can walk a whole grocery store. Doesn't make the need to buy groceries go away."

"And they'd let me *use* them?" As stupid as it was, Percy could barely contain his excitement. To hear Hazel and his parents tell it, Percy was simply too weak and sickly to even *try* to go to a grocery store.

"Uh, yeah, of course. It's a customer service thing. If loaning 'em out means they get a sale, they'll loan 'em out." He stuck his hands in his pocket, twisting on his ankles. "Although, full disclosure, I mostly know about them because when I was a shithead teenager I used to take my friends for joyrides in them."

Percy tsked at him, but couldn't summon up much anger, seeing as he already seemed sorry for it.

He was going to do this. Pain or no pain, he was going to go to a grocery store with his boyfriend. They were going to fill their shared fridge together. Buy junk food. Together, like a normal couple.

Mostly.

"And you . . . you don't mind pushing me around? You don't find that weird?"

"Percy," Brandon said, taking him by both hands and staring into his eyes sincerely. "Percy. *No.* Never. That's Hazel talking." He pressed a kiss to Percy's lips. "I want to spend time with you, Percy. I don't mind putting out a little extra effort to make it happen. Promise." And then he got that mischievous smile of his, that smile that made Percy's whole world warm and playful and good. "Just so long as you don't make me shop at Whole Foods."

CHAPTER
THIRTY-FIVE

Brandon couldn't sleep.

His bed felt hard, lumpy. His sheets kept getting him tangled. His blankets were too heavy. His pillows were either too flat or too puffy.

He tossed from side to side. Stared at the ceiling and the walls.

Kept thinking about his meeting tomorrow with Judy . . . and the fact that he hadn't quite told Percy the whole truth about James Ringer.

He'd intended to, he *had*. They'd been down in the basement, talking about Nolan, and Brandon had recounted the entire sad story, right up to the part where James had died. And then he'd frozen, unable to form the words.

Percy had been fascinated, enthusiastic, ecstatic to hear the truth, even if it was sad.

But Brandon couldn't bear to go so far as break his heart. So he'd brushed it off. And now the confession kept cycling over and over in the back of his head.

He'd been thinking about it all night. All through their dinner with Kovie—where she had thoroughly vetted Brandon and Percy's new living situation, then gleefully asked for all the sordid details of Percy's daring solo escape plan, and *then* bought them both triple-thick milkshakes to celebrate—, all through their grocery store stroll, and on the couch, where they'd made it through half of a movie before both admitting they were falling asleep right there.

He didn't want to ruin their happiness, their peace. Or rather . . . *Percy's* happiness, *Percy's* peace, because sitting on this secret had completely obliterated his own.

If Percy could just be here beside him, his closeness might ease

Brandon's restlessness enough that he could sleep. Sleep, and hope that his guilt and anxiety didn't follow him into his dreams.

He didn't want to be alone right now, dammit.

Did he have to be?

He rolled over to stare at his closed door.

Sure, Percy obviously still needed the space of having his own room. Brandon was hardly gonna fault him for wanting to transition into the whole idea of living with a person, especially when it had happened without notice or planning. He would have his own space as long as he needed it.

But Brandon asking to make an exception for tonight, when he needed Percy . . . that wasn't violating those boundaries, was it?

Well, he could always ask, and if Percy said no, then that would be it. He'd respect that.

He'd told Percy it was okay to ask for help, for extra care and extra effort. If it was okay for Percy, then it had to be okay for Brandon too. He pulled himself out of bed, bringing his pillow with him because the two Percy had were the only two that didn't reek of potpourri, and last Brandon had seen, Percy was using both of them.

They'd left one of the lights in the kitchen on, and it cast shadows down the hall, making the house look warm and alive. The opposite of Brandon's shadowed, silent room. He'd felt haunted his whole life in this house, but now it wasn't anything but his own bitter guilt clinging to him.

He knocked lightly on Percy's door. Waited a few seconds in the quiet before he turned the old brass knob and pushed it open. Percy's lights weren't on, but his curtains were pulled and he had cracked one of the windows, letting in the full moonlight and the warming breeze.

"Perce?" he murmured. "You awake?"

"Mm," Perce replied sleepily. The mound of flowery quilts he was tucked under stirred. "Mmm?"

"Uhm. I was just wondering if . . ." How could he say this without sounding like he was a five-year-old with nightmares? "You know, if you wanted company."

Nailed it.

Percy's blankets rustled again. "If *I* wanted company?" he asked, sounding much more awake, and thoroughly amused at Brandon's expense.

"Okay. You got me. It's me who wants company. Can I come in for a little while?"

"I *suppose*." Percy flashed him a smile in the dark and lifted his blankets up.

Brandon let out a breath and crossed the room to slide in next to him. All of Dahlia's beds were queens or bigger, so they weren't squashed together like they had been in Percy's room. Brandon wasn't sure whether or not that was something he appreciated. "So . . ." he said, spreading out on his back.

"So . . ." Percy moved himself carefully, sliding over until he was taking possession of most of Brandon's pillow instead of his own two. He laid a hand on Brandon's stomach. Something in Brandon *twinged*, and he didn't know whether he was about to pop a boner or start crying.

But if he didn't come out with his secret *right fucking now*, they were going to end up having sex—like he had to assume Percy thought he wanted by being here—and then his chance would be gone.

"I didn't tell you everything," he burst out. "About my grandfather. There's . . . something else, Perce. Something I wish I didn't have to tell you. Something I wish wasn't true."

Percy's fingers twitched. "What is it?" They twitched again when Brandon couldn't get himself to say it. "Brandon, *tell me*."

"Percy, I'm sorry, I'm so sorry, I'm sorry, I'm sorry . . . but James Ringer, he killed himself. The motorcycle crash he died in . . . it wasn't an accident. They forced him to break it off with his male lover. Threatened him . . ."

Saying the words aloud had Brandon crying all over again, big wet cleansing tears that made his throat close up. But he kept going anyway. "Nolan said people got in his head about what would happen to Dahlia and my mother if anyone found out about them. About *him*. And his manager kept pushing his image with the marriage and the baby in the tabloids, trying to make him straight, and he just couldn't do it. He couldn't live as the person everyone said he had to be, and he couldn't risk slipping up and ruining her." He gasped in a breath. Percy rubbed his hand up and down Brandon's chest. "He couldn't live like that. Couldn't risk hurting her. He didn't make it."

He expected Percy to say something. He wasn't sure what. Just something.

Something that wasn't, "You made it, though."

"It's not about me," Brandon said eventually, his voice hoarse.

"It's a little about you." Percy moved closer, resting his chin on Brandon's shoulder. "And I . . . think I always suspected. About his death, I mean. The way he looked sometimes, or the way he answered questions about himself, his personal life. He would brush things off with a joke, or, or he would flirt his way out of it, but it was always clear he was dodging, if you paid attention. Especially in *that* interview."

"*The* interview?"

Percy nodded. "I wasn't sure, of course. But there were hints. Things most people may have brushed off because they wanted to keep a specific image of him."

Brandon closed his hand over Percy's. "But not you."

"No, not me." Percy's voice was soft and sad. "I wasn't interested in sewing together rosy Hays Code-approved pieces of him. I wanted reality. Sometimes reality has ugly endings."

"How do you reconcile that?" Brandon couldn't help asking. "All the good stuff and then *that*?"

"*That* doesn't change the fact that I'm here, sixty years later, watching his films," Percy said gently. "What he did when he was alive isn't tarnished by his suicide, not to me. And don't think I'm trying to either romanticize it or dismiss it, because I'm not. It happened. It was a choice he made. I wish he'd thought he had other ones."

"And that's it for you?"

"That's it." Percy turned his hand up to squeeze Brandon's. "Is there more for *you*?"

Brandon shrugged, jostling Percy. "I guess I just . . . I just always thought I'd die and be gone the same way he was. The same age. The same everything. I went around my whole life hearing people tell me I looked young and tragic just like he did, that I had the same chip on my shoulder, that I would screw it all up the same as he did. End up like him. And then I find out it wasn't some freak accident or, or *fate*, or whatever, what happened to him. It was *him*. He's the one who let go. He *did* screw up. He—"

"Brandon."

"—left Dahlia, and Nolan, and—"

"*Brandon.*" Percy pushed himself up on his other arm with a groan of effort. "Brandon, stop. I know this is upsetting for you, and I know you've got connections and problems with James I could never even dream of understanding, all right? But you have to find your even ground with him. One moment you want to know everything about him, and the next you're willing to write all of that off and throw him under the bus for one mistake, one choice."

"He *died*, though. That's not just one choice."

Percy frowned at him. "How can you say that? Of course it was. For him, it was. You said it yourself: he didn't see another way out. Maybe it wasn't *fair*—to your grandmother. Maybe even to you. But you're so fixated on how he died, and how you thought *you* were going to die, that you can't see anything else. *Couldn't*," he corrected himself. "But I know you see other parts of him—the complexity of him— now. You have to let your fixation on this one thing, this one day out of thousands, go." He pushed Brandon's hand off his and moved up to touch the side of Brandon's jaw. "He was a whole person, with triumphs and failures and traits and contradictions, Brandon, and *so are you.*"

Brandon sniffled miserably.

"You don't have to use your parents' abusive, homophobic framework to prove you're your own person with your own life to live, Brandon. You can just throw out the ... the ... the *fucking* framework."

The burst of energy he had to throw into swearing made Brandon laugh, even if it sounded hoarse and unenthusiastic. "Better watch it. I'm rubbing off on you."

"Are you?" Percy moved his hand back to Brandon's stomach with a little smirk. "I hadn't noticed."

"Smartass," Brandon mumbled. "Are you going to get tired of watching me figure this out? I can't just magically undo nineteen years of bullshit." He could, eventually. With Percy and Nolan. Maybe Judy too, and Alfred, and the rest of his (good) clients. But it would take time.

"And I can't magically undo twenty-one." Percy gave him a pointed look. "But hey, it's not like we fell in love with each other not knowing about any of this, did we? I figure we can only go up from here."

"I can't *believe* anyone fell in love with a hot fucking mess like me."

"Well, believe it," Percy retorted. "And in return, I'll believe that you fell in love with someone like *me*."

"That reminds me! Kovie said something about you 'buying a boyfriend.' I was gonna tell her that you *bought* a surly celebrity lookalike to fuck. The boyfriend stuff . . . no amount of money from *anybody* could buy that from me. But I gave it to you, free of charge."

"I never doubted it." Percy stroked his belly in lazy, possessive, circles. "Well, okay, I kind of did, but like you said, that's Hazel talking. Truth is, you're in no way tactful enough to fake any of this. Which must mean I'm lovable after all."

"You have a real talent for complimenting me and insulting me at the same time," Brandon grumbled good-naturedly. He stretched his arm out and Percy settled down against him, his hand circling lower. Brandon squirmed. "Speaking of talent . . ."

Percy lifted his head. "Seriously? That's the segue you're going with?"

"It's been a long day, cut me a break."

"I'll consider it." Percy thumbed at the band of his sweatpants, fitting his cool fingertips between it and Brandon's stomach and just resting them there.

Resting them there and driving Brandon *nuts.*

"Perce," he mumbled. "I—"

"Shh. I have a better segue." Percy kissed the corner of his mouth. "You need to stop thinking for a while. Hmm?" His small, cold hands slipped under Brandon's shirt and the waistband of his sweatpants simultaneously, one reaching up to cup his pec while the other scratched through his pubic hair. "Let me take care of you."

"*God*," Brandon groaned, going liquid. Yes, he wanted that. Wanted Percy to take control, guide him, make him feel, wash his mind and spirit clean.

And what was more, he could trust Percy to make that happen.

"Take off your clothes, Brandon."

"Yeah," Brandon agreed, then realized it had been an order, not asking permission. "Oh! Yeah." He shifted, trying to get his shirt and his pants off all at once, and distantly heard Percy laughing at him.

"Shut up." His shirt came loose first, so he balled it up and tossed it aimlessly, then arched his back to shove his sweatpants and boxers down.

"Now get up. Let me look at you."

Brandon swallowed and slid out of bed, his mouth dry.

Percy sat up with his legs under him, folded to one side while he leaned on his hands, taking the weight off his hips. "Turn," he said, the corner of his mouth twitching. But his eyes were focused on Brandon, sharp and certain. They didn't flicker away once as Brandon turned obediently, letting Percy look him over from every angle. Funny how his job could literally be to casually get naked with people who wanted to see him, but *this* made him flush hot.

"Good," Percy murmured when he'd turned a couple times. "I'm going to have to get you to do this at different times of day, see what lighting I like best. I don't know if I'll ever find anything to top moonlight, though."

"Because it's mostly dark and you can't see my nonexistent abs?"

Percy rolled his eyes. "Romantic."

Brandon's mouth trembled and his gaze fell to his feet as tonight's conversation crept back up over him. "Because . . . because it looks like I'm in black and white?" he said, softly.

"Yes, Brandon," Percy replied, evenly, maybe a little impatient. "Because I like the aesthetic, though. Not because I'm pretending you're him."

"Right," Brandon said. He was being stupid, of course. Of course.

"If I wanted *him*, I already had him, right where I was. Alone, in my parents' house. But I don't want him. I want you. Now come to bed so I can touch you." He patted the mattress beside him, and his face was loving and firm, that expression that made Brandon's heart pound and his limbs go limp.

Brandon went to him.

"Good boy," Percy cooed, opening his arms, gathering Brandon against him. "That's it." He petted Brandon's hair, kissed his temples. Nudged him back onto the bed so that he could stroke Brandon's chest and nipples and hips, then down to cup and roll his balls.

Brandon moaned wordlessly, fisting the sheets, and let Percy have his way with him. Let Percy spread his legs and smooth teasing fingers along the insides of his thighs and up again, never touching his aching cock.

"Good boy," he kept saying, over and over, lulling Brandon with it. Words he felt like he'd never heard, not ever. But he believed them now, from Percy.

For Percy, he was good.

"Love you," he moaned, slurred, as Percy guided him to roll onto his front

"I know," Percy murmured back. He let his hands roam over Brandon's back, then knead his ass. Spread him open. Brandon rutted helplessly against the mattress while Percy played with his hole. Percy's soft lips kissed down the center of his back. "You weren't hoping to top at some point, were you?"

Honestly? Yes, but he'd gladly forgotten all thoughts of it the first time he and Percy had made love. This felt so right, being spread out and pinned down for Percy, he didn't need anything else. Couldn't even imagine an alternative.

"Want what you want," he managed to say.

Percy's response was pleased, not surprised. Satisfied . . . and undeniably superior. "That's right." His thumbs tugged at Brandon's hole, opening him up a little roughly. "But then, if that's the case, why don't I have a bottle of lube right now to fuck you with, Brandon?"

The note of disappointment in his voice had Brandon simultaneously aching in shame and panting with want.

When he wasn't completely fuck-drunk, he was going to have to at least make some *show* of standing up for his dignity.

But for now, he'd just let Percy treat him exactly how he liked.

And he'd love every moment of it, too.

The lube was down the hall, but when he tried to wrap a blanket around himself to go there, Percy shook his head. "Go naked," he ordered, the little goddamn devil.

Brandon streaked out. Grabbed the lube. Streaked back. Practically fell all over himself trying to hand his prize to Percy, who was now sitting imperiously on the edge of the bed, naked.

"I've decided you should suck me off while you get your ass ready," he said. He blushed a little as he did, but kept the proud tilt of his chin.

Ten minutes ago Brandon might have given him shit for it, but now? No way.

Well, maybe just a *bit*. Like grazing his knuckles over the flush on Percy's cheeks. Percy batted his hand away, squinting one eye, but his expression leveled back out into self-satisfaction when Brandon arranged himself, kneeling on the floor between Percy's legs, and popped the top on the lube.

"You're so sexy," Percy said. "I could watch you all day."

Now Brandon blushed. "Stop," he protested with a laugh. He coated his fingers with lube, making sure to look Percy right in the eye when he pressed them inside himself.

Percy's eyelashes fluttered, his lower lip drawing in between his teeth. He took his dick in hand, pointed it at Brandon's face. "*No.* Now, be a good boy and open up like you're told."

Yep, Brandon was definitely gonna have to kick up a fuss about this. Later.

Right now he was much too busy fucking himself with two fingers while Percy fed him his cock.

Brandon didn't just look sexy.

He looked absolutely beautiful.

His eyes were bright, his cheeks flushed, his lips swollen as they wrapped around Percy's dick.

And yes, the moonlight was perfect, rolling shadows over Brandon's shoulders, down the slope of his back. Percy had never been with him this late in the evening before, especially not naked. It thrilled him to know that this was a sight he could see, drink in, again and again and again.

"How many fingers are you using?" he asked, running his fingers through Brandon's hair. Brandon moved to pull back and Percy tightened his fingers, wincing through the pain. "No, no. Just tap my thigh. Tell me."

Brandon did him one better: leaned back until the head of Percy's cock was resting on his bottom lip, then stared up into Percy's eyes and slid his tongue twice over it, slow and thorough.

God. Percy fought to keep his voice even. "Use three. I want you ready."

Brandon nodded and swallowed Percy's cock back down, his free hand cupping one of Percy's calves, like he wanted . . .

Percy tilted his head and tried carefully pressing his leg up. Brandon made a noise and shuffled closer, letting Percy hook his thigh on his shoulder. It leaned Percy back, enough that he had to brace himself, but it was a position he could hold. For a while, at least. And it felt *good*, the shift of Brandon's muscles, the warmth of his skin. How easily Percy could bring him closer, if he wanted to.

He wanted to.

He always wanted to.

So he did.

Because he was worthwhile, and he was allowed to want things, ask for them, even demand them.

And Brandon gave.

He grunted and bucked at a particularly good pulse of suction, then used his grip on Brandon's hair to pull his head back. All the way back, this time, until Percy's cockhead popped out of his mouth and he was left gasping and sputtering.

"Get into this bed." Percy let his leg slip and grabbed at Brandon's shoulders to urge him up.

He'd never felt right, ordering Brandon around quite like *this*, when he was paying for the service. But now that they were boyfriends and Brandon could tell him to fuck himself, if that was what he really wanted? Percy felt free to let loose.

Brandon, for his part, looked hypnotized, glazed, wanting. Like the last thing he wanted to do was tell Percy to take his domineering attitude and shove it. When he got himself into the bed, Percy rewarded him with a slow, deep kiss. Tasted his own cock and precum in Brandon's mouth, which only made him hungrier.

"Lay on your side," he directed, gently this time, taking as much care with Brandon, now, as Brandon routinely took with him. Brandon's brow furrowed and he lowered himself down facing Percy until Percy nudged his shoulder. "The *other* side." Brandon licked his lips and rolled. Percy gave his top leg a push until it fell forward, opening him up. "There. That's it." He rubbed his fingertips over Brandon's wet hole, playing with it a little, listening to the soft, dreamy noises Brandon made at every touch. "So beautiful," he whispered into the skin of Brandon's shoulder on a kiss as he laid himself down at Brandon's back, curling over and around him.

There was a bit of a learning curve to this position, but he still managed to get himself into the right spot, where he could slide his dick into Brandon's waiting hole without causing himself pain or pressure.

Brandon whimpered when he did, and Percy murmured into his ear, rubbed calming circles on his tense belly. "Thaaat's it."

It was equally as intense this time as it had been the last. Maybe more, with Brandon twitching and so warm in Percy's arms, tipping his head down to rub his face into the pillows and Percy's outstretched arm.

He was mumbling something, muffled, and Percy reached up to tilt his head back. "What did you say?"

"I said," Brandon licked his lips, "more, please."

Percy smiled at him.

At this angle, all he had to do was use Brandon's body as a lever to ease himself back and forth, working his hips in a way that didn't involve much flexion or driven power. It let him focus on the feeling of Brandon around him, hot and squeezing. Let him focus on the sensation of his chest pressed to Brandon's heaving, trembling back. Let him focus on kissing Brandon, turning his face back and kissing him and *kissing* him as he moaned into Percy's mouth.

He wouldn't change a single thing about this, or them: who they were, separate or together.

Brandon started shaking, sweat slipping down his back and sticking them together. He kept panting Percy's name and asking him for more, but it was just words, Percy thought, just words, because he seemed happy with anything Percy gave him, and that in itself was such a small miraculous thing. That no matter what problems they'd had, they had always given and taken and evened out in the end. Come back together.

Found each other under all the layers of—as Brandon would say—bullshit.

"Can I," Brandon panted, dragging one hand down and shoving it between his legs.

"Yes." Percy rubbed his face against the back of Brandon's neck, his hair sticking to his forehead. "Go ahead."

He felt the shock ripple through Brandon's body when he fisted his cock. Kissed the back of his neck again. Then bit there, his fingers pressing down against the strong line of Brandon's hipbone. It felt like Percy was holding him there, holding him together, even as his right arm was beginning to tingle from the weight of Brandon's head, from the pressure of Brandon's occasional, sloppy kisses against the inside of his elbow.

"Come for me now, beautiful," he whispered into Brandon's ear, then nibbled the lobe, increasing the speed of his thrusts.

Brandon cried out as he came, his whole body shivering and his ass clamping down almost painfully on Percy's cock.

Not too painfully that Percy didn't still come from it, though.

Percy stayed inside him awhile after, running his hand through the hot spattered cum all over Brandon's chest and belly before using his sticky fingers to gently pinch and pull on Brandon's oversensitized cock.

Brandon breathed out a dozy, tortured noise, but didn't fight. Twisted in Percy's grip, but didn't throw him off. Instead he pushed himself closer, burrowing back into Percy's chest.

"Good boy," Percy said, relaxing behind him, letting all his stiff muscles finally unclench. "You're my good boy, Brandon."

"Yeah," Brandon agreed. "I am."

He turned his head enough for Percy to see he was smiling.

CHAPTER
THIRTY-SIX

"**B**randon," Percy said from the door of Brandon's room. "You're freaking out."

"I'm not freaking out." Brandon looked up from where he was buried in one of his drawers, hunting frantically for the jeans that were . . . thrown over the back of the chair by his door. He straightened up and ran a hand through his hair. It was a mess, too. Everything was a mess. "Okay. Okay, maybe I am a little."

He went over to get the jeans and yanked them on. They were fucking wrinkled, of course they were, from being on the chair. Fuck.

"I'm just, what if she fires me?" he said. What the hell else did he need to wear? A real shirt, probably. Yes. He stripped off the T-shirt he'd been sleeping in and went to his closet to find a shirt that wasn't equally wrinkled. Jesus shit, when was the last time he did laundry?

Oh, wait. Hadn't Maggie said she'd thrown a load in?

Which was probably still in the washer.

Growing mold.

"Fuck." He slumped against the wall. Last night had been amazing. Percy had done exactly what Brandon wanted and made him stop thinking. Had driven him so far out of his head all he could really recall was a long stretch of being held down and filled up and taken care of. It had been so good.

And then he'd woken up this morning and reality had crashed down on him. Because what if Judy fired him? What if she didn't approve of him dating—*moving in with*—a client and continuing to work at the agency? Paul Newman had left the agency. What if it hadn't been because he wanted to go, but because Hollywood Doubles didn't allow this kind of thing? What if Ms. Monroe hadn't had the same reaction to Harvey as Theresa had had, or Brandon refusing a client was finally the last straw for her? He knew he really didn't have a long leash of favors to be asking, especially not with his string of bad reviews and worse behavior lately.

If Judy fired him, it wasn't just him he had to worry about anymore. Percy said he had trust funds and bank accounts, and Brandon knew he had enough to throw around, but what if his mom didn't hold to the promise to keep him on his parents' medical insurance? What if Brandon got behind on tax payments, or, or he couldn't buy the right food for Percy? Or—

"Brandon." Percy ducked in front of him and grabbed his face. "Look at me. Breathe."

Brandon breathed.

"Good. Again."

Percy smelled like Brandon's shampoo and soap. Like Dahlia's potpourri. Brandon looped his arms around him and squeezed him close. "I have no idea how to handle this," he admitted.

"It's easy. In through the nose, out through—"

"It's nice to know when you're not paying me money, you pay me in sarcasm, you jackass." Brandon rubbed his cheek on Percy's bony shoulder. "No, I mean . . . how to handle giving a shit about getting fired from a job. Ms. Monroe threatened to fire me before, sort of, but I didn't care near what I do now. I really, really . . . *really* don't want to get fired. And that's a new thing."

"A good thing." Percy stroked his back. "Come on. We'll go and talk to her, and, well, I mean, I can't promise you won't get fired, but I can promise I'll still love you if you do? Mostly."

Brandon lifted his head to squint at him. "*Mostly?*"

"Joking! I'm joking," Percy said, showing his palms. "But you're not hyperventilating anymore, so I've done my job." He patted Brandon briskly on the shoulder, then looked him over with a newly critical eye. "The jeans look good. You need . . ." He turned to survey Brandon's pathetic collection of unwrinkled clothes, selecting a belt— one of the ones from Hepcat, of course—and . . . *oh*, slipping the end into Brandon's belt loops. He threaded it all the way through, then moved Brandon's hands to the buckle so he could do that up himself. "Better. You do need a new shirt, though."

Brandon gave him a wide-eyed look. "I was planning to wear this one. What's wrong with it?" He watched Percy have three seconds of what was sure to be an epic fashion aneurysm before breaking face and laughing. "What, you can joke, but I can't?"

Percy flapped his hands at him. "When you can dress yourself as well as I can, you'll be allowed to joke."

He sifted through Brandon's clothes, humming unhappily at the selections. "You don't have *anything* else?"

"I—wait." Brandon headed into his room. Now that he wasn't panicking, he could sort of remember getting drunk a couple weeks ago and angrily stuffing things in one of his dresser drawers. "Fuuuck," he said, opening one and finding all his Hepcat Vintage purchases inside. "They're all wrinkled as fuck. And I don't think I even own an iron. How do you unwrinkle clothes without an iron? Can you even do that?"

"Brandon," Percy sighed. He vanished back into Brandon's closet and came out with a modern shirt that wasn't too terrible. Or not terrible enough for Percy to make him wear, at least. "We're doing laundry when we get back . . . home. I need to wash things too." He almost sounded excited by the prospect.

Brandon took the shirt and shrugged it on. "I'll show you how to operate the machine, Richie Rich. You can wash as much as you want."

Percy raised an eyebrow at him. Cast a pointed look at the piles of filthy and/or wrinkled clothes strewn around the room. "Are you sure *you* know how to use it?"

"Spare me your judgment, O Hip One." Brandon buttoned the shirt with a flourish. "There. I look acceptable now?"

"Hmm . . ." Percy reached to unbutton the cuffs of his sleeves. It took a few tries, but Brandon patiently waited for him to get them undone and then roll them up a couple times, so Brandon's forearms were bared. After a step back to survey him, Percy tugged the shirt's hem straight and readjusted Brandon's belt so it was situated to his satisfaction. Made sure Brandon's zipper was up.

Then he let his knuckles press down and in a little . . .

And fucking *grinned*.

"Yeah, that looks fine," he said breezily, and strutted out of the room.

Well, now Brandon was anxious *and* horny. He didn't know if it counted as an improvement or not.

And they were gonna be late if he stood here any longer trying to puzzle it out.

Thanks to Percy, they actually wound up being ten minutes early for their meeting. Didn't matter, though, because Judy was already sitting in her usual booth when they arrived. Today, she was wearing a tight olive green dress and hat combo with a black fur collar and thick-framed cat eye glasses.

"Oh my *god*," Percy hissed from beside him. "That's her. Oh *wow* that's her."

"Yeah," Brandon agreed, steeling himself. "That's her all right."

She stood when they approached. She looked . . . nervous, her lips pinched tight and her body language stiff. She had her hands folded in front of her at waist level.

"Brandon," she greeted. "And . . .?"

"Percy, his boyfriend. And can I just say, wow? Wow?" He flushed all across his cheeks. "Sorry, um, serious work-related meeting. I know this. But *wow*."

At least that got Judy to smile. But she wasn't any less tense. If anything, she looked more nervous than before, and confused, to top it off. "Sit," she said, waving at the booth. She returned to her side gracefully, and Brandon slid in so Percy could have the outside of their bench. He was bouncing in his seat like an excited kid, beaming a thousand-watt smile right at Judy.

She offered a hand across the table, and Brandon swore Percy blushed from head to toe as he rushed to shake it.

"So Brandon . . . I take it you're 'pulling a Newman'?"

Brandon gulped. "Y-yes and no?"

Her brow knitted.

"Well I mean, Percy was a client of mine, and it's true we're dating now and he's not paying Hollywood Doubles or . . . uh, me, to see me anymore. But I'm not leaving the agency for him, either. I mean, I don't . . . I don't want to leave the agency, but I guess if I have to then I have to, like, I guess you're my boss, so it's up to you . . ."

Judy held up a hand. "Wait. You don't want to leave the agency?"

Brandon blinked at her. "Well, no. I mean, no way. If that's okay. Percy's okay with it." Beside him, Percy nodded vigorously.

"So . . ." Judy murmured, " . . . you didn't call me here so you could quit?"

"No!" Brandon cried. "I called you to apologize for how I've been acting lately, and for all the bad reviews pouring in. I called you to tell you I'm gonna work hard to clean up my act and get back on track."

Judy's shoulders relaxed a little. A small, sad smile tugged at her lips. "Theresa told me about Harvey." She reached across the table, offering him her hand, which he took. Under the table, Percy squeezed his knee. "As soon as I heard, I understood. I appreciate your apology and think it shows character, Brandon, but I wouldn't have expected or demanded one, considering the circumstances. I think a few weeks of being terrible at your job is warranted, don't you?"

Brandon opened his mouth. Closed it. Opened it again. "I, uh. I guess?" It took him a few seconds to work it through his head, what she was saying. And he thought it was that she wasn't going to write him off. That she wasn't done with him. That she wasn't going to fire him, toss him out, because he'd screwed up. "So I'm not . . . I'm not fired?"

"Of course not," she said, closing her other hand on top of their clasped ones. "Brandon. Of *course* not. I thought you wanted to tell me you were done. That you weren't going to stick with this after all. I came to wish you well, and tell you there were no hard feelings . . . and that I was sorry for not protecting you. Theresa and I both are."

Tears welled in Brandon's eyes. He let them; what was one more crying jag to add to the past few days' list? "It's not your fault—not either of you. And I know it's not mine, either. Well, except the being terrible at my job part. But yeah, I am. I am going to stick with it."

"And it's okay that he and I are together?" Percy asked. He sounded sincerely nervous.

"So long as you're not still paying him under the table, losing the agency their cut, that's all they care." She pursed her lips. "That's the *official* policy as outlined in his contract. My personal policy, or advice, or whatever?" Now she turned to Percy with a smile. "Don't try to talk him out of his work if that's not what he wants for himself. Believe me, sweetheart, I've been in a few relationships where that has happened, and it never turns out well for anyone."

"No, I wouldn't. I swear." Percy met her eyes squarely, his fingers closing tighter on Brandon's knee, making Brandon gravitate toward him, same as always.

"Good. Now, if you happen to be considering stopping taking clients of your *own* accord, Brandon, like I've decided to now that I'm going steady with a certain someone. . . Well, I'm staying on as manager of Hollywood Doubles and you'll always have my support."

"And mine," Percy added. "All I want is for him to do what makes him truly happy. And, to be honest?"

He glanced at Brandon with a small smile. Still a nervous smile, but a pleased one, too. Pleased and *proud*. Brandon didn't think he'd ever seen so much pride on one person's face.

"To be honest," Percy murmured, holding Brandon's eyes, "I'm glad he's happy doing this."

At that, Brandon really did start to cry. Then it sort of poured out of him, the whole story. They both knew the bare bones, the DNA half, but now he told them the rest: how he'd grown up with his parents and his parents' friends and the whole goddamn world telling him who James Ringer was—a user and a cheater and a playboy who'd never really loved Dahlia—and by extension what Brandon was. How his parents had thrown him out. How he had wanted to tell Judy the first time they'd come here that he could understand a little of what she went through with her folks. How he'd lived with Dahlia, how he'd wanted to keep the house and sell the collection. How he'd been scared to death that the truth about him would get out somehow, whether it was Vince looking for publicity or otherwise. He told them about Cyrus's blackmail.

And even though Judy assured him that she wouldn't let Vince *or* Cyrus—who she assured him would be fired as soon as possible—go public with Brandon's identity, he told them how he didn't think he *cared* anymore, if people knew who he was, because he wasn't ashamed of it. Of James or this job.

Or himself.

Judy's gray eyes were wide by the time he finished. Her stunned silence made Brandon fumble for Percy's hand under the table, anxiety threatening to grip him again.

Then she smiled.

"*Well*," she said. "That explains a lot."

"Tell me about it," Percy said.

And Brandon had to laugh.

EPILOGUE

Not long after Percy started his first archiving class that fall, the two of them had a crazy, brilliant idea.

A couple months after *that*, they used the equipment at his school to pull the infamous James Ringer interview off Percy's ultra-rare VHS tape, both of them hunched intently over it like they were lifting the world's most precious diamond, and uploaded it online.

Shortly after it went viral, they launched their Kickstarter, which funded 200% in eight hours.

One of its biggest donors was Judy Monroe.

Brandon had *told* her about it, sure, but he hadn't expected her to give them that much. Enough to name her one of the founders of the James Ringer and Dahlia Delair Memorial Estate, which, all things going well, would be opening next year in a gorgeous gallery space in Bergamot Station. And, all things going better, would have Percy attached to it as its official, full-time curator.

He also hadn't expected her to tell all her friends and favorite clients. Nor for Kovie—who gleefully took full advantage of the fact that Percy no longer had visiting hours or curfews by visiting him and Brandon as often as possible—to tell all of *her* friends. Turns out a bunch of elderly vintage film enthusiasts allied with a bunch of twentysomething hipsters was pretty much an unstoppable force for crowdfunding. They even had enough money to start looking into the possibility of expanding the collection beyond just James Ringer and the stuff in Brandon's basement to include objects and ephemera from queer film history in general. Brandon was thinking maybe, eventually, with all of the proceeds, they would be able to open an actual permanent museum of their own one day.

Nolan, still wiping his eyes after seeing *the interview*, had been the one to come up with that. "Why not host it in the house?" he'd said. "It's famous enough. And it's got more than enough room for the two of you and a bunch of stuff, huh?"

"Don't put that in his head!" Maggie had said, playfully swatting his arm. "Do you know how much cleaning I'd have to do if they did that?"

"Brandon's the messy one, not me!" Percy'd called from the living room, sending Nolan into a fit of coughing laughter.

He and Percy had taken instantly to one another, bonding over the collection and all its various pieces, most of which Brandon got to see once Percy had unearthed them from the basement, lovingly dusted, researched, and catalogued them, and then boxed and brought them upstairs to prepare them for the future move to the gallery.

Brandon was navigating around the ever-growing piles of boxes now, holding a tray full of . . . *something* . . . that Kovie had made for the party. Puffs that smelled amazing and had a bunch of vegetables in them, that was all he knew. He added them to one of the already laden-to-the-brim tables on the patio.

Their *Night with Mr. Ringer* party for their funders was kicking off in less than an hour. Brandon had hired a pool cleaner especially for the occasion, and Maggie had brought her son, her husband, and her sister-in-law in to help them get everything scrubbed down and company-ready, since they were supposed to look professional, here. Kovie had chipped in the party planner her parents used, and Judy had shown up early, dressed to the nines . . . with Theresa on her arm.

Yeah. So *that* was why Theresa had wanted to rave about her fantastic Saturday night date.

"Yooo." Kovie sidled up to Brandon's side as he grabbed another tray of the something-puffs from the kitchen counter. Her cocktail dress was sun-yellow, and Judy had waylaid her as soon as she was through the door to interrogate her about where she'd gotten it. "Where did you say you put that margarita mix?"

"Uh, I didn't put it anywhere. It's—hey Percy!" Brandon called out the patio doors, spotting him over by Nolan's lawn chair. "Where's the margarita mix?"

Percy shrugged and pointed at Kovie, who waved and stuck her tongue out at him.

"I told you we should've hired a bartender," she told Brandon. "Next time we're hiring a bartender."

"Oh are we?"

"Absolutely. Next time you put on a we-are-unexpectedly-rich party, I am *so* hiring a bartender."

"Yeah, we're gonna be 'rich' for about . . ." Brandon checked an imaginary watch, " . . . four more days." Then they would write a check to the gallery to reserve their half a year of display time. And then, later, they would have to pay a moving company to get it all safely from Brandon's house to the gallery, where it would be—fingers crossed—set up under Percy's supervision.

The rest of the money would sit in an account, untouched, until they could put it toward the museum, whether it ended up being at Brandon's house or not. It would happen someday. It'd work out.

It would all work out.

For both of them. For *all* of them.

"Okay. Bartender," he agreed. "For now I'm hiring *you* to find the margarita mix before we get swamped."

Kovie pursed her lips, blowing a somehow polite raspberry. "Puh-*lease*. Like you're gonna pay me anything." She swung in to kiss his cheek with a sparkling grin, then headed back to the poolside.

"I'll pay you with my eternal gratitude," he called.

She flipped him off over her shoulder.

He laughed and turned to scoop the tray back up.

"She is right, you know," Percy said from right behind him. Brandon almost dropped the tray, tried to pick it up again, then decided *fuck it* and considered it a casualty of the moment.

He turned to look at Percy, because seriously, how could he *not*? Perce had had all his stuff moved from his parents' place: clothes, movies, books, and that included the set of outfits Brandon assumed were previously reserved for Percy's parents' parties. Like the suit he had on now, all crisp and clean and perfectly tailored.

Tailored well enough it made Brandon's mouth water. Made him want to get on his knees and ask very nicely for . . . something. Lots of things. Some of the many, many things they'd tried out together.

Brandon needed to stop himself right there before things got out of hand.

It was already too late for his dignity, which he'd never really managed to scrape up enough protest to defend once Percy got started on him. Right now, Percy's smirk told Brandon he knew *exactly* what he was thinking.

Brandon picked up one of the puffs. With a napkin. Otherwise Judy would make faces at him. "Right about what?"

Percy plucked the puff from his fingers and put it back on the tray. "Those are for *guests*. And she's right about not accepting your eternal gratitude as payment. You've sworn to me several times that I'll be the recipient of that, and it is *surprisingly* short-lived, for eternal." He wrapped an arm around Brandon's waist and sank against him, staring out the French patio doors at the pool, where Judy and Theresa were sitting side by side with their feet in the water. "You're very good *at first . . .*"

"Hey, come on now. For you, Perce? I'm *always* good." Brandon tugged on his tie.

"We'll see how well you do tonight during the party," Percy said in that prim, superior way of his, the one that was affectionate and teasing and endearingly snooty. "But I suppose it's true. For me, you are very, very good."

Brandon, Pavlovian dog that he was, found his toes curling just at the words.

But words were as far as it went, because Kovie poked her head through the patio door. "C'mon out. Nolan thinks he's got your projector working. Wants to do a test run before anyone else gets here."

They followed her out to Dahlia's patio, lit up with bright blue pool water reflections and cheesy little paper lanterns. Nolan had set up a projector to play on one of the house's white walls, showing clips from James Ringer's movies and snippets of behind the scenes footage.

Percy squeezed Brandon's hand when the image of his face—six feet tall and larger than life—first appeared on the wall. Brandon knew the clip instantly. Recognized his checked shirt and the way he nervously chewed his lower lip.

He looked down, a moment. Looked up and smiled, a little wistfully, before his expression flipped to that practiced, cocky look. The one Brandon used to paste on when he got fired, when he got told he was just as much of a waste of space as his grandfather. The one he'd perfected all on his own, only to find it doubled on film. The one that was just begging to be punched in the face.

Except now Brandon saw it for what it was: a brave, conflicted young man overcoming his insecurity and his fear to become something bigger and *more*.

"Well, ah, that's a dangerous sorta question now, isn't it?" His voice echoed from the speakers and washed over all of them. He stared down at his folded hands for a second, then half-grinned and looked back up. Into the camera. Did that *"squinty head-tilt thing"* Percy had once accused Brandon of doing. "I have a girl, of course. Dahlia Delair, yes. Oh, I'd say it's serious, alright. She understands me better than anyone, see. And I suppose all I have to say is, as long as she understands, as long as I've got *her* on my side, then that's enough. I'll be just fine. I'll . . ."

He blinked suddenly, and his gaze slid away, somewhere far.

Then he laughed. Gently. At himself, maybe. "Thank you, yes. You bet." He peeled up out of his chair, reaching to shake someone's hand. "Heaven and Earth couldn't stop me. Only her. For her, *I'd* stop Heaven and Earth." There was a low murmur, a scattered catch of sound, a voice that wasn't his.

Then James Ringer's voice again. "Oh, that was fast." He came through strong and clear at first, but he was off-screen and growing quickly distant, distorted, under the crackly rattle of his microphone being taken off him. "That's all you've got for me?" he asked, fading. "I'm finished?"

Never, Brandon thought, lacing his fingers together with Percy's, clinging to him tight. *Not so long as I'm here.*

Not so long as Dahlia's life's work was preserved and Nolan was here to pass on his last truth, and people like Judy and Kovie were here to listen. Not so long as Alfred—and all the others like him—carried his bittersweet memory faithfully in their hearts all these years. Not so long as his celluloid spirit guided people like Percy safely to adulthood, to happiness and freedom.

Not so long as I have you to thank for everything good in my life. Brandon's teary-eyed gaze landed on Percy's, and they both smiled: sad, for the moment, but here. Here, together. Thanks to him.

This is all *thanks to you.*

And wasn't it funny: the jackass, dogged conspiracy theorists had been right all along.

James Ringer lived.

Dear Reader,

Thank you for reading Heidi Belleau and Sam Schooler's *Dead Ringer*!

We know your time is precious and you have many, many entertainment options, so it means a lot that you've chosen to spend your time reading. We really hope you enjoyed it.

We'd be honored if you'd consider posting a review—good or bad—on sites like **Amazon, Barnes & Noble, Kobo, Goodreads, Twitter, Facebook, Tumblr,** and your blog or website. We'd also be honored if you told your friends and family about this book. Word of mouth is a book's lifeblood!

For more information on upcoming releases, author interviews, blog tours, contests, giveaways, and more, please sign up for our weekly, spam-free newsletter and visit us around the web:

Newsletter: tinyurl.com/RiptideSignup
Twitter: twitter.com/RiptideBooks
Facebook: facebook.com/RiptidePublishing
Goodreads: tinyurl.com/RiptideOnGoodreads
Tumblr: riptidepublishing.tumblr.com

Thank you so much for Reading the Rainbow!

RiptidePublishing.com

ACKNOWLEDGMENTS

This book couldn't have been possible without the help and guidance of our beta readers: Jules, who cheerlead and asked tough questions and picked at our grammar, and Nikki, who provided us with feedback on our representation of disability. We'd also be remiss not to thank Ridley, who took the time and effort way waaaay back in the book's early planning stages to send us a list of resources on disability in relationships, sex, and of course Romance, which gave us a foundation to stand on (and hopefully kept us from making too many egregious errors right off the bat). Any remaining mistakes are all ours.

We'd also like to thank the entire team at Riptide for turning our draft into a book: our editor Sarah Frantz Lyons, Chris Muldoon and everyone else who provided notes on the text along the way, and the creative team behind the cover art.

A hundred million thank yous!

ALSO BY
HEIDI BELLEAU

Straight Shooter
Wallflower
Apple Polisher

With Lisa Henry
Tinman
The Harder they Fall
Bliss
King of Dublin

With Rachel Haimowitz
The Burnt Toast B&B
Flesh Cartel

With Violetta Vane
Mark of the Gladiator
The Druid Stone

ALSO BY
SAM SCHOOLER

Blasphemer, Sinner, Saint, with Heidi Belleau (in the *Bump in the Night* anthology)
Writing Your Own Ransom Note

ABOUT THE
AUTHORS

HEIDI BELLEAU was born and raised in small town New Brunswick, graduated with a degree in History from Simon Fraser University in British Columbia, and now lives outside of Edmonton, Alberta with her tradesman husband and two kids. A proud bisexual woman, her writing reflects everything she loves: diverse casts of queer characters, a sense of history and place, equal parts witty and filthy dialogue, the occasional mythological twist, and most of all, love—in all its weird and wonderful forms.

You can visit her online at HeidiBelleau.com, or follow her on Twitter: @HeidiBelleau. She's always available by email at heidi.heloise.belleau@gmail.com.

SAM SCHOOLER is an Ohioan university student studying journalism with a minor in American Sign Language and a specialization in African American studies. She is both queer and genderqueer, and has found a home in writing trope-themed New Adult stories about people of all genders and orientations. She has a wicked and extremely noticeable soft spot for werewolves. After graduation, she intends to flee to Canada to join her spouse Alex and escape the customs regulations that keep her separated from her truest love: Kinder Eggs. Jeremy Renner played her in a movie once.

For her backlist and news about her upcoming books, go to samschooler.com. If you're feeling daring, follow her on Twitter as @samschoolering to get the full immersive experience.

CPSIA information can be obtained at www.ICGtesting.com
Printed in the USA
LVOW08s1137111015

457798LV00006B/628/P